TALES

TALES
from
AFRICA

DOUGLAS COLLINS

Kenway Publications

Published by
Kenway Publications
Brick Court
Mpaka Road/Woodvale Grove
Westlands
P.O. Box 45314, Nairobi

First published 1995

ISBN 9966 46 526 X

Typeset by
Typedesign Limited
Kijabe Street, Barot House
P.O. Box 8519, Nairobi

Design and Layout by
Jessie Kirika

Printed by
English Press Ltd.
Enterprise Road, Industrial Area
P.O. Box 30127, Nairobi

Contents

Author's Foreword and Acknowledgements

These pages contain a whimsical anthology of my fifty-four years in Africa, mostly in tents and under thorn trees. The stories are about saints and sinners; eccentrics and gentlemen; comedy and tragedy; success and failure, fast adventure leavened with tedium.

I have written of the assorted faces of Africa, from as far north as the Horn, the Somalilands — the legendary Land of Punt — to as far south as the Limpopo.

I have served in Africa as soldier, administrative officer and professional hunter. I lived in an old Arab house in Lamu for fifteen years, where I learned of sheikhs and slaves, met hippies, drunks and made friends.

The stories are mere memories, which bring pleasure to me as I recall them, and which, I sincerely hope, will bring pleasure and an occasional smile to those who read them.

My thanks are due to Jarrolds Publishers (Hutchinson) and the Adventurers' Club, both of London, and the Amwell Press, Clinton, New Jersey, USA, for permission to include extracts from *A Tear for Somalia* and to the Amwell Press for extracts from *Another Tear for Africa.*

I am enormously indebted to my friend Mary Nicholas, whose drawings enhance and lend lustre to the book. I also reserve a kindly word for my patient editor, David Round-Turner, who has been quick to spot author's errors. Any errors, of fact or time, which remain are mine alone.

Douglas Collins
Vipingo, Kenya, 1995

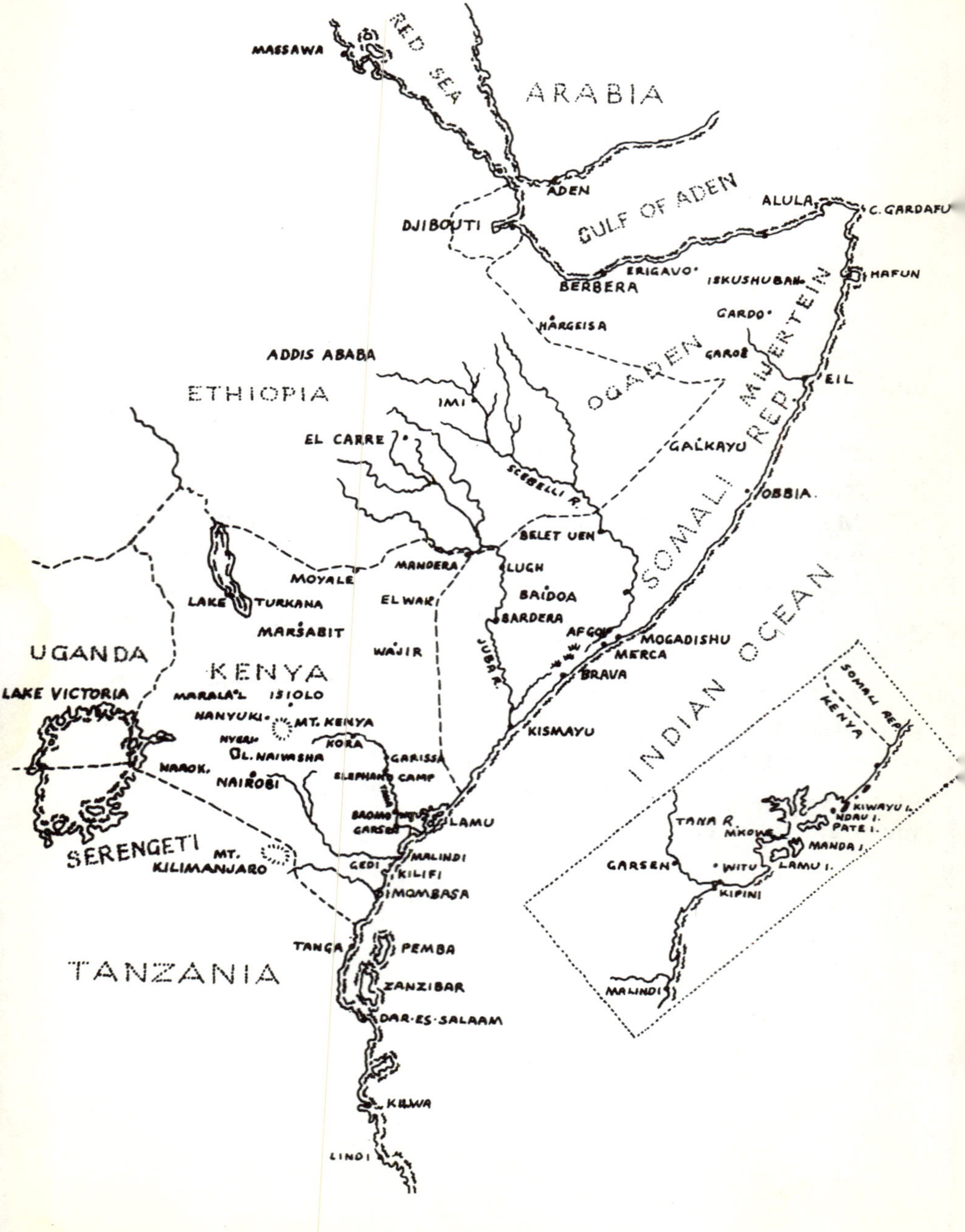

MASSAWA
RED SEA
ARABIA
ADEN
GULF OF ADEN
ALULA
C. GARDAFU
DJIBOUTI
ERIGAVO
BERBERA
ISKUSHUBAN
HAFUN
HARGEISA
GARDO
ADDIS ABABA
GAROE
OGADEN
MIJERTEIN
EIL
ETHIOPIA
IMI
EL CARRE
GALKAYU
SCEBELLI R.
OBBIA
SOMALI REP.
BELET UEN
MANDERA
LUGH
MOYALE
BAIDOA
LAKE TURKANA
EL WAK
BARDERA
MARSABIT
AFGOI
MOGADISHU
MERCA
WAJIR
JUBA R.
BRAVA
INDIAN OCEAN
UGANDA
KENYA
LAKE VICTORIA
MARALAL
ISIOLO
NANYUKI
MT. KENYA
KISMAYU
KORA
L. NAIVASHA
GARISSA
NAROK
NAIROBI
ELEPHANT CAMP
LAMU
GARSEN
SERENGETI
MT. KILIMANJARO
MALINDI
GEDI
KILIFI
MOMBASA
TANGA
PEMBA
TANZANIA
ZANZIBAR
DAR-ES-SALAAM
KILWA
LINDI
SOMALI REP.
KENYA
KIWAYU I.
NDAU I.
PATE I.
TANA R.
MKOWE
MANDA I.
GARSEN
WITU
LAMU I.
KIPINI
MALINDI

One

SOMALIA

My First Safari

1941. The scene of this story is at Afgoi in Somalia, as it was called then, on the banks of the Uebe Scebelli river and beyond. Aged 21, I had just arrived there seconded from my regiment, the South Staffords, to the Somalia Gendarmerie. Major Ray Mayers, called Indo Adde *(White Eyes) by the Somalis, was the Civil Affairs Officer-in-Charge.*

Almost fifty years before this, Winston Churchill had called the Somalilands 'a desert of rocks and thorn trees and peopled by rifle-armed fanatics'. That was the time of Mohammed Abdulla Hasan, the so-called Mad Mullah, who with his dervishes in the north fought against the British, Italians and the Habash (Ethiopians), in his Jehad *against the Gal — the Infidels. Those tribes who did not join his banner, notably the Ishaak, Gadabursi, Issa and Osman Mohamed — indeed they fought against him — suffered grievously from his cruelty. This country was splashed with blood. I was to find that it had altered little since then, for when I left ten years later, in spite of strenuous disarmament operations, it was much the same.*

1991. Yet another fifty years on and civil war has torn the country apart from Berbera in the north on the Gulf of Aden to Kismayu in the south on the Indian Ocean. But this time the splashes of blood are bigger, for the Russians, Americans and Europeans in their infinite wisdom have supplied them with fighter planes, tanks, artillery and automatic weapons. Tribe against tribe. Clan against clan.

The Somalis themselves have a saying that the Prophet said that when God created man He picked up dust from all parts of the earth. Some of it was black, some red and some white, but all men were made of that dust and were brothers. He then had a small handful left over. He laughed as he threw it in the air where a dust-devil carried it afar. Thus were the Somalis created

* * * * *

My training programme for the Gendarmerie platoon was now in

3

operation and working smoothly. Early one morning as we were stripping the Italian Breda machine gun, Indo Adde strolled along. He looked worried and seemed angry.

'Would you come along with me to the office, Dougie?' he asked, as I fell in step with him. He told me that three Garre tribesmen had just arrived in from their dry weather grazing near Ardegle. They were part of a manyatta there and apparently had been attacked by a large raiding party of Galgail — their traditional enemies.

'They might be exaggerating but they say they're the only surviving male members of their clan. We'll question them. I'd like you to listen to their story.'

In his office I saw the Garre chief, Abdi Omar, together with his headman, Ali Hersi. Their faces betrayed their bitterness at the news brought in by the three warriors who stood in the middle of the room, dressed in their travel-stained robes. They each carried a stabbing spear, a long thin pliant shaft, cut from the *dibi* or *makari* tree, dried, polished and greased with ghee — unclarified butter. The blade was about a foot long. They had knives thrust into their leather belts — the Somali dagger, about eighteen inches long, double-edged with a horn handle. They wore them strapped to their waist belts by a thong sewn to the sheath. One of them was wounded in the arm, which had recently been bandaged.

The wounded Somali spoke excitedly. 'It was the day before yesterday,' said Omar, the interpreter, 'when the sixth hour was near. They are of the clan Garuras, and they were grazing 'bout three herds of camels near Donca Adega ...'

'About sixty miles north of here,' muttered Indo Adde. 'It is now eight o'clock. Assuming they escaped from the fight round about 6 a.m. it's taken them roughly fourteen hours to get here.' Mentally I worked this out and looked up at the three Garre in admiration. They had averaged about four and a half miles an hour which was some going, considering the distance they had covered. Omar continued: 'There were about twenty fighting men in the *Rer*, twelve women and some old, old men and a few *yeros*. They had only poor manyatta as little water — they move all time and so bad *zariba* (thorn fence) round peoples.'

'He means,' explained Indo Adde, 'that the Rer or clan, continually on the move for grazing and water, only made a temporary boma and did not bother building themselves a good thorn zariba which would have afforded them more protection from the raiders.'

At this point the wounded Somali trembled. Gripping his spear with clenched hand he called out violently *'Silei! Silei!'*

'What does Silei mean, Omar?' rapped out Indo Adde.

'It means torture, Sahib.' A further torrent of despairing words came from the Garre spokesman. Blood was slowly seeping through the bandage on his arm, staining the white linen crimson. His face was grey with pain and fatigue. He swayed on his feet.

'Tell him to sit down, Omar. Give him a chair,' said Indo Adde gently.

'He say, Sahib, that those men not killed by Galgails were all tortured.'

'What clan were the Galgail?'

'Dirasama, Sahib.'

'How many fighting men?'

'Bout forty spearmen and p'raps twenty bowmen, Sahib.'

'Any rifles?'

'No, Sahib.'

'Any other weapons?'

'Yes, Sahib. They throw boms-boms (grenades) in zariba before attack.'

'Who was leading the Dirasama?'

'Aden Yebir, Sahib.'

'How does he know?'

'He recognised that man, Sahib. He say he saw him at *baraza* (meeting place), two months ago when you awarded the Garre seven hundred camels as *dia* (blood money) from Galgails.'

'Ask the other two separately if he speaks the truth.'

'They say, yes, Sahib.'

'Ask Chief Abdi Omar if he remembers the Galgail Aden Yeber attending my last baraza?'

'He say yes, Sahib. I 'member also.'

'H'm.' Indo Adde tugged at his ear reflectively. 'I think on this occasion we're getting the truth for a change. Have you any questions, Dougie?'

'Just one. How does he know the survivors of the fight were tortured?'

'Good point. Ask him Omar.'

That worthy took his *mswake* — a thin stick cut from an evergreen tree — out of his mouth with which he had been polishing the nearly whiteness of his teeth and put the question to the Garre tribesman. He raised his head slowly and looked at us. His eyes were twin pools of pain and despair.

'I saw,' he said dully. 'I heard. *Wa runtis,* (it is true). *Illahha, hagge by Jira?'* (Where is God?')

'Right Omar.' Indo Adde spoke incisively. 'Now listen, and listen carefully.

'Sergeant! Take these three Garre to your lines, feed them and look after them. Call the dresser and have a new bandage put on that man's arm. I don't want them to go to the village or speak to anyone. All understood?' The Garre Chief and his Headman nodded assent. The Sergeant saluted and herded the three Garre outside. They were out on their feet.

'Abdi Omar.' Indo Adde now addressed the Garre Chief.

'I want twenty camels with five *lenders* (camel men) here at the office within the hour.' He and his Headman salaamed and went out.

'Omar. Call back the Sergeant. Now Dougie. You are on the wing. You're off on safari. It is now nine o'clock. I want you to be off by eleven. Ah, Sergeant. I want one section of *Illalo* (tribal scouts) ready within one hour to go on safari with the Collins Sahib. You will go with them. You'll probably be away a week to ten days. Issue fifty rounds of ammunition to each man. Get ten *barrimils* (drums) of water ready for loading on the camels. Off you go. How many Gendarmes can you spare, Dougie?'

'Let me think for a moment,' I replied. I was excited by the thoughts of my first safari with the possibility of a fight at the end of it. 'I've got three sick. Two on leave. Lance-Corporal Buno is on a course. That leaves me with twenty-five men including the Sergeant. I've got a permanent twenty-four hour guard on the armoury of one NCO and three men. That cuts it down to seventeen men. I could take Sergeant Mulei and fourteen askaris.'

'Good! Get hold of your sergeant now and tell him to have his men ready. Full marching order but I'll leave all the details to you. I suggest you take rations for fourteen days. Buzz off and get your own Kag ready and then come back here where I'll brief you'. I salute happily. A safari. A foot safari with camels at last. At long last I was going into the bush. I ran off to my bungalow.

'Yusuf,' I called. 'O Yusufo! *Dakao* (hurry). *Funga kitanda na chop-box yangu na pata wote tayari kwa safari,*' I ordered. In my excitement I retrieved the chop-box from the kitchen and hurriedly threw in tins of bully-beef, milk, sausages, tinned peas, a packet of tea and sugar and also packets of biscuits and dates. Into my valise I put a torch, extra stockings, a change of khaki drill uniform, shaving kit, towel, soap and a pair of field-glasses. Yusuf, I thought, can now do his damndest. I had the essentials. Telling him to pull finger I returned to the office for my briefing. Indo Adde wasted no time.

'If the alleged attack has in fact taken place, and I do not think the Garre were lying, I want the Galgail, particularly the Dirasama clan made an example of. Haji Mohamed Elmi, I am sure, is behind all this. Arrest Aden Yebir if you can but don't go out of your way to chase him if he's left the vicinity of Donca Adega. If you do arrest him I'll only put him in jail and that means nothing at all to a Somali. He'd probably welcome the free prison rations.

'Take away his stock though, that's a different matter. Particularly camels. That really hurts them. A Somali reckons his principal wealth in his camels. That will be your primary job. Any Galgail camels near the Donca Adega area confiscate and bring in here. Quite apart from the attack on the Garre the Galgail have flagrantly disregarded my express instructions not to graze in Garre country and that in itself constitutes an offence. Firstly, seize any stock whatsoever in that area and, second, arrest any Galgail who took part in the affray. Here's a map to take with you. You will see that Donca Adega is about sixty miles north of here. Follow the Afgoi road until you reach Balad for about thirty miles. Then you cut in on this track you see here through Deimadera and Ambohile until you reach Donca Adega. You should come across water at Deimadera but don't count on it. You have your Mannlicher Schoenauer rifle

7

which will be adequate for your own personal protection. You've got your own two sections of Gendarmerie plus a section of my Illalos and it will be useful for shooting meat to supplement your rations. The Wakamba, especially, are big meat eaters and anything you can shoot for them will keep them happy.

'I don't think the Galgail will risk an attack on your force but they may try something once you have seized their stock. Put out night sentries when you camp and don't get yourself surprised in the bush. It conceals hostile movement and favours surprise in attack. Protection from all directions is essential and dispositions must be as elastic as possible to meet sudden emergencies. It's quite impossible to carry out a patrol in any set formation for any length of time owing to the distances that have to be covered and the exhaustion of the men as they march through thick bush. You will find file or single file the only way and then if you are attacked form the good old British Square and let them have it! The bush is damned thick in that area and you will find visibility limited to fifteen yards, sometimes even less. Happy? Good. Now let's see what progress is being made about getting you off.'

My Gendarmerie under Sergeant Mulei were working with a will, helping the camel men rope up their camels whilst the Illalos were sorting out the various rations and water *barrimils* into separate camel loads. The Somali camel as a baggage animal is invaluable and can carry up to four hundred pounds. They are quite gentle and only grumble and become fractious when they are overloaded. For loading, the *herio* or baggage saddle is used: it is a set of three fibre or grass mats which are tied on the camel's back to form a pad. The load is then evenly distributed and balanced on each side with the whole securely lashed. The supercilious, ungainly looking Master of the waterless deserts averages about two and a half to three miles an hour. A unique survival animal, it can go up to two months without water. For the nomads it is invaluable for they can live off the milk and it can provide clothing, footwear and at the same time transport their *gurigi* or portable houses.

The Somali usually carry their water in vessels of wood and plaited bark called *hans*, but they often leak and are apt to taint the water. I was lucky, I thought, in having Indo Adde's military-type barrimils with secure screw tops. They each contained eight gallons of water. Five of the camels had been cut out a little apart from the rest and the owner, helped by a couple of Illalos, was busy lashing the barrimils, one on each side of his camels.

At length our caravan was ready for safari with the four groups of five camels tied nose to tail. I sent one section of Gendarmerie as point under Sergeant Mulei a couple of hundred yards ahead with one of the Illalos to act as a scout. The section of Illalos were to acompany the camels with the camel men. The remaining Gendarmerie section to bring up the rear.

With a little coaxing the camels lumbered to their feet and we were off. As we crossed the bridge over the Uebe Scebelli river I glanced at my watch. The time was a few minutes after 11 a.m. Passing through the village, the long, winding, red sandy road lay ahead of us. Omar, the interpreter, walked alongside me and as we pushed along slowly he chattered incessantly, for the Somalis are great talkers and story-tellers. I began to learn something about bushlore.

Little ground squirrels and sand lizards scuttled out of our path. The Somalis, I learned, were generally uninterested in birds, mostly calling all the varieties *shimber,* but as a greater bustard, a large grey bird, bigger than a turkey, stalked in between the thorn scrub bordering each side of the road I made a mental note that Omar called it *chugli.* We flushed a brace of lesser bustard which spiralled up in the air with their harsh discordant cries. One flew over us, closed its wings, then plummeted to earth away to our left. Becoming a little tired of the pungent smell of camels we increased our pace until we caught up with the point section ahead. Sandgrouse, lying very close, their speckled colour camouflaged perfectly against the sand, fluttered out of our way with their characteristic throaty chuckle as they took wing.

We disturbed a gerenuk doe with a few-weeks-old fawn taking shade under a low acacia. The gerenuk, meaning giraffe-necked in Somali, is also known as Waller's gazelle. With an extraordinarily long neck and by standing on its hind legs it will browse off the lower branches of trees, mostly acacia. The doe moved off with a peculiar, inelegant trot-like gait with long neck extended and its head low. She had a handsome light chestnut-coloured coat, darker on the sides and with a fawnish colour on the underparts. The dainty little fawn stood watching us for a moment, through enormous limpid eyes, then trotted away after its mother.

Looking back, I saw we had outstripped the camels. We had a welcome five minutes to rest by the roadside to allow them to catch up. Off again, and the keen-eyed Omar spotted movement to our left. With jutting chin he indicated a herd of some twenty reticulated giraffe browsing on the acacias. They moved off as we went past, with an odd, slow-motion gait, appearing almost to float through the bush. With their liver and white markings they are far more handsome than the giraffe in Kenya and Tanzania. Omar told me their hides are highly prized by the Somali for making sandals and buckets for water. We crossed a *lac,* a dried watercourse, with the sun now high. Here a family of warthog, the boar with huge tushes, dashed from cover to trot up the dried-out stream bed. Ugly animals, with their long heads and unsightly warts, but so comical as the boar and sow, followed in single file by a litter of eight piglets, all with little tufted tails erect, made for safety. Omar spat.

'*Donfar,*' he said contemptuously as I half brought up the Mannlicher to my shoulder, thinking of meat for the evening. He was horrified.

'We Somalis no eat. Unclean. Later we see kudu, p'raps *arrigas* (oryx). You shoot then, Sahib.'

It was now one o'clock, with the sun a big flaming eye in the sky. My shirt, wet with perspiration stuck lovingly to my back. Little rivulets of sweat ran down my chest. I thought I could now

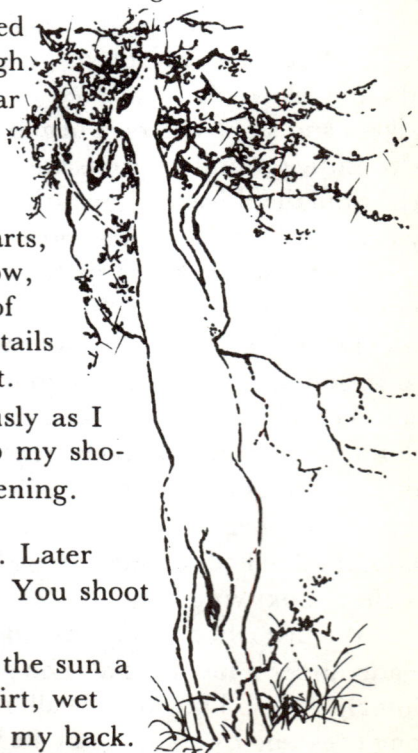

call midday halt without loss of *heshima,* or face. Here the bush was fairly thick and dotted with 'hig aloe,' a *sansevieria* shrub with sharply pointed leaves, and blossoms of red and yellow. The informative Omar explained that the lesser kudu abounded in that country and ate the leaves of that particular shrub.

Really thick, the bush now, and so we plodded on till we reached a pleasant little clearing, clumped with bunches of *durr* grass which Omar said the camels could graze on.

Calling the caravan to a halt, I gratefully stretched out under a large shady acacia, thankfully seeking the shade it afforded from that hellish, energy-sapping sun. Sergeant Mulei came up and saluted.

'We'll make camp here for one hour, Sergeant, and have tea,' I said. The camels were off-loaded and hobbled by a short piece of rope tied round the front legs which allowed them to take short, jerky steps to graze, but kept them close to our midday camp. Yusuf opened up the chop-box, taking out the kettle and a few bits and pieces. Within twenty minutes I was munching away at a packet of dates and drinking tea. Delicious tea which assuaged my thirst. On my orders neither the Wakamba Gendarmes nor the Somali Illalos had so far touched their water-bottles so I perforce had to follow suit, but it had taken all my will-power to keep my hands off the bottle as it slapped away on my buttocks during the march. Lazily resting, I squirmed my way under the acacia, its shadow diminishing as the sun rose higher. My siesta ended when Sergeant Mulei reported that he had seen kudu beyond the grazing camels. This was a chance not to be lost, for if I shot a kudu as rations for the evening we could tie it on one of the camels when we re-loaded them. The Sergeant took us over the durr grass, through a clump of thorns, past the grazing camels, where we crouched down. We looked out over a small open glade and, following the line of his pointing arm, I saw three forms partially visible in the bush and about seventy yards away. They moved in to the open and I saw my first kudu. One was a bull. A good head with ivory-tipped spiralled horns. He was grazing with two does.

'*Nyama,*' (meat), hissed the Sergeant in Swahili.

'*Illib,*' echoed Omar in Somali as I pushed forward the safety catch and took careful aim behind the bull's shoulder.

The Mannlicher cracked, followed by an immediate 'thunk' which told me that the bullet had gone home. The poise of the elegant head faltered, he staggered then bounded away followed by his consorts. I was dumbfounded. I just couldn't have missed at that range.

'*Napiga. Napiga,*' (a hit, a hit), shouted the Sergeant racing forward with Omar and myself tearing after him. There he lay, a hundred yards further on with his pretty striped coat stained crimson over the heart. Several of the Somali antelopes are lovely creatures but I award the palm of beauty to the lesser kudu. The Sergeant pumped me by the hand. He was overjoyed.

'Nyama,' he kept saying, 'Nyama.' Omar was upset. 'Dead, Sahib,' he said. 'Dead. I can't *chinja* it so we Muslims no eat.' Evidently any game killed for the Somalis must be properly *bismillah'd* before it dies. Its head must be turned towards Mecca and then with ceremony its throat cut. He looked so woebegone that I promised to shoot the Somalis another antelope later on but I mentally resolved that it would not be another kudu — they were too lovely for that.

Aided by a couple of Gendarmes we carried the kudu to our midday resting place and I gave orders to load up. The camel chosen to carry the kudu was already carrying two sacks of maize meal and it objected most strongly to an additional burden. He roared, gurgled, spat and buck-jumped to show his displeasure, dislodging the kudu twice. It was then tied on again so tightly that he finally submitted though with very bad grace. We moved on with the heat of the sun still searing down on us. Nothing else moved but the caravan, and Omar said that all the game was now resting in the thickets during the heat. We marched on following the remorseless red sandy road until the sun lost its fierceness and mercifully the heat was less oppressive.

Three dikdik dashed across the road, bounding at speed in a series of stiff-legged jumps. Myriads of pink and white butterflies gladdened the eye as they fluttered on sansevieria blossom. As the heat diminished the desert began to live again. Hornbills appeared, weaving and dipping their undulating way over us. I saw my first hoopoe with its feathered, crested crown. Francolin scurried underfoot and seldom took to the air. A covey of sandgrouse passed high overhead winging their way to the now distant river. Weaver birds flew and twittered among a colony of nests in a large acacia; each nest as light as gossamer as it swayed suspended from a single thorn. I picked up a feather of dark blue, lying like a glittering jewel in our path as we marched on. It was good to be alive and I rejoiced with the birds whose presence was rarely lacking, except during the oppressive midday heat. At length, an hour before sunset, I reckoned we had covered some fifteen miles and when we reached a clearing in the bush fringed by large acacias I decided to make camp.

The camels came to a grumbling halt and needed no word of

command from their *lenders* to fall to their knees
for the off-loading. It was a pleasant camping site
and I was not at all enthusiastic when Omar asked
me to try and shoot meat for the Somalis.

Leaving the Illalo Sergeant to supervise the
off-loading and pitching camp I posted my sentries, then resignedly made my way to the edge of
the plain followed by Omar and the inexhaustible
Sergeant Mulei. We immediately saw a flock of
eight ostriches, one cock resplendent in his
black and white plumage and his seven dowdier-looking
consorts. With their huge, naked thighs they looked like a troop of
ballet dancers. Suddenly, taking alarm at our approach they were
off, dodging this way and that, helped along by their flapping wings.
Mulei had his nose to the ground like a trained bloodhound and
pointed out what I took to be recent spoor.

'*Ba'id,*' shouted Omar excitedly, only to be crushed by a reprov-
ing look for his noisy outburst from Mulei.

'Oryx,' he breathed in Swahili. He pronounced it 'arrigas.'

Weaving our way through the scattered bush we came suddenly across a small herd. They were wary but under Mulei's expert
tuition we approached upwind until we were within a hundred yards
of them. The Beisa oryx is a splendid-looking animal with black and
white face markings in striking contrast. The long, slender, scimitar-
like horns curve slightly backwards and are annulated half-way up
from the base. The males have heavier horns than the females. Lying down I cuddled the Mannlicher into my shoulder, drawing a
bead on a fine buck in the herd. He went down. The herd panicked
and dashed off, the wounded bull taking a line of his own as he fell
then struggled lamely to his feet. Reloading I gave him another which
felled him and then we closed in. He was wonderfully tenacious of
life as he stood up again, then lowering those sharp, curved horns,
he gallantly faced us. Mulei and Omar circled him, approaching from
the rear whilst I covered them. A quick rush and they seized him
by the horns. Omar drew his dagger, quickly despatching him as
he struggled to the last. He severed the jugular vein and so the blood

flowed through a Muslim hand. He uttered an invocation to Allah. Waving aloft the blood-stained dagger he boasted:

'O Be'id, thy horns are sharp — but my knife is sharper.
'*Ilib, ilib, Ilah Mahaddi!* (meat, meat, thanks to God!)

The Law of the Bush. Kill or be killed, I mused regretfully as I looked down at the oryx, his emerald eyes now glazed by the death which had so suddenly come to him. Leaving Mulei with the carcass to keep scavenging hyenas and vultures away, Omar and I slowly walked back to camp only to meet a baggage camel led by two jubilant Illalos. Hearing the shots they had anticipated meat for the evening.

The camp was bustling with activity on our return. Most of the Wakamba were cutting down *Jirin* trees and building a large circular zariba, carefully laying down the branches so that the long, wicked thorns pointed outwards. The rest had already skinned the kudu and were cutting it up. The Illalos were carrying the rations and water barrimils into the half-built zariba whilst the lenders were keeping an eye on their hobbled camels outside.

Sitting on my camp-chair, I contentedly sipped the tea Yusuf had prepared. The sunset glow faded. A jackal barked away, short, staccato yaps which were answered by the hyena's long drawn out hunting call from the direction of the dead oryx.

'*Waraba, waraba,*' laughed Omar.

'*Fisi, fisi.*' echoed the Wakamba, showing their filed teeth as they happily cut up their meat.

'What is so funny about the hyena, Omar?' I asked curiously.

'He he and she at same time, Sahib,' he laughed, while the Wakamba, thinking this the biggest joke in history, roared their appreciation at Omar's description of the allegedly hermaphroditical hyena.

'*Cheka. Cheka.* That is why he laughs for he got both kuma and plick,' explained Mulei with a huge grin who had just reported in with the oryx lashed to the back of a camel. More shrieks of merriment from the Wakamba. Omar further explained that generally hyenas are loathed as unclean and hated as stock killers, but they are considered to have brains like men and to possess infinite guile.

The zariba was complete, a thorn fence about six foot high and twenty yards across into which the lenders now herded the camels for the night. Three camp fires were burning and crackling brightly. One for the Wakamba, one for the Somalis and my own kitchen fire. I made my way through the belching, gurgling camels, for we all shared the zariba. Most of them were contentedly crouched, wetly chewing their cud and drooling green saliva from their rubbery lips as they regurgitated from their stomachs the acacia leaves and durr grass they had just eaten. Their acid-sharp, pungent smell pervaded the whole camp. I ordered the Gendarmes and Illalos to dig shallow rifle pits spaced at regular intervals facing outwards on the inside of the thorn perimeter. They would sleep in them with one arm through their rifle sling. My own bed looked inviting so I stripped off my uniform, slipped into my *lungi* and flopped down.

A sonorous call from Omar and the Illaloes and lenders came for evening prayer.

'Allah! Allah!' he called as they gathered in a half circle round him, each man kneeling on his prayer carpet of tanned leather. At another call from him they all stood up gazing meditatively into the night, their hands crossed on their chests for several seconds. Then they knelt again, each man bending forward three times, pressing his forehead on the sand.

'Allah! Allah! Allah Akbar!' Omar called again. Their prayers went on for the best part of half an hour. The pagan Wakamba were busy eating from strips of oryx meat tossed on the flames.

'Dinner, Sahib,' said Yusuf quietly. I sat up on my bed and ate oryx steak and liver which was really good. As I sipped away at my coffee, Mulei came over with a cracked oryx leg bone, which had been cooked in the ashes, and a clean sliver of wood and invited me to eat again. I poked out the marrow which made one of the most delicious meals I have ever tasted. I thanked him and told him to instruct the early morning sentry to wake me at dawn. I was replete. The camp settled down for the night but not so the hyena. They soon winded the fresh meat, having finished off the offal where I had shot the oryx. The night was made hideous with their concert, an uncanny wailing which they kept up for most of the night. There was a sliver of a moon and the stars shone friendlily. I could make

16

cut the Great Bear and the Southern Cross.

I slept, lulled to slumber by the hollow sound of the bells as the camels settled down for the night. Yusuf woke me with tea. Then came the dawn, grey-veiled and silent, while a little wind stole past. The desert was filled with the soft, shy colours of early morning. The camp awoke and hummed with life. Sergeant Mulei, none too gently, woke the Wakamba still sleeping and the Illalo Sergeant in his gutteral Somali rasped out '*Ka Ka*' (get up, get up). The duty sentry relaxed and spat. Hastily donning my soiled uniform I walked around the zariba. The camels came to life as the herios were lifted on to their backs, grunting complainingly as the ropes were tightened around their bellies. A furtive hyena skulked off followed by two jackals — his scavenging accomplices. Half a dozen vultures with a hop, skip and a jump soared into the air.

Loaded now, the camels lumbered to their feet and we were off just before six. Loitering a while and letting them get into their stride I called Mulei over and asked him to show and familiarize me with the various spoor I had noticed around camp. He showed me lion, leopard and hyena as well as jackal and the smaller cats — civet and serval. We hurried on and caught up with the swaying camel convoy ahead. The bush grew dense again with the curved, clawing fingers of the 'wait a bit' thorns reaching out in places over the road. With startling suddenness a large flock of vulturine guinea fowl burst out of the thorn scrub to wing away in all directions with their rattling cry of alarm; brilliantly-coloured birds with their neck feathers of black and white and breasts of cobalt blue. A parrot, swift of flight, just a flash of green and orange, flew through a flock of bee-eaters, lovely gregarious birds, circling in the sky then swooping down in carmined streaks to snatch up insects off the bushes. Doves, grey and lilac, fluttered in our path, whilst from the road-side came a fragrant aroma as the camel loads caught and bruised the branches of overhanging aromatic shrubs.

Ahead, the Wakamba point section, their bellies full of meat and hearts as light as mine, were singing endlessly and repetitively the old King's African Rifles marching song:

Funga safari, funga safari
Amri ya KAR, Amri ya KAR

Amri Ya Bwana, Amri Ya Bwana,
Amri ya KAR

Oh, I thought, let the senior officers in Mogadishu have their
crumpets, their wives, their Italian mistresses, their Somali mistresses,
their elevenses for gin and their dusty files of bumph. What cared
I? What could they know of the loveliness of the desert? A red ant
hill, towering above us, leaned grotesquely over the road as we swung
past, the camels lurching to one side to avoid dislodging their loads.
The old enemy, the inexorable sun, began its tireless climb into the
sky and after marching for another two hours we thankfully reached the Deimadera track, which wound its way at a right angle from
the road. Here we found a large *deshek,* or water pan, the edges
caked hard and criss-crossed by huge cracks in the dried-out mud.
A little green stagnant water remained in the middle. A Somali *karia*
was encamped in an open space near by. Calling halt, for it was
now close on eleven, I flung myself under a large candelabra tree
and watched the swaying camels arrive. Omar and three Illalos came
up with three wild-looking Somali warriors.

They each carried a spear and from their belts protruded a knife
and a throwing stick. Porcupine quills decorated their long, bushy
hair and their robes were of a reddish colour. They carried the usual
praying mat of tanned leather folded on their shoulders. Threaded
on their wrists were their ornamental head-rests carved from the
'Malmal', a myrhh tree. Tied above the muscle on the left arm was
a small leather pouch containing Koranic charms. They stood a few
yards to my front, aloof and proud, whilst all the time their wild,
untamed eyes were flickering from me to my mixed body of Wakamba Gendarmerie and Illalos, assessing their numbers. One of them
stood like a stork, his right leg folded up, resting on his left knee.
He cleaned his teeth with his tooth stick then spat out the fibre and
continued polishing.

'*Nabat!*' I said. There was no reply. They looked at me
contemptuously.

'Omar, their tribe?' I asked.

'Rahanwein.' This from the warrior cleaning his teeth. He smiled and spat again. In my direction this time.

18

'Where do they come from?'

'They say nowhere, Sahib,' replied Omar.

'Where are they going?'

'They say nowhere, Sahib,' (Oh, give me patience, I prayed). Omar came to my help.

'I already asked women and children — they are Galgail, Sahib. See that camel? It has Galgail brand on neck — two lines and a dot. This Galgail karia Sahib. These mens lie.'

'Sergeant Mulei,' I called. He ran up, saluted by smacking the butt of his riffle as he stood quivering to attention.

'Disarm these three Somalis and tie them up with camel rope. We are taking them prisoner.'

The Sergeant turned about and yelled: 'Kayanda, Toto, Buno, Mrefu, Yulu — kuja. Fix bayonets. *Kwa ngufu toa mkuke na visu yao na funga hawa,*' he ordered. Menaced by the glittering steel the three Somalis lost a little of their arrogance. They were disarmed none-too-gently and while three Gendarmes presented the points of their bayonets at their chests, the other two quickly and expertly tied their wrists behind them. They looked at me venomously, their eyes narrowed and glittering with enmity.

'Ask them their tribe again, Omar,' I said.

'Galgail,' they spat out.

'Clan, Omar?'

'Diraisama,' they hissed.

'What do they know of the fight between the Garre and the Galgail at Donca Adega a few days ago?'

'They say they know nothing, Sahib.'

'What are they doing on this side of the road in Garre country?'

'They say they are Galgail, Sahib. They can water and graze where they like.'

Good, I thought. I've established their tribe and clan and they admit trespassing in Garre country. For all I know they may themselves have taken part in the fight at Donca Adega, only fifteen miles from here. I pondered on the situation. An Illalo brought me up a *tebed,* a vessel made out of camel leather which the Somalis use for drinking milk and carrying ghee. It was brimful of foamy camel's milk straight from the udder. I drank deeply, watched begrudgingly by the three Galgail.

'Omar,' I paused in between mighty draughts of milk. 'How many camels do you think the Galgail are grazing here?' He turned round, surveyed the scattered karia and large zariba then began his estimation, ticking off the numbers on his fingers.

"Kow, laba, sadeh, afarr, shan — five hundred Sahib. Mebbe more. They are also 'bout thirty women, many children and p'raps forty spearmen but most of these out grazing camels.'

'Call up the two Sergeants.' At Omar's call they marched up together and saluted.

'Sergeant Mulei. Put a guard on these three prisoners, then organise the rest of our force in building a strong zariba. We camp here for the night.'

'Mag'a?' I addressed the Illalo Sergeant for I did not know his name. 'Gared Mohamed, Sahib,' he replied. 'Kabil-ka? Clan?' 'Makahil, Sahib.' I mused on this for I intended at first light to seize one half of the camels here as a preliminary to my first punitive measure against the Galgail. Could I trust the Galgail Sergeant though?

'Omar. Ask him how long he has been an Illalo Sergeant and how many Galgail Illalos have I got with me apart from himself.'

'He say, Sahib, he Illalo Sergeant since the Inglesi first came. Before that he Sergeant-Major of Dubas for seven years with Italianos. He says other Illalos Rahanwein, Garre, Geledi and Uadan. No more Galgails.'

I'll take a risk on it, I thought. I don't like splitting my force but I'll send him back to Afgoi with the Illalos, less three which I can use as Scouts. If they get off at first light they will be able to make camp within striking distance of Afgoi.

'Right, Omar. Thank him and tell him to dismiss.' After he had left I idly watched marabou storks, cruising and wheeling lazily at a great height over the karia. Scavengers, they are unlovely birds — more of a vulture than a stork with their backs a slaty-green colour and white bodies. Their heads, neck and chest are bare giving them an obscene look. A single bird was standing on one leg, halfway between myself and the karia. It had an attitude of profound meditation. Omar disturbed my own thoughts.

'What you going do, Sahib?' He was nobody's fool Omar, and he had obviously deduced from my questioning of Sergeant Garad that in all probability I would punish the Galgail Diraisama for their trespass into Garre country. I decided not to enlighten him.

'Nothing yet,' I said. He was disappointed and looked at me reproachfully as he salaamed and walked away. It was now lunch time but the camel's milk had so filled me that I had no further appetite. I detided to walk around the karia. Omar, thinking perhaps he could get some information out of me if he persisted, came along. He had, apparently, forgotten my seeming lack of confidence in him for he was at his most talkative and eager to please. We reached the karia.

'Galgail karia only arrive yesterday, Sahib. Look, women still building.' He explained that when the Somali makes camp the women sweep it before constructing their tents, the gurigi which are carried by the camels. They then thrust into the ground forked stakes and over these they place boughs; fixed into the ground are props for the door frames. They then tie the first sticks and boughs together, then the props of the door frames. Then one by one they place over these bent sticks or saplings and the smaller boughs. These are then all tied together. Over this framework they then place camel mats. If there is no rain about, as at present, they do not bother surrounding the tents with earth to keep out the water. When the exterior of the tent is finished they cut branches which they place on the floor to sleep on. This is called the *daragad*.

A Somali family never lives alone in the bush. Several assemble to form a rer or karia. The first work of the families is to make two enclosures. A small one for the sheep and goats, and a larger one for the cattle and camels. When there are no lion about each tent has its own entrance through the zariba, but if lion are troublesome there is only one communal entrance. All the inhabitants sleep inside the enclosure.

Early in the morning the men and yeros take out the stock to graze and have nothing else to do. All the work is done by the women. Walking about the karia, watching with interest the women performing their various tasks, I saw only two fighting men who watchfully followed my movements with sullen eyes. I assumed the remainder were out with the camel herds. A small Somali child, standing by its mother, suddenly caught sight of me, burst into tears and fled into one of the tents.

Not so the Somali *gabdo*, the unmarried girls. They were far from shy. Born courtesans, the dusky beauties with their bold, almond-shaped eyes and swaying, seductive forms followed me wherever I went. As a general rule they like amourettes with strangers, following the well-known Arab proverb — 'the newcomer filleth the eye'. However in cases of scandal, the woman's tribe revenges its honour on the man.

Sauntering back to camp I gave nods of approval and a word of encouragement to the Illalos and Wakamba alike who had done a prodigious job in almost completing the zariba. The weapon pits had been scooped out of the sand and on the inside my own little camp was organised with my bed under a convenient acacia in one corner. I cleaned the Mannlicher and laid it on the bed. Yusuf produced tea. From him I learned that the Galgail karia-folk were troubled by leopard and regularly lost one or two goats or sheep each week whenever they were encamped in this area.

The three Galgail prisoners, their hands tied behind their backs were sitting in the middle of the karia. They had been roped to short stakes driven deep in the ground. A sentry stood nearby.

I was a little embarrassed to find a bevy of giggling Somali girls in camp inspecting my bed with much interest. Shooing them away, for I had sterner things in mind, I sat down and wrote a brief sitrep to Indo Adde which I would dispatch at first light by an Illalo runner.

The first of the returning Galgail stock then burst through the scrub bordering the far side of the clearing. First came the sheep and goats in a bleating rush for the green, stagnant water in the deshek from which they drank thirstily. Next came the camels in a long, padding, straggling herd. Hundreds of them. Many of the she-camels had their young with them and I saw twins; tiny, woolly, spindly-legged miniature camels nuzzling mother's udder as they suckled. The air was filled with their plaintive bellowings as they entered the Galgail karia, herded in by the warriors and yero with their piercing whistles. I counted about forty fighting men for the most part armed with their formidable stabbing spears and daggers. Some carried bows and arrows.

The arrows, carried in leather quivers, were slung over the shoulders of the bowmen. The arrow tips are poisoned with the *wabayo*, made virulent by boiling the roots of the *waba* tree — a round evergreen not unlike a bay tree. This poisonous juice renders any wound uncurable and death occurs usually within an hour. Omar told me that to test the efficacy of the poison a little is inserted into the ear of a sickly sheep or goat, which usually dies in half an hour. If they had rifles, then they must have hidden them. All in all not so formidable, I thought, as in the far country, bordering Ethiopia, where I had heard as many as two hundred raiders at a time, the scourge of the Ogaden, the dreaded *shifta*, mostly armed with rifles and some automatics, would raid down deep into Somali country. In their wake they would leave a trail of utter devastation as they killed and tortured the men, raped and absconded with the women and — bitterest blow of all to the tribes — looted their camel herds.

It was time for the milking. All the girls and married women gave a hand. Omar brought me up another tebed and, as I drank slowly, my plan of action for first light began to form. We would strike camp and load up our camels for a quick start. I reckoned there would be about five hundred camels in the Galgail herd. I intended to seize half. The Wakamba Gendarmes would cover the seizure and shoot down any resisting Galgail. As soon as those Illalos I had detailed had started with the camels to Afgoi, we would continue our march to Donca Adega.

We settled down for the night. I slept fitfully and inspected the sentries at 2 a.m. At about 4.30 a.m. I was awakened by the frantic bleating of sheep and goats coming from the Galgail karia. A grunting sawing roar shattered the stillness of the outside night, which set off again the terrified cries from the Galgail karia. The flickering flames from the camp fires cast leaping shadows in the dark as the lenders began to saddle up our baggage camels.

'Shabel!' exclaimed Yusuf, bringing tea. The leopard's sawing coughs decreased in intensity as, with a series of harsh coughs, he made off into the night. Our camp fires and movement had evidently deterred him from his intended nocturnal attack and the spotted killer went in search of easier, safer prey.

Dressing quickly, I despatched the Illalo runner with a chit for Indo Adde at Afgoi. I then gave my instructions to Omar and the two Sergeants. A smile of approval appeared on the attentive face of Omar as they listened.

False dawn lit the night sky as we formed up and quietly marched down to the sleeping Galgail karia. We entered, an Illalo pulling away the tangle of thorns protecting the entrance. Two sleepy sentries were unceremoniously bundled into one of the tents whilst half the Illalos, with rifles and bayonets fixed, kept guard at the other entrances. Others kicked and prodded the camels to their feet. Dawn broke. Grumbling and complaining the camels lurched to their feet and within a short space of time half of them were outside the karia. Herded by the Illalos I had detailed they started in the direction of Afgoi. The Galgail, angry and fully awake, now tried to recover their camels but were penned in the zariba by the glittering bayonets. They endeavoured to break out through the thorn fence but a couple of shots from the watchful Wakamba drove them back.

As my own caravan of baggage camels got underway I withdrew the Wakamba guarding the karia entrance and the Galgail warriors poured out in a torrent of raging fury. A spearman, bolder than the rest, bounded forward coughing out his tribal war cry, and took Sergeant Mulei's bullet. He dropped his spear, clawed at his chest and sprawlingly sank to the ground. The Mannlicher spoke and a bowman, notching his poisoned arrow, fell over backwards as the bullet went home. Sullenly they broke and dispersed. Some to take refuge in the karia and others after their camels, now a dust cloud over the scrub and making good time on their way to Afgoi. Staying behind with the reargard of the Wakamba we also made good time in the opposite direction and only lessened our pace when pursuit seemed unlikely. Leaving Sergeant Mulei in charge of the rear party I moved ahead past the camels with a Wakamba orderly. The Sergeant, a look of concern on his normally cheerful face, had insisted on a bodyguard for me after that sharp little action. I now saw that each Galgail prisoner had had his hands re-tied to his front, and that each man was attached by a short rope tied to the tails of three camels.

Omar was jubilant. 'Good, Sahib, good,' he kept repeating. He was of the Rahanwein tribe who, like the Garre, had suffered grievously in the past from the depredations of the truculent, avaricious Galgail.

Moving briskly, still keyed up with that little brush with the hostiles, we remained alert for a possible counter-attack.

It was Kayanda, my orderly, who first spotted them. Kayanda, the clown of the platoon, who had raised a laugh a little while back by aping the unfortunate Galgail prisoners as will-nilly they shuffled along, tied to the camels' tails. The Wakamba are born mimics and imitators and Kayanda was no exception. He pointed far ahead with his rifle. I followed the line of the upward-slanting barrel and saw a cloud of tiny specks wheeling high in the sky

'*Ndege ya nyama,*' said Private Kayanda Toto. Vultures. They never lie. Their presence always means something. The remains of a lion kill; a Somali karia; a wounded animal, or the birth of an animal such as oryx, kudu or gerenuk as the mother gently licks its newly-born, trembly offspring, the while keeping a watchful eye and lowered head on the voracious vultures as they plane down from space to greedily clean up the afterbirth. We covered another mile and I could now see and distinguish the wheeling vultures and marabou storks. Quite suddenly I smelt it. Death. I remembered it from the approaches to Dunkirk in France. That familiar sweet, quite unmistakeable smell of the dead. Kayanda raised his perspiring face and sniffed.

'*Watu, watu walikufa,*' he said for once in serious mood. Omar came up and looked at me. Calling up Sergeant Mulei the four of us increased our pace. A spotted hyena, the waraba, the largest of the hyena family, its unprepossessing, ungainly shape with its blotchy body and short round ears, loped across the path ahead of us. Nearer now to that awful unknown. The sweet, sickly stench came stronger. Jackals, several of them, slunk out of our way when suddenly we were clear of the bush and on a large open plain. A Somali karia, abandoned, with no visible signs of life looked lonely on our approach. Several vultures taxied away and, with beating wings, lifted themselves in the air. Two more hyenas shambled away. The stench was now unbearable.

It was then that I saw them — or what remained of them. Five bloated, broken bodies were scattered around the karia, face upwards on the ground. They had been crucified. Their arms and legs had been spread-eagled, tied and pegged down. I thought that the scavengers, fearing their human smell, had probably left them for the first few days and then, as the last agonised movements and tortured screams ceased for ever, they had grown bolder and closed in for their unholy feast. A bloodied thigh bone, snapped off its body by the hyena's powerful jaws, lay to my left with the foot pathetically intact.

Horrified, I moved closer. A face here half eaten away; a full face still left there, bloated out of shape but with the agonised expression still frozen as death mercifully came.

They had been castrated and, spewing out of the mouths, still recognisable as such, were their testicles. I paled, felt an overwhelming wave of nausea to rush off behind a convenient ant hill where I was violently sick. Then, recovering, I returned to that awful place of death.

'*Ilah ha isha Samaiyai mianu arka hain?*' (God made the eye, shall He not see) spat out Omar. His eyes were bitter. The baggage animals approached with the leading camel shying at the death smell. The Illalo I had retained as a scout approached and I could see his face turn from a bronze colour to grey. Trembling violently he screamed unintelligibly. Foam flecked his lips and his eyes went mad. Throwing away his rifle he drew his knife and rushed at the bound Galgail prisoners a few paces away, screaming with hate in his violence.

'Sergeant Mulei,' I shouted urgently. The Sergeant reacted quickly, bounded forward and thrust his rifle between the Illalo's legs as he sped past, bringing him heavily to the ground. A Wakamba stabbed his boot on his knife hand as the sobbing, fighting Illalo was overpowered and held down by a pile of Wakamba.

'Rope. Tie him,' I ordered.

'He Garre, Sahib,' explained Omar simply. 'He Garre Giumbulul. This is Clan.'

'Let's get away from here,' I said urgently to no on in particular. Moving quickly, making a detour, I hastened away and along the path. About half a mile from that place of death, Donca Adega, we found another deshek in a smaller clearing. It was quite dry. A little mud remained at the bottom. Giving orders to off-load and make camp, I then thought out my future actions. First things first, I thought, calling up Sergeant Mulei. I told him to bring the Galgail prisoners to me. Still defiant, they looked contemptuously at me. One smiled. A thin, sneering smile. I burned with anger. In our kit we carried half a dozen *pangas,* large chopping knives, which we used to cut down thorn trees for constructing zaribas during our line of march. They would now come in handy.

'Sergeant Mulei,' I said. 'Take a half section of your men and get these Galgail to dig a grave and bury the Garre. They are to dig deeply. After that they will cover the grave with stones so that the hyenas and jackals will not be able to get at the remains. Neither you nor your men will help. If they refuse shoot them and bury them all together. Understand?'

'*Fahamu,*' replied Sergeant with a grim smile. He was happy. Those three blue-blooded, murdering aristocratic dogs of Somalis would work all right — or else.

'Omar. You have heard my words. Tell them to the Galgail.' He complied.

'Get cracking Sergeant,' I said. Slipping a round in the breech of his .303 rifle, he held it at high point, then reversing it suddenly hit the still-smiling Somali over the face with the butt as they hustled them away. I told Omar to bring up the Garre Illalo for questioning. He looked broken and stared glassily at me from defeated, apathetic eyes.

'Tell him I'm sorry for what's happened but I want him to help me contact the Galgail and punish them and recover the looted Garre stock.' He brightened up at this and began to take an interest in life again.

'How big was this Garre karia?'

'He say 'bout five hundred camels, Sahib. He himself owned fifty of them which were herded by his two brothers. They were both killed by Galgails.'

'How many fighting men had the Garre? How many women

and children?'

'He say 'bout twenty spearmen, Sahib and 'bout fifteen women, some old men and yeros.'

'Where does he think they have gone?'

'Not sure, Sahib, but he think Bulo Garas. 'Bout forty-five miles from here where there is water and big, very big Garre karia. Too big for Galgails to attack.'

'Where does he think the Galgail fighting men have gone with the looted Garre stock?'

'Not sure Sahib, but p'raps crossed road into Galgails country. P'raps best go to Bulo Garas and ask there. Also water at Bulo Garas.' At the mention of water I started guiltily. Once leaving Afgoi events had moved so rapidly that I'd completely forgotten to check up on this most important item.

'How much water have we got left?' I asked anxiously.

'Not know, Sahib. Will go and count,' he replied striding off He returned quickly, concern showing on his face. 'Bad, Sahib, bad Only half barrimil left. 'Nuff for tea tonight then little in water-bottles, after that finish.' I cursed savagely. I had only myself to blame. What a clot, I thought. Here we are right out in the middle of the bush with little or no water. Walking over to the barrimils I kicked them in a panic. All empty but one and that sounded only half full as I rocked it from side to side. Calling up a Wakamba I made him carry it and have it placed under my bed, giving instructions to the sentry that it was not to be touched.

'Where is the nearest water from here, Omar?' I asked apprehensively.

Bulo Garas, Sahib — 'bout forty-five miles away.' It would be dusk before the gruesome job of digging a communal grave for the Garre was finished. Well, I thought, there's nothing for it. We'll push off for Bulo Garas at first light, getting information from the Garre there. They would be only too keen to help contact the Galgail and in so doing recover their stock. Calling up Omar and my orderly, Private Kayanda, we followed the track back to see how the burial party was progressing. They had almost finished. The three Galgail looked much the worse for wear after their several hours work — probably the first manual work they had ever done in their lives.

Gone were their *maridadi* porcupine hair quills, and gone was their arrogance. Sergeant Mulei had done a good job, I thought.

In order to finish the cairn before dusk, we all now helped in piling the flat, grey stones high on the grave. In spite of the violence of their end they had at least found a decent resting place in the brooding desert. More than can be said for some of the Somalis in the bush. It is customary for them, when on long treks, to leave any old people behind who are unable to keep up for the lions or hyenas to finish off. However, a person subjected to a violent death traditionally should be buried before sundown and I hoped that these Garre slain, in spite of being so cruelly treated, would find unlimited hours in the hereafter. We piled the last few stones on the grave, then made our way back to camp. The sun had set; already the scavengers were giving call.

I had Sergeant Mulei fall in the Wakamba. Examining each man's water-bottle, I found they were all empty. Filling each bottle from the remaining barrimil left that empty too. It served little use in lecturing them, but I did so, pointing out that their irresponsibility in squandering the water had put us all in a most dangerous situation. Childlike, they lived only for the day. The *serikali* (government) would provide. Were they not wearing the King's uniform? Were they not receiving their pay and their rations every month, and their uniforms half-yearly? I watched as they thought it out, wide-eyed and solemn-faced, wondering why their officer Sahib was scolding them over a little water. In their own country, lush with banana trees, papaya and the like, the river flowed past their huts. Their women drew the water and brought it home to brew the *pombe* (millet beer). Here they drank their fill, smoking, yarning, idling. They gave up trying to work it out and chorused '*Ndio, effendi*' after my little lecture.

There they stood awaiting my dismisal. Eat, drink, the occasional whore and the askari is happy. If he over ate when those black bellies would swell out like 44-gallon petrol drums, the platoon dresser would give them some white powdered *dawa* and their stomach aches would go. If they ever drank, mostly pombe, or much worse, Nubian gin, which was sold illicitly in Afgoi village, they would suffer imperial hangovers. If they had a whore and caught a dose of clap then that was the biggest joke in history. The kindly, benevolent

29

Serikali would send them to hospital in Mogadishu where they would lie beween clean sheets and have the little, healing needle jabbed twice a day in their backsides until they were better. True, their pay was stopped in hospital but for those few ecstatic, vigorous minutes of lusty passion it was well worth it. Happy, likeable, wayward. I dismissed them wearily.

Calling up Yusuf, I asked him if there was any water left over in the kettle for tea.

'*Bio damai.* Water finish,' he said happily. They were all the same, I thought. They love being the bearer of bad news. They seem to take a fiendish delight in watching the Sahib's reactions to the news that this is finished or that is finished, when one is miles in the blue and it is quite impossible to obtain further supplies.

'Open up a tin of fruit for dinner,' I told him sourly. I could eat the fruit and drink the juice. 'Gone. Finish. You eat, Sahib,' he replied, happier still and proud of his few words of English.

'Damn you, Yusuf,' I snapped crossly. 'Open up a tin of peas then.'

'Can do, Sahib,' replied the imperturble Somali Jeeves. I ate the cold peas moodily, forkful by forkful as I speared them from the tin. I then drank the green juice thirstily and threw the empty can away. A superb starling, resplendent in red and blue jacket and green waistcoat, with inquisitive yellow eyes, alighted from a nearby acacia, walked over to the can to eat the few morsels I had left. It was night again. The hyenas started up and went through their whole reper- toire. They shrieked, howled, cackled and laughed in a frenzy of mad orchestration at being cheated out of the human remains they had previously dined off. I slept miserably and fitfully with my thirst unassuaged. My sub-conscious anxiety over water made me to dream vividly of pint upon pint of cold beer. Delicious ice-cold beer. Each pint in a frosted pewter tankard.

I awoke with a dry mouth and with some difficulty opened my eyelids which had stuck together. It was five in the morning. I gave orders to load up the camels. The usual drill followed but with little enthusiasm as though all realized the plight we were in and the waterless miles ahead of us. We left without the usual refreshing, sugared and energy-giving tea. The sun, friendly no longer, rose and climbed inexorably. I was too miserable to take notice of the game as I fought back the temptation to uncork my water-bottle and drink for I had given orders that the Wakamba were not to open their bottles until we halted.

On we marched until eleven, through that parched and cruel bush, along the winding, monotonous, never-ending track. It was too much of an effort now to raise my arm to brush aside the clutching 'wait a bit' curved thorns. Staggering through them doggedly, they gashed my face and tore into my tunic. I now panted with the heat and that awful, raging thirst. Sergeant Mulei came up and raspingly begged me to halt. His face was a perspiring black mask, his uniform black too, with his sweat. He forgot to salute.

'*Bado nusu saa,*' I croaked. In half an hour's time. I wiped the sweat out of my eyes and went forward again, looking with a longing ache at an invitingly low, shady acacia by the side of the track. We must cover the miles. Cover the miles. Cover the miles, I kept repeating to myself. A hornbill gave his harsh mocking cry as he dipped overhead.

The sun flared down hellishly until my eyeballs grew hot in their sockets. Heat waves shimmered and danced relentlessly to my front. My mouth was long since dry of spittle. I wanted to vomit but couldn't. Trying to screw up my eyelids, I blundered into a thorn bush again and blood mingled with the sweat on my face.

'Sahib,' Omar rasped out behind me. I turned listlessly to look at him dully.

'*Dombir,*' he croaked, pointing to a tuber partly exposed in the hot, red sand. Already the Garre Illalo had his knife out and was digging it up, frantic in his eagerness. Omar joined him. They drove their knives deep in the sand as the long, putty-coloured root became fully exposed. They slashed pieces off, ate and spat out the flakes of root. He offered me a piece, urging me to eat. Biting into it I found it had a bitter taste but it contained moisture, wonderful, life-giving moisture. Gesturing to Sergeant Mulei to off-load, I slumped under the nearest acacia, unmindful of the fallen thorns. Snatching at my water-bottle I drew out the cork, letting the water tickle, drop by precious drop down my parched throat. There was a little left. Licking the cork I replaced it firmly and shoved the bottle upright

in the sand as I stretched out. The sun's fiery heat
penetrated the canopy of thorns affording little shade
as I squirmed still further under the tree. Taking
off my boots I sighed with relief. I was too tired to
brush off the ants which persistently crawled over
me.

At length, recovering somewhat, I called
Sergeant Mulei over and gave him orders to
get the Wakamba collecting as many tubers
as they could and to put them in empty ration sacks to load when we moved off. I tried
to doze but the reeling heat of the sun and
the ants would not let me. The Garre Illalo
brought over a camel mat and flung it over the umbrella-shaped tree
as I panted gratefully in the extra shade it afforded. With an agonis-
ing motion the sun passed its zenith and began its slow fall from the
sky as though begrudging its power over the parched land it held
in thraldom. I sat up with an effort, rearranging the camel mat on
the acacia so that the small shadow now fully covered my resting place.
The askaris were lying here and there, each man under his own
stunted little thorn tree. Even the camels were couched, tired, for
this was their fourth day without water. I thought we had covered
about twenty miles so far, which left about twenty-five before we
reached Bulo Garas and water. It was essential that we covered
another ten miles at least today for we couldn't take another full day
tomorrow without water. I began to worry again. What would we
do if the deshek at Bulo Garas had dried out? That would mean there
would be no Garre karia there — no life-giving milk from the she
camels. I again reproached myself bitterly. What a God-forsaken
place the desert was. No place for weaklings. I began to see how the
Somali had retained his tough virility over the centuries. The survival of the fittest. The old people who couldn't keep up with the
caravans left behind for the hyenas to pull down and finish off.
They died the hard way. An inadequately protected karia attacked
by a stronger force of feuding Somalis. They too died the hard way

by rifle, spear, arrow and knife.

Slowly conserving my energy, I pulled on my socks and boots, giving the order to saddle up. Still with the thirst on me I ambled over to where my chop-box lay. Six tins of bully-beef — no future there for the salted beef would only increase that awful craving. Four tins of milk — puncturing one with my knife, I drank the warm contents, greedily sucking through the small hole in the tin and loving-ly rolling it round my tongue, savouring its refreshing goodness.

It took much longer to load the camels as the askaris and lenders worked lethargically. I dragged myself reluctantly from the shade of the friendly little acacia. Left right; left right; left right; back came the torture. My shorts and tunic chafed as the sweat again broke out, seeping in little rivulets down my body. The Mannlicher, weighing about seven pounds, now seemed to weigh fifty — a long piece of iron piping, hot to the touch as the sling cut into my shoulder, first the left and then the right, as I constantly changed its position. It required an effort of will not to call halt each time I passed under a large acacia overhanging the track whose shadow beckoned friendli-ly and afforded a fleeting second's respite from the sun. We left the weary miles behind — but slowly now. Oh, blessed relief as the sun, lower and less fierce in the sky lost its heat and a small breeze sprang up, a zephyr which gently played on our faces, cooling the heat within us. On and on. We were now moving like automatons, mechanical perspiring machines. My legs felt rubbery whilst my boots seemed to sink deeper with each step I took into that cursed sand.

'Walk the Somali off his feet,' the Colonel had told us. 'En-dure the hardships he does.' Walk him off his feet mocked a go-away-bird. Hardships, hardships, hardships. Walk, walk, walk. Walk him off his feet, feet, feet. Shaaged, shaaged, shaaged, echoed the hornbill.

The sun sank fiery red over the horizon in a blaze of defiance and I sobbed my relief as the air cooled a little. The unending nightmare continued. I half stumbled and recovered. There was nothing to be seen but the dense thorn scrub on either side of the camel track winding and twisting ahead of us. I was now dream mar-ching as in a coma in the fading sunset, devoid of all thought with that constant, raging thirst still upon me.

It grew dark. The stars came out and nightjars like huge moths flitted silently across our path. My watch told me it was 7 p.m. and I realized that we had just about completed the remaining miles for the day. The bush thinned a little. Wearily, and so thankfully, I called halt then lay down, pillowing my head on the near empty water-bottle. The Wakamba fell in their tracks and scrambling to my feet I ordered Sergeant Mulei to post a sentry, and then exhorting the others to one last effort we built a zariba, slashing away at the sullen thorns with panga and knife.

I drank the remainder of my water, gasping with pleasure as it trickled down my parched throat. Stumbling to my bed I slept as one already dead.

Dawn came and mechanically we saddled up, kicking the camels to their feet as they protestingly roared their complaints. There was no cheerfulness in camp now and no singing. Two of the Wakamba were limping with large open sores on their feet.

We staggered on. Bulo Garas must be reached before the sun began to burn down again or we would surely die. A hyena wailed his way through the bush and was answered by the long drawn out hunting cry of another. I shuddered, frightened now and started to walk in a panic. Outstripping the others, I then heard Omar calling hoarsely, 'Sahib, Sahib.' The caravan had stopped. Stumbling back I saw that one of the Wakamba was on the ground groaning incoherently. He seemed older than the others for his tarbush had fallen off showing the curly wool of his hair sprinkled with grey. He was far gone.

'*Funga huyu juu ya ngamia,*' I panted. A camel was brought to his knees at the lender's rasped out word of command. Somehow we hoisted up the Wakamba, lashing him on with rope — then on again as the caravan lurched forward.

One hour, two hours, three hours with the sun rising higher and ever hotter until I wanted to fall down and rest and to hell with the hyenas. I felt madness was not far away. Then came the miracle. We were clear of that dense, lonely bush and saw the vultures ahead, wheeling high in the sky above a large karia in the middle of an open plain.

I could now make out a clump of doum palms near a deshek with a herd of sheep and goats near the crusted edge. We ran forward, askaris and camels in a stumbling group of men and animals. Dropping our rifles we threw ourselves in. Filthy green slimy water covered by the dung from thousands of camels, cattle, sheep and goats but — water. I lay on my back, wallowing in the filth of it, filling my mouth as my head rolled from side to side. I spat out hardened goat droppings ... Our relief was infectious.

'Sahib, Sahib,' laughed Omar, *'Anah Gel.'* I squelched my way out of that wonderful slime and with trembling hands grasped the tebed of camel's milk offered to me by a smiling Somali girl. Burying my face in it I drank deeply.

'*Garre,* Sahib, *Garre,*' smiled Omar happily. The Wakamba askaris now laughed and joked as two of them dragged their half-conscious comrade to the water's edge where he drank, lying on his belly to suck up the water. We were soon surrounded by the Garre warriors left behind to guard the karia — the old men and women, the girls and the yeros, all wildly excited and conversing with Omar in their gutteral tongue. Calling up Sergeant Mulei, I told him to put a guard on the Galgail prisoners. Many willing helpers soon had our camp finished and the zariba constructed near to that of the Garre. I then collapsed on my bed, sleeping until late in the afternoon. I surfaced and held a baraza with the Garre: from them I ascertained that the survivors had made their way here from Donca Adega. The clan had lost most of their stock to the Galgail raiders who had now rejoined their own clans in Galgail country. The three prisoners had been identified as part of the raiding party. I promised that Indo Ade would bring them to justice as soon as we returned to Afgoi. I also promised to return to them their looted stock. At this, all the fighting men, some eighty of them, rushed forward with their spears. I would have no lack of volunteers for the job in hand.

The following day we rested, then moved on to Galgail country. My force now consisted of the Wakamba sections plus twenty Garre spearmen and a similar number of women. We moved off, refreshed and in high spirits, making good time across counry as we hit the Afgoi road about midday. We had our customary halt, leaving camp soon after three in the afternoon where we halted for the night at a place called Billo Toani, which consisted of the usual clearing and a deserted Galgail karia.

I asked Omar to question the Garre as to the proximity of the Galgail karia and their stock. He said that the bulk of them were not more than eight miles away at the most. Before turning in for the night I held yet another baraza, outlining my plans for the seizure of the Galgail stock in the morning.

Immediately on making contact I would split up my sixty-odd men into three parties. Party No. 1 under Sergeant Mulei would do a pincer movement to the left of the grazing stock, with riflemen and Garra levies. Party No. 2 under the Garre Illalo, consisting of roughly the same number, would do a pincer movement to the right: both parties to seize as many camels as they could handle and to herd them into the karia here. The third party would remain with me. Neither party was to fire or attack the Galgail unless they started hostilities.

Moving off before first light we contacted the Galgail stock a little later. Immediately both parties fanned out to the left and to the right of them, penetrating deep to the rear so as to seize the bulk of the camels. I brought our baggage camels to a halt, constructed a large zariba and had some anxious minutes when I heard rifle fire in the far distance.

Well before midday, a great cloud of dust heralded the approach of the Sergeant's party with a straggling herd of camels. About three hundred of them I thought, making a rough estimate as they streamed into the waiting karia. Questioning Mulei, I gathered the Galgail herdsmen had tried to close but had been driven off by his riflemen. There were no casualties and I congratulated him. He smiled his pleasure. Another anxious hour passed, then came the second party, whistling and yelling as they herded in score upon score of camels. There must have been at least five hundred, I estimated. The Garre Illalo came up, almost incoherent with delight at the serious blow we had dealt the Galgail. Most of the stock we had recovered were Garre camels from Donca Adega.

Leaving our temporary camp we now set off in the direction of Afgoi with a strong rearguard. The noise from the camels was indescribable but it was sweet music in my ears and sweeter still in the ears of the Garre. They had forgotten the massacre at Donca Adega for here they were with what they worshipped most in life

— camels. They had most of their own back and the balance belonged to their hated traditional enemies. They were jubilant. In a frenzy of delight a warrior would suddenly leap high in the air, spinning as he came down, brandishing his spear and screaming out his tribal war cry.

Milk was there for the asking from the she-camels and we drank our fill from the tebeds as we moved. The air was choked with the dust churned up by their countless pads, and it took me some time to weave my way through them until I reached the leaders way out in front. Here I pressed on with Omar and my orderly to reconnoitre what I hoped would be our last camp before Afgoi was reached. Omar assured me that there was another open plain about a mile ahead. He was right. Here we would build yet another zariba in the middle of it, so that any attacking Galgail would have to cross open country before they could press home any attack. The camels arrived and everything was finished by tea-time. I gave orders for a camel to be killed and roasted, later sharing its succulent sweet meat with the men.

Night came swiftly. Posting double sentries I slept, happy in the thought that the safari had been successful and was now almost over. At about midnight I was awakened by a strange noise I could not identify, which turned out to be two camels making love. Evidently one of our baggage animals considered he has been celibate long enough and now with a harem of several hundred females to choose from had straddled one sitting on the ground a few yards from my bed. He was performing a rocking motion, blowing out his neck and making the most terrible love calls. He looked so ludicrous that I burst out laughing in spite of being so rudely awakened. I left the two strange lovers to it and tried to sleep again.

Dozing off, I felt a hand on my shoulder and muttered an impatient curse. It was the Garre sentry. 'Libah, Sahib, Libah,' he whispered urgently. Fully awake now, I heard a succession of deep grunts coming from the lion's belly as he softly padded outside the zariba. My bed was not placed in the middle of things but away to one side of the thorns, Yusuf no doubt thinking it wise to keep me as far away as possible from the massed herd of camels sharing camp.

The lion coughed again, menacingly. The camels milled in fright. I reached for the Mannlicher, slipping off the safety-catch. Omar, feeling much more secure from the centre of the zariba, called out in typical Somali bravado, 'Oh lion, splendid lion, where art thou? A feast. A feast of eight hundred camels awaits thy Greatness.' This brought a laugh from the awakening askaris but these died away when the lion, hungry and determined on meat, grunted again. The grunts reaching a frightening intensity as he tried to panic the camels into breaking out of the zariba. The roaring coughs culminated in an ear-splitting, utterly terrifying roar as he uncoiled his muscled springs and leapt over the six foot-high thorn fence and in amongst us.

I had half expected an attack on the zarìba by the Galgail in an effort to recover their stock and this I was prepared for. But the unknown quantity, to me, of the lion and its totally unexpected attack in all its ferocity paralysed me with fright as I saw a blur of death curving over the thorn wall. Remember, I had only been in Africa a few weeks and the only lions I had seen previous to this were in Regent's Park at the London Zoo, where I seemed to remember they spent their time yawning and watching the visitors through the bars on the cage with amber, indifferent eyes

Now the flickering flames from the fires outlined his shape in those few terrifying seconds. The magnificent head, the out-stretched, death-dealing forepaws, that splendidly-muscled body as he stood there for a moment, sure of his power. He was a picture of rage, muscles tense and ready for action. Suddenly his tail stiffened, then with blazing amber eyes he leapt for the kill on a terrified she-camel only yards from my bed. A quick blow from his forepaw broke her neck. He then buried his fangs in her throat.

I fired and as he half-turned for a second charge, the watchful Garre Illalo rushed forward, burying his spear in his side. He roared in a paroxysm of pain and rage, standing on his hind legs and biting savagely at the haft of the spear. I fired again for the throat. He thrashed about then sounded his death cry — a long drawn-out moan — and died. I walked up to him and gazed my fill, for he was magnificent. I felt no regret for the circumstances of his death which had a glamour all their own. My very first lion.

Early the next morning I was awakened by the hum of a truck as Indo Adde pulled into camp in a red cloud of dust. He was enthusiastic over the way the safari had gone. With his usual thoughtfulness he had brought up water, rations, beer and a bottle of whisky. We chatted and later savaged the beer. Would I care to accompany him back to Afgoi in the truck? I was tempted and briefly considered the offer but then declined; I thought it better to finish the safari on foot with my Wakamba. I asked him to take two of the Wakamba back with him, one suffering from malaria and the other with a poisoned foot; also the three Galgail prisoners whom I would be glad to get rid of. I opened more beer. Indo Adde seemed in no hurry to get back to Afgoi and I was glad of his company.

'You've had a damned hard safari with excellent results. Congratulations,' he said. 'The count has been handed to me. Of the eight hundred camels you seized, five hundred were looted from the Garre karia at Donca Adega, which left three hundred with the Galgail brand plus the two hundred and fifty from the first Galgail karia. In all, five hundred and fifty Galgail camels. I'd like you to attend my baraza tomorrow. No, make that the day after to give you a rest. The five hundred Garre camels will be handed back to them and the Galgail camels will be confiscated as a communal fine for their attack on the Garre. I have given Haji Mohamed Elmi, Chief of the Galgail, ten days in which to find a further 1,100 as dia — or blood money — for the eleven Garre his warriors killed. The news of your safari is all over Afgoi and beyond. Before we came the Italians never really enforced the payment of blood money and the Galgail had things their own way for too long.

"Kill," Haji Mohamed told his warriors. "Kill and loot, for who will enforce the payment of dia? The Garre? They're too weak. The Serikali? Bah — the Residente never leaves Afgoi — he doesn't seek trouble."

'Well, Haji Mohamed has been badly shaken. He is going frantic and sending out runners to all his clans. Stop the killing he is saying. Not only is the Residente enforcing the payment of dia but we also have to pay an additional 100 camels for every cursed Garre we kill. He has now lost face and after this will not be the power in these parts he once was. Yes. Between us we have stopped the Galgail-Garre feud.'

It was evening and Indo Adde had long since departed. I was savouring a whisky with cool, clean water. I wondered then if the feuding and bloodshed between the tribes would end. Not only the Galgail and Garre but all the tribes, clans and sections in this turbulent, unhappy land, for killing between them was a way of life.

Fifty years later I am still wondering.

Death of a Patriot

The Somalis have a saying that the Prophet said that when God created Man He picked up dust from all parts of the earth. Some of it was black, some red and some white, but all men were made of that dust and were brothers. He then had a small handful left over He laughed as He threw it in the air where a dust-devil carried it afar. Thus were the Somalilands and the Somalis created. Theirs is a land, particularly in the north — the Mijertein of many hundreds of miles of desolation, with the bitter desert on the morrow turning again into a shudder of blinding sunglare. The dried dust of camel dung and sand blows over the land tearing more of the hard shale from the earth, so that the long ridges of limestone appear through the shale-like bones. When the moon comes up these bones show themselves white and grey against the pink sand.

Iskushuban in Somali means 'Meeting of the Waters.' Rather a misnomer this for apart from a rock-girt pool, fed by underground springs from the far north of the country, there is no other permanent water to be found for hundreds of miles.

It was here that I was posted, in complete isolation once more, for I had already served in far-flung desert outposts like Cape Guardafui, Alula and Bender Kassim (Bosasso). I lived here in a theatrical, Beau Geste-like fort the Italians had built, stuck high on a stabilised sand dune and overlooking the junction of two dried river beds called lacs. In the courtyard of the fort was a huge statue of Mussolini, minus the head. The Somalis told me that South African troops, during their Mijertein campaign some years ago, had attached a steel towrope to the neck and with the aid of a ten-ton truck had forcibly decapitated Il Duce — a grim forboding of the violent end that awaited him in later years.

As far as I can recall I had only one European visitor during my stay there. He was on the wing to Bendir Kassim, still further

41

to the north to take up his posting.

An old friend, for we had crossed over from Ireland together from our respective regiments on being seconded to the Somalia Gendarmerie. Gerald Hanley, the wit and raconteur and in later years the well-known author. It was good to see him. It was good to see anyone in this lonely wilderness with the *kherif*, the hot desert wind, moaning over the land like some demented Djinn.

The Irish are splendid drinkers but poor cricketers. Naturally, during his three-day stay with me I cajoled him into nets which were placed just in front of Mussolini's headless statue which made a satisfying long stop. My Somali troops were enthusiastic over football but cricket they did not like, and so I was hard pushed to have someone to bowl at me.

After Gerald had gone, the long, lonely days, lonelier nights, weeks and months passed pleasantly enough for I was fortunate enough to have as my District Clerk a most likeable and intelligent Somali named Abdiraschid Shermarke Ali. He was about my age, good company and we spent many a pleasant evening together.

It was at Iskushuban that I first tangled with the Somali Youth League. This political party was originated by progressive young Somalis in 1943 with the aim to prepare themselves for independence. The movement was approved of by the British Administration. Abdiraschid was one of the up-and-coming Somali politicians; also the SYL President. He was a good Moslem for he neither drank nor smoked and was utterly sincere.

Inevitably, from time to time my authority was undermined as he impatiently wished the Somalis to take over the reins of Government — particularly when in the Court House for here I was a Magistrate as well as an Army officer. One day, holding court, I was taking down evidence from several tribesmen who had taken part in an affray over the disputed ownership of a well. One man had been killed and two others badly knifed.

'Your name?' I asked the first accused.

'Abdi Mohamed,' he replied.

'Your tribe?'

'Somali,' he replied. Thinking he had misunderstood my, as yet elementary, Somali I repeated the question.

'Somali,' he replied again. Quite emphatic this time. I called upon my interpreter to help.

'Omar. Tell all the accused that I am not an idiot in that I know they are all Somalis, but in order to get at the facts of this particular case I must know their tribes or clans if you like. As you know it is customary. Please ask him again.'

'Somali,' he said defiantly and with some truculence.

'Question the others,' I said testily for I had not experienced this non-cooperation over revealing their tribes before.

'Somali!'they all replied in unison. I cogitated for I was not a little put out.

'Court dismissed', I said. 'Place them on remand for three days.'

It was a Monday, I suddenly remembered, and Abdiraschid was coming to my house that night for our lessons in Somali and English. I would ask his advice. Punctually at 7 p.m. he arrived carrying half a dozen books I had loaned him, including an illustrated clan map of the Scottish Highlands, showing the various tartans and history of the inter-tribal feuds. My predecessor was a Scot and must have left it after his handover to me as he hurried away to the fleshpots of Mogadishu.

I poured out two large tumblers of camel's milk. Being a devout Muslim he didn't drink. I did, but Gerald had helped me to finish off my last remaining bottle of whisky; perforce I was left with camel's milk. I told him of my dilemma over the court case and as I was completely mystified as to why none of the accused would give their tribe, could he help? He smiled. Like most Somalis he had a marvellous sense of humour.

'I told them not to,' he said. I was indignant and told him so. He held out the illustrated Scottish clan map which he said he had been studying with great interest.

'Tell me about the clans of the Scots,' he said. 'Well,' I replied. 'I am not a Scot but being a romantic and interested in them and their country I will do my best.

'First of all I would say that the clan system in Scotland, allied to the tartan kilt and the playing of the war pipes is a most laudable thing — and yet it destroyed their unity as a country due to tribal fighting among themselves and therefore being unable to resist the might of England when they invaded.'

'Carry on, Sahib?' He smiled again.

'Well, it was all a question of jealousy. Each and every clan was so jealous of the other that they had no unity.' At this Abdiraschid grew quite excited as the Somalis do when under emotional stress. His eyes shone as he stood up and gesticulated. No one could but doubt his luminous sincerity.

'Exactly,' he said. 'The prideful clan system destroyed Scotland but it shall not destroy Somalia, and it is for this reason that I have sent messages by fast camel to all four corners of the country. No man will give the name of his tribe, clan or section. They will say they are all Somalis.'

I pondered his words. I was sympathetic to these aspirations and had only a couple of months left to serve at Iskushuban. Independence would be theirs some day and I had no wish to quarrel with this friend of mine. I changed the subject for I thought he was right then and decades later was certain that he was right.

'Have you heard any news of the Government lorry up from Mogadishu?' I asked. 'It is now a month overdue. The askaris have not been paid and their rations are running short. So are mine. For

the last month I have been living on stringy goat meat, a few dates and camel's milk. I've nothing to drink either — and my God! Do you know what date it is tomorrow? Christmas Day! Christmas Day! Come round and have dinner with me. I'll try and shoot something.'

Abdiraschid looked thoughtful. 'I too have little to eat. The rice ration is finished. Mebbe the lorry has been hijacked. Mebbe broken down. Allah alone knows.' Perhaps Allah knew. I certainly didn't for without transport and a signals set we might as well have been on the moon.

Early the next morning, Christmas Day, I took out the shotgun in an effort to bag something for dinner. If I could get a Speke's gazelle or even a greater bustard we would have a feast. On my last leave in Kenya I had brought a few seeds back with me including peas for my minute garden. They had flowered, the pods ripened to become swollen with the succulent peas. They were now ready. My mouth watered for I was hungry. I walked miles from the fort but there was nothing to be seen. That is hunting. Some days are good and some are bad. Wearily I trekked back to the fort with the sun high now but nearing the rock-girt pool I checked that my shotgun was on safe, laid it by a rock, took off my clothes and dived in quite naked.

The cool water revived me but I still felt miserable when I thought of goat again for Christmas dinner. Lying on my back in the water and contemplating my navel I looked up. A dot appeared in the sky. It approached closer. Closer still as it swerved when it saw water. I heard a honk. It was a goose! I had no compunction. No pity in my heart whatsoever in spite of the fact that this was the first goose I had ever seen at Iskushuban. It was possibly the only goose in the whole of Northern Somalia. Allah alone knew where it came from. Scrambling out of the pool I snatched up the gun and pushed the safety catch forward as it circled and came in low. I gave it the choke barrel and it fell next to me in the water. I grew quite lighthearted for I was possibly the only Englishman to have shot a goose when in the nude in the whole of Somaliland. Possibly in the whole of Africa. We had our Christmas dinner. Goose and green peas. The few potatoes I had left over were mouldy and so the one course of vegetables would have to suffice.

My cook had not seen a goose before. I showed him how to pluck it and then to singe it. I told him to roast it. My mouth watered. I gave him all my precious pods of peas. Three large double handfuls. I showed him how to shell them. I stressed that one ate the peas and threw away the shells. He had not seen peas before. In my excitement and anticipation at such a noble repast for the evening I quite forgot to tell him to boil the peas. Obviously I had been at Iskushuban and other isolated stations for too long, for this omission had disastrous consequences. He roasted the goose to perfection but fried the peas in ghee. They were inedible. Quite black. As black as sin. They were as hard as buckshot and, as Abdiraschid said in between mouthfuls of succulent goose, they resembled goat droppings.

Came the day when I was relieved. Abdiraschid went his way and I went mine. Long years at Bardera and Isha Baidoa in the south followed by more years in the Ogaden and finally back to the Mijertein again. Abdiraschid was to be cheated out of his dream of independence for another ten years, for after the British left the League of Nations decided that Italy would administer the country for another ten years. After that period independence was finally theirs.

In the meantime I became a white hunter operating in Kenya, Uganda and Tanganyika, as it was then. One of my safaris took me to the Northern Frontier close to the Somalia border.

By this time I had competely lost contact with my old Somali friend.

Age dims the memory somewhat but it was probably in 1960 that I was introduced in Nairobi to a Spartan-like character from the States who had just graduated from Yale University, majoring in fine arts. I say Spartan-like for he was built like a Greek god and was as tough as one. About six foot tall, brown hair with classical features, wide-set eyes, mobile mouth and a strong jaw. He was also arrogant and obviously thought the sun shone on his backside alone. I was still reasonably tough, but was more than twenty years his senior, and when he said he wished me to take him on a foot safari to my old haunts in the Northern Frontier, would I be up to it? He anticipated walking about forty miles a day. He looked at me rather disparagingly. I thought a little gamesmanship was called for.

Once in the bush I gave him a pair of Somali sandals to march in. I made sure that they were a size too small. After the end of a month's marching I would say honours were about even. Particularly so when one looks at a photograph of the condition of his feet taken by himself in that classical book of his, *The End of the Game*.

Peter Hill Beard on safari proved to be a masochist. (He blames his English public school for this for he went to Felstead). Now, a white hunter's job on safari was to be able to cope with anything — including a masochistic client, but he did give me some sleepless nights for he was one of those rare characters who are quite without fear. On safari that can be dangerous. Nevertheless he survived my safari and others he undertook and is now recognised as one of the world's most brilliant photographers.

It was towards the end of the safari when an incident occurred which really impressed him. It was dusk. A Somali warrior, travel-stained and weary, loped into camp with a message for me tied to the haft of his spear. I sat him down, gave him tea and dates which he wolfed as if there were no tomorrow. I enquired of his name and tribe and introduced him to Peter. They shook hands. It was quite amusing I thought. The Somali was a superb physical specimen and they eyed each other as two gladiators might have done before entering the arena at the Roman Games. Excitedly I read the note. It was from no less a person than Abdiraschid Ali Shermarke, my old friend at Iskushuban all those years ago.

He was now Prime Minister of the Somali Republic. He was on safari in Jubaland over the border and had heard that I was on safari thereabouts. I looked at the date, did a bit of mental arithmetic to find out that his runner had covered some 150 miles in three days. I told Peter. He was suitably impressed.

'The *habari*,' he said excitedly. 'Read the habari out loud.' I did so. After the customary greetings and salaams and regrets that we had not kept in touch over the long years would I consider the offer of moving with my safari outfit to the Republic across the border? If agreeable I would be under the umbrella of the Prime Minister himself who would give me all the help and facilities he was capable of. I could base myself anywhere I wished in the country and, as I knew, the hunting in Jubaland was just as good as the country I was hunting now. It was a most generous offer. It took me no time at all to make up my mind. I had always had a nostalgic longing to get back there and to renew friendships with a people I admired and liked. Many of my old clients, too, I knew were looking for fresh hunting grounds and the rarer type of game. I thought Kismayu on the coast would make a good base from which to hunt Jubaland itself. Further north beyond Mogadishu on the plains I could find Pelzeln's, Speke's and Peter's gazelle, Soemmerring's gazelle and the rare dibatag.

Further north still on the escarpment from the Ras Hafun and on the range of incense-clad hills sweeping down to the sea, all country I had trekked over, I would find the rare and elusive Beira antelope. Like Pelzeln's, Speke's and the dibatag, the only country in the world where they are to be found.

The following day I penned my reply, saying that if convenient I would meet the Prime Minister in Mogadishu in one month's time. The Somali, now rested, then tied my message to his spear and I made a friend for life by producing an old army haversack which I insisted he take with him on his long trek back over the border and beyond. In it I crammed a packet of tea, matches, sugar, coffee, bread, biscuits, raisins and dates, all unheard of luxury for him, in the wilderness through which he would be trekking. Off he loped, just as effortlessly as when he had arrived.

On my arrival in Mogadishu a month later, I found that my old friend had changed but little over the years in spite of the high office he now held. The following night in order to celebrate our reunion he had organised a small party to attend a banquet he had arranged for me at Afgoi, where I had first been posted in 1941.

Happily, after a few more days in Mogadishu and meeting old friends, I returned to Nairobi. There followed a frenetic week organising my move, mailing old clients in the States and elsewhere to tell them of my plans for hunting in the Somali Republic. Then came the heart-breaking news.

The Prime Minister of the Somali Republic, whilst visiting the far north in the Mijertein, had been gunned down and killed by his own bodyguard. Many years later I heard that his assassination had been instigated by the Russians, who then put their puppet Siad Barre in power. Abdiraschid's dream of a Greater Somalia inhabited by united Somalis was cruelly wrecked by power politics, and his death was a tragedy for his country.

The Cricket Match

This was not England, rural England in Nottinghamshire at Bestwood Park, with the grey smoke from the tall brick chimneys of the Hall curling lazily into the sky and the Estate church clock chiming the hour. There was no verdant green grass to lie on, nor the shady elm or oak to rest under. There was no green and gold pavilion and at the start of the season no apple blossom nor could one hear the first liquid notes of the calling cuckoo. There was no emerald green sacred square, meticulously cut and rolled, with the lines of the creases showing sharp and white. There were no buttercups and daisies on the outfield and beyond, in the surrounding woods, no bluebells and rhododendrons.

This was the tip of the Horn of Africa. To our front the Gulf of Aden and the sandy shore which was our cricket ground, with the smoky range of mountains on either side covered with frankincense, incense and myrhh trees as they grew on the rocky, precipitous slopes up to Cape Guardafui. Nearer and frowning down on us was Bolimoch, or elephant's head, a rocky promontory fashioned by some impish djinn, like the head of an elephant with the trunk dipping into the sea.

At our backs the ripples of sand dunes danced in the heat haze and beyond — miles and miles of desert wastes.

Alula (meaning pearl in Somali), had not seen cricket before. With the exception of myself, the only other man present to have even heard of the game was my aged interpreter, Haji Dif, who in his youth had spent many years at sea and once had resided in Cardiff. He was a splendid character, and if his translation of the Somali language into English was not of a very high standard, it was nevertheless most amusing, as he slipped into slang with the words often larded with sea oaths he had learnt before the mast.

Just about the whole village had turned out, although this first game interfered with their afternoon's siesta. The boundary of the ground I had marked out with whitewashed stones and it was now a blaze of colour.

The young warriors in their spotless white *tobes*, the girls and women in their brightly coloured *khangas*, looking like a swarm of exotic birds as they chatted away. A cluster of grey-bearded Chiefs and Akils were in one corner, about eight of them, all trying to shade under Sultan Mohamed Bogor's umbrella.

Away on the far boundary was a group of Arabs. Wild-looking men, with long, matted black hair and elf locks, kohl-fringed eyes and barefooted in their stained brown gowns. A couple of little dancing boys lay at their feet. The Arabs wore carved, silver-handled daggers in their girdles and during their stay I had taken the precaution of locking up their long muskets in the station armoury. They were traders from over the Gulf of Aden. From the Oman, Muscat and the Yemen. They had arrived in their ocean-going dhows by the trade winds which filled the huge, triangular, lateen sail their dhows carried. They were here to barter their dates with the Somalis for incense, myrhh, aromatic gums, pearls, dried shark fins and the fat-tailed sheep from the Somali hinterland. Others had called in to water on their way further south — to Mogadishu, Lamu and Mombasa with their cargoes of brightly-coloured carpets and rugs.

Yet another group, quite on their own were the Midgans — the hunters — and the Tomals, the blacksmiths, silversmiths and spear makers. The despised social outcasts in the class-conscious strata of Somali society.

Sindbad, the diminutive, young Somali punkah-wallah from the office, staggered along manfully behind me, carrying my leather bag of cricket gear. Idris Ibrahim, my ever pompous clerk, who was to score, strolled up importantly with a cheap exercise book and

sharpened pencil.

On the improvised, sandy cricket field paraded my platoon of Gendarmerie, less the office guard, armed and in their sections. Drawn up opposite them were the Illalos or tribal scouts in their serried ranks, also armed. On my approach, and at Sergeant Ali Jama's word of command, they came to attention and sloped arms. The Sergeant marched up to me and saluted. I raised my cricket cap and told him to order the men at ease and to pile arms.

'Why in heaven's name did the troops bring their rifles?' I enquired of Haji Dif. 'We're going to play a game, not fight a battle.'

'They just bloody higgerent, Sahib,' replied that worthy.

Ordering Sergeant Ali Jama to choose ten Gendarmes, including himself, whom I would captain, I then turned to the corporal in charge of the Illalos, telling him to do the same. Carlo would captain the Illalo side.

Carlo was an Italian. Quite mad and I had to agree with the few lines about him my predecessor, Pip, had written in his handing over notes: 'By profession a barber in Mogadishu. Evidently his business hadn't thrived for he was a damned awful barber and so had applied for, and obtained, the post of lighthouse-keeper at Cape Guardafui, which is in your parish some twenty miles to the south. Drinks gin and grappa which he makes himself. Stationed at Guardafui for two years. Has a persecution mania for he is under the delusion that his three Somali assistants want him poisoned. Speaks a little English. Only reason he stays on is to save up sufficient money to open up a barber's shop in Rome. If he ever makes it I pity the Romans. To keep his hand in at hairdressing he catches his pet cockerel once a month and trims its head feathers. Quite mad but harmless. Should be relieved.'

To give him a break, I had brought him down from his lonely eyrie, for it was Christmas 1942 and I thought if he took part in a game of cricket his morale would benefit. However, he had spent most of his time so far finishing off my meagre stocks of gin and listening to my old wind-up HMV gramophone, playing the six records to have survived the perilous camel safari when I had first arrived here. His favourite record was *I dream of Jeanie with the light brown hair* by Stephen Foster, the American song writer. To my astonishment, when he finally turned up on the ground he didn't seem to be at all enthusiastic when I appointed him captain of the Illalos. He swayed slightly and smelt of gin.

Spinning a coin in front of him, I asked 'Heads or Tails' 'Who ees Jeanie?' he asked dreamily. He was far gone.

Relegating him on the spot, I called over the Illalos corporal. Picking up a bat I said: 'This is called a bat. Think of it as a camel. Now, when I throw it on the ground, will the hump come up first or the flat belly?' The corporal saluted.

'Allah only knows, Sahib,' he replied gravely. I gave up and put them in to bat. Haji Dif was to do his best by umpiring both ends. The Illalos' two opening batsmen padded up. One had his pads on upside down. The game began. I opened the bowling from the lagoon end and bowled three Illalos in my first over. Just like teaching them to shoot, I thought. Hopeless to begin with and then one has to look to one's own laurels to beat them. The next over was from the Elephant's Head end. Three wickets for no runs. As a Gendarme prepared to bowl, I noticed that the two fieldsmen I had carefully placed in the slips were holding hands, fingers interlaced, a Moslem custom between close friends.

'Umpire Dif,' I called. 'Tell those two wets in the slips to wake up or I will confine them to barracks after the match. How can they hope to catch the ball holding hands?' The two Gendarmes sheepishly unlaced their fingers and the game was resumed. The bowler wouldn't, or couldn't, bring his arm over when he delivered the ball. He ran with long, loping strides, stopped dead at the bowling crease to then hurl the ball at the batsman. Used to spear throwing, the ball was delivered with remarkable velocity. Shades of Harold Larwood at Trent Bridge and bodyline. The first three deliveries screamed past for four byes each. Three wickets for twelve runs. The Illalo batsman, by some fluke, then connected with the fourth delivery and they began running. They ran five runs with none of the fielders bothering to chase the ball which skidded to an abrupt stop in a dollop of soft camel dung, way past cover.

'Umpire Dif,' I shouted peevishly again. ''Tell the fielders to chase the ball and return it to the bowler.' Half-heartedly a Gendarme complied with the umpire's constructions to throw the ball back to the bowler. All my team then seemed to go into a huddle in the middle of the wicket, stopping play.

'Oh no,' I groaned inwardly. Not a mutiny. Not a mutiny on Christmas Day. I glanced at the piled arms on the edge of the boundary and noticed with relief that the sentry there seemed to be alert. What the devil do I do now, I thought. I could hardly put about half my command on a charge. How would I word the charge, anyway?

'What's the matter now?' I called to the long-suffering Umpire Dif. Full of beer, turkey and Christmas pudding, I was feeling rather testy.

''They say, Sahib, that they Mijertein Somalis. You know. Blue bloods and superior to the rest of the tribes. They are just a lot of bloody landlubbers so what can you expect? They like defending themselves with the Inglesi spear (the bat) and throwing the grenade (the ball), at the enemy, but they refuse to chase the bloody grenade after the enemy hits it. They say that job for slaves — for Tomals and Midgans.' I groaned. Class distinction was fast disappearing in England, but evidently not in Somaliland. I tried to argue with them but they were adamant. It's a question of caste, they said. There is only one thing for it I thought. Prisoners. I put the question to Umpire Dif.

'How many chaps have we got in clink, Umpire?' 'Mebbe nine, mebbe ten,' he replied.

'Right. Send a fast runner over to the jail and tell the prison warder I want all his prisoners here for cricket. Dakso! (hurry).'

Calling the two teams around me I endeavoured yet again to explain to them the etiquette of the game. The sun seared down.

Ten prisoners were soon hustled up by their armed escort of three warders. The Gendarmerie fielders retired happily, having won their point. Only Sergeant Ali Jama stood his ground. Probably thinking of his stripes, I thought sourly. The prisoners, under protest, took their places in the field, anxiously watched over by the warders on the boundary.

''Mebbe better put pads on that mans, Sahib,' said Umpire Dif, pointing to a fierce-looking Somali, looking wildly around him. 'He on remand for murder, knifed man dead at Ollok last week.

He mebbe try and escape. Not run far as wicket-keeper in pads. Rest just no good bums. Camel and goat thieves — OK?'

'OK' I replied weakly.

'Game. Two bloody balls to come you lubbers,' said the umpire, bending professionally over the wicket. The last two balls went through for byes again, the alleged murderer making little or no effort to stop the ball as it whizzed past him. I placed a longstop on the boundary. I bowled another Illalo with the first ball of my over.

He walked back to the pavilion, a small stunted thorn tree, giving shade about the size of a small carpet. Four wickets down for 25 runs.

In came Carlo, weaving slightly.

He took his stance and theatrically flourished his bat. He hit my second ball for four and looked around for applause. There was none. The spectators were getting restive, dwindling away in twos and threes. A fastish ball this time which ran up the splice of his bat to strike him on the nose, which spurted blood in a steady trickle, staining his shirt and the sand crimson. I ran towards him with a handkerchief but he hysterically waved me away. He threw his bat down, screaming *'Berdio. Cattivo. Molto Cattivo.'* He then took off for my house and refuge in a shambling run, holding his nose.

A loud 'Ah! Ah!' went up from the spectators. The atmosphere was now tense. Those leaving the ground came streaming back.

The greybeards all had their heads together. Everyone rose excitedly to their feet. So this was 'kriket.' They had seen blood and now approved. First blood to the Gendarmerie, or should one say to the prisoners? This was then the equivalent to their own mock battles.

'Ah! Ah! *I Dil,'* screamed the warriors.

'Lulululula' trilled the women.

Umpire Dif looked round disapprovingly. He might have been at Lord's.

Battle was joined.

A hit. Three runs. The new batsman, a tall, well-built Illalo, with a halo of fuzzy-wuzzy hair through which was stuck a porcupine quill, twirled his bat over his head and looked aggressively about him. Short on the leg side. A mighty crack, a dull thud and a wretched prisoner, lazily scratching his navel, stopped the ball on his shin-bone and collapsed. He was carried off. The batsmen ran three. The applause and screams were now terrific. The warriors on the boundary leapt stiff-legged, high in the air, coughing out their war-cries and brandishing their spears. They looked as though they might invade the ground at any moment. The Arab traders apprehensively fingered their silver-handled daggers. Sultan Mohamed Bogor excitedly waved his fly-whisk.

The last ball of my over. I ran up to the wicket, wet with perspiration and my shirt clinging lovingly to my back. A rap on the pads. I appealed. Umpire Dif's finger shot up.

'Out, by God!' he said. Puzzled, the Illalo stood his ground. 'Out!' repeated Umpire Dif. 'Leg before the bloody wicket. *Isakatag!*' (Go). He went.

The game progressed. The Illalos being all out for 57 runs, without further casualties. Hot sweet tea, lemonade and dates were handed round. At last the prisoners enjoyed themselves.

Just after 5.30 p.m. I opened our innings with Sergeant Ali. The opening bowler bounded gracefully up to the wicket, stopped, and hurled the ball at my head. Being a left hand bat this was just the ticket. I ducked, swung, the ball connected with the meat of the bat and hurtled to the boundary, scattering the Sultan and the rest of the ancients. Hysterical animal noises came from the Midgans and Tomals from the other side of the ground, delighted that their overlords had been made to take evasive action.

The Sultan scowled his displeasure.

The second ball, quite wide, whizzed past my ear for the customary four byes. The third ball was short of a length. It hit a stone under the mat and struck me on the chest. I staggered. The crowd went wild. The fourth ball I pulled out of the ground for six and the fifth I drove hard back to the bowler who, doubling up with pain, incredibly held it to his stomach. A perfect caught and bowled. One wicket for 14 runs. Walking up to the Illalo bowler I clapped him on the shoulder. He grimaced his pleasure as Umpire Dif handed me my blazer. Walking back to the thorn tree pavilion a herd of sheep and goats invaded the ground, holding up the game for a few minutes. The flaming sun hung suspended over the sea, then slowly dipped into the ocean. Four more byes from the last ball of the over. Sergeant Ali then faced the bowling. Ones and twos off the edge of his bat, then his wicket shattered. He strode off giving the jubilant bowler a disdainful look.

A procession now as the bowlers took command. Their bowling, or rather throwing, being hostile and accurate. Most of the runs as usual came from byes and seven wickets were soon down for 45 runs. The score crept along with yet another wicket falling. Eight for 50. A pye-dog then ran off with the ball which was retrieved by one of the Midgans, the Somalis refusing to touch it for the dog, to them, was an unclean animal. A new ball had to be produced. A solitary gull winged overhead. Another wicket. Nine for 53.

The moon came out as the last man came in. He faced a hostile bowler on a bumpy pitch with the stars now appearing one by one overhead. I couldn't follow the flight of the ball as it whistled past for the usual four byes, chased by a tired perspiring fielder.

The score was even.

A rap on the pads and an appeal.

'Out,' said Umpire Dif, pocketing the bails, suddenly remembering the camel I had presented them all for Christmas which had yet to be killed. 'Kriket' was all very well but the succulent meat from a camel, roasted over a pit fire much better!

The Colonel's Inspection

'Well, Collins. You've had a long spell here at Alula — this so-called pearl of the Indian Ocean.' He smiled sardonically. 'Are you fit?' He looked at me sharply. I nodded dumbly.

The guard commander turned out the guard and presented arms. Although obviously tired from his long journey he inspected them. Minutely. Each man stiffened to attention and gazed rigidly to his front. Gendarme Ali Jama had the top button of his tunic undone. The Colonel flicked at the offending buttonhole with his swagger cane.

'Do it up,' he said. Ali Jama quivered with fright, endeavoured to right the frightful enormity with fumbling fingers, then dropped his rifle.

'Pick it up,' rasped the Colonel. I blushed.

'Dismiss the guard,' he ordered. I marched to their front, right-turned and stood to attention.

'Guard – dis – miss,' I shouted. The guard commander and three men turned sharply to their right. Ali Jama turned to the left. Chaos.

'As you were,' I roared. 'Guard dis – miss.' They marched off. I ushered the Colonel into the house. Haji Dif, my interpreter, fussed around, shaking hands with his escort. The Colonel looked at his watch. 'Lunch in an hour and kit inspection at 1600 hrs,' he said. I showed them to their rooms.

We had lunch. The Colonel had brought up wine, tinned tongue, lettuce, tomatoes, potatoes and even radishes. All the things I had dreamed about for so long. He and Tony, my relief, ate heartily and made small talk. I ate sparingly and remained silent. After over a year waiting for this moment I now resented their presence. I wanted to be alone again.

Kit inspection followed. There were eight spoons missing.

'Haji Dif,' called the Colonel. 'Ask these askaris where their spoons are.' They remained silent.

'My fault, Sir,' I mumbled. 'I borrowed them for tunny bait.' He cocked a quizzical eyebrow at me. I focused my eyes mesmerically on the red band encircling his cap. Tony sniggered.

'You did what?' he snapped. I found my tongue at last to explain in great detail how a spinning spoon was ideal for attracting tunny with which the sea off Alula abounded. He was no Isaac Walton fan and was not amused.

'The Hospital,' he said. We inspected it.

'The Lines,' he said. We inspected them.

'The Latrines,' he said. We inspected them. They smelt.

'The Armoury,' he said. We inspected it. In a corner stood half a dozen spare .256 carbines with bayonets attached. A spider had woven an intricate laced web festooning the bayonet points, slightly rusted.

'Pretty, Sir,' I remarked lamely as he poked the web to pieces with his cane.

'The Jail,' he said. I sweated. The Head Warder herded his prisoners into the courtyard. Their warrants were in order.

'Any complaints?' he barked. Their spokesman, the prisoner on remand for murder, handcuffed, hobbled forward and spoke for about ten minutes. He bared his shin, pointing dramatically to a grubby bandage.

'Well?' he asked Haji Dif.

'He bloody fool, Colonel Sahib,' lied Haji loyally.

'No griff. Fargone.' He tapped his head significantly. He was rewarded with a black look and a grunt.

'Nur.' The Colonel called his own orderly-cum-interpreter. Nur was a Sergeant. One of the de-tribalised, flat-nosed Riverines from the Juba south of Mogadishu. He quickly ground the cigarette he was surreptitiously smoking under his heel and came forward. He saluted oilily, darting Haji Dif a spiteful look. The Colonel didn't miss a trick.

'And if you smoke again when you are on parade with me I'll have those stripes off you before you can say knife. Do you understand?' Nur was shaken and now eager to please.

'They complain about torture called 'kriket', Colonel Sahib.

They say this Tenente far worse than Italian officers. He say they tortured every Saturday. They request you remove him and replace him with an officer full of the milk of human kindness.' Tony burst out laughing. The Colonel smiled frostily and said he would investigate their complaints. He suddenly asked me to tell him about the alleged murderer.

'I have taken great pains over his case, sir, and the whole file is in the office if you wish to peruse it. It was a particularly brutal murder. You've only got to look at his face. Of the Suacron tribe he raped a young girl of the Isman Mohamed and then killed her. It's caused a lot of ill-feeling here and if I may suggest it might be a good thing if we take him back with us to Mogadishu to stand trial before a higher court than mine.' He suddenly turned to Tony, who never had been a ball of fire, the little I knew of him.

'You've heard Collins' summing up of the alleged murderer. Now, what would be your verdict in Mogadishu if you were an assessor?' 'I really don't know,' Tony replied lamely. The Colonel was obviously curious.

'And if you read his file on him and agreed with the findings that he had, indeed, committed this murder in the most brutal circumstances what then would be your reaction?' Tony now looked really embarrassed. 'I'm not sure,' he said.

'No! ' said the Colonel bitterly. 'You are not sure. I have many of my command like you. Damned lot of women.' He now looked at me. His glance flickered over the two small Staffordshire knots on the lapels of my khaki drill bush jacket. The hangman's noose, some old sweats called it.

'Right, Collins. We get to Mogadishu and just suppose that you were a rank higher and our legal Johnnies agreed to you sitting in judgement with a couple of assessors, what would be your verdict?'

'I'd recommend he be hanged, sir, for I just could not find one extenuating circumstance when taking the initial proceedings here.' He brightened up. The sun was now sinking.

'We'll call it a day,' he said. 'A shower and then a little serious drinking, Captain, on your promotion. You may put up another pip immediately for I had a pleasing letter from the Commodore at Aden in regard to your conduct over the survivors from the torpedoed oil tanker *Belita*. I'll show it to you tonight.' The tip of his cane flicked one of the knots. His face hardened. 'You are a first class magistrate and you now have the rank. Use your knot,' he said with grim humour. So ended the inspection.

'Cigarette?' The Colonel produced a carton of Players. Tony accepted one and they lit up.

'No thank you, Sir, I don't smoke,' I replied. The three of us were in my sitting room. I moodily watched a praying mantis fly to its inevitable death against the bright lure of the pressure lamp. He produced a bottle of Scotch. 'Have a whisky,' he spoke encouragingly.

'Er, no thank you sir. Not at the moment,' I said. He helped himself and passed the bottle to Tony. I stared at the wall. At the grotesque leaping shadows cast by the lamplight. Absent-mindedly, picking up the Colonel's glass I drank deeply, gasping with pleasure as the unaccustomed drink hit my stomach. The Colonel's wise eyes looked sharply at me as he poured himself another drink in the glass Tony produced for him.

'Don't mind me,' he said good-humouredly as I stammered my apologies. He pushed the bottle over to me.

'Glad to see you've put your third pip up.' He fumbled in the pocket of his tunic and produced two letters. 'The reason for your promotion,' he said. 'Read them.'

The first letter was from The Secretariat, Aden, and signed by the Chief Secretary.

I am directed to transmit to you for necessary action, a copy of a letter No. 70/1 of 27 December 1942, from the Commodore Aden, regarding the recent assistance rendered to the survivors from a sunk Allied merchant ship by Lieut Collins (The South Staffordshire Regiment), the Political Officer at Alula.
... and the other:

I desire to bring to your Excellency's notice the recent assistance rendered to the survivors from a sunk Allied merchant ship by Lieut Collins (The South Staffordshire Regiment), the Political Officer at Alula.

2. The survivors landed from this ship's lifeboats in the

vicinity of Alula and were helped in every possible way and most hospitably treated by Lieut Collins who did not hesitate to give his own scanty stock of provisions to these men.

3. The Captain and Officers of the ship are most enthusiastic in their gratitude to Lieut Collins and in the circumstances I respectfully request that the conduct of this Officer may be brought to the favourable notice of the authorities concerned.

The Colonel gave me a charming smile. 'Congratulations,' he said. He passed round the bottle again.

'Only one thing intrigues me. What on earth did you give them at your table?'

'Camel's milk, fish, dates, goat and army plum jam,' I said. We all laughed. The serious drinking started. He produced another bottle.

He was a handsome man. About sixty I would judge. He looked like a character out of Beau Geste. Tall and lean. A brick-red face. Iron grey hair cut short, cold blue eyes and a bristling moustache. He had three rows of medal ribbons including the DSO and MC with two bars which showed he had earned them the hard way. Looking at him I wondered why he, still only a full Colonel with his record, commanded the Somalia Gendarmerie in this undoubted backwater of the war. Had I been able to read his mind I would have known that he just didn't care and was resigned to the failure he saw within himself. He could not quite believe in this failure himself. Anyway, he would always ask himself after half a bottle of whisky what the hell is failure anyway? And what is success? He was a bachelor but quite liked women though not in the mess. They must know their place. I wondered if he knew about Amiina for he was a crafty old devil. Had the news filtered down to Mogadishu on a dust devil? An NCO on leave who would speak to other NCOs, who in turn might make some mention of his officer there.

Scandal in Mogadishu, particularly among the wives was rife. They were bored and had nothing else to do but gossip. I thought not for he was friendly enough when off parade and after all he had just promoted me and for this I was thankful. He held his drink well, even when drunk. He was in the South Wales Borderers and would bore those around him by telling them of the action at Rorke's Drift in South Africa in the Zulu wars. He was proud of his country, his flag and above all his regiment as he would recall how they had won seven VCs there before breakfast, as he put it. He never mentioned the rest of the battalion at Isandalwana a few days before who were cut to pieces by the Zulu Impis.

He was well liked for he would always back you up. He believed that the British still had a message for all the peoples of the Empire. But some were now unsure — even some of his own officers— here in this damned God-forsaken country for they were becoming afraid of this benevolent rule over the long years and thought the time had come to give up the colonies, thereby destroying all the good things achieved. The Colonel loathed and detested them.

We were now all well on the wing. He passed the bottle round again. I was determined to drink drink for drink with him. Tony was not a drinking man and began to wilt.

'We won't have dinner,' he said. 'I've brought up some duck pâté. Have your cook prepare toasties. Dinner will spoil the party. We'll have a good breakfast for the road back. Your cook will find kidneys, bacon and fresh eggs my bearer gave him.'

He now began on his stories. The Empire. The Army. The flag. His regiment. Tony groaned, half asleep and knocked over the Colonel's glass. He didn't apologise. Petulantly he ased: 'Why do we have to talk about the wretched Empire? I don't believe in it.' I kicked his leg under the table but he was too far gone to notice. He had probably heard all the Colonel's stories at the stations they had stopped at *en route*. Garoe, Galkari, Gardo and Iskushuban.

'What's that? What?' the Colonel was dumbfounded. He righted his glass and poured himself another large tot. His hand was as steady as a rock.

'If you can't take your drink like a gentleman, I suggest you retire to your quarters,' he said. Tony took the hint. Mumbling his goodnights he staggered out of the room.

We finished off the second bottle of whisky at about two in the morning. Before he could break open the third bottle I explained tactfully that as he wished to leave after breakfast I still had to hand over the station cash and handing over notes.

'We'll stay another day,' he said. Somehow I got Tony out of bed to tackle that splendid breakfast which I enjoyed as did the Colonel. Tony had black coffee. Accompanied by our hangovers we did most of the office work. The Colonel announced briskly that he'd take a walk followed by a swim.

At tea time, old Haji Dif, almost in tears, gave me two beautiful Somali daggers in their decorative skin sheaths. I presented him with a wrist-watch which I'd had sent over from Aden by dhow several months ago. We shook hands in the Moslem fashion, that is after the normal handclasp we pressed thumbs which is one of the superstitions of the country relating to 'Hhudur', the Prophet. Hhudur is a man, yet not a man. A Prophet, yet not as great as Jesus or Mohamed. According to legend he is gifted with eternal life to which God has attached certain conditions. He must never stay long in the same place but must wander as the wind wanders, disappearing and appearing at will. Sometimes he will ride on the dust-devils so common here. He must never marry or settle down. The Somalis believe that Hhudur often visits in the guise of a beggar. He prays for those who are kind to him and they amass great wealth. Those that are unkind to him are ruined. No one can tell who Hhudur may be or where he is. There is only one way of recognising him. In his right thumb there is no bone, only flesh, and if one shakes hands with him his thumb will bend backwards. If anyone finds Hhudur in this way he is supposed to grasp his hand until Hhudur's blessing is given, saying, 'I will not let thee go except thou bless me.'

It was now sundown on my last day at Alula. The Colonel heard the bugler blowing the sad notes of the *Tamaam* parade and he went on to the roof-top of my old crenellated Italian house. He looked down below at the flag beyond which the sun was sinking. It fluttered slowly down as the bugle notes called over the bitter desert. The sun was never allowed to set on the Union Jack. The Colonel stood to attention, bareheaded, pride and loneliness stirring in him. The sun did not set on the flag, he reflected sadly. But it had begun to set in the hearts of those who saluted it and the Empire it had represented and he could not understand that terrible sunset.

Love at Alula

1942. I had been at Alula for eight months living on camel's milk, fish, goatmeat and dates with my platoon of Somalis. Mogadishu, the capital of Somalia and headquarters of the British Military Administration was a thousand miles to the south and we lesser mortals occupying these far-flung desert outposts were conveniently forgotten, for the ration lorry containing pay for the troops, their own rations and my NAAFI supplies had not been seen or heard of since my arrival. Perhaps it had broken down. Perhaps it had been shot up or looted. Perhaps it was at Hordio to the south awaiting camels to bring up these precious commodities, for here the road ended. I was without communications for I had no radio and so we just soldiered on with the troops getting restless with no pay, and I also restless without a drink or mail. I longed for company but had none; the nearest British officer was stationed at Bender Kassim, a hundred miles on the coast to the west. I am sure he had his problems too. His predecessor had shot himself.

Alula, meaning pearl in Somali, was situated on the northernmost tip of the Horn of Africa and in the misty past this whole area was called by the ancient Egyptians The Land of Punt. To the north my district embraced the coastal villages of Durbu, Merhagno and Ghessili; to the south Bereda, Damo and Tohen. East to the desert wilderness of the hinterland the Alula District joined up with Iskushuban, some hundred miles as the vulture flies over an impenetrable mountain range. By day I could work off my frustrated energy by a three-day march to the lighthouse at Cape Guardafui, not too far from Tohen. On the station itself I could keep myself occupied with bayonet practice, field exercises, the shooting range and keeping the old Breda machine gun I had been bequeathed in working order, so that I could repel any hoped-for attack the Japanese might make from their marauding submarines in the Gulf of Aden.

Anything, but anything, to relieve the awful boredom and to keep my Somalis occupied.

The long, lonely nights were the worst. I would dream of an apple, a pear, an orange, grapes, or even a potato. I would have nightmares over a sirloin of beef with all the trimmings, lamb chops with mint sauce, a roast loin of pork and the like. I also dreamed of women. Also of cheese like poor old Ben Gunn on Treasure Island. It is said by some that the Northern Somali girls were the most beautiful in the world. I would not dispute this.

I resolved to find one.

My mind went back over the months. During the unbearable nights I had thought of her. Of her swaying, seductive walk, her generous breasts beneath the revealing *maro addi,* the sarong-like garment she wore. Of the provocative look she gave me on the day I bought a camel for the troops for Christmas. I had not seen her since. I had, however, found out her name.

The sun was just setting when I left the house one evening for my walk along the beach. Just before its flaming orb seemingly dipped in the vastness of the ocean it changed the sea into a golden colour tinged with pink. A long echelon of cormorants, stretching as far as the eye could see, winged their way to Bolimoch, the nearby rocky promontory that was their home, now silhouetted in bold relief against the clear evening sky.

I walked barefoot along the shore to the blue lagoon about a mile to the south, clad in my *lungi* with my shirt worn outside in Somali fashion. It was the hour for prayer. I heard the muezzin calling from the village mosque the familiar, *'Allah Akbar, Allah Akbar, La Allah, Il Allah, La Allah, Il Allah, U Mohamed Rassul Allah.'* (God is great, there is no God but God and Mohamed is the Prophet of God). A quickening breeze whipped up little swirls of sand as I passed. An old, grey-headed Suacron fisherman, his net thrown over his shoulder and carrying several silver fish threaded on a line, gave me the traditional Moslem salutation of *'Alikam Asalam.'* I returned his 'To You be Peace, Salaam,' as he trudged homewards. The beach was now deserted. I approached the date palms, their nodding heads fringing the lagoon with the surf pounding in unison to my heartbeats and the thrill of longing that was in me crashed like a thousand thoughts through my mind as all the inhibitions of the past lonely nights choked me with that familiar ache.

It was then that I saw her.

Taller than I, she stood looking out to sea with her back to the prow of a gaily-painted dhow careened on its side. Motionless. As if she were the dhow's figurehead.

I approached nearer, walking noiselessly on the soft sand. Her coiffure was partly disarranged and the imprisoned long black hair, as though impatient to escape, had cascaded to her shoulders. A single desert rose crimsoned behind her ear, enhancing the dark beauty of her face. Playfully, the freshening kherif caressed her one-piece dress which was knotted over the right shoulder and girdled round the waist so that it clung to her lissome body, outlining the generous rounded breasts, the superb thighs and long slim legs. The very fronds of the palm trees seemed to stand still as I drank in the beauty of her.

She must have sensed my presence for with a quick, startled motion she suddenly turned and saw me. As I walked up to her she swept a coloured head-dress over the lower part of her face so that

I was confronted by two bold, slanted, kohl-rimmed eyes which stared steadily at me. I was tongue-tied and neither of us spoke for seconds. Her eyes then brimmed with laughter and she broke a long silence by saying provocatively, '*Nabat! Abdi Melik, so dowow*, (come near). Dids't the Galgail cut out thy tongue then?'

'Nay, Amiina, and why dost thou hide thine?' I ventured, gently removing the yashmak from her face, catching an elusive, fragrant scent of myrrh as I did so. We both laughed.

She had the Mijertein Somali's aristocratic aquiline nose, a generous mouth and flawless, even teeth revealing the dark gloss of her gums. An amber bead necklace encircled her neck.

'Come, sit thee down,' I said. 'Now tell me why dost thou call me Abdi Melik, and what dost thou know of the Galgail?'

'Everyone calls thee Abdi Melik, which is thy Somali name and dost not all the Somali clans throughout the land know of thy fight with the Galgail far to the south and before thee came up to our country. The kherif travels fast and the dust-devils brought us the news of how thee seized their camels in their thousands,' she replied admiringly.

Somali flattery perhaps, but her honeyed tongue was as music to my ears and a balmy sedative which assuaged my lonely heart.

'How many years art thou?' I asked.

'Seventeen, and thou?'

'Twenty-two' 'Art thou married?' 'Nay. And thou?' 'Nay.' 'It is well, Abdi Melik. Knowest that I am a *Jiradah* (Princes). My father is Mohamed Bogor, Sultan of the Mijertein, and his camel herds are countless, his cattle fat and his sheep and goats are as many as the stars in the Heavens yonder.' Here she pointed a shapely rounded arm to the galaxy of stars above us.

'Knowest thou also that this dhow is his. Aye, and others like it at Bendir Kassim, Ollok and Hafun.'

She lay back, resting her head on a coil of rope by the dhow, glancing at me sensuously through half-lowered eyelids. Tracing a pattern in the sand with her forefinger, she began to sing a *balwo*, a lyrical Somali love poem. It had a distinct tune with a syncopated rhythm and it was with difficulty that I caught the words as she softly sang them:

If I set myself to write
Of the love that holds my heart
A wondrous great *kitab* (book),
Could not contain it all.

I long for thee as one
Whose dhow in the *kherif*
Is blown adrift and lost
In the grey and empty sea.

The curving of my breasts
Like apples sweet and small
Are thine to caress
When night turns dusk to dark.

Then lay between these breasts
And call thy life fulfilled
And never be denied
This well of happiness.

'Abdi Melik,' she asked shyly yet imperiously after a pause. 'How dost the Inglesi make love?'

I gasped with desire, then gently eased her forward and in so doing the top of her dress loosened, exposing her breasts which rose and fell like twin cupolas to her eager breathing. Our two hearts hammered together as I murmured, 'With kisses. Thus and this and thus.' I kissed first the tip of her left breast, next the right one, then transferred my mouth to hers which opened with all its fresh moistness at my eager questing. Her eyes widened, then grew dark under my caresses. I was lost. Love-lost in the fragrant, ambrosial scent and voluptuousness of her as we impetuously loved on the beach.

How long we lay there I do not know for time was endless. It meant nothing in an ecstasy such as this. Screened by the dhow, the kherif mourned its loneliness to the outside world. I lost my own loneliness. Lost it deep buried into the open well of her mouth as my kisses rained in there. Amiina herself broke the spell by whispering, *'War Abdi Melik, awa wa addo,'* (Oh! How the moon shines), then kissing me passionately. 'Oh God, I love thee.' Drunk with happiness, I replied with a long, slow kiss. 'I love thee too, Amiina.'

The brilliant moon now riding high above us bathed us both in her friendly light. Drawing my lungi over us both we slept, lulled to sleep by the Trade Winds whispering in the palms and the incessant breaking of the surf. All too soon from the Suacron fishing village behind us a cockcrow heralded the false dawn and she stirred sleepily in my arms.

'Abdi Melik,' she whispered, *'I si, I si,'* (give me, give me). Her lips parted and her kisses infused me with a passion more than I could bear — soon, too soon to be extinguished as love itself rested. Urgently now the cock crowed its strident reveille again. The sun's first blush peeped over the sea. Pulling Amiina protestingly to her feet I stripped in a second whilst she disrobed, letting fall her shift as she looked shyly at me — a bronze Aphrodite.

Hand in hand we ran to the sea, splashing through the shallows and surf, then swimming to a wrecked dhow where we rested, panting with exhilaration and laughing with the joy of being young and in love.

'Ahalki an tagno,' (let us return), I smiled at her.

'Edinku sidas shada eg! wainu ta-gaina,' (Say ye so? — Lo we go), she laughed, diving in the shining waves and heading for the beach.

We dressed quickly and ran up to the house, past the astonished sentry, who gave me a belated butt salute as we went by; and so began my love affair with Amiina. The nights now were no longer long for I would teach her English and she, in turn, helped along my elementary Somali.

From her I learned much of the folklore of the Somalis; that the legendary figures of the Somali race — Darod and Isshak — came from Arabia and she herself claimed to be able to trace her ancestry back to those Arabian aristocrats. She possessed all the physical beauty rhapsodized by the younger set of advanced Somali poets in their short love poems — the belwo. A poet will write some of his best belwo to an unapproachable beauty knowing that his love for her is hopeless, perhaps because of his financial standing but more likely because of his inferior tribe. The Somalis are very class conscious. He would base his romantic love on the curve of a breast or the flicker of an eyelash. These Somali love-poems are mostly of physical love, passionate and sincere. It is not done to use vulgar expressions, thereby offending public taste. It must be remembered that poetry requires no special materials nor carrying space other than the talent of the composer, which is carried in his memory. Since the Somali is constantly moving his tents in the search for grazing and water this is important, for he must carry as little equipment as possible on his burden camels. Also poetry costs nothing — quite a factor to the nomadic Somali in his insecure and poor life.

Generally, marriages are not undertaken lightly and are mostly arranged by the parents with a view to mutual financial advantage. The arrangements are complex and are decided upon by the man himself, the girl's father and also the tribal *Akils* or Elders. Much must be arranged and then settled; the bride price *(yarad)*, the token payment made *(gabati)*, by the man on his engagement and the percentage he has to find of his estate, the *mehr*, which is made out to his wife on marriage. A dowry, or *dibat* is given to the couple by the bride's family.

Usually the girl before marriage is gentle, but afterwards, like some of her European sisters, she often develops into a shrew, becoming irritable and a nagger. The reason for this is that her position is caused by economic necessity as well as tradition. Her status is decidedly inferior to that of man. For example in any tribal affray or blood feud, should a woman be killed accidentally, or taken captive, her loss is reckoned at fifty camels. A man is worth one hundred. This is called *dia* — or blood money. For this reason I think some Somali women prefer an affair, or marriage to a European, for unlike the Somali who, if he treated his wife with unusual thoughtfulness, would be laughed at by the rest of his tribe. A European would show her the kindness and consideration he normally shows to his own woman, to which the Somali girl is unaccustomed.

And so it was with Amiina and myself, for in my love-making I showed her all the gentle intimacies she would not have known otherwise.

I took delight in composing poems to her, as close to the belwo as I could get. In one of them I described her charms:

73

As lovely as a dhow at sea
Thy young beauty is to me
Tall, with all the gerenuk's grace
A daughter of the Darod race.

Black hair, fine as gossamer thread,
Eyes that speak of things unsaid
High cheek bones with straight nose
On thy mouth — the desert rose.

Teeth as white as the lul
Hidden in its secret pool,
Dark shining gums, cheek copper-lush
Beautiful as the desert's blush.

With rounded neck, arms and hips
You sway your form like the desert ships
And when the sun unveils its light,
I long again for the approach of night.

Twin breasts; neither large nor small
Supporting nipples too proud to fall,
At the touch a little wide,
Allah keep them in their pride.

Long-limbed, your thighs a dream,
I have a djinn for it would seem
I cannot sleep, Amiina
These nights in Paradise.

The months flew by now as she accompanied me on my safaris
of absolute happiness. North along the coast by leisurely camel
caravan. To Bereda, Ollok and Damo, the little Suacron fishing
villages nestling in the dunes with the Indian Ocean sparkling sap-
phire blue beneath us. We explored a cave to the south which Amiina
called 'Gadka Darod' (Darod's cave), and one late afternoon, sip-
ing clove-scented tea underneath the date palms at Ghessili, she told

me the full story of her tribe. Amiina, like all Somalis was a born story-teller and I always listened enthralled. Later that evening with the moon playing hide and seek in the palm fronds above us, she danced for me the Butterfly Dance of the Mijertein Somalis.

A few weeks later and back at Alula I was standing on the top of my house scanning the emptiness on all four points of the compass. I stiffened. A camel convoy was approaching from the south. It heralded the arrival of the Colonel with my relief. I learned that I had been posted to that most turbulent District — El Carre in the Ogaden and far to the south. As the vulture flies about eight hundred miles.

On foot, by camel convoy and hitching a ride on the infrequent traders' lorries, Amiina was to find me there later.

Fate

Batch shot himself at Gardo. He was the first of a few other unfortunates to do so. I can well picture the scene. Garoe, Galkayu, Iskushuban and Gardo all had picturesque Beaus Geste-like Italian forts, isolated, each as desolate as the other. I had served in two of them for lengthy periods. Just like living inside a camel, for during the *Jilal* (dry season) there were thousand upon thousand of them watering at the wells. This was the Mijertein and Sheikh Mohammed Abdille Hassan's — the Mad Mullah — territory exactly one hundred years ago.

Outside the fort at Gardo the wind would be lonely again. This hot wind, the *kherif,* would moan, seizing grains of sand to spray them against the latticed windows of Batch's living quarters. The pressure lamp would probably be blown out from where it hung suspended from its wire hook on the scabrous ceiling. He would then be left in darkness, for his servant had left and he did not know how to start it up again. By the light of the moon he would see a colony of ants carrying away the crumbs left over from his supper. Possibly a scorpion under the raffia mat which served as a carpet and always on the walls the geckos chasing and eating flies and mosquitoes.

Every evening he would hear the bugler blowing the sad notes on the *Tamaam* parade and he would see the flag on which the sun was sinking. It would flutter down slowly, reluctantly, as if knowing that in the future another country's flag would replace it. The sun was never allowed to set on the Union Jack. For the first few months he would probably take the salute at the parade. Immaculate as ever — but then his morale would go. Perhaps he would not shave for a few days. Always a moderate drinker perhaps he would now hit the bottle. Every morning in his office he would not be able to cope with the trickery, lies and deceit of the Somalis, nor have the ability to stop the bitter, bloody tribal fights which went on over the ownership of camels, water rights and the sparse grazing.

Hundreds of nights alone gave one the terrible knowledge of self; with this knowledge would come a sick reality that there was no point in being alive. The Italians, during their regime in these parts, were far more *simpatico* to their officers than the British, for they would keep them at such stations for only a few months and always with a detachment of Italian troops as well as their Somali levies. Batch would be the only white man there. He would be surrounded by savages, desert, camels and acres of dung. This was not his scene. He was not fitted for it in physical strength, guile nor inclination. He could not cope. He would give up before he had a chance to achieve anything for he had no perseverance, no stamina and no mental strength. He then became mad and shot himself through the chest with his revolver, but that attempted suicide proved to be another failure, for he survived.

But this was all in the future. In 1941 when our draft arrived in the capital, Mogadishu, a hot, odiferous, colourful city, built on the shores of the Indian Ocean and founded in the 9th century, being then the seat of the Sultans of Zanzibar, we came from all regiments. Mainly from the English counties, several from Scots and Irish regiments, a sprinkling from the Brigade of Guards and just one from the Royal Artillery. Batch. We were all now crammed together in the Somalia Gendarmerie Headquarters and about to be welcomed and addressed by the Colonel. Idly I glanced around me. Batch seated in the front row stood out like a light. He was a character. Another Beau Nash. A dandy and his sartorial elegance even outshone the few Guards officers there. He was taller than most. Well over six feet, blond, good-looking with aristocratic features. Slenderly-built he had the bearing of a cavalryman with his khaki drill uniform superbly cut and tailored to perfection. His Sam Browne belt seemingly was of liquid gloss and, through the open window, a darting ray of sunlight played on his highly-polished buttons and his Gunner's badge on his dress cap of crimson and blue, which he wore at a jaunty angle. He was smoking a cigarette in a long ivory holder. His trousered legs with knife-like creases were negligently crossed. I noticed with amusement that he was wearing pale yellow socks and his expensive-looking calfskin shoes could only have been made by Lobb of London.

In spite of his lackadaisical manner and rather affected speech — for he couldn't or wouldn't pronounce his 'rs,' he was well liked by all. He was not vain. He was too ingenuous for that but what impressed all of us was his charming manners and affability. If one did pull his leg he would blush as easily as a girl and tend to stammer. What we didn't know then was that he could never make up his mind on anything, nor could he come to a decision or accept responsibility. Therein lay his tragedy.

'Good morning, gentlemen,' greeted the Colonel.

'You may sit. My name is Patrick. I am Colonel Commandant of the Somalia Gendarmerie — Military Wing — as opposed to the Police.' He gave a disdainful sniff.

'As you know you are all seconded to this Unit from your various regiments.'

He looked like a character out of Beau Geste. A brick-red face, iron-grey hair, cold blue eyes and bristling moustache. Tall, he had three rows of gongs including the Military Cross and two bars. The others that mattered had also been earned·the hard way. He was most impressive.

'I will now try and put you all in the picture. Here we come under Middle East Command and the country we are to administer is Somalia or ex-Italian Somaliland. Also the Ogaden and the Reserved Area of Ethiopia (which the Somalis dispute) have all been placed under British Military Administration since a few months ago when we defeated the Italian armies in the field. To the north of us is British Somaliland which will eventually revert to British Colonial Office control. Further north still the smaller territory of the Afars and Issas under the French. To the south we have the Northern Frontier District of Kenya. All these territories form the geographical feature known as the Horn of Africa, or, as the ancient Egyptians called it, The Land of Punt.

'This is a vast area consisting mostly of semi-desert scrub country and is inhabited by Somalis who are Muslims and follow the nomadic way of life common to peoples of the desert the world over. Fifty years ago, Winston Churchill called this country a desert of rocks and thorn trees and peopled by rifle-armed fanatics. It has altered little since then. The perennial needs of the tribes for water and good grazing for their vast camel herds, cattle, sheep and goats has led to the development of a complicated, but well-defined, series of tribal migrations. For example, tribes from British Somaliland move south into the Ogaden Haud during the rainy season and tribes from the hinterland of Somalia move towards the fertile valleys of the Juba and Uebe Scebelli rivers when their own lands become parched.

'This almost constant flow of tribal migrations naturally causes bloody clashes between the rival tribal clans in search of grazing and water. These fights have been going on for centuries. Now that the whole of the Italian Administration has collapsed and disappeared, matters have worsened.

'To touch upon the Ogaden Province. Bounded on the north by British Somaliland, to the east and south-east by Somalia and the hostile country of Ethiopia itself, this area in itself is an enormous slice of territory. Although claimed by the Ethiopians, geographically and ethnically it is a Somali country. Of the population of some 320,000, all but a few thousand are nomadic Somali tribesmen solely dependent on livestock for their existence. It is quite remarkable how little the close contact between the Ogaden and Ethiopia has affected the people, for they retain all the characteristics and customs of the Somali and adhere to the Muslim faith. Their neighbours, the Ethiopians, are Coptic Christians and the enmity between them goes back to the distant past. The Ethiopians have not bothered them much about government or law and order but they do sweep down from the highlands in large raiding parties to exact tribute in the shape of livestock, and in so doing cause hardship and casualties. Those of you who are stationed up there will find enough fighting to keep you occupied and tribal fighting is no picnic I assure you.' He lit a cigarette.

'I am sorry. You may smoke if you wish.'

Batch awoke and lit another cigarette. The Colonel continued.

'Most of you will be leaving Mogadishu immediately. Some to form part of a force for disarming operations. Get into the bush which I have just described to you — there's some 300,000 square miles of it. Plenty of scope. Get to know your tribes. Respect their religion.

Learn their language. It's not written so use your imagination. Seventy per cent of the population are nomads so you won't get any information sitting on your backsides. We've no tents. Live under thorn trees as they do. Chase them up. They have some 1,000 rifles still, several thousand hand grenades and a few hundred automatic weapons — mostly booty from the Italians. We want them recovered There is trouble here, here and there and there,' he continued, stabbing a large map on the wall violently with the end of his swagger cane.

'The Aulihan are fighting the Merehan. The Garre are fighting the Galgail. The Uaden are fighting the Geledi. The Omar Mohamed are fighting the Habr Ghidir Saad and the shifta in the Ogaden are fighting for the hell of it. Stop it. We are here to bring back law and order. Get in the information at your stations and you will then soon bring the various situations you have to deal with under control. The Somali doesn't give a damn for our flag, or any flag for that matter. Make him. It's up to each and everyone of you. Shoot better than he can. Ride better. On your foot safaris walk him off his feet. Endure the hardships he does. Then you will get his loyalty. I emphasise again, you must first get his loyalty.' His cold blue eyes flickered over us.

'Most of you will be completely on your own with just a platoon of Somali askaris. You will be hundreds of miles from your neighbour. You will have no wireless sets and little or no transport for some time to come. You will know loneliness, for the desert is lonely. I will endeavour to relieve those of you from the more isolated stations as and when I can. God alone knows though where your reliefs will come from. Where you will have a platoon of Somalis the Italians had a couple of companies. They had the men to spare. We haven't. Any questions?'

Batch put out his cigarette, uncoiled himself from his chair and stood to attention.

'Sir,' he said, 'as you see my wegiment is Woyal Artillery. I am a gunner. I am not infantwy and I don't like the idea of walking miles in the bush without my twansport and my guns. Chasing savages is a beastly sort of a job. With due wespect Sir, I wish to make this verbal application to weturn to my wegiment.' He sat down. There was silence then a gale of laughter. The Colonel smiled frostily and looked at Batch. He looked at him for along time.

'Any more idiotic questions? No? Glad to have met you all. Good luck. You'll need it.'

I wondered then how Batch, with his natural tendency to eccentricity would cope if he were posted to one of the more isolated stations where obviously it would be developed to an extravagant degree. Surprisingly he was one of the more fortunate ones, being posted to Mogadishu itself as Court Prosecutor of all things. How he coped with that job I would not know for after a few months at a place called Afgoi I was posted to Alula in the far north. So far north that if you took another step further over the sand dunes you would find yourself paddling in the Gulf of Aden.

Batch, though, would be in his element. In Mogadishu there was the Officers' Club. The ex-Italian Tennis Club. The old, but quite spacious Croce Del Sud Hotel, built by the Italians and opposite the cathedral. Half a dozen decent Italian restaurants serving good wines, pasta drenched with spicy sauces and parmesan cheese, ravioli, canneloni, delicious scampi, lobster, crab and prawns. Liberal helpings of ice cream as only the Italians can make it and an assortments of tempting *dolcis*. The great Escoffier himself would have approved. Then there was the night club on the beach — the Lido — where he could dance away the night long with the attractive nubile Somali girls or, if his tastes did not run in that direction, then there would be the lovely Italian girls. The British were not strictly speaking allowed to fraternise with the enemy — the Italians, but I am certain any vigilant Military Policeman who saw Batch dallying with his Italian *amore* would have smiled (if Military Policemen can smile) and discreetly turned his back. The Italian *mamas* would not have minded, for Batch in all his elegance and impeccable manners was obviously a Cavellere — a gentleman — and the war would not last for ever ...

It was a year and a half later when I saw him again and then in all unlikely places on the cricket field — or sand, I should say, for now on local leave I had been asked to turn out for one of the teams in Mogadishu.

We were batting and as I took my stance at the wicket I spotted him in the deep. Naturally he had spotted the one and only thorn tree for shade. Just as elegant as ever in cream shirt and flannels and wearing round his waist the garishly coloured MCC tie. He waved to me and then loped over to greet me effusively so that play was held up for a few moments. I was well on my way to fifty when to my astonishment the opposing captain tossed Batch the ball. Languidly coming in from a short run his arm came over. Straight up and down. No guile about Batch. I dispatched it for six. Two more for my fifty. I saw a look of hurt on his face. One should not do that to friends. His second ball was short of a length and as I turned to hook the ball must have hit something under the matting for it never left the ground and clean bowled me. He rushed up apologising, saying how sorry he was that I had not made my fifty and how simply beastly he felt about the whole thing. All this with complete sincerity. That was Batch.

On my return from my Kenya leave I was to find that my application to return to my regiment and posting to a more active sphere had been turned down. Several others suffered the same fate, including Batch. We were then given our new postings. I had hoped that mine would have been south to Brava, Merca or Kismayu — attractive places and comparatively civilised for at these places would be several other British officers. This was not to be. I was posted up north again in the Mijertein to a place called Iskushuban. Batch was posted to Gardo. I swear I saw him shudder. I was to leave the following day and Batch three days later. He saw me off from the Transport Depot. He was in the desert. I gave him a compass. There is but one main track, I explained, and it goes due north to Gardo. 'Just like London to Brighton. I'm sorry we can't go in convoy but I gather your replacement askaris won't be ready for another three days. Don't worry. Just head up north and follow my tracks.' He looked quite dazed.

Three days later, after having bad two punctures and constantly filling the panting radiator on my ancient Italian diesel, I arrived at Gardo. The battlemented fort looked lonely as we approached with the Union Jack lying limply against the flag-pole. Fitz, who I remembered from the draft, rushed out to greet me. We shook hands.

'Are you here to relieve me? the wompo? the mail?' he asked

breathlessly.

'All aboard,' I reassured him. Plus a basket of vegetables and fruit. I had rememberd to bring up a basket to each of the stations until I reached Iskushuban. He almost swooned with delight. Also told him that Batch would be relieving him in three days time.

'Poor devil,' he said. 'He'll go round the bend at this bloody place. You'll stay the night?' he asked pleadingly.

'Glad to,' I said, for why the hell should I press on? What was a lost hour, a day, a week or even a month in this loneliness? We offloaded his wompo — the drink — the mail then the fruit and vegetables. I left him for a moment, a peeled banana in one hand and a hammer in the other frantically opening a box marked 'gin.' Fitz had been at Gardo over a year and that evening bombarded me with questions. Was it true that Ian MacDonald had won the MC in the Ogaden? It was. Was it true that old Fellows-Smith had ended up in the bug-house? It was. Was this true? Was that true? We talked and talked until there was nothing else to talk about. Then we started up all over again. I noticed on the wall leading to his bedroom a vulgar painting of a naked Italian soldier. He wore only a sun helmet. In his right hand he carried a rifle with fixed bayonet. In his left hand was a Chianti bottle, tilted so that the red wine was spilling like blood on the yellow sand. The soldier had a shaggy black beard and he was laughing showing good teeth. Printed in large letters underneath were the words *Il Taverno degle Insabbiata* and *Qui Rido Io*. I pondered over the translation and finally came up with 'The Tavern of the Besanded. Here laugh I.' I took some comfort that the Italians here had gone round the bend too but the fastidious Batch, I thought, would definitely disapprove. Some of the Italians had been frightened of these deserts and their fanatical tribes. No Italian officer was left more than six months in any of these isolated outposts and during their tour of duty would always have a sprinkl ing of Italian soldiers under command as well as their Somali levies to boost morale generally.

That night Fitz's one solitary pressure lamp died down. We were now in moonlight. He made no move and so I pumped it. The sudden glare lit up the drab room with scabrous' walls. Several cockroaches scuttled across the floor. Two Praying Mantis, emerald green, one male and one female settled on the neck of the brandy bottle, their beady eyes in their triangular faces revolving round the room. The female was slightly larger than the male. With minute tongues they licked each other and then proceeded to fornicate. At the *moment critique* the female, with spikes on the inside of her forelegs clutched the male even closer and began to eat him. Chop by delicate chop. Charming. Batch would not like that either. I flicked the remnants of the male and his greedy consort off the bottle with my forefinger as I poured us out another large tot. They joined the moths which had fluttered through the lattices of the windows, attracted by the pressure lamp to burn their wings against the hot glass as they dropped fluttering on the stone floor. A solitary jackal yelped into the night and then came the first of the camels. Thousands upon

thousands of them, plaintively burping, groaning and moaning as they were herded to the adjacent wells outside. I again felt sorry for Batch for in this sordid atmosphere he would think he was living inside one.

We finished off the bottle of Old and Bold brandy and I produced another. I knew there was something I had forgotten to tell Batch and that was if he ran out of paraffin for his pressure lamp then this brandy could be used in its place.

The servant came in to announce that supper was ready. Fitz was evidently far gone by this time for he had forgotten about eating. His face lengthened when the usual goat was served but enthused over the dish of vegetables. Carrots, peas and potatoes. He said he hadn't had his greens for six months. I rocked with laughter. Helping himself to another spoonful of vegetables he suddenly sat bolt upright on his chair. He was quite agitated.

'Do you hear them?' he asked excitedly.

'As a matter of fact I don't — hear what?' I was puzzled for all I could hear was the constant noise from the milling camels.

'Those damned ducks. Every time I have supper — usually about now — they perch on the roof of the fort and start up their infernal quacking. They are driving me mad.' He was quite put about. So was I, for apart from the chain of wells close by and about a hundred feet deep, the water being hoisted hand over hand in glistening goat-skin buckets, there was no other water to be found for many miles at Garoe to the south and Iskushuban to the north.

'Yusuf,' I called to my servant. He was in the kitchen adjoining.

'Bring my shotgun and the ammunition for it.' After my year at Alula I knew the drill by now. I loaded the gun and walked outside. Looking on the battlemented roof just to make sure that the ducks were not perching there, I took a brain shot at the man in the moon and pulled both triggers, then ejected the empty cartridge cases. The night was shattered by the yelping of the pye-dogs from the village area, and the Corporal of the Guard's hoarse words of command as he turned out the guard. The alarm whistle shrilled. The guard came over at the double. I assured the corporal that we were not under attack and that all was well. He saluted, relaxed and they returned to their post.

"Sorry Fitz,' I said walking back in the room, 'but I missed both barrels.'

'Ah well,' he replied philosophically, 'I didn't really expect roast duck with our green peas would be possible.' He then fell asleep in his chair. I went to bed. At first light I woke up, shaved, had a shower and climbed into my uniform. I had a fearful hangover but wanted to be off before the sun rose. The old enemy.

Fitz was still asleep in his chair when I walked into the living room with my cup of tea. He snored gently. His stockings had fallen crumpled round his ankles. The sordid debris from the evening's drinking was still on the table. An empty bottle of Old and Bold brandy and a second, almost finished, stood together like Humpty-Dumpties. The pressure lamp had burnt itself out and the glass was discoloured with a sooty film. A circle of dead moths lay around it. Through the open window I saw the Guard Commander change his sentry. I woke him up to say goodbye to him. No. I wouldn't bother about breakfast for I had many miles to cover before I reached Iskushuban.

I had been there about three months when the news filtered through by bush telegraph over Batch's attempted suicide. The bullet had missed the heart and miraculously he was still alive. A trader's lorry luckily passing through at the same time had carried the news, driving non-stop to Mogadishu. The British Military Administration there had signalled Aden and the RAF had sent in a plane to evacuate him there. When he had recovered physically they had requested the senior RAF doctor in charge to have him returned for court martial. The request was refused, which reflects great credit on the humane doctor who had replied that he was well physically but not mentally.

There my saga of Batch might have come to a close but there is a short epilogue.

Two years later when I had been posted to the Ogaden more news came through about him. He had cheated the vultures in Mogadishu by obtaining a posting back to his regiment in Burma, where he had been killed by the Japanese.

A Bunch of Bananas

Pat Lyons, of Irish origin, was one of the four brothers who formed the North Kenya Polo Club and team in 1938. They played at Mweiga with their headquarters at Nyeri.

When I met up with him in 1941, he would be in his mid-forties, I would judge. A smallish man, not quite handsome but of striking appearance in a horsy way. Greying wiry hair cut short, clean-shaven with fierce bushy eyebows. He had the blue, laughing eyes of his race except for the left one, which was covered by a black patch. He had a touchy temper, a rasping voice and could be abrasive with an ironic sense of humour. He was generally popular and well-liked. At that time he was Town Major of Kismayu, a coastal town off the Somalia hinterland. The Civil Affairs Officer there was Ray Mayers, called Indo Adde (white eyes), by the Somalis and in later years was to be regarded as one of the most brilliant administrators in the country — particularly in the turbulent Ogaden Province. He and Pat had been friends from the early years together in Kenya.

Stationed further north in Mogadishu was their superior, the Brigadier, OC Troops, and his wife who was known as Bullshit Barbara. They lived in Cockroach Castle, formerly the residence of the Italian Governor before the Italian surrender. The Brigadier, a regular soldier and strict disciplinarian was not generally disliked, but Bullshit Barbara was and by none more so than Pat Lyons. Their paths, I should imagine, must have crossed in the past somewhere. One of the reasons she was so disliked was over the issue of NAAFI supplies. Probably the kindest thing one could say about this was that she invariably got her figures wrong when putting in her indent and so received far more than her entitlement in the way of liquor. This did not amuse the troops.

Over their usual sundowners in Kismayu, the two old friends were discussing the invitation they had received from the Brigadier for drinks and dinner at Cockroach Castle to mark the occasion of Bullshit Barbara's birthday. What they did not know was that the Brigadier had commissioned Bruno Di Sopra, a local Italian artist, to paint a portrait of her in oils. Di Sopra, apart from being a brilliant portrait painter was also very suave with a quiet sense of humour. He would have made a good diplomat. He had taken one look at her and with tongue in cheek said that whilst he admired her classical beauty her hands were undoubtedly her biggest asset. He really did not have to rhapsodise here for her hands were really most elegant. He would like to paint them. A slightly mollified Brigadier then told him to go ahead on painting them but that the painting should be finished for presentation on her birthday.

Pat Lyons was quite adamant in his refusal to attend the party while Ray Mayers was equally determined that his old friend should patch up his quarrel with the Brigadier's wife.

Finally, the Mayers' famous persuasive charm, possibly aided by the drinks they had, had won him over and they made arrangements to motor up to Mogadishu in Pat's staff car the following day for the party to be held that evening. Naturally they made brief stops to visit with old friends at the coastal villages of Merca and Brava on their way. Finally they arrived at the party a little late but in good form.

Entering the imposing portals of Cockroach Castle they were each handed a glass of champagne, after which they edged their way to where the Brigadier, his wife, his ADC and a few acolytes stood admiring the painting which was hung in a prominent position in the Hall. There were the usual murmured platitudes and all agreed that Di Sopra had excelled himself. Pat Lyons moved closer. He squinted at the picture with his one good eye.

'Bruno Di Sopra, my eye' he said in that rasping, penetrative voice of his.

'The man's gone mad. Been in the country too long. What the hell is the feller thinking about? The only thing we have in Somalia are bananas, and yet he paints a damned great bunch of them to hang in Cockroach Castle!'

The Long Drop

The Beaver came from Yorkshire where, apparently, his father owned a mill. He was a huge, shambling, ape-like man aged twenty-two. Blond shaggy unkempt hair adorned a moon-like red face with pimples and child-like blue eyes. He had attended Rugby School but the years he had spent there had obviously been of little benefit to him. Neither had the short time with his regiment, The Green Howards, and I suspect the Colonel at British Military Headquarters in Mogadishu had sent him to me in desperation. He had seen no active service. He couldn't or wouldn't learn the local language and made no effort to understand the Somalis in his platoon who were new and strange to him. He was slow, plodding and dim, hated the life and all he seemed to think about, when he thought at all, was Yorkshire, the mill, the world of good clothing, food, drink and their lovely home. He had been with me now for three months and I despaired.

You reach El Carre, where I was then stationed, north through Bardera, Lugh Ferrandi, Dolo and Lama Scillindi. It is some twenty miles from Imi on the Uebe Scebelli (Leopard River) where lies the cairn of stones marking the last resting place of Mohamed Abdullah Hassan — the so-called Mad Mullah. It is in the Ogaden and beyond in the misty distance lie tier upon tier of mountains. Ethiopia. The station was the stronghold of Ray Mayers, my predecessor and mentor. The boma, consisting of battlemented stone houses, huddled together for protection against Ethiopian raiders, the marauding shifta, nestled under overhanging red sandstone cliffs. I had taken over from Ray as Civil Affairs Officer some several months previously.

Among many innovations, for Ray was both able and energetic, he had deepened an existing dry well in the boma compound but after his labour had toiled down with pick and shovel for about a hundred feet, it still remained dry. One of his failures, but nothing daunted and always philosophical, he had turned it into a long drop, or lavatory, over which his *fundis* had constructed an intricately carved thunder box which resembled a small throne. It was a work of art. The whole was housed under rondavel with a neat thatched roof. Inside were shelves on which were placed old newspapers and magazines. It was most comfortable. Ray always used to proudly say that it was the deepest long drop in the whole of East Africa. I would not dispute it. The Beaver evidently thought so too and in his leisure hours he would sit for lengthy periods on the throne pawing through the equivalent of Comic Cuts or whatever it was he read.

Then came the news from the Rer Wafata, one of our friendly tribes. A raiding party of over one hundred shifta had swooped down on them from over the border killing and maiming the men, women and children and looting their entire stock of camels. The Rer Wafata grazing grounds were only some twenty miles east from El Carre itself and the insolence of this provocative attack left me shaking with anger. More so for I thought that any possible attack would come from the north or the west where I had strong patrols out.

Only the Beaver and myself were left on the station with a weakened company. On my orders the office sentry sounded the alarm and after many precious minutes the Beaver came lumbering into the office. I snatched up a map.

'This is where you go on patrol,' I said. Briefing him I explained the position. One of our patrols was due to return any day. We knew he route they would be taking and the Beaver with a small escort would head for them. They would then combine forces, get behind the shifta and ambush them on their way back to their mountainous stronghold in the Ethiopian foothills.

'Ah,' the Beaver said, 'Ah.' He hadn't understood a word I said. I looked at him hopelessly. I couldn't possibly send such an imbecile into that hostile country and against such a merciless enemy. He would be cut to pieces.

'As you were,' I said resignedly. 'You will remain here in charge of the station. It is now the 28th. Here are the keys to the safe and the armoury. You will pay out the Chiefs, staff and the remaining askaris at the end of the month. George, the clerk, will make out the nominal rolls for you. On all payments made get their signatures or thumbprints. I should be back in several days time.' He could come to no harm in the boma, I thought. I still did not know the Beaver.

In half an hour I had collected my mounted escort with sufficient water and the minimum of rations. We cantered off, through the frowning El Mara pass, the foothills dotted with Cape chestnuts and the occasional cedar tree. Once through the pass we were clear of the foothills and the Adamboi plains lay ahead of us. Rer Wafata country.

Through my binoculars I could see in the hazy distance a column of baggage camels and men. The returning patrol. We intercepted them and after some hard riding and marching we made for my ambush point — but we were too late. The shifta, in spite of having hundreds of looted camels to herd, had moved fast and evaded us.

Tired and dispirited we camped out in the bush that night. Before turning in. a mounted Illalo (a tribal policeman), rode into camp with an urgent message from the Beaver. It was unbelievable.

'Armoury and safe keys lost down long drop. Cannot pay out. What shall I do?' Savagely, I penned a curt chit back: 'Recover keys and pay out as ordered. Shall be back in three days. If these orders are not executed on my return I will place you under close arrest.' After a quick bite of food and tea the Illalo galloped off.

The Sergeant Major greeted me upon my return. There was no Beaver. He had been evacuated to hospital in Mogadishu minus his shaggy hair, his eyebrows and a lot of his facial skin. I gathered he would recover.

What had happened evidently was this: in his slow ponderous fashion he had mulled over my chit, dawdled, but finally had come up with a novel solution. He would have the thunder box removed from over the hole for space in order to lower a sweeper on a camel rope down the long drop. First of all though (and this was a kindly thought), he would fumigate the gloomy depths below. He next gave orders to have a 44-gallon drum of petrol rolled up. The cap was removed and the whole of the contents poured down.

He made a torch of rolled-up papers, lit it and dropped it down.
He then peered hopefully over the top.

Night of the Long Knives

The Somali Republic became an Independent State on 1 July 1960. The Somalis occupy the eastern horn of Africa — the largest single homogeneous area on the continent. Their country consists for the most part of desert and scant pastures with two rivers, the Juba and the Uebe Scebelli, both in the southern part of the country. North or South, both areas have been the playground of international politics for over a hundred years.

The Somalis themselves are more akin to the Arabs, from whom they claim their ancestry, than to their Bantu neighbours to the south on whom they look down. They are far more militant, intelligent and better organised, making tough and ruthless fighters, and with their powers of endurance and knowledge of the bush they are truly fearsome opponents.

Going back some 500 years the Somali coast has always been a formidable barrier to the unwelcome intruder for, as early as 1506, Brava, to the south of Mogadishu, fiercely resisted a Portuguese invasion. Their Somali army of some 6,000 spearmen killed forty Portuguese and wounded many others.

Sailing north in their galleons the Portuguese then attempted a landing off Mogadishu where the beach teemed with armed Somalis, many of them horsemen. Wisely the Portuguese withdrew.

Burton and Speke were to meet for the first time in Aden (opposite my old station of Alula on the northernmost Somali coast), for an expedition together in Somaliland which was a complete disaster for, at Berbera; Issa tribesmen made a night attack on their encampment. Lieutenants Stroyan and Herne were killed, Burton wounded in the jaw by a spear, Speke wounded and taken prisoner, subsequently escaping only to be wrongly accused by Burton of cowardice — yet in the fight both men showed their courage.

Jubaland(once part of the old Northern Frontier District of

Kenya) was transferred by Great Britain to Italy in 1924, and thereafter was colonised by them with the rest of the northern Italian possessions, as was the British Protectorate whose borders are washed by the Gulf of Aden and the French Colony bordering the Red Sea.

It was only when Italy surrendered during the Second World War that the whole of what was the Italian Colony came under British Administration in 1941. History does indeed repeat itself for disarmament operations were necessary then in restoring normal conditions. This was undertaken satisfactorily by a small mixed force of mainly Somalis with some Wakamba who were then part of the newly-formed Somalia Gendarmerie. Never more than a battalion strong it was commanded by British Officers.

During my two decades living with them in their desolate country as soldier, Political Officer and professional hunter, I always found them staunch and loyal under dangerous conditions. However, I also found them fiendishly clever at pitting one officer against his neighbour with their charmingly deceitful characters. So it proves again in 1993 for they have now succeeded in causing a rift between the United Nations and Italy whose troops there are attempting to keep the peace.

At the end of the Second World War the Four Powers — Britain, France, Soviet Russia and the United States — were unable to find common ground on the disposal of ex-Somaliland. France suggested the continuation of Italian rule, the USA wanted direct International Administration and Britain proposed a temporary Trusteeship for a Greater Somalia, lumping together British Somaliland, Italian Somaliland, French Somaliland, the Ogaden and the Northern Frontier District of Kenya. All territories in the main populated by Somalis. Indeed the Somali national flag is a white five-pointed star on a blue background, representing each of these five territories so dear to the hearts of all Somalis. This eminently suitable proposal was disbanded because once again the Big Powers failed to agree. Molotov of the Soviet Union was scathing in his remarks that Britain was trying to expand the British Empire.

In January 1948, the four Big Powers held a Commission in Mogadishu to ascertain the wishes of the people as to their future. The Commission asked that those political parties that wished to do so should be permitted to hold public demonstrations. The up-and-coming Somali Youth League, of which my old clerk from my Iskushuban days was a founder member, as well as being by now the Prime Minister of the country, Abdiraschid Shermarke Ali, received much authority as did other political parties. At the same time unauthorised counter-demonstrations were staged by those Italian colonialists who had stayed behind after the defeat of Italy, together with their Somali supporters.

With the volatile, excitable temperament of the Somali matters got out of hand and widespread disturbances followed.

A night of horror resulted in the deaths of fifty-one Italians and seventeen Somalis.

Most of the Italian dead died under the spears and long, wicked-looking, double-edged knives for there were few, if any, illegal firearms in Mogadishu at that time.

The Moonflower

Caressed and enticed
By a wandering moonbeam,
Its cream pale loveliness
Slowly unfolds.
Reluctantly it would seem
As though shy
To display its chaste purity
To my tempted eye.
Yet I would not profane
A single bloom,
Nor even touch a petal.
Just a sigh
As I wistfully pass by
Its elusive fragrance
Lost for ever
For tomorrow I know
It will die.

The Beachcomber

Give me a beach
With virgin sand,
A turquoise sea
And a fish to land;
Ghost crabs a-scurrying
Driftwood and shells,
Sounding softly towards evening
Camel bells.
The sun slowly sinking
With the stars twinkling
At a crescent moon
Aromatic seaweed my bed
A soft dune for my pillow
Lulled to sleep
By the Song of the Sea.

Two

OF WILDLIFE AND HUNTING

The Life and Death of George Adamson

It was in 1941 when I first met him briefly. At a coastal town in Somalia called Kismayu. We were both in the army and I was passing through on my way further north.

Almost two decades passed by which time he was a Game Warden in Kenya, and had spent most of those years in the Northern Frontier. It was here that our tracks crossed occasionally at places like Isiolo, Garissa, Wajir, El Wak, Marsabit, Maralal, Moyale, Mandera, Garba Tulla, and as far north as Lake Rudolf, now Lake Turkana. Always at isolated outposts, for both of us by then had chosen to live that way.

In 1986 I had retired and was living in an old Arab house I had bought on Lamu Island. After some time beachcombing and lotus-eating on that small island I grew restless and yearned again for the bush and desert.

In that same year a wandering dust-devil brought me welcome news from the Trustees of the Kora National Reserve, some one hundred and fifty miles, as the vulture flies, to the north. Would I team up with the Old Man at his Kampi Ya Simba? Evidently he had suffered a further loss since his wife Joy had been murdered at her own camp in the Northern Frontier years before. His only brother Terence (one of the unsung heroes at Kora), an indefatigable bushman who had cut all the tracks and roads in the Reserve; had built the airstrip there, as well as the camp, and had kept the ramshackle Land Rovers and tractor in repair, had died two months previously. I was to learn afterwards that he was a dowser of repute and this stood him in good stead when the Old Man could not contact his lions.

Instead of dowsing for water, Terence would dowse for the missing lion or lions. Poring over a large-scale map on a camp table, a gold ring at the end of his sensitive plumb-bob in the one hand and a photograph of the missing animals in the other, he would painstakingly and meticulously cover the area where they were thought to be. When the gold ring rotated he knew then their whereabouts within a few miles. I was to be told later that his pin-pointing was accurate eight times out of ten. To me this sounded far-fetched and unbelievable, as I am sure it would to many others, but then once at Kora I was to find out that this was but one of the enigmas I would be confronted with in connection with the Old Man and his lions.

To add to these misfortunes, his mercurial assistant and pro-tégé. Tony Fitzjohn had been declared *persona non grata* by the Kenya Government and was having to move with his attractive and hard-working girlfriend, Kim Ellis.

With his long mane of silvered grey hair, moustache and pointed white beard, the familiar figure still looked the same. All in all, I thought the years had dealt with him in kindly fashion. His blue eyes twinkled as he shook my hand with his well-remembered shy smile. He said he was glad to see me. Once in the mess the legendary hospitality was there too. He had only one helper in the camp and she came over as he made the introductions. Her name was Sabine, a Kenya girl. About twenty, I would judge, small, attractive and, like the Old Man, with an engaging shy smile. She would be with us for some months and of all the many guests we had in the year to come she would prove to be the most endearing. He asked her to bring us drinks and within a few moments a large pink gin was in my hands. He had remembered my tastes.

Over a frugal lunch on my first day, made palatable by the fruit and vegetables I had brought up with me — for there were no luxuries here unless a kind visitor came armed with the odd bottle and supplies, we ate sparingly. With the wind rattling the palm thatch above the mess as we ate, the Old Man and Sabine fed the 'family'. Nuts out of a tin for the tame ground squirrels, hornbills, doves, go-away birds and vulturine guinea fowl in their hundreds. Even the greedy and mischievous vervet monkeys shared our food and my precious bananas disappeared as they spirited them away until

Sabine, bless her heart, placed the remainder in a wired-in cupboard. All were made welcome, fed and watered at the Old Man's table at this St Francis-like sanctuary.

After lunch, and before our Egyptian physical training, he put me in the picture. I learned that poaching was worse than I had believed possible. From the Somalis certainly, but the real damage was being done by organised gangs employed by wealthy Africans in Nairobi.

Evidently when George had first arrived at this comparatively small reserve, it held about eighty rhinoceros. They had all been butchered. Every one of them. He estimated that eighty per cent of the elephant population had been killed also. Bulls, cows and calves carrying tiny pathetic toothpicks; for the poachers were quite merciless.

As soon as I could get out on safari I found that the few elephant left, mostly cows and calves, were always on the move; so terrified were they. I remembered the old days — the Golden Years when the vast herds would amble down to the river as the sun went down. Here they would drink in the shallows to then bathe in the deeper waters, the old bulls entering first to pound the sandy river bed with their ponderous feet, so driving away any lurking crocodiles which are quite capable of taking a baby elephant. After the drinking and the bathing, and just as leisurely, they would then feed off the doum palm nuts which were a delicacy. If there were insuffecent windfalls on the ground then their domed foreheads would butt the slender boles so that they were then showered with a fresh supply. After the feeding they would sleep on the river bank to return slowly to their grazing grounds deep in the bush.

Not any more. The pitifully small herds of several animals each would hurry to the river. A few quick furtive intakes of water and then just as quickly rush back to the far bush where they hoped to find sanctuary.

Of the smaller animals a few zebra remained, waterbuck, gerenuk, impala, Grant's gazelle, oryx, lesser kudu, bushbuck and giraffe. Thankfully, the ubiquitous tiny dikdik were to be observed everywhere. Leopard had been completely poached out for the value of their skins and only on one occasion did I see cheetah. Crocodile, those baleful killers, were just as numerous as I remembered and from time to time took their toll of the Somalis' domestic stock, small game and sometimes the Somalis or Riverines themselves.

With just the three of us in camp those were idyllic days, and as we had our sundowners with the sun sinking into a sea of bush, the Old Man and I would start yarning and story telling, with young Sabine listening wide-eyed and drinking in every word. Once when he was a little late at the rickety drinks table, for we heard his battered old typewriter clattering away from his thatched hut, I apologised to her, saying that she must be bored at listening to we two old fuddyduddies yarning away every night. She gave me that direct look of hers and a small smile appeared on her lips as she said: 'I have never been so happy in all my life.'

I remember all his stories, two of them particularly well. One was true to life and one imagined. One was slightly *risqué;* the other typical of the man with his simple sense of humour. The ritual would start with the fumbling of his old briar pipe until it was drawing to his satisfaction. I was smoking in those days and ran out of cigarettes. George was short of tobacco and came the time when he ran out. I then remembered an old-timer from my Somaliland days who was in the same predicament. He smoked dried, aromatic elephant dung. George had enough tobacco to last him that night and the following day. I suffered in silence. Sabine then measured us out a modest tot of whisky and added a little water for the both of us. She did not drink herself. The next night I collected a couple of handfuls of dried elephant droppings, soaked them in a little brandy we had and put the mixture out in the sun. Sabine made me some cigarette papers. I put the Kampi Ya Simba smoking mixture into George's now empty tin and rolled myself one. He filled up and took a few tentative puffs.

'Good Lord,' he said. 'Not bad, Dougie. Not bad at all. Reminds me of Balkan Sobranie for it is slightly aromatic. When you next go into Mwingi though, there should be a few tins of Sweet Nut awaiting me there and of course there will be cigarettes for you also.' He puffed away happily. He then smiled and looked at both of us.

'Did you ever know Van der Merwe?' he asked. Sabine shook her head. I nodded. That is, I knew of him. That comical, rather thick Afrikaans character who was always putting his foot in it.

'Well, many years ago, Van der Merwe was the manager of a large gold mine down south. One late afternoon he received notice he was to expect two most important visitors. The mine owner's wife and daughter no less. He was to take them by lift down the mine and to show them everything of interest. Naturally Van der Merwe was thrilled. He was unmarried and in his thirties. He had seen the daughter from a distance and she was built like a destroyer. All the right lines. Such a visit could lead to anything. Promotion? An illicit liaison, for he noticed that she had a roving eye. Marriage even, for then he would be made for life.

'They were late to arrive but he had all their gear ready. Overalls, mine helmets and the like. They descended safely into the bowels of the earth and Van Der Merwe excelled himself in showing his VIPs everything as he had been instructed. They both thanked him prettily and the wife looked at her watch. She had an appointment in Johannesburg and her daughter a date in the same town. The sun had gone down. Van Der Merwe pressed the button for the lift. Nothing happened. He pressed it again. He noticed that the mine lights were out. A short somewhere. He despaired. He would get the sack he knew. Next to the lift was the old original mine shaft with an iron rung ladder reaching to the surface. Through the aperture, high above them the stars started to twinkle. Van der Merwe pointed to it and stammered his apologies. The good lady was kind to him for she said that both her daughter and herself were trained mountaineers and to climb to the top would be no effort on their part. Van der Merwe shuddered. She said she would go first, followed by her daughter and then Van der Merwe. Half-way up they rested. Van der Merwe, thinking to distract them from their doubtless perilous predicament, looked up through the shaft aperture and said that he could see Uranus. Whereupon the attractive daughter, rather sourly, thinking she would be late for her date replied that she could see Mars too.' Sabine giggled delightedly. Another pipeful of the Balkan Sobranie special, another cigarette of the same mixture, another drink and we waited for the next gem.

'One day, again a long time ago, in the thirties I think it was, I was motoring from Mombasa to Malindi where Terence had a little cottage at Leopard Point. The two of us were in a clapped-out old banger I had then. You must know in those days there was no tarmac — just a red, dusty track. I'd had a couple of whiskies at Mombasa Club — Terence as you know neither smoked nor drank. He was driving. We were about halfway to Malindi. No houses in those days. No hospitals or dispensaries. No hotels. Just a few African huts every mile or so.

'All of a sudden I spotted an upturned bicycle in the ditch. I told Terence to stop and back up a bit. We got out of the car and walked up to the bicycle. We could smell the booze — you would call it wompo Dougie — but it was *chang'a* — a poisonous spirit, the African's drink, but really only good for putting in pressure lamps. Good Lord, but it's potent and the whole place reeked of it. We approached closer and then we saw a drunken African under the bicycle. Entwined in and out of the bicycle and round and round the African was just about the biggest python I have ever seen. It had tried to swallow him, but he was a big chap and had got no further than the top of his left thigh. I produced my .38 and with a stick turned the python's head slightly to one side and blew its head off. We then tugged and pulled it off the swallowed thigh. There were a few slight lacerations on his leg but nothing much, which I doctored with iodine from my Red Cross box. All this time the African was snoring away in drunken bliss and from his mouth came those dreadful fumes. He was as drunk as a fiddler's bitch. I placed half a dozen aspirins in his fist and we drove off. I have always wondered when he sobered up. A smashed bicycle and a dead python on top of him. I dug Terence in the ribs. "Probably take a page out of your book Terence, and swear off alcohol for life!"' The Old Man chuckled reminiscently.

I thought about the story and knowing him so well did not for one moment doubt the authenticity of it. So typical of his puckish sense of humour — and kindness in remembering the aspirins!

'One more for the Malindi road.' I looked at Sabine suggestively. She upturned the empty whisky bottle. 'Good Lord,' (the Old Man's favourite expression). 'Have we finished it?' He looked quite concerned.

'Ah well, we'd better have supper as there is no more whisky left.' 'Indeed there is,' I replied. 'Several bottles, for you are forgetting the consignment I brought on the plane.' I rushed off to get a bottle.

'Just one more story,' Sabine begged. 'Hamisi has just told me that the bit of goat I gave him to make up into a stew was on the tough side and it's not quite ready.' She poured us out another. The Old Man recharged his pipe. From the magic outside a lion grunted in the distance. Long drawn out moans which went on and on. They sounded just like a drum being beaten.

'Tom Tom,' he said. He knew them all, their distinctive roars and grunts... he sipped his whisky reflectively. Sabine brought us a plate of scrambled egg sandwiches. She sat down, arms round her legs as she waited for the last story of the evening. Tom Tom grunted again. Nearer this time. He was probably coming into camp for his supper which would be the goat carcass old Hamisi had saved after cutting off our small portion for the stew.

The Old Man smiled reminiscently.

'Gin,' he said. 'Just like Worcestershire sauce. So necessary in the bush for the sauce is good against the heat of the day and the gin keeps off the mosquitoes.' He looked at me.

'I'm sure you agree, Dougie?' I did indeed. I wasn't sure about the Worcestershire sauce and his theory, but a couple of gins at midday and a couple of whiskies as sundowners were all part of the magic of the bush and helped along the evenings in companionable fashion, for we had no music here, no shows, no television, no pubs. You made your own amusement and entertained yourselves.

'Gin,' he said again. 'I do like a couple at midday but Joy disapproved and she used to hide the bottles. She was clever and I'm damned if I could find them — unless Hamisi saw her and then he would tell me. Mark you, when I knew she was coming, every Christmas, I used to hide my own bottles. Bury 'em. But do you know last Christmas I'm damned if I could remember where I had buried them. The outlook was bleak. Terence, of course, couldn't stand her and just before she came he would tear off in his little Suzuki for his cottage at Malindi. The way he drove you would think the Devil was after him. A pity that, for he would have dowsed and found them for me. Well, here she was and it was Christmas Day and no booze. Suddenly I remembered I had hidden a bottle of Gordons in the workshop. I went over and spotted it. At least the label said it was Gordons — boar's head, juniper berriers and so on. What I had forgotten was that when I drank the last tot I filled it up with brake fluid. I screwed off the top and had a large swig. Good Lord, it nearly killed me! However, Hamisi there' — he pointed with his pipe stem to where old Hamisi was crouched over the camp fire trying to cook tenderness into the tough goat — 'saved the day. He saw me burying a bottle underneath the waste-paper basket in my hut.' We laughed and had supper. An explosive roar then made the jelly shake on the table. An effort from Sabine. Tom Tom had arrived. He had his supper too.

So that, then, was the pattern of the delightful time I spent at Kampi Ya Simba. A few weeks later guests began to arrive. Some invited, some not. Some good, some bad and some indifferent. For some were helpful and some plain lazy. In the evenings, now with about a dozen around the little table, and the female acolytes vying with each other as to who would pour out the Old Man's drinks, came the little quarrels and bickerings. The Old Man didn't seem to notice this but went on in his own benign, kindly way. Essentially a loner, I thought at times such as these that a little solitude would be helpful and so I would load up Terence's Suzuki, his chop box, a bottle and a few tins of rations to motor some thirty miles upriver where we had a gang working on demarcating the northern boundary of the reserve. After two or three weeks I would return to camp when things were less hectic.

The three cubs, which we had in the wired-in compound, were by now about half-grown and all of us would take turns to go on walks with them. Abdi, the Boran tracker, was particularly good and fond of them. It was his job to clean out their pen and to see they had plenty of water. Once I had become used to them jumping on my back when I least expected it, I, too, grew fond of them. But I never trusted them.

Africans in general look upon the plains game, eland, Tommy, impala and the rest of them as something to eat. No more, no less. The dangerous game they look upon as a nuisance and something to kill when they have the right weapons. Not Abdi. He was a jewel, that little Boran, and after the tragedy when the cubs were darted and placed unconscious in the plane for their long flight o Botswana, he thought they were dead and cried. Unbelievable, but true.

All animals react to fear in a person. They know immediately when you are frightened of them. Any horseman will tell you that. They also know when you dislike them. I disliked the vervet monkeys and this dislike was reciprocated. It took Sabine and I a couple of days to clean up in the store after they had pulled away the protective wire covering the windows. In the store were drums of maize meal, sugar, rice, beans, corn, tea and so on. We were often visited by Police, Game Rangers and the like who invariably were out of rations for themselves and petrol for their Land Rovers. They shamelessly begged off the Old Man who never once refused them although they were issued with their own Government rations which they probably sold. Such frequent handouts must have made quite a dent in his Game Department pension.

The drums had open tops. Again the contents were wired in but those mischievous little devils had torn that off too and so there was a scene of desolation. Flour, maize meal, beans, corn, the lot strewn all over the floor and our nicely-stacked tins of food chucked all over the place. As I say, I hated them and they in turn hated me. At supper, one in particular would perch just above my place at the table, high above on the pole supporting the thatched roof. The horror would then proceed to pee in my soup or whatever it was I was eating. It was like musical chairs, for I continually, and uncharitably perhaps, changed places with the helpers or guests, but to no avail. They concentrated on my plate only. The Old Man's shoulders would shake with silent laughter and Sabine would be in hysterics.

Over drinks one night at supper time the Old Man asked me if I would care to accompany him the following day in an effort to find his favourite lioness, Coretta, and her six consorts. He had neither seen nor heard of them for two months now and was worried. A freshly-killed camel was ready should we come across them. We would take both Land Rovers and stay out that night in the bush. Happily I agreed. He gave me further instructions that night. At dawn I had the camel carcass loaded in the back of my Land Rover with a stout chain round its neck as he had suggested. Once again I eyed the worn-out tyres dubiously as I thought of the luggahs, the sharp flint-like rocks and the thorns we would be motoring over. He led the way south, the track winding in and out as it followed the course of the river. We drove here and we drove there with the Old Man using his bull-horn at likely looking places.

'Coretta,' he would call. 'Coretta.' There was no answer. All that day we searched and when the sun was going down we finally came to a large plain. I opened a few tins and we had a meal of sorts. Later, with the sun now sinking in a sea of bush he tried yet again.

'Coretta,' he called almost despairingly. 'Coretta.' I felt for him. Dusk now and I produced a comforting bottle of whisky. We had taken our first sips when out of the velvet night I saw seven shapes approaching. His own eyes were not as sharp as mine. He saw me staring ahead.

'See anything?' he asked eagerly. 'Seven Somali donkeys,' I replied. 'It looks as though they are trespassing again over the river but I don't see any Somalis with them.' They came closer. Lithe, tawny shapes. They were not donkeys.

'Good God!' I said. 'Lions.' I then corrected myself and said, 'Seven lionesses.'

'Coretta,' the Old Man beamed happily, puffing away furiously at his pipe. 'I had a feeling they might be on this plain and they must have heard me calling them.' He put down his glass of whisky on the bonnet of the car, picked up his stick and walked over to them.

'Come and meet the family,' he called over his shoulder. On the bonnet of the car I had my own whisky and his old .303 rifle. I disregarded the whisky and picked up the rifle. I mentally congratulated myself that I had zeroed it in recently. I thought now I might be needing it. Previously at the camp when feeding the released lions we had opened the small gate and thrown them their portions, or heaved a leg of goat or two over the wire itself. Now here he was walking in the dusk to greet them. Not only that: I saw in astonishment that he was patting them on their heads as though he was at a dog show and judging Great Danes. He now came back with them trotting at his heels.

Bugger that for a game of soldiers, I thought as I clutched the rifle in one hand and my glass of whisky in the other. He smiled at my discomfiture.

'You've nothing to worry about, for Coretta has such a gentle nature. Replace your rifle in the rack, Dougie, drink your whisky and follow me in the Land Rover. At the end of the plain there is a good stout acacia. I will show you. Back up to it and we'll chuck out the carcass and chain it to the tree.'

It was now quite dark, but after motoring behind the Old Man I spotted his acacia in the headlights, turned, and backed up to it as he had instructed. We both got out with the pride of lionesses looking on hungrily as we tried to unravel the chain in the darkness. It was hopeless for it had become entangled with the spare wheel. The pride, I thought, were growing restive. The Old Man was quite unperturbed. Calmly puffing away he said: 'It really doesn't matter. We'll camp here for the night and they can feed from the back of your Land Rover!' I felt quite relieved when he made the suggestion that we both sleep on top of his own Land Rover where he had two mattresses and an ingeniously constructed super-structure with shelving for our thermos flask soup, coffee, sandwiches and the like.

Under the stars, that night proved to be both exciting and exhilarating with the pride feeding under our noses. Ignoring the grunts, snarls and bickering as they fought for the choicer pieces of the camel, I slept. Came the dawn and I saw that the whole pride had moved off in the direction of the river. I stirred myself, clambered down from my lofty perch and made a fire from brushwood which was lying about in plenty. The Old Man produced a battered kettle with the lid tied to the handle with a piece of string, tea and sugar mixed up together in a page of newspaper and a tin of condensed milk. I emptied the contents in the kettle, placed it on the fire and brewed up. I then produced a couple of enamel mugs from the chop box and we sipped our early morning tea. It tasted like nectar.

The camel's rib cage, with some meat still remaining, I tugged out of the back of the Land Rover. The Old Man eyed this speculatively to remind me that the pride would be ready for another meal after slaking their thirst at the river. We then managed to unravel that damned chain. One end was tied to the back bumper bar and the other end round the carcass.

'We'll give it a tow. I think I know where to find them,' he said. Even now I was not wholly convinced on his quite remarkable powers of contacting the pride. During our drive from camp the previous day I had noticed dozens of tracks leading from the one we motored on to the river. Motoring back in the direction of camp he unhesitatingly chose one of them. With the river glinting quite close we rounded a bend and there they were, all waiting for us on the sandy track. I was completely won over.

Once a month I would take one of the Land Rovers to Mwingi on the main Garissa road for supplies and from time to time we would hear of shifta attacks on vehicles on this same road we used, as also on vehicles plying the road from Nairobi to Garissa. Even buses, whilst escorted by Police, for on two occasions they too were attacked with the passengers being killed or wounded and all their belongings looted. On another occasion two Police Land Rovers were ambushed, and all the occupants killed.

As the Old Man's armoury consisted only of one .303 Lee En-field rifle of 1914-1918 vintage, one double-barrelled .470 with a damaged stock, a .22 and his own .38 revolver I was hardly armed and equipped to deal with roving bands of shifta and poachers armed with automatic rifles. These raids now came in a little close to the Reserve itself. I became worried for the safety of the camp. I deepened the weapon pits at the four corners of the camp, sandbagged them and hoped for the best. I tackled the Old Man as to why he did not ask for a permanent well-armed guard. He was hesitant in reply-ing. Finally he admitted that he just could not afford them for as usual he would be supplying them with rations and petrol for their transport. I could see his point.

The months went by and the raids slackened off somewhat. The shifta menace seemed to have died down. Came the time when I was offered a paid job at a place called Mamarehe, just outside the Serengeti National Park in Tanzania. It would be for six months. There were several helpers and guests in camp at that time, two of whom I knew were quite responsible. Sabine had left. I discussed the matter with the Old Man and we both agreed that as the shifta threat had slackened off it would be possible for me to go. Here I was working on information received by his informer who used to work for him in the Game Department — as also from my own source of intelligence from Somalis I knew in the bush. He asked me to come back and to this I agreed. I have always regretted the move in the light of the tragedy which happened.

Some six months later I was back at Muthaiga Club in the Military Wing and making arrangements to rejoin the Old Man. Then the terrible news came through. George Adamson, Bwana Game, that well-loved and indomitable Old Man, had been murdered not far from his camp. One of his guests had just motored from camp to the airstrip to pick up guests when she was ambushed. They had heard the automatic rifle fire in the camp. It was on 21 August 1989 at high noon.

The Old Man reckoned not on the odds. Taking his patly-ly inadequate .38 revolver and three of his middle-aged staff with him, armed with the old .303, the damaged elephant gun and the

.22, he drove off to rescue his guests.

The automatic weapons were waiting for him. He was cut down by a hail of bullets and killed on the spot. So were two members of his staff. One escaped. I will not dwell further on what happened for all details have been in the press and media and by and large the accounts are accurate.

All I wish to say is this: there have been many heroes in history going back as far as you care to do so. Military men mostly. Marshal Ney at Waterloo was called the bravest of the brave as he repeatedly led his cavalry against the British Squares. But then he was a soldier. That was his job, leading men, getting killed or surviving, possibly being wounded, decorated and so on. The Old Man was a civilian. He was aged 83 years. I think his chivalrous action was the bravest I have ever heard of or read about.

Once again the Koru Trust contacted me. Would I go up there yet again, organise the funeral arrangements and look after the camp until the time came to close it down, for by now it was considered a security risk? It was of some comfort to know that the surviving members of the Old Man's staff had asked for me. I couldn't refuse.

Motoring as far as Mwingi on the tarmac road I turned in left and then followed the familiar track into camp. It was late afternoon. The staff rushed up to me and asked what was to become of them. They were confused, demoralised and frightened. I could not blame them. So were my police guard of six armed constables. I had asked for no less than ten with a senior NCO. I had a welcome cup of tea and then held a baraza.

Without the Old Man's comforting presence I felt a little lost but I dared not let my feelings show. I explained to them that we wouldn't be here for long. Some of them had been with him for twenty years. If the camp was to be closed down then I would arrange transport to take them back to a riverine village called Isako where they had their families. They would be rationed and they would be paid. For every year of service there would be a month's extra pay. I would try and persuade the Trust to pay them extra on top of this. They cheered up a little.

The corporal of the police guard, in his early thirties, approached me. He was truculent. They had already been here a week. When were they to be relieved? They were all obviously terrified out of their wits. This was not their country and the Somalis they feared. I told him it was not my country but off and on I had been up here some fifty years — not a week. I further told him his fortune and if his attitude did not improve I would have his stripes. Later they deserted. After old Hamisi the cook had fed me I turned in early. I slept uneasily that night.

Then came the television crews. Before and after the funeral I did not like this avalanche. Japanese, French and Australian. I suppose it was inevitable because of his worldwide fame but to me it was macabre and out of place with their security an additional worry. I also resented their probing questions and the photographs and murmured platitudes beside those peaceful graves.

There were many at the funeral. Mostly his old friends from Kenya but others from the four quarters of the globe. I met Virginia and Bill Travers. They had brought with them tea and sugar for the staff plus a shirt each and a bottle of whisky for myself — a kindly thought. Ken Smith, a retired Game Warden, was there as also Ruth Woodley, Doddie, Ilke and Kim and a host of others.

At the graveside I comforted young Sabine who loved him as a guru. Old Hamisi the cook broke down and I saw tears from little Abdi, the Boran lion helper. At this time there were no lions in the compound itself, for the three half-grown cubs had already been sent down by air to Botswana to start a new life there under the guidance of a youngster, Gareth Patterson, who is now dedicated to their care.

Mostly by air the Captains and the Kings departed and once more I was left alone. The days I found bearable but the nights were an aching loneliness I had never known before. Fiona Alexander, the pilot of one of the light planes, told me that she had seen a concentration of the rebel Somali army on the other side of the river and a night later we heard firing from that direction. It was about this time that the guard bolted and I was left for three days and nights without any guard whatsoever. A new guard was then sent up but they were as terrified as the others and of little use. The staff remained staunch due to the efforts of old Hamisi the cook who harangued them. I shall always be grateful to him.

In the meantime I had remembered Terence by placing a cairn of attractive quartz stones over his grave with his headstone embedded in cement. As also a young lion called Super Cub. The Old Man was in the middle of them. Just the three of them together. I had also planted desert roses round the three graves.

I had now received instructions to pull out and to abandon the camp. The day after the funeral I resolved to take what might be a last farewell of him. For watering the desert roses I had a couple of buckets of water placed in the same beaten-up Land Rover in which he was killed, with the shattered windscreen and the cruel bullet-perforated doors. I took little Abdi with me. Old Hamisi was still too upset to go.

There had been a high wind the previous night. The sun was setting when we left camp, following the winding pink sandy track to the graves. I ordered the guard to remain in the car and Abdi and I each carried a bucket over.

It was then I saw a pride of lions had visited the graves that same night after the funeral. Were they watching the whole sad affair from the inselberg overlooking the camp? How did they know he had been killed? These questions must remain unanswered. I approached the Old Man's grave with Abdi, placing our feet carefully so as not to disturb the spoor. Quite a few of the bunches of flowers and wreaths had been blown off the cairn of stones but most had been replaced. I remembered one wreath in particular, for it was larger and heavier than the others. It was made up of wild flowers together with a cream satin bow and streamers. I seem to remember **Johnny Baxendale, the Old Man's godson,** placing it there. This too must have been blown off for some distance but replaced — but not in the same position I remembered from the day before. From where it had been carried back we saw the spoor of a large male lion and on closed inspection saw the indentations of the teeth marks on both the wreath itself and on the ribbons. Apart from our own tracks there were no others. No jackal or hyena. Just a large pride of lions, replacing the wreaths and flowers and all the signs where they had laid down to spend the night there. It was uncanny. I just could not believe it.

I looked at little Abdi questioningly for he knew lion better than I and could read sign better. He said quite simply: '*Simba ya Bwana George walarudi kwa piga salaama kwake.*' (The lions of Bwana George returned to say salaams). I thought he was going to cry again. I placed my arm around his shoulder and we left with the wind getting up again causing the doum palms to sway, while the whistling thorns made their own weird, sad music.

Bwana Game. George Adamson had guarded his lions for a lifetime and they were now guarding him. They had remembered.

Duel in the Sun

The big buffalo was coming hard. I had moved my hunting camp from the Masai plains where my young American client, Robert Thompson of Nevada, USA had obtained good trophies, but he now wanted an outstanding buffalo. His father, Wilbur, had been out with me years ago and had bagged a forty-eight incher and the boy wanted to beat his dad. Quite a tall order, for a buff with a spread of forty-eight inches was good. Very good. I smiled wryly. An American trait, this, of wanting something bigger and better than one's neighbour. That the neighbour in this case was his father made no difference.

My new camp in the Loita Hills in the heart of a cedar forest had produced a dramatically changed landscape. Here the air was cool and fresh with a wealth of colour in the undergrowth. Above the tents the cedars soared like giant Christmas trees, tall and straight and the wood from them on the camp fire crackled fiercely, giving off an aromatic smoke. The trees were festooned with moss, lichens and here and there a wild orchid. Down below a little stream gurgled and sang as it flowed over polished black stones forming little pools fringed with delicate ferns. It was a scenic fairyland.

On our daily treks through the forest we had seen many buffalo: bulls, cows and calves, with their attendant white egrets often giving their presence away, but always the big bull I had set my heart on for the youngster eluded me. We had been charged twice at close quarters; dangerous situations when it had only been Buno's uncanny knowledge which had extracted us from a possible goring or even death. Buno was my gunbearer. A Mkamba from a tribe of hunters. He had been my eyes, ears, tracker and friend for thirty years. He was small, black and insignificant-looking with a face like a pickled walnut but he was the best in the business being half-buffalo himself for he saw like one, smelled like one and heard like one. No

mean hunter myself, I always found this intuition of his quite uncanny for he even thought like one: in any given set of circumstances
he seemed to know what a buffalo will or will not do. He was quite
fearless and had the heart of a lion. Like me he was pushing the
years now.

My second tracker, much younger than the two of us, was the
Masai, Ole Legis, who was born in these parts and always joined
me when I was hunting in his area. He was now ranging far and
wide in his own tireless efforts to locate the big herd he knew of,
but they seemed to have moved off.

In spite of our many frustrations these were happy days for both
of us — particularly for young Bob, only twenty-one years old who
was learning and seeing something different on each and every trek.
The long walks had given him blisters but I had shown him how
to soap the inside of his socks — an old army trick this and it had
worked. He had stopped asking questions as we trekked for I had
simply pointed out to him that we were here to walk silently, to listen
and to observe for that, I had emphasized, was the essence of good
hunting. He was amazed at the way we interpreted sign. On one
occasion I pointed out to him a scarab or dung beetle, rolling its
eggs in a coating of mud and duiker droppings. Laboriously pro-
pelling it to some unknown place only the beetle knew of. I explained to him that the ancient Egyptians regarded these beetles as sacred
for they saw in the rotating ball of mud, dung and eggs, similarity
to the sun and their sun god, Ra. Thus to them the beetle was the
reincarnation of the Creator of the Universe and so popularised their
scarab amulets.

We would trek patiently and tirelessly through the waiting, watching, listening bush. Once Buno stopped to point out a young
wildbeest fawn a few days old, lying concealed in the grass with only the tips of its ears showing. Try as he would he could not spot
it until Buno had walked him right up to it. Of the lesser game we
observed warthog, the amusing bat-eared foxes, hares, dikdik, duiker
and, pasing a rocky kopje — klipspringers. They were standing on
high rocks, their speckled yellow colour silhouetted against the
skyline. We had started to climb to get a better look but they had

bounded away, bouncing on the tips of their hooves and sounding their warning snorts.

He was a good boy, a little spoilt, but the bush soon knocked that out of him; I grew fond of him, his lanky frame, tousled brown hair, freckles and wide-spaced grey eyes. In the evenings, pleasantly tired after our long treks, he would ignore the chair placed for him by old Ali, my head steward, to sit cross-legged on the ground next to me, not wishing to miss a single word as, absent-mindedly I suppose, I would recall my hunting stories and anecdotes. Sipping sparingly of his beer, he suddenly asked:

'How many days have we left on our safari, Bwana?'

'Only three,' I said.

'Only three,' he echoed with obviously a feeling of sadness that our safari would soon be over.

'I shall miss you, boy. I shall miss you,' I said. We sat in a companionable silence for some time.

'I wonder what is keeping Ole Legis?' I mused. 'It's not like him to keep me waiting for I told him that our time was now short.'

Suddenly to our left where a strip of forest grew about two hundred yards from the camp, a bushbuck barked. I stiffened. It barked again. Urgently this time. The moon sailed from behind a dark cloud and we could see up to fifty yards around us. We heard a faint rustle in the grasses. Something approached and suddenly a lone figure was revealed. It grew closer Tall, dark and carrying a long spear glinting in the moonlight. Nearer now, coming on with long springy strides. It was Ole Legis the tracker. Of a copper colour, straight nose, eyes set wide apart and tall like most of them. About forty years old, slim with magnificently wide shoulders and hard, muscled legs. He now stood in front of us like a stork with

his left foot braced against the inside of his right knee, negligently leaning on his spear. I called for beer. He drank long and thirstily. I let him finish his bottle of Tusker and then we spoke. Young Bob was all ears and I now addressed him with quiet satisfaction.

'Good news. Ole Legis has contacted the herd he has been looking for and has seen at least seven shootable bulls in it. He followed them all this afternoon to where they watered and bedded down for the night. No question, of course, of using the hunting car. I reckon it's about a four-hour walk from here. If we leave camp at five o'clock tomorrow morning we should catch them out in the open and before they return to the forest for shade. Good night. Sleep well. With luck we shall be calling tomorrow the Day of the Buffalo.' I heaved myself out of the chair. My right leg had gone stiff on me as usual. I kneaded the heart-shaped scar above my knee. A buffalo had broken the leg for me years ago.

A few minutes before five we left camp. Just the four of us, with Ole Legis in the lead. From camp the game track down to the stream was rough and wet; during the night there had been a spattering of rain so that soon we were mud-spattered and damp from the rain dripping from the cedars above. We crossed the stream, wading through it up to our knees. Treacherous going in the darkness. Up a steep incline then plunging deep down again into a ravine, heavily bushed and hard of going. We toiled on for another three hours and mostly through thickly-bushed, broken country. Over a rocky volcanic ledge and then down another gully where we heard the warning grunt of a leopard. Now we slid, clinging to the vines so as not to lose our footing. The effort was beginning to tell on me and my injured leg was now dragging a little. I slipped in crossing another deep stream. Ole Legis, with tireless, springy strides was way ahead.

He turned to look back impatiently. Young Bob too turned and with some concern saw me up to my waist in water, though I managed to hold my rifle aloft. He turned back to grasp my outstretched hand, pulling me out of the stream and up the bank. I thanked him with a tired smile. Safari can make a man or break one. It seemed that this safari would be the making of Bob as his father had hoped. For the first time he issued a word of command. He knew me well enough by now. He knew my pride. He knew I would go on until I dropped. There was no way I would admit to being bushed. I was the professional.

'Buno,' he said, gesturing at me. Buno nodded and understood for he too was about bushed. *'Ngoja kidogo,'* he said sinking on his haunches.

Pale and almost spent I looked at him gratefully, my eloquent eyes thanking him for the words which would not come. I sat down and lit a cigarette. Buno took a pinch of snuff from a cartridge case hanging from a thong round his neck. He hawked and spat. Ole Legis looked down at us disdainfully. He was a Masai and could go on for ever. I wished I had met him twenty years before. I'd have given him a run for his money. After fifteen minutes I rose to my feet and we were off again. The rising sun dried out our clothes and warmed out the dampness underfoot which made the going easier. We pressed on. Both Buno and I were feeling our grey-hued years now. Wearily I glanced at my watch. It was just after nine and I reckoned we must have covered about fifteen miles and could not be too far from the Tanzanian border.

Now the country opened up. Finally we came across a plain. Ahead, Ole Legis pointed with his spear. I stumbled ahead of the little column. Fumblingly I reached for the binoculars slung around my neck. My hands shook slightly as I focused them. About half a mile ahead a large herd of buffalo were grazing. Undisturbed. There must have been over two hundred of them. I could see at least two shootable bulls and knew there would be others.

Shaking the little bag of wood ashes tied on my wrist I tested the wind. It was favourable and so we began the stalk. We were quite close to them when they disappeared from view behind two small hills. I checked the wind again. It still held true. At a crouch we ascended one of the hills. We still couldn't see them but we tensed as we heard them grazing quite close.

Without warning we then heard the most violent smashing noises, accompanied by hoarse bellows of rage. I flopped down or. my belly to squirm ahead thinking 'stuff this for game of soldiers'. I was too old for this cowboys and Indians caper. The others followed me.

More bellows and smashing sounds. Bob crawled alongside to look at me enquiringly. I thought I knew what might be happening but was not sure. I shrugged my shoulders and looked at Buno. At the look of enquiry on my face that worthy, his red-rimmed eyes closed to slits, a grin on the gash of his mouth showing broken, discoloured teeth, ruined over the years by biting off the crimped tops of beer bottles, shook with silent laughter. He had a wonderful sense of humour, that old Mkamba gunbearer in his tatty hunting clothes, for he knew exactly what was happening and the Bwana was not sure. One up to him and not for the first time. He looked back at me and once more silently rocked with mirth. Forward once more and we now reached the summit of the small hill and took cover behind a bush. We looked down below.

It was an unforgettable sight. With the rest of the herd looking on as at some medieval lists in the animal kingdom, two bull buffalos were fighting it out for the herd leadership. The rising sun shone on their huge, immensely strong bodies on short, powerful legs, horns interlocked, each massive bull weighing almost a ton as they pushed and strove against each other. I whispered to Buno to produce Bob's cine-camera from the haversack he was carrying.

'A sight I've never seen before and one we'll never see again,' I whispered in his ear. 'Get cracking with your filming. We'll sort one of those bulls out afterwards.'

I could see that both had magnificent trophy horns. The two adversaries broke apart, backed off, only to launch themselves furiously at each other again. Meeting head on like two crashing

locomotives. This was the noise we had first heard. For sheer animal fury and unbridled savagery I had never witnesed anything like this. We forgot entirely about shooting, for a sight such as this could only be seen once in a lifetime. The sun rose higher. The darkness of their bodies glistened with sweat. The duel could only have one ending. Death for one of them. Once more they backed apart to meet head on again with that same sickening crunch. First one gave ground and then the other. Finally, one of them slipped on the wet grass and in a flash his opponent raked him with a cruel, curved horn. Raked him deeply to open up a mortal gash along the length of the belly so that we could see the sudden spurt of blood followed by the intestines as part ballooned out from the wound.

With a hoarse bellow, the badly-gored bull, somehow staggered back on his feet to run unsteadily from the field of battle. To run unknowingly and uncaringly to where we lay hidden.

The victor, feet apart, chest heaving, watched his retreat as he ambled back to the waiting herd. At a nod from me to Buno, the cine-camera was quickly replaced by the double .470 Express. The wounded bull, leaving a trial of crimson in his wake came closer now. He did not see us for his eyes were glassy. He was dying.

'Take him,' I said. The report from the heavy rifle reverberated over the plain followed by pandemonium as the entire herd panicked to rocket away in the direction of the forest. The bull dropped and remained motionless. Slowly we walked down to the dead animal approaching from the rear. I allowed Bob and Buno to break into an excited run as they approached him. I knew this one was dead for I had heard the death bellow. Ole Legis, his work done, strode majestically by my side.

Before us lay the magnificent vanquished bull. The Old One. The leader of the herd until half an hour ago. Now beaten by the younger bull's superior fighting ability and youth. Youth. The older animals making way for their younger rivals. The Law of the Bush. Kill or be killed. There he lay. Still looking truculent in death with the great crimson gash along his belly, and the neat hole in the heart region which had ended it all.

'What will he go, Bwana? What will he go?' Bob danced up

and down in his excitement. 'Will he go bigger than my Dad's? Just look at that boss and the length of horn.' I smiled at his eagerness, my eyes taking in the measurements.

'H'm', I said. 'I'm really going to be unpopular in some circles. You've already got a better lion and leopard than your father and this old bull will certainly beat his forty-eight incher.' I spanned the massive boss with outstretched thumb and little finger to then assess the outside span of horns.

'Bwana. Bwana.' Bob begged with impatience.

'H'm. The boss will go fourteen inches and I reckon the horn span fifty inches.' Rather slyly I then produced a small metal tape out of my pocket and assisted by both Buno and Bob took careful measurements. The tape revealed that the boss was exactly fourteen inches as I had estimated but the greatest width on the outside curve of horn was fifty-two inches. Bob was speechless.

'One for the book. One for the Rowland Ward's *Records of Big Game*. He'll be well up there,' I announced. They shook hands all around and following my example, Bob thanked Ole Legis for all the hard work he had put in contacting the herd.

'What do we do now?' Bob still looked with disbelief at his trophy. 'How do we handle this monster so far from camp?'

It was eleven o'clock. I issued a few instructions to Ole Legis who hiched his dull red shuka up to his thighs and left at a tireless lope in the direction of the camp. I explained to Bob: 'At the rate he's going, cutting corners, he'll be back in camp in less than two hours. He will then bring out the driver in the hunting car. Not the way we came of course. Wouldn't get a bloody tank through that lot.' I waved back and to my right.

'I remember this bit of country now. The main road to the border is just over yonder hill and as far as I remember, the driver will have only one small stream to cross. Ole Legis will find a shallow ford for him and I guess they will be here early this afternoon. In the meantime you might like to give Buno a hand with the skinning. You'll want the horns, headskin and probably two front feet?' Bob nodded.

'We'll have the tongue and tail for our table. Both are far better than from a domestic ox. If Escoffier ever knew about buffalo tongue and tail he'd go wild with delight. The camp staff will have the rest of the meat and they too will go wild with delight for buffalo meat is their favourite. You will be a very popular young man in camp tonight. Oh, by the way, when you have taken off the head-skin, you might make a present of the rest to Ole Legis for making a shield. He'd appreciate that.'

I left them to it. Found a shady tree, propped myself against the trunk and had a couple of sips of brandy from my hip flask. I needed it, for that gruelling trek had really taken it out of me. I thought I'd make this my last safari. After that I'd be a courier. Milk run, ice-cream safaris to the parks. Just like London to Brighton. Tented camps and lodges and nothing more dangerous than a hangover.

Having met young Bob, Buno and Ole Legis and seen a glimpse of Masailand, you might well ask who the narrator of this story is. I would reply: a colonial relic and sometimes White Hunter, now aged and of no consequence.

The Banker

Being conversant with the aphorism over the correct order of food, and having had excellent African cooks on safari in my hunting days and then in tented camps and lodges, I have had few complaints over meals. Cooking is one of my hobbies but I probably tend to give myself too many bouquets when I occasionally turn out, with or without the help of my cook, something unusual and better than average.

This being the case it is always upsetting when guests turn up their noses at something I have suggested or at the various dishes I have had prepared for them. In a way one feels sorry for them, for you know, they invariably have an inferiority complex. Possibly having lived on the very basics in the days of their youth, and now having made a pile of brass, they hate to remember the days when they were poor and so put on the airs of landed gentry — or so they fondly imagine. Meeting all types, as I have over the years, I am a great believer in that old northern saying: 'there's nowt so queer as folk.'

About this time combis (or minibuses if you like), were taking over from the traditional safari vehicles, Land Rovers or Toyotas, in transporting victims from Nairobi to Masai Mara and other parks or reserves on their milk run, ice-cream safaris. The tourists were usually packed like sardines in a can, festooned with cameras and light meters. Some of the ladies sported floppy hats with pastel shades of ribbon around the side, while the men wore stiff-brimmed safari hats adorned with imitation leopard skin bands which they misguidedly thought were masculine and the sort of sartorial headwear Ernest Hemingway might have worn.

Imagine my surprise therefore when, late one afternoon, a minibus painted in black and white zebra stripes came panting into

Elephant Camp. Two rather past middle-age guests tottered out while their driver sat looking bewildered and possibly wondering where the hell he was. Obviously he wasn't at all happy at landing up in this wild and desolate country.

After the usual introductions, a booking voucher for three days was thrust under my nose accompanied by a chit from headquarters explaining that these were VIPs and would I kindly treat them as such. From the beginning it was quite obvious that they were discontented with their lot and one could, I suppose, call them professional complainers. They complained about the corrugations on the road from Thika into camp; their driver had lost them twice as well as having two punctures; it was too hot in this desolation. Why were there no fans in their tents? They had found a drowned mosquito in their thermos of iced water and so on.

I gathered the man was an ex-banker, now retired. He was fat and bald with ice-cold eyes behind gold-rimmed spectacles through which he obviously viewed everything with grave suspicion. Added to this was a mouth like a sprung mole trap. I would hate to have had to have approached him for an overdraft. He completely bullied and dominated his mousy-looking little wife so that she in turn would try and take it out on anyone else. The least charitable thing one could say about them was that they were not a happy combination to have in camp.

That night over a drink in the bar, the retired banker growled, 'Whatddywegotfordinner?' Now my regular cook, old Christopher whom I had had for years, was off sick but in his place I had engaged one John Williams, a Luo. John was a dream of a cook — if a little on the expensive side and it so happened I had briefed him about supper that same morning. I ticked off the various courses we had arranged on my fingers.

'First the soup — which I call Isle of Zanzibar soup.' (John Williams here in his enthusiasm had gone a little berserk with cloves, sticking too many on top of a Kenya ham so that the basis consisted of slices of ham plus the cloves). Tasting it I thought it too pungent but a tin of cream, a little sherry and more vegetables in the stock made the whole a gastronomic dream.

'Secondly,' I said. 'The soufflé. A cheese soufflé. A savoury soufflé and speciality of my cook. To quote from an old grand-mother of mine — as light as love.' Here I looked at them hopefully at this dubious turn of wit but they both remained quite devoid of expression.

'Thirdly, roast Molo lamb from the Kenya Highlands. Quite as good as English and possibly better than New Zealand or Welsh — but a Welshman of course would never agree to that. Served with roast potatoes, garden peas and a choice of mint sauce or red cur-rent jelly — just as you prefer.

'Fourthly, Crêpes Suzettes, another speciality of the cook. You will have these served so thin they will melt in your mouths. They will be flavoured with curacao and a little mandarin orange juice.

'Fifthly, a choice of Kenya cheeses with butter and crackers to be followed by our own blend of Kenya coffee.'

After my lengthy discourse on our supper I was quite exhausted but the very river seemed to gurgle its approval. Lolling back in my chair and lighting a much-needed cigarette, I called the barman for a double Glenfiddich.

I didn't offer my guests one as they had not returned the com-pliment after the first drink I had bought them. Charitably, I thought the banker couldn't afford to buy me one. I then told the barman to take a bottle of beer with my compliments to John Williams in the kitchen. 'Wedontlikelamb,' was the quite extraordinary reply I received.

Bugger my old boots, I thought, and shuddered but kept my temper while remembering an old chum of mine, one Tony O'Brien, a tough hunter if ever there was one, who had chucked his client in the Tana River after he had annoyed him. The crocodiles didn't get him but he almost drowned which didn't do Tony's hunting career much good.

No. I was the diplomat, so squaring my shoulders I looked at the river in supplication and another gurgle of encouragement seemed to come back. This is where I start the Camel Dust, I thought. Bags of it. Acres of it. Manfully I rose to the occasion.

'Well now.' I smiled winningly. 'I will not disappoint you. It so happened just before your safari here I had occasion to make a reconnaissance to the Somalia border where an old friend of mine, a Sultan no less, presented me with a baby camel. These camels are of a special breed and quite a delicacy. They are fattened up in special pens for their nobility to eat. I suppose it's something similar to the Japanese custom with their Kobe beef — but of course they sell that commercially. Now, the cook still has the time. Would you like to try it roasted? It has been said that it tastes something like lamb but then I am no judge. I would like your opinion. You, my dear madam and dear sir, will probably be the very first Americans ever to eat roast camel hump — incidentally called by the French *Bosse de Chameau Rotie* — but then I am sure you know that.'

I could read their thoughts. This really would be something to tell the folks back home. They almost waxed enthusiastic.

'Say,' said the banker. 'Yeah, we'd sure like that.' His wife nodded dutifully in agreement. I had John Williams called up from his kitchen and spoke to him in Swahili.

'In one hour's time John, serve supper as we arranged. Should the *wageni* (guests) here ask what the meat is tell them *Bosse de Chameau Rotie*, which to you, chum, means *Nyama ya Ngamia* or, in Inglesi, camel's meat. Forget about the mint sauce and serve it with the red currant jelly.' Like most cooks John Williams was fat. He understood and laughed so that his belly wobbled like a large blancmange.

'And take another bottle of beer back with you to the kitchen,' I invited.

The supper was a terrific success and using as a shield my large kikoi-clad backside, I managed to carve the lamb without the guests observing the joint too closely.

At the end of the meal the banker, with a rare gesture of affection, laid a hand on his wife's arm with the contented remark that the camel was sure good and not a bit like lamb. 'Will you have another helping, dear?' She simpered. 'I agree with you, dear. I will.'

The Lion Hunt

The hunter was right. The lion had found the scent of the drag from the stream. He was seven years old. In his prime with all the splendid powers of him. Coil upon coil of hard muscle in his heavy shoulders and forelegs. From the tip of his scarred nose to the black tuft of his tail, he measured ten feet. A magnificent black mane covered his head, neck and chest. There was violent death in his four hundred and fifty pounds weight for the zebra, kongoni or wildebeest which he'd kill with ease. Stalking them to within twenty yards or less, flat on his belly through the yellow grass which blended perfectly with the gold of his body. Releasing his muscles suddenly, a series of breath-taking bounds would land him on the doomed animal's back as they both would crash to the ground. An enormous velvety paw would then cover the animal's nose to suffocate it or he might chop through the vertebrae.

The plains were alive with fear of his presence, but silent except for the drumming of hooves as the zebra rushed wildly into the enveloping night. He ignored them, coughing menacingly as he followed the drag. Nose close to the ground. Blazing yellow eyes looking everywhere at once. For three days now he had not eaten. His stomach cried out for meat. Two nights ago he had suddenly been confronted by a bull buffalo at his night watering place. This lion feared nothing. Neither did the buffalo whose courage is beyond dispute with his brute strength, superior weight, viciously curved horns and massive boss. Several twitches of the tufted tail, stiff now as the lion had made his leap, but on this occasion had underestimated his prey. As the flying death had landed on his back, the buffalo had rolled over before the fangs and claws could do him any real damage. It was only the lion's quick thinking, agility and smooth reflexes which had saved him from being crushed under a ton of ill-tempered fury. Again they faced each other. Bared fangs and raking claws against curved horns and massive boss. Hate against hate for these two were traditional enemies. It was just bad luck for the lion that he was hunting on his own. With a second lion or even a lioness to help him he would have made the kill. Even now, with the hunger still on him, he had almost charged again but had thought better of it. There was easier, safer prey to pick up. With a snarl of frustrated hate in his yellow eyes he had backed away from the menacing blur of the buffalo. Now he was to find other meat. The hunter's bait.

The hyenas had winded it first. Four of them. Spotted and ungainly-looking but with formidable jaws and jagged teeth in their white gums. As the lion approached, silent now, they were leaping up at the dangling legs from where it had been tied in a tree, in an effort to get at the meat. Three of them were quick to lope off as the black-maned killer bore down savagely upon them. The pangs of his hunger and the recent experience with the buffalo had changed him from a normally lazy, even-tempered animal into an ill-tempered executioner. The fourth hyena, his powerful jaws clamped on one of the zebra's hind legs, was swinging off the ground and was just not quick enough to get out of the way. A quick, short charge. A flashing forepaw of incredible speed, a chop through the neck and the hyena lay dead before him. Exulting in his strength and vindication of his prowess, he gave a full-blooded roar. A series of violent eruptions discharged explosively from his empty belly, causing the three remaining scavengers, skulking in the darkness, to retreat still further. Standing on his hind legs, he hooked the claws of his forepaws into the lower part of the striped carcass, tearing hungrily at the soft belly of the zebra.

They left camp at five in the morning. The hunter drove with his sidelights only, easing the car over the known track. Nightjars with their peculiar notes in harmony with the mysteries of the night, fluttered out of their way — weird, uncanny birds with their silent moth-like flight.

There were four of them. The hunter himself, now pushing sixty, and his young client in his early twenties. They had been on safari now in the Masai country for only three days. They were still weighing each other up, like two dogs, still not sure whether they liked each other and not, as yet, using first names. The two Africans were Wakamba gunbearers. One was about the same age as the hunter and had been with him for many years, and his companion about the same age as the client and still a learner.

After driving for half an hour the hunter pulled up by a stream. Three of them got out of the car with the grass wet underfoot. It was as cold as charity. The hunter himself loaded the rifles and applied the safety catches. The client had elected to use the hunter's double Express .470. The hunter himself carried its twin. The learner gunbearer still remained in the car, wrapped in his blanket. The other two, led by the old gunbearer, followed by the client with the hunter in the rear proceeded in Indian file at right angles to the stream. False dawn lightened the sky but it was still not light enough for the hunter to pick out anything as he looked over the open sights of his double. The stars were still there but fading now. The first piece of lavatory paper, carefully placed when they had swung the bait and prepared the blind, lightly brushed the client's cheek, causing him to start for an instance. The old gunbearer had avoided it. On another hundred yards and a cobweb which he had avoided too, now smothered the client's face, its diaphanous, silken fingers closing over his eyes and mouth. Impatiently he thrust aside the wispy net only to fall to his knees in an antbear hole. The hunter drew up alongside, clutched his arm and helped him up. On they went, following the spectral lanterns of pink paper dancing beckoningly ahead of them. Frightening in its suddeness, a francolin whirled up at their feet to rocket away in the now lightening sky. The old gunbearer stopped. He stiffened. Raising his chin he pointed with it to his front.

In between themselves and the blind and about fifty yards away, stood the lion. Motionless. Looking at them. He had left the bait nearby and was returning to drink at the stream. A little wind played over his mane, ruffling the blackness of it. Darting shafts of dawn lit up the gold of his body. The client stared unbelievingly at the savage beauty of him. Stared at the open mouth, the two-inch teeth and the muzzle stained red with the zebra's blood. Stared into the cruel yellow eyes and felt sick with fear.

The hunter swore softly under his breath. Always the unexpected in hunting he thought, thinking of the blind a couple of hundred yards ahead with the peepholes and perfect rests for the rifles. Without taking his eyes off the lion he came abreast of the client. The old gunbearer dropped on the track to give them a clear field of fire.

'Shoot him.' the hunter said.

'Shoot him,' echoed back the whistling thorns.

'Shoot him,' the hunter said again. Urgently this time. The client raised his rifle to his shoulder, aimed and gentled the trigger. Nothing happened. Out of the corner of his eye the hunter looked at the client's rifle.

'The safety catch,' he said. 'For God's sake release the safety catch.' The lion charged.

The hunter took a step to one side as the heavy double blasted in his ear. The lion seemed to crumple, but then came on at them with deep, vibrating grunts of hate. Fast and low in the grass. Tufted tail held out stiffly behind him like a banner. Thirty yards from them now when the hunter fired his own .470. First the left barrel and then the right. Badly hurt the lion swerved, roaring in pain and in a flash of yellow disappeared in the thick stuff. The hunter broke his rifle, ejected the spent cartridge cases to reload with two spare rounds he carried in between the first and second fingers of his left hand. The old gunbearer stood up and grinned. It was all in a day's work to him. Grasping the badly shaken client by the arm he led him back along the track in the direction of the car. Backing slowly, his eyes on the thicket where the lion had disappeared, the hunter covered them as he edged in the same direction. After what seemed an age they reached the stream and the car. The hunter lit a cigarette.

'Coffee,' he said to the young learner hunter. Gradually the colour came back to the client's face as he stammered out his apologies for forgetting the safety catch and for firing only one barrel. The hunter looked at him with indifference.

'Have some coffee,' he said.

'What do we do now? What do we do now?' the client was almost hysterical.

'Finish this coffee and cigarette and then my old gunbearer and

I go in and get him. That's what you're paying me for. You managed a reasonable shot and I got two in him. This particular lion is a courageous animal and if he's not already dead, we've a fight on our hands. He's got guts. As I say, if he's not dead he will be stiffening up by now and feeling sorry for himself with all the fight knocked out of him. Callous? Possibly, but that's the way it is, for you don't court danger needlessly in this game. The old cemetery in Nairobi is full of those who did. I don't want to join them.' He threw away his cigarette stub, drained his coffee and handed the mug to the young gunbearer. Next he produced an old army greatcoat from behind the seat of the car. He put it on, buttoning it up to the neck. Then he swung his arms, picked up his rifle to sight down the barrel. Even wearing the thick, cumbersome coat, the rifle came easily into his shoulder.

'So as to give him something to chew on if he gets that far,' he said.

'Protects to some extent my throat and belly. *Hiya Mzee,*' he addressed the old gunbearer. That worthy shrugged and spat.

'*Kazi ya mume,*' he said. 'Man's work.'

'I'm coming with you,' the client said. The hunter spoke to him sharply.

'You do not come with me. Let me make that quite clear. A wounded lion is as dangerous as they come, particularly in the thick stuff where I expect to find him. He is now in the driving seat and will choose his own place where to ambush us if he's not too sick or dead. This sort of hunting calls for quick shooting. Accurate shooting and I don't want one of your bullets up my backside. That old Mkamba and I have worked out a drill over the years and a third body just gets in the way. Two are just right. Three an army. More movement in our approach, more noise and that sort of thing. When you hear the shooting bring up the car and don't wreck it in those thorns. Do you understand?' The client nodded. He looked relieved.

The hunter now opened the breech of his .470 to re-check the rounds in the chamber. He then took out of his cartridge belt a further two soft-nosed rounds which he again carried in between the fingers of his left hand for quick loading. He nodded to the old gunbearer. They walked straight to the place where the lion had been wounded. Frothy blood streaked the grass crimson. A little further on more blood, dark and clotted. Here the lion had been sick.

'Lung and deep body wound,' he said to the old Mkamba who nodded in agreement. Another hundred yards he had been sick again. Here he had rested for a short time where the blood-stained grasses had been flattened. But he'd dragged himself off again. The old Mkamba's bird sharp eyes were focused on the give-away blood spoor. The hunter's eyes were ahead. Always straining ahead for the lion. He held his rifle at high point, safety catch off, right forefinger resting lightly on the trigger guard.

Thick now, the bush. The hunter's belly touched the other's buttocks. He could smell the rancidity of him and wondered when he had last had a bath. Keyed up. Nerves taut, they proceeded with pitiful slowness. The old Mkamba just in front at a half crouch and with immense concentration, his black face gleaming with sweat which he would wipe off impatiently with the back of his hand.

All at once a twitching black tuft of a tail told them where he was. Dangerously close. About eight yards. The old Wakamba dived down in front and the lion, badly wounded, was partially paralysed. Helpless to attack and yet when he saw his enemies he tore and ripped up the grass around him with his claws. Courageously he tried to get to grips with them, rising and getting up his head so that the hunter got the chance he was waiting for and mercifully ended it all with a neckshot. They took several paces forward where he now lay at their feet. All dignity gone with death. Truly, the hunter thought to himself, all the joy in this game is the hunting. The planning. The anticipation. The unknown. Not in the actual killing. He felt strangely deflated and sad. He did not mind killing the killer leopard or the vindictive buffalo but not the lion for he had a presence and a dignity which both the others lacked.

A few minutes later they heard the hunting car threading its way though the thorns and bush. He shouted out that the lion was dead and that they could bring the car alongside. The client got out cautiously.

'Congratulations,' said the hunter with false heartiness. 'Take your pictures. I'm going to have another coffee. No thank you, I never have my picture taken with the client's trophies, particularly not the King as you refer to him.'

He sipped his coffee and listened morosely to the cameras clicking and the cine-camera whirring.

'A King indeed,' he thought bitterly. 'A fallen King. A King covered with black hair for his crown. Killed by trickery. Superior intelligence and superior weapons.' He spread out his hands to look at them. Puny. Stunted harmless nails.

'What chance would we have against the King without our rifles?' he mocked himself. Wearily he then helped in loading the five hundred pounds of dead weight in the hunting car. He then motored ahead to the blind which the two gunbearers destroyed. They then cut down the zebra bait. It was now eleven o'clock. He motored in the direction of camp. After about a mile the client realized it.

'Hell,' he said. 'We're going back to camp and it's only eleven o'clock. Why? I paid you to hunt.'

The hunter looked at him coldly, spat out of the open window.

'I need a drink,' he said.

Birth of an Elephant

The vulture, voracious and keen-eyed, turned in space on pinioned wings as it soared a mile high over the Tana River. The longest in Kenya, with its source on Mount Kenya and the Aberdare range, as it winds some three hundred miles to exhaust itself into the Indian Ocean at Kipini. The huge bird was hungry as it looked down on the mighty river with loops and sinuous curves like those of a giant python. From its source the river flows north but soon turns south-by-south-east, which is then its direction for the remainder its life-giving waters. It is a river of moods; during the heavy rains of May and June it is violent, vaguely evil and of a destructive urgency, for it then becomes a raging torrent of turbulent brown waters. A fiend of merciless energy as it sweeps everything before its flooded banks. The slender-bolled doum palms, the shady *makunga* trees, with roots eaten away by the incessant pounding of the waters as they are toppled into the depths. Whole shambas of maize, millet, cotton, bananas, papaya and mango trees would be engulfed as well as the riverine villages — drowning humans, camels, cattle, sheep and goats as well as the game animals. All later to be devoured by crocodiles lurking in its murky depths.

Yet during the *jilal*, the dry season, its waters are clear, luminous and flecked with gold in the early evenings as the sun sets. Limpid and friendly, with even the stars seeming to drink from its calm, now slow-moving waters. At this time of the year, the river is the only ribbon of life for the tribes — the riverines themselves, the Boni, the Sanyo, the Orma, the Galla and the nomadic Somali. It sustains their countless thousands of camels, cattle and sheep and goat herds. To the north and the north-east stretches an enormous semi-desert country reaching to the borders of Ethiopia and the Somali Republic. This country, still called by the old-timers the Northern

Frontier District, but since independence now called by the less glamorous title of the North-eastern Province, is a magical wasteland of sand, of thorns,of red termite anthills with their crazy turrets, of dust-devils, of twisted anguished trees whose roots search for water, which occasionally seeps through to their thirsty roots if God so wills.

It is a land of searing dry heat, of thrusting volcanic rocks, of luggahs with wind-creaking doum palms listing over the banks, and here and there the evergreen trees bearing the lovely desert rose. A splash of deep pink in this wild-looking country. It is populated mainly by the Somalis, nomadic and warlike. Further north and bordering Ethiopia are the savage Suk and Turkana, the Rendille and the Samburu; also the Ethiopian border raiders, the Gelubba, who would raid far to the south, slashing and killing indiscriminately for sport. The looted stock of course a bonus, but the biggest prize of all the testicles from their unfortunate victims. These tribes, fighters all, had but one thing in common — a mutual hatred of each other and a lust for raping and killing in their constant search for grazing and water.

Only three decades ago, this vast country could justly be called the Kingdom of the Elephants for they loved its scant, hot pastures dotted with aloes, the low thorny *jirin* bush, the nuts from the doum palms, the fibres from the baobab trees and the wild sisal.

About half-way from its source, the river forks to form Balamballa Island, about eight miles long and a mile wide. A further fifty miles to the south lies the frontier town of Garissa. It was on this island, some way about the turn of the century, that an elephant was conceived and born. In later years he would be called 'Shaitani'. The Devil who Disappears. The Killer. This rogue elephant with the fabulous ivory, would be spoken of with awed reverence as possessing supernatural powers by both Europeans and Africans alike, for he had killed many men — for men, and men alone, aided by the weapons they possessed, menaced his existence and that of the herd he led.

At the time of his birth, during the end of March and just before the heavy rains, the herds were first forewarned of the dangers to come by the Arab slavers with their black-powder rifles. Slavery had

142

been declared illegal, on paper at least some years before, but in these wild, isolated parts it had not yet been fully stamped out. The elephant hunters, armed with more lethal weapons, had not yet appeared on the scene, and it was to be a hundred years later that poaching and killing, on a scale never known before in their twenty-odd million years of existence, almost decimated the elephant.

Yet when Shaitani was conceived on the island, the surroundings were peaceful and idyllic under a clump of doum palms much sought out by elephant, both for the nuts they produced and for the shade. Their bolls, tall and slender, soared grandly aloft in serried ranks, crowned with their tufts of feathered fronds, stencilled against the blue African sky. On every side of the undergrowth beneath other variant trees, rose the heady perfume of wild flowering shrubs and sweet-scented thyme. A sprinkling of white, yellow and purple dotted the river bank where wild flowers grew in profusion.

It was here at this picturesque place in the fading light when both colours and outline are softened by the afterglow that Shaitani's mother, in season, had been seeking out his father. They had been mating for weeks past, for they had a special affinity, being mutually attracted. He had been patiently waiting for her at their love-trysts — for the mating of wild elephants is a very private affair. When she had commenced their love play, encouraging him by her advances, coy retreats and by the erotic use of her trunk, then kissing in the mouth, he had finally mounted her. All six tons of impetuous passion, and as she received him enthusiastically he had then consummated the preliminaries to their love-play. He repeated the performance twelve times during the next two days, after which they browsed and grazed together to continue mating during their honeymoon.

Fourteen months later, with the female heavy in pregnancy, the bull left her to join the other tuskers whilst she moved in with the females. Here she was cosseted in the maternity ward with the pregnant cows. Prior to the birth of Shaitani she sought out the privacy of a shaded thicket and, with the other cows acting as guards — the mothers, aunts, sisters and even daughters — with her forefeet she scraped a small area to clear it of twigs, thorns and pebbles.

The moment of birth was quite a family event with all the

females of the herd, some one hundred and twenty strong, venting their pleasure by shrill trumpetings and bellowings until his mother caught him in her trunk to amble in the bushes and away from those ponderous feet. Within thirty minutes he was able to stand and at this point began to suckle from the mammary glands between his mother's forelegs. This is the time when the calf is at its most vulnerable from lion, hyena and hunting dogs, but always fiercely protected by its mother and other attendants, in particular from two aunts who were his godmothers.

High in the leafy branches of the shade trees the bush cuckoos sang their welcoming duets, to be joined below by the vulturine

guineafowl with their high-pitched rattling calls and the harsh cries of the francolin. From nearby acacias came the calls of the red-eyed mourning doves, which had started at dawn to continue through the hot drowsiness of afternoon, until the cool lilac of evening. Even at this hour one continued his insistent mockery of *koo-koo-koo, who are you? who are you?* as Shaitani made his appearance on earth.

Just after the birthing, the vulture, still lazily riding the air currents saw the milling cow herd and planed down through the sky to investigate, its dark brown shape throwing a moving shadow on the sand below. Quickly it spotted the red, slimy smear of afterbirth and landed on extended talons. With a few clumsy hops assisted by beating wings, it attacked a foraging jackal — after the same meal.

Simon Sykes

That brilliant intellectual and erudite rake, Sir Richard Burton, had such a command of languages that at the end of two months it was said that he could learn a new one. At the end of his life he was believed to speak and write no less than twenty-nine. I feel so sorry for poor Speke who was his complete opposite, methodical, abstemious and respectable and could speak but two, and those badly. The gods must have laughed ironically when that Don Quixote and his Sancho Panza set off on their ill-fated safari together.

I speak with some authority here for in those bitter-sweet golden years which I spent mainly on my own in the Somalilands, I too, once misguidedly went on a two months foot safari with a friend. A good friend, just the two of us with our Somali askaris. The safari soon developed into a battle of endurance. After a month we just could not agree at what time we would break camp in the morning; at what time we would halt during the midday heat and for how long; the time for calling a halt when the sun started to go down; which of the two of us would supervise the building of the zariba for protection against shifta and lion. We were both of the same rank, but who was really in charge? On the long, weary marches we would eye each other surreptitiously as to who would be the first to uncork and drink from the swinging water-bottle at hip and so on.

For a few days before the safari came to an end, in the evenings I would have my orderly take my camp bed from out of the zariba where it was next to my friend's and place it a hundred yards away under a lone thorn tree. We had only one Dietz lamp between us and at night he liked to read by it. I didn't. He won that round, for at night a marauding lion came unpleasantly close and I had to pick up my bed hurriedly and carry it back into the safety of the zariba. Of course we were both very young and both out to impress

our Somalis how tough we were. The Somalis are the toughest of the tough and in the end walked us both off our feet.

But I digress. It was also said of Burton that at one time he lived in an enclosure with thirty monkeys in order to study the noises they made. He even succeeded in writing a short monkey vocabulary. I must confess to being more like Speke for like him I could speak but two languages, apart from my mother tongue — Somali and Swahili — and both badly.

This brings me to Simon. He was a Sykes' monkey. A large and handsome monkey of a deep blue-grey colour with the limbs, crown and end of tail black. His eyebrows were striped whitish-grey with a pure white gorget round his throat. He would be about twice as big as the mischievous little black-faced vervets gambolling in the trees about camp, and the same size as his cousin, the golden monkey.

I first came across Simon looking lonely and quite forlorn on Charles' and Penny's grave on the outskirts of the camp in the shade on an immense wild fig tree. Here I should mention that they were my predecessors at Elephant Camp on the Tana River, with Charles dying there several months before. It was during the heavy rains with no clients that Penny, in her grief-stricken loneliness had finally succumbed and committed suicide. I had arrived the following day, read her note in which she expressed the wish to be buried in her kikoi with Charles. Naturally, I had respected her wishes and had fashioned a concrete plinth over the mound on which I had inscribed their names. It was a sad story.

I saw Simon as I approached through the line of doum palms soaring up tall and straight with their fan-shaped fronds stencilled by the dying rays of the setting sun. I approached closer. Simon did not move. In my hand was a bunch of woodland flowers I intended to place in the little jar I had embedded in the concrete. Closer now and Simon still did not move. I placed the flowers in the jar and it was only then that he moved, raising his head a little to watch me as though in sympathy at what I was doing. He tried to talk to me with a cricket-like *tick, tick, tick,* followed by a whistling chatter and looking at me with sad, eloquent eyes. I tried to talk back as I sat on the concrete plinth with him, but it was of no use. I was poor Speke and not the intellectual Sir Richard Burton.

'Did you know Charles and Penny?' I asked him. More little noises and a movement of the front paws, one of which he held out to me.

'You DID know them!' I exclaimed, 'and I am sure they fed you too?' More little noises. He looked at me hopefully. It was now dusk and through the grove of palms I could see the light from the pressure lamp my servant had placed in my little mud and wattle thatched home by the river.

'Well, let's go home then — I am sure you have been there before.' He followed me chattering away happily. I poured myself a whisky and gave him a banana which he peeled daintily. Quite unlike those horrible, red-bottomed baboons with their close-set, crafty eyes. I have little doubt that if I offered them one they would snatch it away and probably bite my finger in so doing. Not Simon. He was a gentleman.

If I was typing in the office, he would watch me quietly, half-concealed by the foliage of the tree he was sitting in with his long tail hanging down. When I left he would follow me home and as our friendship developed he would join me (well, almost) for tea. I never got him trained sufficiently to use cup and saucer, but he would sit on my trestle table to share a fruit cake with me and his manners were impeccable. I would cut two slices, one for Simon and one for myself. I would hand him his on a side plate from which he would nibble at genteelly. Never would he grab my piece, nor the remainder of the cake, until a further piece was offered him.

The white elephant of a camp closed down years ago now. It was inevitable, for all the elephant had been poached. The rhinoceros and leopard had gone years before, and all we had left were the crocodiles, lion, the other smaller predators, a few water-buck, oryx on the plains, the odd Grevy zebra and that was about all. Except for Simon, of course.

Should you ever make a safari to Garissa in the Northern Fron-tier, cross over the bridge the South African Engineers constructed during the last war and then motor downriver for some twelve miles. On the right hand side of the road you will find my markers of the two huge boulder-like skulls of poached elephant. Turn in here and follow more skulls on either side of the track until you reach the long-**deserted campsite. You will most probably think it macabre and** unfeeling of me to blaze such a trail but this was my mute protest **at the slaughter of elephants. Once the campsite is reached you will** see the concrete plinths on which stood the tents, the dining room, the bar and my old home. Look also for an enormous wild fig tree and there, overgrown and forgotten by most, you will find Charles' and Penny's grave. Should you see a Sykes' monkey in the vicinity just call out 'Simon'. Engage him in conversation, give him what food you can spare from your lunch box and give him my salaams, for he is probably lonely.

Birds

That well-known ornithologist, John Williams, in his *Field Guide to the Birds of East and Central Africa* states that there are no fewer than one thousand and thirty-three full species of birds in the relatively small country of Kenya. I can recognise about fifty of them. This sounds a terrible admission, considering my fifty years in East Africa mostly spent in the bush and under thorn trees. Paradoxically, I put this down to lack of interest, laziness and hard work. I will try to explain. Many of those years were spent in footslogging in the Somalilands from water-hole to water-hole, and during those weary marches with the Big Eye burning down relentlessly one walked as an automaton, conserving energy as best as possible and hoping against hope that the water ahead had not dried up. Then the long years spent in professional hunting. So enjoyable and yet I know of no harder work. Up before dawn, Saturdays and Sundays included, for a month, two months and sometimes as long as three months. Spending the whole day in the veld, returning at dusk for a shower and supper and then the endless conversation in entertaining the clients until late in the evening. Too exhausted to write up any field notes on any of the 'little brown jobs' I may have seen out of the corner of my eye.

Having said that, with hunting banned, so as to give the poachers more scope in their murderous activities, came the easy life of lotus-eating at Lamu and in various lodges and tented camps, mainly on the Tana River.

One can say with some justification that the bird life then in the bush, particularly on the Tana, did regiment one's life up to a point.

You awake, but leisurely this time, at dawn with the familiar honking of the Egyptian geese. Leisurely again you shave, shower and dress and then have a bowl of camel's milk (or something equally sustaining) for breakfast. Midday then comes and soon it will be time for lunch. You have already observed the flights of thousands upon thousands of sandgrouse, with their throaty chuckles, winging their way in for their delicate sips of water in the shallows just in front of camp. Now is the time for the emerald-spotted and tambourine doves you have been listening to, for they suddenly develop thirsts and flutter down from the nearby acacias to drink.

You approve of their action and call your servant to bring you a pink gin. You, too, drink. Suddenly, for no apparent reason, all the doves take to the wing, a frantic flight of metallic blue, brown and white, washed with grey. You train your binoculars high in the sky, a couple of miles away over the river where marabou storks and vultures circle. They have probably found yet another dead elephant killed by the pitiless poachers. There is nothing you can do for you are not even allowed a rifle in camp. Morosely you call for another pink gin. Don't cry for me (or rather the elephants) Argentina.

Everything sleeps during the midday heat after lunch and so you, too, do what comes naturally. A little Egyptian physical training when you go into reverse for fifty-odd years and study again for the Staff College. You awaken at teatime to listen to the re-awakening of the birds. The geese, having fed all day, usually make off about now. A couple of hours or so later you have your first whisky wompo. Looking over the languorous sweep of the river you see echelons of egrets, their white feathers flashing in the now dying rays of the sun, winging their way homewards followed by a trio of noisy Hadada ibis with their croak-like cries.

Dark now when you hear the tiny Scops owl perched in his usual place in a tree above your house calling softly to the river — *ke-oo, ke-oo, ke-oo.* A stone curlew, with the most plaintive, mournful cry of all to emanate from the bush, and one I love above all the others, now joins in to make a soft duet as supper is served.

It was during one of these idyllic days in camp when I was on my own, for the rains had just started and so had little to do but philosophise on the past sands of time, when the lonely fisherman appeared. I sensed straight away that we had something in common, that bird and I.

He was long-legged and yellow-billed. A yellow-billed stork or wood ibis, red-faced, pinkish-white with black wings and tail. Handsome. Not for him a mate for company, for as I subsequently found out, he was always on his own. A true loner. Also the most persistent and unsuccessful fisherman I have ever known. I watched him for hours through my binoculars. Solemnly striding up and down on his spindly legs, with his bill open just below the surface of the water. His beat was a short one, about thirty yards. Left-right. Left-right and so on. About turn. Left-right. Left-right ...

The only catch I ever saw him make was on the fifth day and it was a small, modest catfish. On this momentous occasion he chopped at it in his bill for fully five minutes before swallowing it. After that he stood on one leg in apparent satisfaction for a full half-hour, contemplating the scenery with equanimity. How I so wished I could speak with that bird! I wanted to ask him all sorts of questions. Was he ever disappointed with his life? Was he ever upset that he was so unlucky with his fishing? Was he ever hungry? Did he ever pine for company, for a mate? Had he a nest or a home anywhere? Was he very old? So many questions had to remain unanswered. I then came to the conclusion that seemingly he was quite happy with his way of life, although he never caught another fish while I was observing him. Though what could be more disappointing in life than a belly full of fish and an aim fulfilled?

The Egyptian goose mates for life. This short sentence expresses all the admiration and affection I feel for this most handsome of our East African geese with its rich brown plumage and contrasting pure white shoulders which are so conspicuous when in flight. After my lonely fisherman had left me, probably to try his luck on another stretch of the river, I had occasion to observe a pair of these geese on the far bank of the river. They stayed for about a month. Elsewhere I had seen them in fairly large flocks but I cannot recall ever having seen a single bird. I grew fond of my two residents for they were quite inseparable. They would always arrive together to saunter up the gently sloping bank as they fed. If one got a little too far ahead, the other would quicken its pace to catch up. When they stopped to preen their feathers they were never more than a pace apart and when taking to the air with their loud honking cries, there was never more than a couple of seconds between take-off. More often than not they would fly off simultaneously.

It was a constant delight for me to observe them which I did with envy because of their obvious devotion to each other. Or could one say love? Is it possible for geese to fall in love? What a charming thought!

In support of this theory, I well remember, soon afterwards, a French guest shooting one of them. This was just before the ban on hunting when I would sometimes be called upon to take out shooting safaris, although I restricted these as far as possible to bird shooting because of the paucity of the bigger game due to poachers. This particular couple, a Frenchman and his wife, had taken out bird licences. At the time I was recovering from a bout of malaria and I had sent Buno, my old gunbearer, down country on compassionate leave. This being the case I allowed them to go out with one of my more reliable camp employees, assuming that walking a few miles from camp they could come to no harm. On the other hand they could do no harm themselves, armed with shotguns and shooting birds. I briefed them what they were allowed to shoot; fifteen birds per gun and I suggested they concentrate on vulturine guineafowl, yellow-necked francolin and sandgrouse for all these species were in abundance. Moreover, they were all good table birds. I warned them they were not allowed to shoot greater bustard and on no account would they shoot my two resident Egyptian geese which I took pains to describe in detail. Fever or not, I cursed myself afterwards for not accompanying them.

As dusk was approaching I heard a few shots down river and not too far from camp, but thought little of it. Feeling a little stronger I staggered out of my bed to sit on the verandah. It was then I saw the intrepid hunting party approaching on the path which led in front of my house to the main camp. They were carrying an assorted number of birds, but Madame herself was proudly swinging by the neck one of my Egyptian geese, its breast and white shoulders now stained crimson. As they passed she jocularly remarked that she would have the liver for hors-d'oeuvres that evening. Evidently she had been thinking on the same lines as Fulbert-Dumonteil, who wanted the whole of natural history and its subjects in our frying pans or cooking pots. I could have cheerfully shot her and so add to the list.

It was almost dark yet the surviving goose did not fly off to disappear as perhaps one would expect. It flew up and down the river, approaching close to my house as if to reproach me for the death of its mate. It called away in such a heart-breaking manner that I have never forgotten the incident. Even as the setting sun lost itself in the sea of thorn bush and it was quite dark, that bird still made its plaintive cries as it continued its lonely, hopeless quest.

On my hunting safaris I would never allow them to be shot and if they should be observed near water when I was out with a guest I either ignored them in spite of his protestations or, like Nelson, turned a blind eye.

However, on one occasion though, I found myself in an awkward predicament which fortunately had a happier ending than the one related above.

Rounding an acute bend on the red, sandy road, driving rather fast, we suddenly came upon a deshek or rainwater pool fringed with umbrella-like acacia thorn trees. It was a charming spot and as it was about midday I decided upon a cold pink gin and then lunch. I parked in the shade of one of the acacias before I spotted a brace of Egyptian geese. My Italian guest, though, saw them immediately and reached for his scope-mounted .22 with that gleam in his eye I now knew so well.

I spoke little Italian and he even less English. Nevertheless in my limited Italian I protested that this particular species of goose mated for life and that it would be a crime to shoot one. My pleas were like water off a lily trotter's back, for all I got in reply was —

'Cosa Che? Cosa Che? Eh? Bang! Bang! Finito, No? Allora mangiare.' With that, riding breeches and boots and festooned with hunting knives, he leapt out of the car, whipped his little rifle to his shoulder and prepared to shoot. I shrugged and gestured to the bonnet of the Land Rover, indicating that he would have a much steadier aim that way, although legally on the face of it, I was committing a game offence.

'Gratzie,' he smiled, expressing his appreciation of my thoughtfulness, but, bless his warm, impulsive Mediterranean heart, he still had perfidious Albion to cope with. Standing behind him, and just as his finger tightened on the trigger, I leant against the car so that not unnaturally he missed his shot. With loud protesting honks the two geese flew off safely into the blue. There were no recriminations for his shot had disturbed a large flock of guineafowl from where they had been resting unseen in some thick bush so off he happily rushed to massacre a few of those. Buno and I smiled at each other conspiratorily. He mixed me a drink with ice from the little refrigerator humming away happily in the Land Rover and at a nod from me helped himself to a Tusker beer. Guineafowl, if they take to the wing, fly like old Caproni bombers but if they decide to run then they go like greyhounds. The dashing Alfredo would have his work cut out and if he didn't make it for lunch then we would have tea ready for him. It was a pleasant way to spend an afternoon.

Never cheat on a honeyguide. This is one of the first things to remember when out on foot in the African veld or bush, whether hunting, photographing or just observing. After sitting and listening around camp fires over the years to many of the stories told to me by old Buno, in which fact, fiction and superstition were intermingled, I never did. He was quite a character, that old gnome of a gunbearer from Ukambani, small and slight of build, with the heart of a lion, an engaging sense of humour. If oft-times some of his tales were so wildly outrageous as to be unbelievable, when relating his experiences with the honeyguide, his cracked, walnut of a face would take on a grave mien and he would be deadly serious.

The greater or black-throated honeyguide is an inconspicuous ordinary-looking bird about eight inches long. The upper body parts are of sombre brown, lighter below and with a black throat in the adult male. There is an indistinct yellow patch on the shoulders. The bill is bright pink. There's nothing remarkable about that, you may say, but like the conjuring cuckoo, it too performs the unique egg trick by laying its eggs in the nests of woodpeckers, barbets and bee-eaters. Now for its second trick.

From its special calling place, often high in the branches of an acacia thorn tree, it will perch for long periods, chirping a very distinct and rather imperious two-note call of *wait-er, wait-er* repeated incessantly. I personally always found this most amusing for its call reminded me of Aunt Sophia (a most eccentric and autocratic old lady) who, when she occasionally gave me lunch in town would make the same bird-like calls when she wanted to attract the attention of a waiter.

Once the bird has spotted you it becomes quite agitated, changing its monotonous little call to chatters and twitters as it flutters from branch to branch in order to attract your attention. When you decide to follow it, suitably armed with either panga or axe to be used for chopping out the nest, usually from the limb of a dead tree or the like, it is then just a question of follow-your-leader.

If there is any hesitancy or waiting on your part, then the bird will immediately fly back to you, chattering angrily and scolding you for your apparent lack of attention and interest in finding the honey.

Once the nest or hive is reached the bird becomes wildly excited and after you extract the most delicious, sweet acacia honey, it is most important to feed your little friend on the honey, comb and grubs.

Should you cheat the bird out of its well-earned reward, then if followed again it will remember your lack of manners. It may lead you to a sleeping leopard up a tree and instead of the honey trickling down your throat, you may have a fur collar of fury wrapping itself around the same part of your anatomy. Or perhaps the angry bird will lead you to a deadly green mamba, perfectly camouflaged so that it looks like one of the tree's slender branches where you may put your hand when climbing. Or again, to a malevolent buffalo, hiding in the thick bush under your honey tree ... such will be the revenge of the cheated honeyguide.

This clever bird does not rely entirely on human help in extracting the honey for it has a curious association with the ratel, or honey badger. This stout, stocky animal with thick, subcutaneous fat beneath its tough hide, is quite impervious to bee stings. Only about a foot high, it is both courageous and bold, and does not know the meaning of the word fear and is capable of attacking even a buffalo, biting the groin and genital organs in its ferocious energy. (What a good recommendation this is for the efficacy of honey!). Once the honeyguide has located the hive it then attracts the mammal in the same way it does the human. Then the ratel, a good climber, digs out the hive with its powerful claws and both share the feast. Neither my old gunbearer's fund of stories nor history relates what happens to the aggressive ratel should it cheat the bird by eating all the honey!

Passing by

She dropped in
  From the sky
Just one of the many
  Passing by.
Yet a smile like a token
  A few words spoken
And my heart stood still
  With her loveliness.
She stayed but a while
  But that memories smile
Lingers on
  In my loneliness.

The Mosque Swallow

It was growing night
  When I saw the mosque swallow,
Swiftly moving, speeding, diving
  In freedom of flight.

Lost for a frantic moment
  In a wisp of cloud,
To re-appear when I felt
  A painful sense of emptiness.
For I would fain be a swallow
  Unfettered and unchained,
Detached from all earthly cares and pain
  To fly at will to those I love.

But pursuit of happiness
  Comes slow to start,
So, swallow go
  With my imprisoned heart.

Three

LAMU

Lamu Island

Lamu Island. The word Lamu is said to come from the *Banu Lami,* an Arab tribe from the Persian Gulf whose people settled here many centuries ago. An older name was *Kiwa Ndeo,* and by some it was also called the Proud Isle.

It stands on a concave curve off the East African Coast in the Indian Ocean some four hundred kilometres north of Mombasa, *Mvita,* the Island of War. The mainland lies close by on the north and west, separated only by a narrow channel known as the *Mkanda.* The east of this channel curves round to the north and here is found the island of Manda — roughly the same size as Lamu. This channel sweeps into Manda Bay, and the wider Siyu channel in turn separates the larger island of Pate from the mainland. North of Pate are the islands of Uvondo, Ndau and Kiwaiyu. Still following the coastline northwards are the Bajun islands strung like pearls; some inhabited, some not, and extend to the border of the Somali Republic and beyond.

Possibly the oldest strain of negroid blood that can now be traced is represented by the Wasanye. Next in order come the Wadahhalo and the Watwa, who appear to be branches of the riverine Pokomo who may be the parent stock of the Giriama and the Nyika.

The Waboni, who claim to have possessed the Watwa as serfs at one time, appear to be the next until they in turn were broken up by the next Hamitic wave, the Wakatwa, who are described as having originated from that division of the Swahili known as the Bajun.

Of the origins of the Bajun there are two explanations. One is the legend of the Wakatwa Sheikh who ruled the town of Chumwona near Kismayu in the Somali Republic. This Sheikh was reputed to have had certain privileges on the occasion of the marriage of virgins. A jealous worthy, who preferred his lady intact, introduced a youth dressed as a woman to the presence of the Sheikh after the marriage ceremony. The youth was armed and duly assassinated the Sheikh, and 'the consequence was' — a civil war between the factions which ended in the Wakiliyu and the Wadili remaining in the north, white the other sections moved to the south and became the ancestors of the present day Bajun and Watikuu.

The second explanation is that about Hejira 295, owing to religious differences, the Banu Yuni were driven from Ii Hasha in Arabia and, settling first at Mogadishu, worked their way down the coast to the Watikuu area, since when the Watikuu have called themselves Banu Yuni and are now known as the Bajun.

On the island of Pate, in addition to the Bajun, there were settlements of II Barwa and II Famadwi, with their sub-division Il Weli and Nufafi from Mogadishu; as also the negro Pokomo and Waboni. The original name of Pate was *Kiwang'aa*, the island that shines, *Kiwa* being the abbreviated form of *Kisiwa*. This may still be recognised in Kiwayuu — the island on top, i.e. above Pate and Ndau, and in the old name of Lamu — *Kiwandia*.

The pre-Islam inhabitants of the island of Lamu were known as the Kinamti and lived in a town now buried under the sand of Hedabu Hill, the name of which was Mrio. The Kinamti claim to have originated in Arabia and to have introduced the coconut. Legend has it that they were wrecked on the island and that their dhow's cargo consisted of coconut seedlings. The town of Mrio is completely buried and no one knows the reason for its abandonment. One story is that it was buried by a sandstorm in a single night for 'Sodom and Gomorrah' reasons and knowing something of the island this I can well believe! Another reason is that the wells became contaminated; yet another version is that some form of pestilence caused its downfall. Whatever the reasons it now provides an elevated and cool site for the District Commissioner's house.

There is no definite information as to the origin of the settlement on Manda Island, but the ruined town of that name is very ancient and thought to be Persian. The Manda people seem to have had no friends in the archipelago and there is a half-forgotten tradition of a daughter of the ruler of Manda crossing to Pate and being shot at with arrows by the Waboni.

It is probable that the East Coast of Africa was known to the Phoenicians as an extension of the area called Paunit, or Punt, by the ancient Egyptians after Paunt, the son of Ham. Paunit was generally regarded as extending from Southern Arabia to the opposite coast of Africa and thence through what was Abyssinia now Ethiopia to the borders of ancient Egypt. A large portion of the east coast to the south may well have been included in Paunit by the ancients. There are phallic columns at Lamu, Malindi and Gede, and there is a ruined mosque on the island of Mgeni, off the coast of Somalia which, it is said, was connected with the worship of Astarte, the Phoenician Goddess of Love.

Ethnologists believe that, from time immemorial, North and East Africa have been the subjects of waves of Hamitic and Semitic migrations proceeding in a southerly direction and that it may be possible to connect all the peoples of that part of the world one with the other, and all with their common ancestor, Noah.

In the handbook of the British Museum Ethnographical Collection the cradle of the Negro proper is described as being about the great lakes of Central Africa, and it is surmised that the black races, developing from their centre, expanded until they came into contact with the Hamites spreading south, thus producing mixed races at the point of contact. It is also thought that pioneer parties of Hamites may have pressed forward until they lost touch with their main body and, being cut off by the Negro peoples, threw in their lot with them thus producing a number of tribes of varying degrees of Hamitic and Negro blood.

The maps and writing of Ptolemy prove that many of the ports and places of call on the East African coast were known to the Romans in the second century of the Christian era.

It is said that *Mtepi*, the nailless dhow of the Bajun, was introduced to this coast by the castaway crews of Malayan vessels as it has affinities with the Malay *proa*.

Chinese coins, beads, Persian and Chinese pottery connect the coast with visits from corsairs or traders from the Far East, but there is nothing to indicate how far back these trade connections date. These examples show that many old civilisations, pushing out their trade routes, came in contact with the East African coast, going as far south as Sofala, the port for Zimbabwe, which the Portuguese believed to be identical with Phir, to which King Solomon sent his ships in quest of 'gold, ivory and peacocks feathers.'

The oldest tradition is that the people of Lamu were traders and town dwellers who were engaged, through the medium of a hybrid population, in commerce with the interior and acted as middlemen for the external sea-carried trade, particularly in slaves.

Nowadays Lamu township is run down. Its patrimony has an apathetic, dreary air of decay and little remains of the former prosperity and magnificence it once knew in the Golden Age. One might compare it to an aged duchess who has fallen on hard times. She has had to sell her tiara, has mislaid her string of pearls and cannot find her lorgnette. Yet the memories of prosperity are still remembered by a few of the ancients who still cling to life and, in spite of everything, many of the old customs are tenaciously held on to.

Many of the population seem to be sunk in apathy. This is not surprising, nor is it entirely their fault as some of them are riddled by disease. Particularly, the inhabitants of Pate, Siyu and Lamu itself present an exceptionally deplorable picture. The amount of ophthalmia and elephantiasis has to be seen to be believed and to these must be added the ills of malaria, worm infestation and the like.

And yet if one chooses to turn a blind or tolerant eye on this air of neglect and decay to visit and roam around some of the old palatial Arab houses still standing, or the hoary crumbling ruins to be found on most of the islands, one cannot help but be charmed by the mysterious beauty that is still there. The houses themselves, beautifully designed with the walls spaced with graceful arches, the rooms long and narrow, as their supports are of mangrove poles — *boriti* — which are seldom cut over twelve feet in length. Light and ventilation was not forgotten for they are both cool and airy with the thickness of the walls proving an adequate protection against the blazing sun outside. Most had sunken baths and adequate toilet facilities. On the ground floor, sometimes covering an entire wall, can be seen the delightfully-carved miniature arches called *vidaki,* whilst other most attractive wall decorations are the moulded and carved friezes of various designs called *makshi.* A sad little verse of poetry illustrates the present state of some of these most beautiful homes:

> *The lighted mansions are uninhabited,*
> *The young bats cling above,*
> *You hear no whisperings or shoutings;*
> *Spiders crawl over the beds —*
> *The wall niches for porcelain in the houses*
> *Are now the resting-place for nestlings,*
> *Owls hoot within the houses and*
> *Mannikin birds and ducks dwell therein*

And yet the old culture still remains and the magic comes back, however elusive, as one views the antiquity of the place. The narrow alleys designed for shade, the forbidding-looking fort, until quite recently the prison, and the line of cannon on the old harbour wall, as if their questing mouths were still protecting the island from the invaders of old.

Government is making preparations to remove the administration and some of the other services to Makowe on the mainland; indeed the prison has already been built there and the prisoners transferred. What effect this exodus of Government servants will have on the economy of the island is problematic.

There are still a few wealthy individuals left, mostly of Arab origin, and abject poverty is all too evident, but the unfortunate individuals without a roof over their heads can always find a mat to sleep on in any of the twenty-two mosques. It should also be remembered that the Muslim faith is so much more compassionate to those unfortunates than their Christian brethren.

Lest it be thought from the foregoing that I am a prophet of doom I add to hasten that this is not the case.

Over the centuries, of all the islanders the Bajun have always been the most energetic in their specialised work of fishing and their light dhows, when weather permits, still leave early in the morning to bring back their catches of sailfish, tunny, kingfish, tewa, tangu and a dozen other different varieties; others specialize in catching lobsters, crabs, octopus and prawns.

Then there are those traditional craftsmen, the wood carvers of doors, beds, stools, dressers, tables, chairs and small *objets d'art*, for which Lamu is justly famous. They are also indefatigable workers.

A most heartening sign of the times here is that quite a few of the youngsters are not happy with their future and more and more of them are taking up contract jobs in Saudi Arabia, where they manage to find work at wages unheard of on the island, or, for that matter, in Kenya generally. They have my admiration for not only do they save a good percentage of their wages but also remit money to their parents, wives and relatives here. Indeed some of the more fortunate are in a position to arrange flights from Mombasa to Mecca so that their kin may make the coveted pilgrimage for the Haj.

It must be remembered, too, that although dhow traffic has declined during the past decades, some large ocean-going craft are still being built at Lamu and Matandoni nearby, and during the fifteen years I lived there I witnessed the launching of several of them.

The Mpekatoni agricultural settlement scheme has been under way for several years now and its farmers are mainly those hardy workers, the Kikuyu, who will ensure that the produce grown will mean that no one will starve on the archipelago.

It is also of interest and some significance, I think, to note that the 1914-18 war had no effect on Lamu; as also the Second World War. It would seem, therefore, that the last fighting was a punitive expedition in 1890, and this some fifty miles from Lamu when a party under the German, Kuntzel, was massacred by the people of Witu, which was then burnt to the ground. So for a period of one hundred years, if not enjoying the prosperity they had known hitherto, the peoples of the island have enjoyed a longer period of peace than ever before in their turbulent history of blood, intrigue and treachery.

But rich or poor, peace or war, in the evenings with the crescent moon — the symbol of Islam, riding high above the Proud Island with all its timeless charm, the Muezzins call the last prayer of the day and each and every individual here of the Muslim faith knows in his heart of hearts that everything may be safely left to Allah. Such is their faith.

Lamu Days

I am an early riser. My day at Lamu usually starts off at 6 a.m., but this morning the Muezzin awakes me at 4 a.m. with his thin, unwelcome but urgent call from the Pwani Mosque (the Mosque by the sea), said by some to be the oldest in Lamu. It is only about fifty yards from my house. I can also hear similar calls from about half a dozen other mosques a little further away, for this island, supporting about 10,000 inhabitants, boasts no less than twenty-two mosques. All as it should be I suppose, for after Mecca and Medina in Arabia, Lamu is listed as third in the holy cities of the Muslim world. There are five calls to prayers daily. Two in the morning — the El Fajiri and El Dhuhur — one in the afternoon, the El Assir, and two in the evening — the Magharib and the Esha.

A cockerel, thinking it is morning too, crows nearby and a donkey makes a rude noise followed by a series of explosive, insane, sickening brays. All this and still two hours to dawn. Peering through my mosquito net, the clock opposite me on the coral, lime-washed wall tells me that the Muezzin is on time and my wrist-watch confirms it. The clock now begins to chime. I count the chimes. It always chimes asthmatically and with some reluctance, four times more than it should. It does so now. It is an ancient American clock and like so many more must have been shipped over in those famed Clipper ships, thence by dhow from Arabia to Zanzibar and then Lamu, about a hundred years ago. I am told that they sold for about two dollars then but now it is worth £100. It hangs on a rusty dhow nail on the wall and is encased in wood, possibly mahogany. Something like a grandfather clock but without the long case. Like the chiming mechanism, the pendulum labours somewhat but its *tock, tock, tock,* has a homely sound. Behind its glass case it has three hands: one for hours, one for minutes and the third points hopefully at the day of the month and for this reason the outside of the dial is numbered one to thirty-one. In the middle of the dial it says REGULATOR. These old clocks have a curious history. Originally made in Connecticut, USA, the firm making them had their premises burnt down. Salvaged from the wreckage were thousands of these quaint clocks. At that time the Americans were trying to establish themselves in these waters (commercially that is, and not to colonise for I would hate to upset our cousins). Oh, to hell with it for why should I worry, and incidentally did you know that Captain Kidd, the most ferocious, bloodthirsty pirate of all to sail these waters was an American? Yes, sir. I always thought the horror was an Englishman and was quite delighted when I learnt that he was a Yank. Don't worry. I've already chalked that one up. He's been dead over 100 years now and so can't make me walk the plank with the tip of a cutlass pricking my backside.

Clocks? Oh, yes. The American Government appointed a Commercial Attaché to their Consulate on the Island of Zanzibar. He was quite young and somewhat of a hustler. He presented a clock to the Sultan who was so intrigued by it that soon the famous Clippers were bringing them over by the thousands.

I now turn my head to read St. Francis' Prayer of Assisi which hangs on the wall behind me. The prayer comforts me and I promise to love everyone in the morning when I get up, in spite of my hangover, for I had punished the wompo last night.

The Muezzin now ceases to call and I try to sleep again but by this time a fearful wailing, shrieking and caterwauling fills the jasmine-scented air. An unsuspecting visitor might think that the clock finally has gone round the bend, with the hands now whizzing backwards for hundreds of years when the people of nearby Pate Island attacked Lamu, and bloody murder was being committed up and down the beach when the Lamuans finally stopped them at Hedabu Hill and so won the day. Not so. Just a couple of cats fornicating outside and underneath my window. At one time I gather there was a plague of rats on the island and the cats were brought in their thousands to kill them. I prefer the rats.

After a restless ratnap I again wake. This time at five minutes

to six. An elusive palm frond from the coconut tree growing below but reaching up to my verandah, wantonly intrudes to caress the outside of my mosquito net. Impatiently I wave both net and palm frond aside to watch the sun rise over Manda Island opposite. A most exquisite dawn of suffused colours. Cerise, mauve and yellow.

A dhow in the channel below, its lateen triangular sail billowing out with the first of the breezes heads majestically out to sea. This tranquil scene is now rudely shattered by a terrible clatter below and outside my front door.

I do not investigate for I know that it is only another wretched donkey knocking the lid off my dustbin to get at the contents. Of necessity they will eat anything. Papaya skins, eggshells, banana peel, mango skins and the like but their favourite breakfast seems to be old copies of the *East African Standard*.

In the Golden Years when on a hunting safari and camped out in the bush, it was always exciting to find piles of aromatic elephant dung, sometimes steaming hot on the sand outside one's tent, but donkey dung calling cards are neither romantic nor aromatic.

Clambering out of bed, I switch on the radio to listen, from the outside verandah, to the BBC news. My tea is late. Mohamed is often late with the early morning tea and I know that as an excuse he will complain of a headache. He's always got a headache, due to no doubt to the chewing of miraa and smoking of bhangi which is the custom here from time immemorial. If he's not got a headache then it's the bellyache and the last time he had this latter he took four days off. After the local *mchawi* — the witch doctor — had finished burning his belly with red hot stones to drive out the *djinn,* not unnaturally he was really ill, for this primitive curative treatment must have been a damned sight more painful than the original bellyache. That, of course, is the whole point of the treatment. I really think he might be a hypochondriac. I glance at St. Francis' prayer again to promise myself that I won't give him hell when he complains of his headache or bellyache.

Particularly so when I think of Colonel Pink, an acquaintance of mine in Somaliland, all those years ago, who was murdered by his cook, strangled by a piano wire. But then he was as queer as a hyena (hyenas, by the way, are supposed to be blessed with both male and female. organs and, according to my old Mkamba gunbearer, that is why they laugh a lot.) No tea — but the news.

Evidently the so-called coup in Kenya is under control. It was started by the NCOs and privates of the Kenya Air Force. The news. A coup this time in the Seychelles, started apparently by NCOs and privates, but this time of the Army. They said their reason for mutinying was because their superior officers had treated them like pigs. Poor chaps! How they would survive, or what their reactions would be, if they ever found themselves on a parade ground under drill instruction from a brutal, tyrannical, foul-mouthed Guards Sergeant Major I cannot imagine. One deduces from all this that these characters are not content to be privates, lance corporals, corporals, sergeants, sergeant majors, lieutenants, captains, majors, colonels or even brigadiers. No. They all want to be Field Marshals like that murderous clown from Uganda, Idi Amin. I switch off the radio. I go to the loo and almost collide with Mohamed carrying the tea tray. I give him a bit of mild hell. He complains of a headache. He rolls his eyes, red-rimmed with bhangi. He should have been an actor.

He then brightens up and says:

'*Leo, siku yangu off*' — (today is my day off). I look at him coldly. I think. I'm never at my best this early.

'*La. Hapana,*' (No!) says I.

'*Ndio,*' (yes!), he insists. He smiles, headache forgotten. I reach for the local paper I had bought yesterday. Thursday. Today IS Friday — the Muslim's Sunday. He's right and I'm wrong and I blame that idiotic clock which at that precise moment chimes the half hour — twice. Resignedly I agree with him, tell him to make my bed, prepare my breakfast and the rest of the day is his. Knowing that he has scored off me he gives a big, triumphant grin, makes the bed in five minutes flat then rushes downstairs to prepare breakfast.

I shave and shower then, clad in my kikoi, I amble downstairs where breakfast awaits. The papaya is a good one, iced, firm and pink-fleshed and lightly sprinkled with sugar. I squeeze half a lime on it. The scrambled eggs perfect on crisp toast well-buttered and the coffee piping hot. I am getting tired of eggs. My imported bacon from Malindi is finished. I dream of kippers, but too far from Aberdeen. Also of kidneys, but these are quite inedible for the beef from the scrub cattle here is as tough as old boots. In fact if you threw one of your sandals in the frying pan I swear you would hardly tell the difference.

Working like a jet-propelled maniac, Mohamed clears away the breakfast things, washes up, says *'Kwa Heri'* and is then off like Sebastian Coe. Headaches, bellyaches forgotten, that boy can really move when he wants to.

I try to map out my day. Big deal. I decide to go swimming but this time to Naazi Moja, in the other direction from Shela. The beach is not as pleasant but there should be no hippies there. Placing my towel, swim trunks, a book, an exercise book and a pencil for notes in a kikapu, lock the front door and set off. Stepping in between the plop, plop, plop of visiting cards left by the donkey I call in first at the Post Office. Once German, once British and now Kenyan. The letter box is painted red and on it is lettered GR. A relic from the colonial days. There is no mail. My children only seem to write when I send them cheques for their birthdays and at Christmas. *Che sera sera.*

I follow the sea-wall for a short while, shod in my rubber sandals made out of an old tyre. Still plenty of tread left on them and probably good for another 1,000 miles I think. Lobb, the shoemaker in London, would have been horrified. However, apart from being a little smelly when hoofing it over the hot sand they are ideal for walking in the shifting soft stuff for which any other type of shoe is not quite so good. The Dunlop Special is both wide, tough and has a good grip — something like a camel's pad.

I now leave the sea-wall and cut in across sand dunes. Finally I reach Bunduki Gunn's old place now owned by Ian Napier. Ian has been away for some time and so I change nearby finding an evergreen bushy tree for my clothes and kikapu. Sunbathing, swimming and sunbathing again I while away the hours; suddenly charmed by the well-known cry of the palm eagle perched high on a coconut tree behind me. Then the shrill *quiket, quiket* call of the Coqui francolin from the scrub and undergrowth nearby. In the shade of the evergreen I sleep, using my rolled up towel as a pillow. There came again from behind me another of those characteristic calls from the bush. This time the emerald-spotted wood dove, a series of insistent, soporific coos, gradually dropping in cadence then quickening towards the end. Lulled to sleep again by these familiar sounds I finally wake up with the sun now low in the sky. I slip on my sandals and shorts, pick up the kikapu and trudge back home.

Entering the house a thirst was upon me and as I opened the door of the refrigerator, the pangs of hunger too assailed me as I remembered I had eaten nothing since breakfast. I looked gloomily at the half-bottle of milk, a bottle of fresh lime, twelve bottles of Tusker beer, four eggs, a few bananas, a couple of mangoes and a pot of Gentleman's Relish — the gift of a recent guest. The admirable Mohamed had forgotten to buy both bread and butter. I took out a bottle of beer, carried it to the upstairs verandah, spannered it open and poured the contents into a pewter tankard. Refreshing, but I was still hungry and after listening to the seven o'clock news I decided to dine out. There were several places I could choose from. Petley's, where the food was good but at tourist prices. The Star, a coffee shop cum-eating house which I found a little seedy. Guy's excellent curry but I have always thought curry essentially a midday meal. Ron Partridge's Equator or the Yoghurt Inn?

Ron Partridge, known locally as 'Akiba,' is another old-timer who used to run the excellent and well-known Equator Club in Nairobi and where, incidentally, he launched a talented Kenya boy, then known as Hank, on his singing, whistling, and guitar-playing career. From there Roger Whittaker has now risen to dizzy heights in the entertainment world of Europe.

Akiba, who died a couple of years ago, had worked at one time or another in most of the lodges in Kenya's parks and elsewhere and whilst one could not compare him to an Escoffier — in any event he was unable to obtain in Lamu the luxury items of food so necessary to compete with such a great cook — he was without doubt, a *maître de cuisine* of some renown. His Equator Inn, just off the sea-front has much charm and originality and he lays claim that his bouillabaisse soup compares to that the purists rave over. In the

174

Mediterranean region, from Marseilles to Toulon the bouillabaisses, however delicious they may be, do not exist for the true connoisseurs of this saffron-flavoured soup. Apart from his cooking Akiba will be missed as a raconteur of some note for I did not know until he told me that the preparation of this soup has divine origins. Its invention being attributed to Venus, the Goddess of Love, who took a fancy one day to prepare the soup as a treat for her husband, Vulcan, mainly with the purpose of inducing sound sleep in him, sleep which Venus planned to exploit for her own ends. There must be a moral to this story somewhere for what the devil do you think Venus was up to? Akiba did not elaborate as he then rushed off to serve other customers. As well as this excellent soup which is suitably smashed with fish, wine, garlic, parsley, saffron, pepper, bay leaves, oil and tomatoes, he used to serve cold lobster and most excellent sailfish which was almost comparable to smoked salmon.

However, having been reckless with money all my life, times were now not what they used to be, and so I reluctantly decided to pay a visit to my favourite little place, the Yoghurt Inn, situated in the poorer quarter of town. I like to refer to it as Fortnum & Mason's. Needless to say it is patronised by hippies and the not-so-wealthy-types visiting Lamu. Chalked on the inside wall was the somewhat cryptic message: *We appreciate hurry, but hurry takes time.* This was perfectly all right with me for I had no car parked anywhere, illegally or otherwise, no train to catch, no phone calls to make, no appointments and little future I'm afraid. In short I had all the time in the world.

In one corner sat a group of hippies. Those who were not eating their waffles and syrup were smoking and gazing vacantly through the wooden lattice in front of them. Full of bhangi and full of dreams. An old Arab sat in another corner sucking noisily at his tea which he had poured into a cracked saucer. He finished it off and belched appreciatively.

My eyes wandered idly over the menus chalked on boards advertising Sweet Menthol cigarettes. The first board read:

Menu 1

White coffee shillings	3/-	Black coffee shillings	2/50
Black tea	1/-	Hot milk	2/-
Icy biscuits	2/-	Potato chop	2/50
Yoghurt	2/-	Sponge cake	2/-
Pineapple pancake	4/-	Fruit salad	2/50
Fresh lemon	1/50	Grape fruit	2/50

Menu 2

Crab salad shillings	30/-	Rice shillings	3/50
Fish salad	20/-	Beef stew	3/50
Prawns	10/-	Bean stew	2/-
Porridge	3/-	Rice pudding	3/-
Chupatti	2/-	Cheese sandwich	5/-
Fried eggs	5/-	Boiled egg	2/-
Pancakes	3/-	Honey	2/-

I did not know what icy biscuits were nor a potato chop.

The Last of the Big Spenders ordered the crab salad followed by pancakes and honey. The honey I knew was especially delicious, wild from the mainland where the bees had sucked it from the acacia blossoms. With an attentive Khalid, the owner, hovering in the background, my supper was excellent and I didn't mind spearing a bee drowned some time past in its own goodness. I then ordered a cup of *buni,* lit a cigarette and thought that all in all, there could be worse places to live than Lamu. The bill came to shillings 37.50. I gave the waiter fifty shillings, told him to keep the change and he smiled, salaamed and thought it was Christmas.

I sauntered back to my own comfortable home, poured myself a liqueur brandy, put on a tape and listened to Trooping the Colour by the Band of the Coldstream Guards. After that I put on a kikoi and scrambled under my mosquito net. With a full moon playing hide-and-seek from behind swaying palm fronds I fell asleep.

The Welsh Falcon

Any visitor to Lamu Island knows that the East African coast has suffered the depredations of many invaders over the centuries. Notably the Portuguese in the 15th century and after that the Omani Arabs from Muscat. Lamu itself was no exception. One can still see traces of their occupation, for mounting and lining the harbour walls are some dozens of old cannon with their still questing mouths looking out over the channel which sweeps in from the sea.

When the Kenya Government banned all hunting in the country, we White Hunters, with all our African staff, found ourselves out of jobs. I had to find somewhere to live, and to live modestly. I chose Lamu. I bought an enchanting old Arab house in town, but after several years I found the life of lotus-eating boring. To escape and get back to my real love, the bush, I found work from time to time as camp manager in various tented camps and lodges, mostly on the Tana River.

However, it was during the time that I was in residence at Lamu itself that the island suffered yet another invasion of the flower children, as I called the hippies. I know that all of us seek happiness in life, an elusive quality that eludes so many, but what made the hippies, like a flight of locusts, alight here I did not know. Unshaven, unkempt for the most part wearing dark glasses, with music machines plugged in their ears, constantly chewing miraa, smoking bhangi and occasional snorts of cocaine, I found them weird. From a combination of these drugs (and if they occasionally removed their dark glasses) their eyes were red-rimmed, bloodshot and lustreless and so if they ever did come across their own mystical Golden Fleece I am sure they would not have recognised it.

At the time I was Honorary British Consul, and perforce had to meet some of them from time to time when inevitably they ran into trouble with the Police. It so happened one day that five of them were thrown into prison. By persuasive talking and by promising the Inspector in charge that I would personally see them on a dhow to the mainland the following day, he released them. By then it was dusk. They had no money and had been kicked out of their seedy lodgings. I had no recourse but to offer them supper and a bed for the night plus money for their dhow and bus from the mainland to Mombasa. It is said that charity is a virtue. I wished I had left them in jail.

That night was a nightmare. Out came the 'joints' where they had been concealed in brassieres, grubby panties and from the lining of baseball caps some affected to wear. Being a staunchly Muslim island drink was always hard to come by and so I served them cokes or fresh lime. When these drinks were finished I gave them beer although I could hardly afford to do so. I kept my one remaining bottle of whisky by my side, explaining that it was all I had and that it had to last me until the end of the month. By the glum, almost hostile looks they gave me they obviously did not believe me. There we all sat on my upstairs verandah, the flower children sucking at their bottles of Tusker, smoking pot and listening to their idiot machines stuck in their ears. Now, I am no intellectual and my most wonderful mother always impressed upon me that it was better to be a good listener than a talker. With only three Europeans on the island at that time I longed for conversation. There was none. They just looked at the lime-washed walls vacantly in a moronic manner as if seeking inspiration. From their passports the Police had handed over to me, I knew that the two girls came from London, one of the youths from Australia and the other two from Sweden. I tried to draw them out. I persisted. In the end I did get a couple of stuttering sentences which invariably finished with that most asinine of English expressions and one which I loathe — 'you know'.

I told them that I didn't know and would they elucidate. A few more nonsensical words. My pet Sykes' monkey I once had at Elephant Camp on the Tana River had more profundity of thought. I gave up and my last precious bottle of whisky suffered. Ashtrays were disregarded, the butts from their bhangi cigarettes thrown on the floor or from the verandah to the street below. I was worried lest any patrolling policeman would get a whiff of the pungent smoke and come to investigate. If this happened then they would be back in prison again and most probably with Her Majesty's Honorary Consul! I called to my servant Mohamed to hurry up supper from the kitchen below. He did so, curry and rice followed by papaya. They ate as though there were no tomorrow. Just before midnight I went to bed, telling Mohamed to keep an eye on them until they finally succumbed to the bhangi.

I wasn't at my best when the soft light of dawn crimsoned the sky, for all through the night the donkeys had excelled themselves with their insane braying just outside my front door. The cats also were in good voice as they fornicated the night away. The Muezzin called the faithful to early morning prayers and this was soon echoed by calls from all over. Moreover nowadays, instead of the lovely clear treble voice of a youngster calling, which was lovely beyond measure, all mosques were fitted with loudspeakers which I found an abomination. This quite horrible cacophony of strident noises, for the donkeys, cats and now cockerels were still at it, would be enough to awaken the long dead. Including my unwelcome guests, too, I thought with some comfort.

Mohamed brought me my early morning tea and said he had taken the guests theirs also. I gave him instructions to hard boil a dozen eggs and to put some bananas into a small kikapu. That would do for their brunch, I thought, for I just couldn't bear their company over the breakfast table. Hastily I shaved, showered and dressed. With Mohamed in attendance I then dug out from their beds my protesting guests. We escorted them to the quayside, saw them on their dhow as I handed over to them their passports, food plus pocket money. I was now feeling quite light-headed. With binoculars slung over my shoulder Mohamed and I had a cup of buni at one of the little coffee houses. He then went back to the house and left me wondering how I would spend the rest of the day.

Feeling a little disgruntled with the sordid evening and angry with myself for so punishing my precious whisky, I wandered to the sea front and sat on one of the cannons. As I say, I was still light-headed and I longed for something to happen to relieve the humdrum monotony of my life here. Anything. Would it be possible, I thought, for those intrepid sailors, the Portuguese, to invade again after some four hundred years? Or perhaps the Omani Arabs? Idly using my binoculars I scanned the channel seawards. I saw a strange ship approaching. It came closer.

From the stern it flew a large, blood-red flag. Good God! I thought not the great red cross billowing out on a white background that the Portuguese galleons flew, but the red flag of the dreaded Omani from Muscat. It came closer and I saw on the prow a great carved falcon. I rubbed my eyes, polished the lens of my binoculars and tried again. Just beneath and behind that most beautifully carved falcon I could now make out her name. In red and gold letters it said 'The Welsh Falcon'. It wasn't a galleon nor a dhow but the most beautiful yacht I had ever seen. So now the Welsh were invading — good for them after all the indignities they had suffered from England over the centuries.

(Many years later from my little cottage perched on coral high above the Indian Ocean at Vipingo, just to the south of Mombasa, I related this story to a couple of most interesting characters. Captain and Mrs Lumsden, both ex-Royal Navy, though in what capacity Mrs. Lumsden served I have quite forgotten. It was just after 4 p.m. and we were having a decorous cup of tea. The Captain, about my age, in his seventies, was a small, blue-eyed, red-faced man. I liked them both. He now looked at me quizzically.

'You must have made a mistake,' he said. 'No ship in these seas would have been allowed to fly a Welsh flag. It must have been the Red Ensign you saw which we Naval types call the Red Duster.'

Now, I know nothing about ships nor naval tradition and so I had to tread warily here. Nevertheless, I insisted that it was a blood-red flag with the crest of a golden falcon. I saw neither the Red Duster nor the Kenya flag, which I suppose it should have flown as well in Kenyan waters. The Captain smiled and said nothing further. He obviously thought that perhaps I had been on the island too long. In this he could have been right.)

I looked again. Down came the anchor. Two jollyboats were lowered full of people and both of these smaller boats too were flying the same flag. All most impressive. They disembarked at the quayside a hundred yards from me. They came my way. Men and women. Mostly Americans I could see but I did recognise one man I knew slightly. He was managing director of one of the big safari firms operating out of Nairobi. He saw me, approached, and the rest of them trooped after him. We shook hands and he made the introductions.

'One of our relics of the Empire,' he said.

'The last of the White Hunters.' I raised my old safari hat and smiled. 'How do you do?' I said. 'Welcome to Lamu Island.'

Two dozen cameras clicked and four dozen eyes looked rather askance at this strange Englishman sitting on top of a cannon.

'Say,' said one of the females. 'How come you are sitting on that cannon? You sure do look cute.' I was feeling better by this time.

'Well Ma'am,' I said. 'As a matter of fact I am a Master Gunner (a lie) and I am the only trained gunlayer on the island (another lie). This being the case, Government have the most extraordinary idea that the Portuguese may invade again. (Here I discoursed on the history of the island and of all the invasions it had suffered in the past). Now. They have given me the job of keeping an eye open. All these cannon, and they are fully primed, are ready for any such event.' I swivelled on the cannon to wave an arm which embraced half-a-dozen layabouts lying in the shade nearby, spitting chewed betel nut juice at scrawny chickens.

'They,' I said, 'are my team. Not much to look at but they will jump to it if I give the order and the occasion calls for it.' There was a roar of laughter.

'Say, honey,' said the same female to her husband, I assumed. 'He sure is cute. Ask him about hunting and all those tiger in the woods. I know you so loved your hunting safaris here.'

After that the questions came fast. Like a machine gun with never a single stoppage. In my old hunting days, ninety per cent of my clients were Americans for they were mad on guns and hunting. After last night it was good to talk to people who showed an interest in something. The sun began to rise higher and they all perched themselves on adjacent cannon and the harbour wall.

'Guns?' one of them asked. It grew hotter. I looked around me. Mohamed evidently having finished his house chores now sat next to them on the sea wall. He understood English and spoke a little. I noticed some of the ladies were getting hot and a little restless. They evidently evinced not the slightest interest in guns or hunting. They wanted to see the town. That is what they had come ashore for. I spoke to their escort making the suggestion that as it was getting hot the ladies might like to look round town. I suggested that they visit the museum which was of considerable interest. Mohamed who was born on the island would be happy to escort them. After that, if they so wished, he could take them to my home which was of considerable antiquity. It also had particularly fine wall carvings and they also might find some of my antiques of interest. After that Mohamed would be pleased to serve them iced drinks. They waxed enthusiastic and thanked me profusely. I gave Mohamed his instructions and off they trooped happily. They were a nice bunch.

I then gestured to a nice shady casuarina tree with two unoccupied benches underneath it. We all sat down companionably.

'Guns?' I queried.

'Yeah,' said the man who had brought up the subject.

'I have a battery of Weatherbys which I used to use out here on my safaris. What do you think to the Weatherby?' Money talks. It did here. I recognised it from the top of his pearly stetson, beautifully tailored safari clothes and hand-tooled boots. But then, they must have all been wealthy or they would not be cruising on that beautiful yacht.

I had nothing to lose and so I smiled and said: 'The Weatherby? It is the most expensive and useless rifle ever made in the States.' There were chortles of amusement at this except from the questioner I liked the look of him for he was good-natured about my disparaging remark.

'How come?' he asked.

'The cartridge carries too much powder and therefore the bullet has far too much velocity; that is for our plains game,' I added.

'Mark you,' I continued. 'I didn't mind them being used in Tanzania, a few miles from Kilimanjaro, for if my client missed the animal he was shooting at, there was always the mountain in the background to stop the bullet.' More laughter and even the questioner gave a wry smile. I continued.

'I have also seen a client who was using a Weatherby place it butt down against a tree and the damned firing mechanism went off. I gave him hell — but he swore it was on safe. I just don't know.'

'The Winchester?' another asked.

'In my opinion the best rifle to come out of the States,' I replied. 'I have one myself and have used it for years. A .375 which I consider the best all-round rifle ever made. Take anything with it.'

'There you are, Wilbur,' cried another, clapping the owner of the Weatherby on the shoulder. 'The Great White Banana has spoken. Now let's ask him about animals. What do you think is the most dangerous?' And so on. I loved it all for we were talking about the life I doted on. The rifles. The animals. The flora. The fauna and the tribes. The sun rose higher.

A smallish bearded man, dressed in grey overalls with serviceable-looking sandals, then rose up from the far bench and came over to me. Obviously he was English. I thought he might be the stoker. He put out his hand.

'We were not really introduced,' he said with a shy, diffident smile and a Welsh accent. 'Thank you for keeping the passengers so interested and it was thoughtful of you to have your servant escort the ladies to the museum, and then to your house for drinks. I am grateful to you. My name is Bailey. Charles Bailey and I own, or rather my father does, the Welsh Falcon. With her sister ship the Welsh Dragon we operate out of Cardiff. This is a sort of trial run in these waters and off the East African coast. Would you care to come aboard and have lunch with us? You seem to be able to keep the passengers happy with your stories and as I am sure you know that is half the battle for they get bored occasionally.'

He raised his voice, looking at his watch.

'Well, gentlemen. I am sure your wives are happy and we will leave one of the jollyboats here for them when they are ready to come back. In the meantime, I have asked this Great White Banana here, as someone rather unkindly called him, to join us for drinks and lunch aboard. I hope I am not rushing you but are you ready for your martinis?' There was a chorus of approval.

Once aboard, the Welsh Falcon was even more impressive than when viewed from the shore. She was spotless. I admired the magnificently carved falcon at close quarters on the prow. Charles took me on a short tour and I was particularly impressed with the wardroom and its heavy mahogany furniture. The whole was a dream. On the deck again some half-a-dozen attractive females, Australian and English I was told, dressed in their skimpy uniforms of red with a falcon crest over the left breast waited in attendance. I was in Paradise. Charles disappeared down below for a few minutes re-appeared followed by a girl with a tray of Bloody Marys. He mixed a mean one.

'You looked as though you could do with one,' he grinned. After that they came up in relays. I told more stories. I was on the wing. Later the wives came back and were enthusiastic about the guided tour Mohamed took them on. They thanked me for the cold drinks at my old Arab house.

We sat down for lunch under an awning forrard. In the golden years, I had lunched at the Savoy, Claridges and the Dorchester and the lunch we had aboard was their equal; as were the wines. I was loath to leave but good manners dictated that I did not overstay my welcome. I thanked them all and told Charles to convey my appreciation to his very own Antonin Careme. He was a surprising man, Charles.

'You mean that French cook who was *tourtier* for a time with the famous Bailly — my French namesake — and afterwards cook to the Prince Regent in London and after that with the Tsar Alexander at St. Petersburg?'

'The very same,' I said. We both smiled. He took me by the arm and said he wanted a word with me in the wardroom. We seated ourselves. One of those lovely girls brought us down a liqueur on a silver salver. We toasted each other.

'Do you want a job?' he asked suddenly. I was quite taken aback. I hedged. 'Most kind of you,' I said, 'but as I am a British citizen as opposed to a Kenyan — even after all these years out here, work permits are very difficult to come by.' However, I was curious.

'What sort of a job?' I enquired tentatively.

'As a lecturer aboard,' he said, 'and work permits do not apply as you would be on the high seas. The passengers like you and you have the knack of keeping them happy. Apart from your knowledge of these parts it may be of interest for you to know that when we up-anchor here we sail north to Mogadishu and Djibouti. You know those countries intimately.' What a wonderful opportunity I thought.

'In that case, yes, and thank you very much,' I said. We shook hands and he said he would be contacting me. I managed to clamber down the rope ladder without disgracing myself and into the jollyboat. That night I slept soundly. The weeks passed and then a month. I heard nothing. Another month — still nothing. I grew bored again and resolved to take a break from the island. I would take the bus called the Disco Dancer from the mainland. Spend a couple of nights at Mombasa Club, thence by the Lunatic Express up to Nairobi and Muthaiga Club. I had many friends here and I told them the story of the Welsh Falcon over drinks.

On my third night there I think it was the Secretary who approached me and asked me if I had read the previous day's copy of the *East African Standard*. I had not. 'There's a copy in the reading room,' he said. I read the article with much sadness.

The Welsh Falcon, whilst at anchor off Djibouti, formerly French Somaliland and known as the country of the Afars and Issas, had caught fire and sank. There were no casualties, I gathered.

The Disco Dancer

There are three ways of escaping from the island as a break from nauseating beach boys, tranvestites, homosexuals, houris and lotus-eaters. Light planes fly every day, or thereabouts, from the airstrip near Makowe on Manda island opposite Lamu, to Malindi, Mombasa or Nairobi.

When the trade winds are favourable, (the south-east monsoon known as the *kusi,* or the north-east monsoon known as the *kaskazi)* one may charter a dhow sailing south to either Malindi or Mombasa, or north, if you so wish, to Kismayu or Mogadishu in the Somali Republic — not to be recommended in the troubled state of that country at present. Flying has been my normal mode of travel. Long-distance dhow travel I consider suitable for the young or the masochistic. The Disco Dancer, though, was a third choice. When Yabollo, an El-Amu acquaintance of mine told me that the Tawakal Bus Company of Lamu had acquired a new coach — The Sweet Coach — rather a misnomer this I thought, with its name painted on the side, Disco Dancer, and the whole daubed in stripes of pink and green and, as though to atone for this violent clash of colour, the rest in modest orange, yellows, and blues, I thought that I simply must make the epic safari from Makowe to Mombasa in this exciting vehicle. I booked a seat just behind the driver. At six o'clock the next morning I was awakened by the raucous cries of the boat touts from the sea front calling up any would-be victims.

'Makowe, Makowe,' they bawled out. By this time my excellent servant, Mohamed, had brought up the early morning tea to the upstairs verandah and was now preparing breakfast below in the dining room. A cup of tea, a quick shave and shower, then dressed in a shirt, shorts and sandals followed by breakfast of an iced papaya with lime, a poached egg on toast with coffee. I left the house in good heart for the jetty. Mohamed followed me with my case over his shoulder. He placed it well forward in the boat as he helped me aboard as I inched my way warily down a flight of sea-swept, slippery and cracked concrete steps. The ancient engine coughs, splutters, then miraculously roars into life. It is packed and you look at your fellow passengers. There are about sixty of them, you assess, plus an apprehensive-looking goat and a couple of dozen unhappy-looking, scrawny fowls. There are traditionally-clad women in their black *buibui*. Only their kohl-fringed eyes showed from the wearing of this voluminous garment. Some were nursing babies. They were all screeching with excitement as they waved their hennaed and bejewelled hands. I also noticed a well-known transvestite homosexual who occasionally puts on belly dancing displays on the island. Probably going to try his luck, I thought, at the night-clubs in Mombasa. A few ancients as well but mostly young El-Amu bloods; many of them armed with noisy transistor radios, also off to taste the fleshpots of Mombasa. There are five other Europeans aboard. Hippy types. The boat sits dangerously low as the *Nakhoda* casts off, then curses as he returns for a semi-hysterical female hippy, beads strewn around her neck and bangles on her ankles who has been taking a long and passionate farewell from her El-Amu boyfriend. She is in tears and blubbers afresh as the *Nakhoda* says a few unkind words to her. We pull her aboard. The boyfriend waves in a nonchalant manner, an insincere sated smile on his face and already wondering what the boat will bring back in the way of female reinforcements. Opposite me sits a little El-Amu boy with a plastic bowl full of samosas on which the flies are already feeding. His rations for the safari, or more likely for sale. Bunches of bananas, kikapus of papaya, mangoes and limes are underfoot. A lilting Welsh voice next but one to me requests a cigarette. I give him one and light it for him. A man of about thirty, dressed in tattered shirt and the usual frayed jeans but, most unusually, sporting a checked cloth cap. A Welshman as I had guessed as I tried to listen to his conversation above the babel. Apparently there is little or no work in England or Wales and so he had been working on oil wells in Australia, of all places. One is always learning, I find, for I never knew there was oil in Australia. On his way out there from London he had flown the cheap way on a Russian Aeroflot plane, spending three days in Moscow which he did not like. He was not impressed by the Russians and thought they led a more miserable existence than the Welsh. He had enjoyed his holiday in Lamu for it was cheap. Well, you meet all types on Lamu, even a detribalised Welshman.

We hit the Makowe jetty with a good healthy thud and there, backed up, is the Disco Dancer in all its garishly-coloured splendour. Two Kenya Police constables armed with automatic rifles keep a watchful eye on things. They are to be our escort evidently, for twice in the last year a bus has been hijacked and shot up by bandits.

The attentive Mohamed places my case on the luggage rack over my head and then, with the help of the driver, forcibly ejects a young Swahili who is occupying my reserved seat. Mohamed wishes me Godspeed, salaams and returns to the boat for Lamu. In the gangway, El-Amu, Arabs, Swahilis and Bantu are pushing, cursing and screaming at each other. Her Majesty's unwanted, unpaid Consul maintains a stiff British upper lip and tries to pretend that the bedlam about him does not exist. Like the boat, the bus is hopelessly overcrowded and one or two hopefuls climb up on top where the heavy luggage is lashed under a tarpaulin, together with the fowls and this and that. I lost sight of the boat. A string bed now goes up as well and Lazarus, the owner, makes sure it is securely tied down before entering himself. Some measure of organisation is now achieved and we all scream good-naturedly at each other with the transistors blaring out their foul music.

From the mainland off Lamu to Mombasa the safari is a long one. Barring accidents, like a blown tyre and ending in a ditch or against a baobab tree or being shot up by bandits, it can take many hours — or even days. I hope that we would arrive in Mombasa safely and hopefully before dark that same day. The driver, a reliable-looking, middle-aged El-Amu impatiently blows the horn of the Disco Dancer and we are off like a panting dragon. We make good time past Makowe Mini Market thence to Makowe village, where we stopped outside a tumble-down, makuti-roofed coffee shop to pick up another couple of victims.

Off we move again with heavy bush on both sides of the road. Dwarfing the bush, the devil had planted hundreds of upside-down trees: these grotesque baobab with giant trunks thrust their root-like branches into the sky. They have always fascinated me. Because there is no timber to be obtained from them most people think they are quite useless. This is not so. Lose yourself in the bush without water and upon spotting a baobab you know that you will be able to survive with the water you may get from the bole. The elephant, of course, know this too and, during the dry season here, particularly in the Tsavo Parks area you may see dozens of trees completely shredded where those wise old pachyderms have tusked their way to get at the fresh reserve of water inside those massive boles. Sometimes, the big mature bulls will tunnel their way through completely and, so, in extremity, this will give you a roof over your head. The rind of the pods hanging down like huge black puddings from the branches may be collected. Cut up, stirred with water and boiled they make a nourishing soup. The kernels roasted and ground are also edible as is the cream of tartar-flavoured tissue in which they are embedded, often used on the coast as fish sauce. The waxy, white flower when chewed allays fever and boiled in water makes a pleasant drink. If you wish to wash the sand out of your hair, the seeds extracted from the pods steeped in water make a most refreshing hair shampoo. Why wait to be rescued? The playful djinn may have laughed when he planted the baobabs but Allah, I think, had the last laugh. The age of these monstrous trees is subject to much conjecture but it can be said with certainty that they may reach a thousand years and possibly more.

In between the baobabs are sometimes to be found the attractive doum palms with their fronds stencilled against the blue of the sky; the massively-bushed mango trees and the slender trunks of the coconut palms. All typical of the forestry in this part of the coastal belt.

A dozen baboons cross the road to our front. One young baboon riding on its mother's back like a miniature jockey, whilst others cling upside down on their mothers' bellies. The Disco Dancer bears down relentlessly on them, scattering all in the bush with their scowling looks and hysterical barks. A line of women with jerricans of water on their heads obtained from a nearby pool plod alongside the road on their way to their village. A herd of waterbuck and topi grazing with their calves in a clearing off the tender green grasses where the long, coarse grass had previously been burnt off. A few more miles further on and I spot a lioness by the side of the road.

'Simba!' I shout and lean over to nudge the Welshman who seemed suitably gratified at being shown game by an old hand. No one else took the slightest notice. Naturally it was only a fleeting glimpse of yellow eyes and bared teeth, for it was no part of the driver's job to stop to view game.

We reach a village called Mkunumbi where we stop to offload a couple of passengers. Now the driver turns left on a narrower road. A deviation this, to hopefully offload passengers for the Mpekatoni Settlement Scheme where the late President, Jomo Kenyatta, settled some 4,000 landless Kikuyu families from upcountry. About 50,000 acres were cut up into small plots where they could grow cotton, maize, simsim, beans, papaya, limes, mangoes, bananas and the like. A German Aid scheme, employing about half a dozen Europeans are doing good work there, initially clearing the bush and pushing through roads and making water available.

It was here that the Disco Dancer almost knocked down a cyclist with the handlebars of his machine festooned with bunches of bananas. As he wobbled unsteadily off the road to safety I noticed that on the back of his T-shirt were the words 'Jesus Loves Me'. It was a close thing and so I thought He probably did. I reflected that just over a hundred years ago all this land we were now traversing was worked by slaves for the wealthy Arabs living on Lamu Island.

After dropping off a few passengers here and there we were soon back on the main road again with the bush on either side now a dull, lifeless grey but enlivened by little green clearings with new grass on which we saw more topi with their attractive coats of a rich, deep rufous with a satin-like sheen and blackish patches on their legs. They must be the most attractive of the hartebeest family with the possible exception of the rare Hunter's hartebeest which are only to be found much further north. Driving away now from the coastal plain with its verdancy fading away as though all colour had been sucked by the relentless sun out of the landscape. Baked hard and white the soil is fractured by deep fissures. Now and then one sees the bones and bleached skulls of some animal.

We reached Witu for a brief stop. Witu is now a broken-down village and had been and still was, the haunt of thieves and brigands. It was not far from here that buses had been shot up and hijacked. During the fifteen minutes we spent here I chatted to a fellow passenger, a young and attractive Kenyan girl who had been collecting shells, beads and so on which she wired together and sold profitably to the tourists. I admired her ingenuity. Another fellow traveller was a Swiss girl with strings of wooden beads around her neck and her hair dressed in blonde plaits. Other hippies were sucking away at their mangoes. Under the watchful eyes of the two armed constables they probably thought it wise not to indulge in smoking their bhangi. As we left I was saddened to see sacks of charcoal stacked on both sides of the road, waiting to be collected by lorry and taken to Mombasa for sale. More desert in the future. We crossed a well-remembered *vlei* from my hunting days. A little water here and some game with saddle-billed storks and lilac-breasted rollers. A few miles ahead I could now see a long line of doum palms which told me that we were approaching the Tana River at Garsen.

I caught my first nostalgic sight of camels and Somali and Orma cattle herds intermingled with sheep and goats. The Somali herdsmen ran from the herds, taking off their turbans and waving them frantically at us for a lift. The Disco Dancer roared on, disdainfully ignoring them. Nearing the river the road was steeply banked, for it is on this stretch, during the rains that the river overflows leaving the road impassable to traffic. Now dried out, the floodwater pans were the home of flocks of white egrets and marabou storks picking up scraps of refuse thrown out by the tribesmen from their temporary huts.

With the aid of an efficient block and tackle attachment we crossed the river, and I remembered nostalgically that in past years it was much more romantic when you were pulled across by sisal ropes to the accompaniment of much stamping of hard, calloused feet and the vigorous blowing of conch shells. On the ferry two little shaven-headed Riverine boys played with their own version of model Disco

Dancers which they had cleverly fashioned out of Cowboy cooking fat tins. A fifteen-minute stop at the small outpost of Garsen village itself with the usual *dukas,* or shops, lining each side of the road on which donkeys, camels, cows, sheep and goats all wilted in the mid-morning heat. Nothing in the way of an alcoholic drink here and so I knocked back a warm Coca Cola, which did little for my morale. The Disco Dancer also had a drink from a plastic bucket of water which was poured down its innards.

On the Malindi road now we flew past the Hola turn-off and once more leaving the river, the country on either side of the road was grey and lifeless with leafless, stunted trees, except for the few candelabra and evergreens relieving the monotony. On through Giriama country. They are a small tribe inhabiting the range of low hills overlooking the fertile belt, which used to be cultivated by slaves of the Swahili and Arabs. The Giriama now live in poor, isolated groups of badly-constructed huts, hidden away and near the Sabaki River. Their women wear a sort of grass kilt and this old tribe in the past were much persecuted by every other tribe they came into contact with. Perhaps it was for this reason that they have bred up a special type of guard dog which is much sought after as a guard and killer of snakes. They are reputed to be the ancestors of the Bisenji dogs which I hear are now shown at Cruft's. There was very little cultivation apparent near the huts we passed and little livestock, but many sacks of charcoal by the roadside and, however reprehensible, the selling of this commodity was probably their only means of livelihood

On through Kongoni village which boasted a mosque and a post office and it was here that we caught a glimpse of the Indian Ocean again on our left. Crossing the Sabaki Creek we now panted into Malindi itself. It was here, hundreds of years previously in the dim past, that the inhabitants of this friendly little village were the first to give that intrepid sailor, Vasco da Gama, aid and a welcome on his voyage to India. Time here for a couple of samosas washed down by a cold Tusker beer. The Disco Dancer was watered again and our driver checked the oil level with the dip stick being wiped clean with a piece of sheep's wool he pulled off the steering wheel, a clever touch, I thought.

One hundred and sixteen kilometres now to go and in gentlemanly fashion, for we had left the dusty murram stretches behind us and for the rest of the safari we were on tarmac. Past Watamu and the Blue Lagoon. Acres of coconut plantations and then Gedi. The ruins of Gedi. The memories came flooding back for I used to visit a lot in my hunting days with clients from the Tana River to the north.

Gedi. Its name means precious in the Galla tongue. A few miles from the sea, it was founded in the late 13th century and flourished until the 17th century when it ceased to be a small city, for it was completely abandoned. Now ruined and deserted, its paths twist among the ruined shells of places and palatial houses. The sunken baths, the mosques, hidden tombs and searing phallic symbols are all that remain of its former magnificence. But the enchanting names remain. The Dated Tomb. The Great Mosque. The Fluted Pillar. The House of the Dhow. The Mosque of the Three Isles. The House of the Cowries. The House of the Ivory Box. The House of the Venetian Bead and so on. And yet in every Garden of Eden there is a serpent and the puff adder — one of our most poisonous snakes — is legend. But, a mere bagatelle compared with more than a legend as to why Gedi was abandoned. Probably I am more sensitive than most, but I do not think so, for many of my hunting clients said they were glad to leave the place with its air of brooding evil and of horrors in the past. It was first said that it was deserted because of pestilence and then lack of water, but this is not so. Then the nightmare story I heard was confirmed by no less than a Professor of History at Nairobi University and a friend of mine.

He said it was on record in the ancient archives that a cannibal tribe from Mozambique — the Zimba — had eaten their way up the coast as far north as Gedi. Here they killed and ate all its inhabitants. Men, women and children. There were no survivors. Gedi had always fascinated me. I dreamed on, drowsy with the heat. My dreams took me 500 miles north of Gedi to the desert country, the Northern Frontier I loved so well. To one of its most northern forts. El Wak. It was here in the late forties that another friend of mine.

'Mad Mac,' a likeable Scot, had built a fort. Working alone, with a couple of African masons, in these lonely desert wastes it had taken him seven years. The fort was a labour of love. A magnificent edifice with walls a foot thick, turrets, look-out towers, gun slits and the like. The Public Works Department boffins in Nairobi said it would collapse after the first heavy rains, but now five decades later it still stands, a picturesque creation to his memory. Mad Mac? After the completion of his fort he had turned Moslem and, of all places, had been posted to Gedi. The lonely years had proved too much for him and living with the martyred ghosts of the past he shot himself there.

I woke up. Civilisation. More mango trees and coconut plantations and here and there a splash of colour from bougainvillaea and flamboyant trees. We passed a gaggle of blue-shirted schoolchildren; the boys wearing pink shorts and the girls pink skirts. Returning to school somewhere from the lunch break. A dense forest reserve now on our right followed by miles and miles of coconut plantations and cashew nut trees. We pant over Kilifi Ferry, with stalls on both sides of the creek selling pineapples, mangoes and bananas but, above all, cashew nuts for they grow in abundance here with the processing factory close by. The coconut and mango trees now give way to sisal plantations. Miles and miles of their orderly rows with formidable sword-like leaves and looking, as I always think, like giant pineapples. As though standing guard over the regiments of pineapples, dotted here and there the giant baobab trees. Takaungu (shades of the Hon Denis Finch Hatton, for it was here he had a tiny cottage), Vipingo and now the old familiar names where, at some stage or another, I had stayed whilst on holiday, but when they were privately owned, and run by retired Kenya settlers where one was always sure of the warmest of welcomes and familiar faces. Shanzu Bay, Bamburi Beach, Whitesands, Ocean View, Coraldene, Mombasa Beach, Nyali and suddenly civilisation. Traffic lights if you please. Get in your lane. The Disco Dancer complies, but somewhat grumpily, I like to imagine.

A little baksheesh discreetly handed over and the driver cheerfully pulls up at the Mombasa Club. Six p.m., I notice. I pat the Disco Dancer affectionately on her flank and thankfully enter for a large whisky and soda, or one or two or more.

The Lust Story

Although I had visited Lamu previously on several occasions in the past, it was not until the seventies that I came here with the idea of making it my home, although scratching beneath the surface here and there I had found many of the inhabitants quite dissolute and the place decadent. However, my marriage had foundered several years before, my livelihood had been abruptly terminated when Government had stopped all hunting, and so I simply had to find an inexpensive place to live. I purchased an old Arab house and on completing the deal wandered into Petley's Inn for a welcome drink.

I suppose you could call me a loner and so I did not particularly want any company, but when I sat down on my own I was soon joined by a beach boy, as is their custom. They are conceited and quite shameless, as I was to find out, and must be amongst the best hustlers in the world.

He was in his early thirties, I would say. Tall, lean, raffish-looking and with a wisp of a beard so that he looked rather like what one would imagine a dissolute Sindbad the Sailor might have looked like. His height was accentuated by the platform shoes he wore. He had on an obviously expensive crimson silk shirt and the usual worn jeans. Round his forehead was tied a red bandanna which he obviously thought gave him a dashing, piratical look. His eyes were bloodshot with smoking bhangi and for his age the lines on his face were etched deeply. He looked dissipated and obviously was, for his profession of a voyeur had aged him. He asked me to buy him a beer. Just like that. No *tafadhali*. No please.

195

No manners. Just an egoistical conceit. He spoke passable English.

I was somewhat taken aback at this shameless approach but for once was quick on the ball for I asked him if he was a Muslim, to which he replied in the affirmative.

'Well then,' I said. 'The Koran states quite clearly that you should not drink anything alcoholic. I will buy you a Coca Cola.' This he accepted with a poor grace. I called over the waiter to order the Coca Cola and a pink gin for myself. I did not wish to appear churlish to one of the locals when I intended to make my home here, but looking at his discontented face realized that I had got off on the wrong foot. However, I did not let this upset me for, as I have said, I did not wish for company in the first place and hoped that when he had finished his coke he would go. Not a bit of it. He chatted away and I soon realized that he was a man of no morals whatsoever. For some twenty minutes he extolled his sexual prowess, which not unnaturally I found nauseating.

These unsavoury characters wait like vultures for the boats or planes to arrive bringing in European women of all nationalities. Some, it has to be said, are past the first bloom of youth and with a slight exaggeration it may be said that they might never see the next rose of summer again. They are, for the most part, desperately looking for sex (for which of course they pay handsomely), thinking that they must make it now for this may well be their last chance in Africa.

With a smug grin my raffish acquaintance admitted that he had done very well during the last season but now that the heavy rains had started his business, as he called it, had now tailed off. I smiled to myself at the simile.

Possibly I'm a little old-fashioned, but tiring of his company I told him what I thought of him and his so-called business and that I did not approve. At this he looked at me in astonishment to remark that he had seen me around for the past week or so and that he took me for an intelligent man for did I not realize what hard work his profession entailed? At this I had to laugh for I had no answer to his query. With tongue in cheek I suppose I could have passed the remark that it was a labour of love.

My laugh must have encouraged him for he then looked at me

speculatively to suggest that I might like to be his boyfriend. Just for the off-season, he added hastily, when he saw the look of disgust on my face. I did not lose my temper for I find that when one is approaching the sere and yellow one tends to become a little more tolerant than hitherto. Besides, it is bad for the blood pressure. I just told him coldly that I was not that way inclined. I suppose I should have left it then but he looked so dejected that I was rather intrigued in spite of myself.

'Why don't you try a worthwhile job?' I asked him. 'Why do you not try your hand at fishing at which so many of the islanders here make a decent living?'

'I am not a Bajun,' he replied contemptuously. I then tried a different tack.

'Well, what about buying yourself a shamba then? You cannot go on for ever in your present profession. You will wear yourself out. With all that money you say you have made and with the dollar cheques coming in from the States, those deutschmarks from German and sterling from England, all from your former clients, surely you can afford one? If not here on the island then on the mainland at Mpekotoni.' He looked at me morosely to say that he was neither a Kikuyu nor a farmer. Moreover he had spent all his money.

By this time I was beginning to lose patience, but I tried one last time for I had just finished reading a book called *A Pilgrimage of Passion,* the life of Wilfred Scawen Blunt, and because of this I thought perhaps I had judged him rather harshly. He obviously had had no advantages in life, with the most elementary of schooling. Wilfred Scawen Blunt on the contrary had come of a fairly wealthy family, had all the advantages of a kind home and good upbringing and had attended one of the better public schools. With all these advantages he admitted quite freely and unashamedly that he had married the Lady Isabella Noel (and what a fascinating, courageous and gifted person she was) for her money and although their marriage had lasted and been a fairly happy one due to his wife's forbearance, he admitted innumerable affairs with others, including some of his wife's closest friends. Then, of course, there was that rascally cocksman, Frank Harris, who in his book *The Loves and Life of Frank Harris,* I think it was called, boasted of his countless affairs.

To go even further. To one who achieved the highest position in the land, Lloyd George. The least one could say about his philandering sex life was that it had not been exemplary. On the subject of immorality one could seemingly go on for ever, so I thought, who was I to judge my acquaintance, Sindbad the Sailor?

Quite involuntarily I asked him if he could write. Indeed he could, Swahili, English and German. He now looked at me with a little animation for I had obviously aroused his interest at last.

'Then write a book,' I said, thinking of Joan and Jackie Collins both of whom had written lurid books on sex unlimited, the titles of which I had quite forgotten. If they could do so then why couldn't this stud sitting beside me? He became quite excited.

'Yes,' he said. 'Yes.' He shook me excitedly by the hand. 'I can describe my visits to Germany. They are all paid for you know, and all my affairs there, for my girl and her friends whom I also service, thought I was the biggest — what you call in English? I forget now ...' Here, he looked almost apologetic for a change.

'Stud,' I replied laconically.

'Stud,' he repeated ecstatically. 'That's it. Stud. I'm probably the biggest stud on the island,' he boasted. He hitched up his crotch to fondle himself as though to re-assure himself that all his necessary equipment was still there. He now threw out his chest and fished in his pocket to produce a slim pen. Probably solid gold, I thought, and a present from one of his admirers. He twiddled it ostentatiously between his fingers. 'What shall I call my book?' he asked eagerly. There was an acquisitive glint in his eyes.

'There is much money in writing and I shall make some to become wealthy and famous,' he babbled on. I did not disillusion him.

'Call it,' I said with tongue in cheek, *'The Last Shaft in Africa.'* He snatched up my packet of Sportsman cigarettes to write the title on the cover. He then helped himself to one and lit up. He looked at me suspiciously.

'Shaft?' he said. 'What is Shaft?'

'Shaft?' I repeated blandly.

'Means an arrow, a sharpened point, or if you like something shaped like a phallic symbol — like the one on the battlements of

Fort Jesus in Mombasa.'

He had seen it and understood. He roared with delighted laughter, stood up with a swagger and left still laughing. He took my cigarettes with him. As I have said, he was quite a hustler.

I have not seen him since. He is probably in Germany writing his best seller. That is, if he does not die at an early age of an overindulgence in sexuality, drugs and stimulants as did the dissolute Sultan Majid of Zanzibar.

The Love Story

After the preceding story which was sordid and depraved, I would like to make amends by writing an Island love story. Now, this immediately poses a problem for I would have liked this to be a happy story but I fear this cannot be, for the only one I know from these parts, like so many historical and star-crossed lovers of the past, is a most unhappy one about an Arabian Princess. It surely must rank with those classics of days long since gone such as Abélard and Héloise, Romeo and Juliet, Paris and Helen and the hauntingly tragical Mayerling affair.

That it did not happen at Lamu is of no consequence. It happened on the larger island of Zanzibar, many miles to the south, in 1858. I make no apology about this for Zanzibar fits in with these tales and its great Sultan at that time, to give him his full title and name: Seyyid Said-bin-Sultan-bin-el-Imam, Ahmed-bin-Said, Sultan of Zanzibar, Imam of Oman; also known as The Lion of Oman, who ruled not only Oman and Zanzibar but the whole of the Lamu archipelago as well.

My story is about one of his daughters. The Seyyida (or Princess) Salme, who married a German, a Foreign Unbeliever, renounced her Muslim faith, was baptised and turned Christian taking the name of Emily Said-Ruete. Unbelievable in itself, and all the more so in that it happened a century-and-a-quarter ago when religious taboos were more rigidly adhered to than nowadays.

It was an aristocratic, leisurely, secure and mainly peaceful life (at least on Zanzibar Island itself) the old Sultan and his family had led before his enforced departure for Oman. His entourage was impressive. One legal, now ailing, wife, the imperious Azze-bint-Seif, the Seyyida, and his innumerable concubines of every shade of colour, from blue-eyed fair Circassians (one of whom was the mother of Salme), handsome brown Galla women to ebony black Abyssinians. The brothers and sisters, the locust-like swarms of half-brothers and sisters, who together with their grandmothers, mothers, uncles, aunts, cousins, nieces and nephews with thousands of slaves to do their instant bidding, occupied the Zanzibar palaces and overflowed into another couple of dozen Royal residences, had all lived in the main happily together under his kindly and benevolent eye.

Salme adored her father; as indeed all of them did. Moreover the foreigners, diplomats, merchants and the sea captains were all impressed by him. When in her teens, Salme described him as the Sultan, the Master, the Father wise and strong, loved and respected, the giver of gifts and protector of all.

Of her brothers, Thuwani the eldest, was stationed in the Oman as Commander of the Sultan's armies there. Khalid had just died, with Majid now appointed Regent in his place pending the Sultan's return and it was Majid who would eventually inherit the Sultanate. Majid. Kind-hearted, easy-going, weak and dissolute. Next came Bargash who had accompanied his father to the Oman. The opposite to Majid for he was fiery, rash, impatient and ambitious for the throne himself. After Khalid's death, the ailing Azze Binte had died during his long absence but before his departure, the Sultan had made provision for this probable eventuality by appointing Chole, his favourite daughter, to take over the authority of all the other women. Chole the beautiful one, older than Salme by a few years and her half-sister. Salme could not remember a time when she had not adored and admired her. To Salme she was a goddess who could do no wrong and in the days of mourning when her mother died not long since past and she had felt alone, it was this older sister she had clung to for support and comfort.

Beit-el-Motoni was her father's favourite palace for it lay beyond the noise, stench and bustle of the town. The entire estate was encircled by a coral wall with the pink flowers of the coral creeper, growing up and above them, sweeping down to the sea. The whole was surrounded by coconut palms, huge shady mango trees, casuarina and cloves, whilst the gardens themselves were a riot of colour. The red, yellow, mauve, orange, purple and gold bourgainvillaea, the exotic frangipani with fragrant wax-like blossoms of white and pink, the flamboyants and always the all-pervading voluptuous scent of jasmine. Here they would play with the kittens, monkeys, tame gazelles, try to catch the strutting peacocks and listen to the cries of the cockatoos and whydah birds. With the lessening of the midday heat they would, suitably veiled and escorted, be allowed out occasionally to ride their father's fiery Arab horses in his private plantations, well away from all the prying eyes of the common folk. Sometimes they would sail the light dhows off the strictly reserved beach in front of the Palace.

Salme recalled a morning long ago at the Motoni Palace when she had escaped from her nurse and had run to see her father without waiting to put on and adjust a jewelled medallion she wore on her forehead. This would have held her twenty plaits together and the jingling gold coins that should have been attached to the end of each one of them. Her father had scolded her for appearing in front of him improperly dressed, and had sent her back in disgrace to her mother.... it was the only time he had ever been angry with her. The only instance of anger that she could remember in all those happy, sunny, carefree days.

The palace itself with latticed windows facing the sea was kept cool by the trade winds. The rooms were filled with clocks, massive camphorwood gilded chests, elegant lacquered beds and divans on which jasmine flowers were spread. Underfoot were the deep-piled Persian carpets of reds and blues and gold. Carved into the lime-washed coral walls were the *vidaka,* hundreds of miniature beautifully-arched or rectangular niches. In them were displayed imported pottery, articles made from gold, silver, brass, bronze, copper and ivory. Friezes were also to be seen, but carved simply since imagery is discouraged by Islam. Their motifs would usually be leaves in a spiral surround, while perhaps a turtle would be carved in the plaster work. Salme, her sister and friends would spend long hours in the sunken baths which were filled daily by the slaves and always those long, languorous days were regulated by the five sessions of prayer as decreed by the Prophet. A settled routine that created a pleasant feeling of safety and permanence. It never occurred to Salme that it would end. But it had.

Sultan Said had never intended to stay away for so long for he loved Zanzibar and was at peace there. But the vexed problem of his native land Oman had held him fast among the barren sands and harsh rocks there. His traditional enemies, the Persians, had defeated his eldest son's armies on land and had scattered the fleet that he himself had taken there to blockade them by sea, and so there had been no alternative for him but to accept the harsh terms the victors had imposed on him. He thought bitterly that his star was on the wane, for years before this defeat he had set out with a large force for nearby Pate Island in the Lamu archipelago, to crush a rising from that most turbulent of islands — but again his forces had been defeated.

Now a broken, humiliated old man, the Lion of Oman had finally turned his fleet of dhows for home. The great dhows sailed out from Muscat, turning their carved and painted prows towards the south. Some weeks later the crew of a fishing boat, casting their nets off the shores of the Seychelles, had sighted the royal ships and, racing before the wind, had taken back the glad news that the Lion of Oman, was returning home.

Then the watching and the waiting and the family quarrels, for with his long absence, the days that had followed his departure had not been happy ones. Lovely Chole had been unable to avoid arousing jealousy and resentment among the less favoured women; quarrels and disagreements had been frequent. Khalid, whilst he had lived, had been over-strict with his new-found authority and had alienated many.

Then it was Majid, dissolute and unheroic, who had done nothing at all to settle any trouble for he just could not be bothered. There were very few on the island who did not pray for Sultan Said's safe return.

When the news came that his dhow had been sighted the palace had been refurbished and a feast prepared. The rich smells of cooking had mingled with the swooning scent of jasmine; the heavy perfumes of musk and sandalwood had drenched the silken garments of the womenfolk. All had laughed and sung as they put on their finest clothes and jewels and with Chole and Salme leading them they had hurried to the gardens of Beit-el-Motoni whilst others stood on the shore, straining their eyes seawards. Waiting ... waiting ... waiting, as though willing the trade winds to fill those huge lateen sails and so hurry them home.

But still no sails were to be seen, and as darkness fell lanterns glowed along the sea-shore and lights glittered on every roof-top and on the balconies of the town houses, as the whole population waited to greet their lord. When dawn broke they were still waiting and watching and then a great shout of joy rose from thousands of throats as at last the triangular lateen sails of the majestic dhows were sighted. For a moment there was a brief, hushed silence when the cries of joy changed terrifyingly to desolate wails of anguish as the fleet drew nearer, when it was seen that from every prow there hung a mourning flag.

Sultan Said, the Lion of Oman, had known that he was never destined to see his spice-scented island again, for in the same hour that the fisherman had sighted the fleet, he had died. His body was already washed and shrouded and after the customary prayers had been said over it, his son Bargash had it enclosed in a coffin made with the planks of wood he had brought over with him from the Oman for that purpose. That night he was buried near the grave of his son, the dead Regent, Khalid. The scheming Bargash, in the usual callous Arab style, now thought of ways and means of dispossessing his elder brother from the Sultanate.

Stricken with grief once more for the father she had so loved, the orphan Salme turned once again to her sister Chole for comfort during those black days of mourning for her father and it was the elder sister, once again, who mothered and petted her, taking her to live with her in her small palace in town — Beit-el-Tani.

The intrigue and the spying now increased in intensity and Salme thought sadly that Bargash had always meant to be Sultan of Zanzibar for he had never had anything but contempt for the weakness of his brother, Majid.

When he had first heard of Khalid's death it may have seemed to him like the beckoning finger of fate as he now thought of ways and means to achieve his ambition. Majid, though, had the advantage of seniority, the Chiefs and the Elders and the British supported him and so Bargash must be content with being heir apparent, but for how long? Of late Salme had been troubled, too, by anxiety and doubt about her beloved sister for she, without doubt, had taken part in this family plotting and scheming and seemed to be letting her emotions overrule her sense of justice.

It had all begun with a quarrel; a trivial difference of opinion between the new Sultan and his beautiful self-willed half-sister over the ownership of a suite of rooms at Beit-el-Motoni which Chole desired for her own. Majid, however, had allocated them to Khalid's widow together with an emerald necklace he had also given her. Chole claimed that this necklace had been left to her in her father's will. Majid had refused to alter his decision over the gift and when he kindly offered Chole a fabulous string of pearls in their place she had thrown them at him. In their father's day such a quarrel would have blown over in a couple of hours. But in the changed atmosphere created by Sultan Said's death, with its legacy of hate, suspicion and jealousy, it had not blown over. What had started as resentment had now turned on Chole's part to a bitter hatred against her once well-beloved brother and she now looked for a weapon to use against him.

She found this in the person of Bargash. Salme was as fond of Majid as Chole had been, until Bargash and this stupid quarrel had come between them. As Chole had now hated him, so too must her friends and partisans of whom Salme had been included. Chole had forced Salme to choose. Herself or Majid and there could be no half measures. The gentle Salme had remonstrated. She had wavered and wept and attempted to avoid a decision, but Chole, much the stronger of the two, had been implacable. In the end she had won and so Said's once happy and united family was now split into opposing factions.

The small white community, mainly British, German and French, in Zanzibar had little or no power to interfere in any family dispute concerning the succession, but they were not without influence, and so Bargash and Chole looked around them for any means that might further their cause. They then decided that they must enlist sympathisers from them. Hitherto, Bargash had always affected to despise the foreigners whilst Chole had refused to meet their women, but now they both started to invite them to their homes for Beit-el-Tani, Chole's small palace, was very near to that owned by Bargash.

At these meetings Salme would watch, listen and smile shyly, envying these women their complete freedom. Chole did not know — no one knew or even suspected — that they were not the only foreigners whom she watched and listened to and smiled at, or who watched and listened and smiled at her! For opposite Beit-el-Tani, and separated only by the narrowest of lanes, was a house owned by Europeans and from her lattice window Salme had watched the gay dinner parties given by Herr Ruete, a blond, handsome young German who worked for a firm of Hamburg merchants and whose unshielded window faced hers. She was aware that he would have caught an occasional glimpse of her, for once the lamps were lit in Beit-el-Tani, the delicate carvings of the lattice shutters made it easy enough for a watcher to see into the rooms they were designed to conceal. But it was only when he took to coming to his window to bow and smile whilst she peeped at him through her lattice did Salme realize that young Wilhelm Ruete must have indeed seen her, was interested in her and wanted to meet her.

Once he had leaned over from his balcony to toss a rose across the lane dividing them. It was so short a distance that he had been able to throw it accurately so that it fell at her feet. For the unhappy Salme this was balm to her. Eagerly she picked it up to discover there was a piece of paper tied to its stem. On this he had written in Arabic a verse from a song that she herself had sung to the strains of a mandolin and which he must have listened to ...

Visit those you love, though your abode be distant
And clouds of darkness have arisen between you
For nothing should restrain a friend
From visiting the friend he loves

Tenderly she had put the rose in water and when it wilted at last she had collected the fallen petals, and carefully drying them, had hidden them in the bottom of her jewel case. To her they had become a talisman against fear of the future, and sometimes when the fever of hate and intrigue that infected the very air of Chole's little palace became more than she could bear, she would take the faded petals from their hiding place to hold them pressed against her cheek, thinking of such things as love and peace and happiness, and of a young man's openly admiring eyes and smiling face. Slowly her thoughts grew. Anything, but anything, would be preferable to living in the poisoned atmosphere of the members of her family. She thought she was different from the Arabs of the Oman who loved violence, cruelty and cunning and yet, too, she was of the same blood. She put this down to the gentleness of her sweet-tempered Circassian mother whose blood would have seemed to have outweighed the fiery strain of her father's line.

Came the day finally when Bargash decided that he was sufficiently strong to come out in open revolt against his brother in his bid for the throne. However, he had badly miscalculated the latter's strong following and the aid he was to receive from the British. He, with his motley followers of freed slaves, petty criminals and El Harth tribesmen was defeated. At a packed Durbar, Majid, kindly and weak as ever, did not have his brother executed to the surprise and disgust of his followers. He merely ordered him to be deported. After taking an emotional and tearful farewell of his sisters he left shortly afterwards on a British warship for India. Here he would bide his time, for he knew that fate had decreed that he would inherit the title.

Now the aftermath had to be faced. Chole and Salme were pardoned by their tolerant brother but at the same time were ostracised for plotting and aiding and abetting the exiled Bargash. By now their riches had been dissipated and many of their slaves whom they had armed and sent to support Bargash had been killed or wounded in the fighting. Their friends avoided them and even the merchants of the town would no longer call at Beit-el-Tani except under cover of darkness.

'It is all over,' Chole had wept. 'Everything is finished. It is the end.' For her this was undeniably true. But for Salme it was to prove another beginning. Fraught with danger, yet a chance of love and happiness, once more she had the leisure hours to steal up to the roof-top after sundown. Not to mourn for Bargash and the ruin of their hopes as Chole was doing, but to watch a young man from Hamburg entertain his friends in a lamp-lit room on the other side of the lane.

Visit those you love, though your abode be distant.
And clouds and darkness have arisen between you.

No man of her own race would say such words to her now, for what Arab of rank would wish to marry a woman who had been concerned in the rebellion against her brother; who was no longer rich nor received by her own relations? The clouds and darkness had indeed fallen on her and, Salme, who was young, sad and very lonely, watched Wilhelm Ruete and dreamed her secret impossible dreams of love and hope. The ladies of the European colony felt sorry for her and were only too happy to visit her when she had made her wishes known. She began to learn to speak English and German.

Putting all taboos and conventions behind her she had started to converse with Wilhelm which led inevitably to clandestine meetings and to them falling in love and consuming that love. It was natural that her European friends had been taken into her confidence and they were only too eager to foster this romantic love affair and to help the young lovers to escape.

A few days later a way was found. Wilhelm had left by himself on a German boat. A British warship had then put in the harbour and Salme took advantage of a Holy Day to go down to the sea with her maid, to make the ritual ablutions proper to the occasion. By secret prior arrangement she was then seized, together with her hysterical maid, and both were bundled aboard by two grinning English matelots. Nelson would have approved. Immediately the ship sailed for Aden where her lover awaited her. They were married and she was baptised a Christian, taking the name of Emily Said-Ruete.

The town did not take it kindly. Anti-European feeling was so high that it was dangerous for a white face to be seen in the streets and a furious mob of Arabs milled around the German Consulate, shouting insults and demanding vengeance.

From Aden the happy couple then embarked on a German boat for Hamburg, and it was there that her first child was born. For a time the young mother was all the rage in German society and was made much of at the Prussian court. The Germans, always eager to extend their influence in Africa, were at that time competing with the British for possessions there and they believed that in this Arab princess they held an ace which, if dealt at the right moment, would defeat the hands of their rivals.

Sadly Salme's brief period of happiness did not last long. After only three years of marriage her husband was unheroically killed in a traffic accident. This left her alone in an alien country with three small children.

The years sped by and on Zanzibar Island, Majid's death at the early age of 36 — due to an excess of sex, sensuality, stimulants and drugs, now made way for the exile, his brother Bargash, to return as Sultan. At last his ambition was realised. By this time the Germans had seized much of the new Sultan's lands on the hinterland and were now ambitious to seize Zanzibar itself so deposing Bargash and his Al Busaid dynasty. To this end they did all they could to provoke Bargash who, as we already know, was a much tougher, character than the deceased weak and pathetic Majid.

Bargash had decided in his calculating way to throw in his lot with the British as his father had done years before and it speaks much for his now, rather surprisngly, mature character that he had a good understanding and working relationship with that very able British Consul — Sir John Kirk. With Kirk advising him he would not be drawn.

As a last throw of the cards the Germans now decided to play their ace in the person of poor Emily Said-Ruette, the former Princess Salme, persuading her to return to Zanzibar. They told her that she might intercede on their behalf with her brother and that her safety would be assured, for by now she was a German subject. In their hearts, and more to the point, from the reports they had from their espionage agents, they knew that the Sultan would never listen to her — mainly because of her heinous crime, in his implacable eyes, in turning Christian and marrying a foreigner. An unbeliever. Nevertheless, their hope was that her presence on the island would end up by irritating him to such a degree that he would have her arrested or even killed. They would then be justified, they reasoned, by declaring war on Zanzibar and killing or imprisoning Bargash.

The Princess arrived in Zanzibar on a German ship and she went ashore to Beit-el-Tani, now sadly bereft of most of the servants and the old faces she remembered so well. Her sister Chole had disappeared and so she could seek no comfort there as she had done so many times in the past. From the palace she sent out messages to her brother, Sultan Bargash, all of which remained unanswered. It was a sad pilgrimage for the widowed princess. Nostalgically she wandered round her old haunts, shunned by most and barely acknowledged by others. Pathetically she still hoped against hope that her brother would see her and so she could warn him against the British and to put his trust in her friends, the Germans. Just as the Germans had hoped, his sister's presence and her constant letters to him caused the implacable Bargash much anger. But they waited in vain for him to lay hands on her. Coached by the British Consul Kirk, who had easily seen through the German planning, Bargash did nothing at all, curbing for once his fiery nature which he replaced with oriental patience and this, with Kirk's good sense, completely baffled them.

At last the Princess, with more pride and dignity than the Germans had shown, withdrew on her own accord from a position which had become intolerable and too unhappy for her to bear. Saying a poignant farewell for the last time to the beautiful and beloved island where she had known so much pleasure and pain, she returned to Germany where she died in 1924, a still lonely and forgotten old lady.

The Baluchi Girl

During the Great Sultan Seyyid Said bin Sultan's benign rule over Zanzibar in the 17th century, in order to keep law and order and to stop his continually warring Arab satellites from attacking each other in his far-flung dependencies to the north — Lamu, Pate and other countless islands — he enlisted Baluchi mercenaries from Baluchistan.

To this day a small family of them live on Lamu island; moreover they reside just opposite my own house. The streets of Lamu are extremely narrow and from my roof-top balcony it is easy to converse with my neighbours opposite.

When I first noticed her she would be about fourteen years old, I judged. She had two elder sisters, two brothers, cheerful smiling little men, and her parents. At that early age she was mature and was an outstanding beauty. An oval, heart-shaped face, flawless skin, almond-shaped eyes and her mouth was a delight. She had long black hair which was sometimes braided but mostly allowed to cascade loose to her waist. Often she would wear a small blossom of jasmine or frangipani behind one ear. Whichever flowers she wore I loved the heavy, scented perfume I caught as it wafted from her balcony to mine. As she would lean over her roof-top balcony, I only ever saw her head and shoulders for being in strict purdah she was never allowed out of the house. She did not affect the traditional dress of the El-Amu females by wearing a black *buibui*, a flowing garment from head to toe allowing just the eyes to show, but wore a bodice, I suppose one might call it, and so her facial beauty, neck and shoulders would be revealed in all her young innocence.

Because of this strict purdah she was painfully shy and so for months we would just smile at each other but after a while, when accompanied on the balcony by her elder married sisters, we would pass the time of day and converse a little in Swahili.

212

One day I was having tea and I invited the three of them over from their balcony to mine. I should have known better, for the invitation was greeted with shock and the most emphatic refusal, as with cries of dismay they fled their balcony to the lower part of their house. After this gaffe I was more decorous but it was months before they would speak to me again. During my periodic visits to England I would bring back with me a few small boxes of expensive chocolates and sweets, a commodity quite unobtainable in Lamu or, for that matter, Mombasa.

Opening the boxes I would throw over the loose goodies to them. Such a scrambling, like three exotic birds as they rushed from the balcony to collect them around their feet. They would then return to eat them and I would be rewarded by their shining eyes, cries of delight and gracious thanks.

Then came her marriage day and by then I suppose she would be about eighteen. The groom came from Mombasa. The festivities

went on for days. I could hear the music and the laughter but could not see anything.

On the last day of the celebrations, at supper time my servant Mohamed served me with a large, ornate dish covered with a dainty Muslim cloth under which was a Baluchi pilau. It was the most delicious I have ever tasted. Mohamed told me that it was a gift from the bride. I felt a childish delight in that I had not been forgotten. I never saw her again.

The Freelanders

The first invaders of Lamu Island were probably the Syrians in about AD 639. They were then followed by the Arabs and Persians. Long after this came the Age of Discovery when Prince Henry the Navigator concentrated all his seafaring activities on Africa. His Portuguese *conquistadores,* steel-clad, rapacious and determined on conquest first arrived on the scene in 1496 and stayed for some 225 years. In 1798 a British Squadron visited the islands in an endeavour to counteract the operations of Napoleon Bonaparte in his effort to conquer the world. At one time there was a French agent in Lamu, ostensibly dealing in slaves. In 1875 Lamu was visited by yet another invader, Ishmael the Khedive of Egypt, but this incursion lasted less than a year. In 1885, the scramble between the European nations for the partitioning among them of Africa was well on its way, with the Germans and British at one time both occupying Lamu and the archipelago, with the British outlasting the Germans and staying until 1963 when Kenya achieved Uhuru.

It was long before Uhuru however, that Lamu was invaded by what I like to call the first of the hippies; except the present day hippies by no means achieved the decadent notoriety of their predecessors who arrived in 1895. In fact their behaviour is decorous in comparison.

So it came about, therefore, that Lamu was suggested as the capital of a socialistic state and that the British Government of the day misguidedly agreed to the idea. An association was set up composed of Europeans of various nationalities, and their state would henceforth be known as Freeland. The leader of the expedition was an Austrian, a Doctor Wilhelm and the project sought to colonise the lands behind the islands of Lamu, Pate and Siu. First they explored the Tana River area but they found it too dangerous, because the lion there were far more aggressive than the ones down-country and the mosquitoes equally ferocious and aggressive. So they decided on Lamu.

It is curious to note that the British Foreign Secretary at that time, Lord Kimberley, instructed the political agent, Arthur Hardinge, to place no obstacles in the way of these would-be colonists who wished to create this Eden east of Suez.

The arrival of their ship in the *mkanda,* the channel of sea which separates Lamu from Manda Island, must have been quite an event. They were a curious bunch of freakish crackpots with advanced political ideas.

Many of them were decidedly eccentric. Their idea of Freeland seemed to be a State in which every individual should not only be absolutely equal but should also do whatever he or she deemed right in their own eyes; which is probably why one of them stepped ashore to declare herself Queen of Lamu. They hired a house on the sea front — which still exists. They called it Freeland House.

Doctor Wilhelm, the nominal Chief of the strange expedition had no real control over the others nor had they any organised plan for what was to be done in their new Utopia. Among the members were three men of some consequence. A Mr Scanenius, the son of a Danish Cabinet Minister; Captain Dugmore, a British Army officer and a surveyor named Glucksellis, an Austro-Hungarian. These latter two persons seemed to be a cut above the others, as we shall learn later.

At this point it is necessary to mention some of the curious habits of the Freelanders. Almost to a man and a woman (with the possible exception of Captain Dugmore and Glucksellis), they were tosspots. Their Lamu headquarters was no less than a Gin Palace and under the influence of gin and possibly any of the local brew, like palm wine, they could lay their hands on, this groggy Band of Hope proposed to one another, and the local populace, their visions of the ideal state in which everything would be literally free. Free grog (or wompo as I call it). Free houses. Freedom from work. Freedom from laws — and Free love. Soon Lamu became a hotbed of scandal, for here they roistered, appalling and angering the local people by their prodigious consumption of alcohol and, possibly a far more commendable feat, by their loose morals. However, heat, grog, the lotus-eating life and above all sexual excesses were wearing them out and soon they found that everything was not as free as they had hoped for by this time they had run out of money and wanted to return home.

The long-suffering people of Lamu could not have learned anything from them to modify their contempt for western culture which had been aroused centuries ago by the Portuguese.

When Hardinge asked Dr Wilhelm why they came to British territory in the first place and had not chosen to go next door to the genial soil of German East Africa, he replied: 'God forbid! and put ourselves under the heel of the brutal German Junkers?'

Evidently he had a point there for when Baron Von Scheele, the German Governor heard of this he said to Hardinge, 'Let the depraved Socialist scoundrels land here and I'll put them in a chain gang!'

Finally the long-suffering British Government paid the Freelanders their fares back home from whence they had come.

The only two men to stay were Captain Dugmore and Glucksellis. They fought for the British against the Arabs in 1895 and later served in Uganda during the mutiny there. Dugmore's last post was as a District Officer in Masailand where he fell ill. He later died in Mombasa. I do not know what happened to Glucksellis.

The Ngoloko

As an old white hunter this, understandably, is my favourite story of Lamu Island. One day, during the long rains, April, I think, it was and most certainly a Friday, the Muslim Sunday, I was having supper at the Yoghurt Inn, my favourite El-Amu restaurant. It was Mohamed's day off and I didn't feel like cooking for myself. Because of the rains there were few visitors on the island and apart from me there were only two other guests at the modest little eating house. They were both locals. One of them caught my eye. Bent and crippled with age, sunken cheeks, milky-rheumy eyes, for he was obviously suffering from ophthalmia as do so many of them here. He was sitting in a corner dreaming away over a small cup of buni — coffee. From his dress I could see he was obviously poor — a *masikini*. I walked over to him, introduced myself and asked if he would like a plate of curried chicken with me. He was hungry and accepted gladly. He moved over on the bench seat to make room for me. His name, unsurprisingly, was Mohamed.

After the meal and the usual belches of appreciation, we chatted away over more buni, exchanging yarns of the bush and for some time I saw him fairly regularly after this.

One of his stories of the *Ngoloko,* also called the *Milhoi,* a mystery of the African bush which happened before the First World War, both intrigued and amused me. He could not remember the name of the European concerned, or what he did at Lamu and for this I could not blame him, for it happened so long ago and my narrator himself must have been in his eighties. He called him the Young Bwana. Anyway, after innumerable cups of buni and by exercising lots of patience as the old man rambled on, I elicited from him the following story. We will let the Young Bwana tell it as I would imagine in his own words as the ancient related them to me.

The day's march is finished, the camp pitched and the

Headman and the Elders of the locality have come and gone. The setting sun lights up the lagoon behind us whilst in the distance the white crests of waves break upon the coral reefs that guard the lonely shore. To my right, on the edge of a red, sandy cliff and almost hidden by grotesque baobab trees and mangrove swamps stands the ruin of an ancient Arab mosque. As eerie a scene as will ever be witnessed. The fast falling night soon eradicates the landscape and it is now time for a sundowner or two, a bath and to drape a kikoi around one. After dinner and a few more sundowners (I gathered from Mohamed that the Young Bwana liked to tipple) and so to bed.

Once more it is morning but the tide is out and we have a frustrating delay of several hours before the safari can embark in two small dhows I have hired for our use. As I walk down to the larger, a black snake slithers across the path.

'A bad omen, Bwana,' says one of the bearers. 'We had best turn back and go another day.' To which I reply:

'Such supersitions are only applicable to you El-Amu and not to me.' This incident is quickly forgotten. The dhows were launched and once we reached the mainland a short march follows and camp is pitched on a knoll from which a good view can be had over a small plain and the more distant bush country beyond. The day passes without anything of special notice but it so happens that there is to be an eclipse of the moon, so instead of turning in at the ordinary time I draw up my chair to the camp-fire to watch the phenomenon. I then pour myself out another sundowner. A dozen Africans are already sitting round the fire, too, roasting mealie cobs and eating them. I quietly smoke my pipe and listen to what they are saying. It is about nothing in particular, but as the shadow gradually sweeps over the face of the moon, one man says that such things are uncanny. They all agree. They talk of the fish recently caught off the island with words of the Koran naturally marked on it; also of a child lately born at Mombasa with three legs, two faces and four eyes. Then someone mentions the black snake seen that morning. What did that portend? Another boy, Asmani, now speaks.

'And did we not start this safari on the fifth day of the week? (according to the Swahili calendar, Friday is equivalent to our Sunday and Saturday is called Jumamosi, or first day; consequently Wednesday is Jumatano, or fifth day and so on) and as the Swahili proverb says "Rats that leave their holes on a Wednesday never return!" '

'True,' says one Juma, 'and when the moon hides her face 'tis a bad time for the children of Adam. We heard the spirits in the baobab trees as we passed beneath them. They knew what was about to happen.'

'To happen to the moon or us?' asks another.

'Who can tell?' continues Juma, 'but when spirits walk abroad 'tis well to be indoors. However, we are all in the hands of Allah.'

It is now just on midnight, the eclipse is full and I am on the point of going to bed when — 'Boom!' We all lift our heads for the sound, though distant, is clear and penetrating.

'What is that?' I ask. No one answers. Then another 'Boom' followed by a series of 'Booms'. Nearer this time and with a note in it that sets one's hair on end.

'What is that?' I repeat more peremptorily.

'The Ngoloko!' whispers someone. A couple of extra logs are thrown on the fire and all close in.

'What is the Ngoloko?'

'Djinn,' replied Mohamed.

'Nonsense,' I protest. 'You are all going daft. You had better go to bed as I am.'

'I am not going to sleep whilst a Ngoloko is about,' says Asmani.

'Nor I,' join in the others.

'Well then, in that case, let us hear about this devil. What do you know, for instance?'

'I know what I have been told and no more. Originally

the Ngoloko was a good spirit and lived with all the others in friendliness and happiness, but one day it did something wrong. It was then chased away and taken up to Heaven. After a while it was driven down again by shooting stars and appeared on earth as a Ngoloko to be shunned by all. That is why the creature lives an isolated life and is seldom met with. When it lies down it sweeps a place clean; it feeds on honey and drinks blood; herds the buffalos and drinks their milk or kills and eats them as it thinks fit. It smells worse than a lion and anyone who has skinned the latter is not likely to forget what it is like. It will change its form so as to enable it to approach its victim and will speak any language under the sun.'

'That reminds me of the Roch in the book of El Bochari,' breaks in Seif Bin Mohamed. 'There we learned that once a wicked people climbed on each others' shoulders until the topmost one put his ear to the roof of the sky to listen to the words of Almighty God who, becoming very angry, told his servants to cast out the intruders. Then the wicked people were bombarded with fire, brimstone and shooting stars until all fell down. The survivors, many blinded, returned to the earth in the shape of the Roch or Ngoloko, destined to live ever after in desolate places.'

'That is all very well,' I interpose, 'but has anyone ever SEEN the Ngoloko?'

Achmed bin Abubaker then began as follows: 'One day, about seven or eight months ago, I went to Mambrui from Malindi, as I often do. I crossed the Sabaki river by the ferry and pursued my way along the sea shore. It was mid-day and very hot. Suddenly I noticed a great figure, human, it appeared, and about eight foot high, standing near a beacon on my left. The giant came towards me and as he did so he changed his form to appear like that of an ordinary man. When he got about fifty paces off he called out to me, 'Achmed bin Abubaker, my dear brother, stop a minute — do.' I stopped. Then I saw that he kept one arm hidden behind his back and that the hand of the other terminated in a great hook. He was clothed and had a gourd slung close under an arm. His hair was of reddish-yellow colour which fell back from his head in a wild tangle as far as his waist. His own colour was that of an ordinary man. His face was that of a human being but very flattish and broad. He had a large thumb on each foot. When I saw this terrible thing advancing on me with a springy walk I thought my last day had come. I covered my eyes in terror and called out

Allahu Akbaru, Allahu Akbaru,
Allahu Akbaru Allahu Akbaru,
Ashah adu Anlaa Ilaha, Illa Illahu
Ashehadu Anlaa Ilaha Illa Illahu,
Ashedadu Anna Muhammada Rasula Illah i
Ashedadu Anna Muhammada Rasula Illah i
Haiya Allah Swalaat
Haiya Allah Swalaat
Hiya Allah Lifalaah,
Hiya Allah Lifalaah
Allah u Akbaru Allah u Akbaru
Allah Akbaru. Allahu Akbaru
La Allah illa Allah

When he heard the translation of the Athani, he knew he was overpowered for he turned aside and went back to a hill. As soon as the way was clear I ran off as fast as I could and after getting to what I thought was a safe distance, looked back. There he was, still climbing up the hill, and as he got near the top he took to his original form and finally crossed over the summit and was lost to sight.'

'Was it male or female?' I enquire.

'I don't know; neither do I care but it was unnatural. As it had long hair and showed remarkable cunning, it must undoubtedly have been a She Devil; but no self-respecting Ngoloko could possibly stand a prayer like that.'

After a short break, Hamis wa Ishmael, who had just joined our group round the fire, starts to relate an adventure of his own. 'It was,' he said, 'about sixteen years ago that I went one day with a Swahili carpenter to cut some wood in a mangrove forest near the Tana river. We came upon a medium-sized marsh bare of trees; we had not been there long before my friend signalled me to keep back as if something were coming. I looked to see a Milhoi or Ngoloko crossing the marsh from the other side. He came up to about six paces from the carpenter and began conversing with him, asking him all about the people in his village by name. It had a shuka or scarf round its neck and partially over the head. I saw the creature had three fingers, one armed with a claw. It also had a gourd under its arm. One eye was blind, the other all askew. There was a certain amount of hair on the cheeks. It had three toes and a thumb and big flapping ears. Its skin was of a grey colour but covered with long, sparse, black hairs. It had no tail. A Galla shuka was the only garment it wore. It was about eight feet high but not very broad. Its arms and legs were thin. I said "I know you to be a Ngoloko," upon hearing which it promptly fled, uttering piercing shrieks and holding up the shuka in its outstretched arms.'

'This is beginning to get interesting,' I remark. 'Can anyone tell me something more?' And, with a little persuasion, for an African is very shy of speaking of a Djinn, Mohamed wa Njamhidi, commented as follows:

'I have been a fisherman all my life and live at Shela where the following occurrence took place but over the *mkanda* on Manda Island. It must have been about twenty years ago when I was not bent and crippled with age as you find me now. I had two fully grown up children. One day I went into the bush to cut wood, leaving them on the sea shore doing something or other to the canoes. After a while they ran up and said, "Did you call, father?" I told them I had not. Then I asked them from what direction they had been hailed. They pointed. They also said they had been called by name. I returned with them to the shore and looked very carefully in the direction indicated. Then

I saw a very tall man standing in the bush. I could see one arm and the hand ended in a hook; the other one was held crosswise and buried in the shaggy chest. I knew at once that it was a Ngoloko and I quickly ran away with the children before he could catch sight of us.'

As I now look back to that night I must confess that it was with a distinctly creepy feeling that after a few more sundowners, I finally turned in. However, rest, breakfast and a bright sun the next morning made any qualms I had entertained the night before look nothing less than absurd. I hunted that day some eight or nine miles away with no luck and on my way back to camp I left the track I had been following and, in spite of the midday heat, struck off after some game I had spotted. By this time I was not much more than half a mile from camp and was crossing one of the bare patches of sand when I came across a spoor such as I had never seen to that day. My boys noticed it too and we all stood looking at it for some little time.

'What has passed here?' I enquired at length.

'The Ngoloko!'

'How old is this spoor?'

'About twelve hours.' Others agreed.

'Twelve hours! Then it was just about the time we heard that booming, grunting noise!'

'Yes, Bwana. We told you it was the Ngoloko and you would not believe us; now you know how it was that we did not sleep.' And I did for the tracks were indisputable; and they were the tracks of a creature I would not dare to meet without a loaded rifle at hand. A reproduction of the footprint was taken on the spot by placing a piece of paper over the track and marking the outline with a pencil. In ordinary soil this would have not been possible; but here, on the crusted sand, conditions were ideal. We followed the spoor for a quarter of a mile, examining, measuring and comparing it with human tracks. As a result of my observations I obtained the following data:

(a) The animal is a biped.

(b) The print had been made by a pad and not a hoof, except that at the point a deep and sharp hole demonstrated the presence of a large nail or claw.

(c) A thumb-mark of considerable dimensions was a special feature; there was no trace of toes, except in one case where very slight indentations by such seemed to have been made.

(d) A heel was observed, but the weight of the animal was usually cast forward on the main portion of the foot and thumb.

(e) Its weight was judged to be at least twice that of a man and probably more.

(f) A certain part of the spoor showed the animal to be walking very slowly on two feet; there the stride measured eighteen inches from tip of the toe of one foot to the heel of the other. It had also taken several gambols at one place and crossed its legs when doing so. When travelling at what I should imagine to be a jog trot, the stride measured eight feet. Two strides were found to be nine feet.

The above facts seemed to be of such interest that I determined to push my investigations further and to my great good luck came upon one, Heri wa Mambruko, whose story I give as far as possible in his own words. It should be remembered however, that the actual details he furnished, are the result of direct questioning. Also it should be added that he never seemed to hesitate, being quite certain and clear in his answers. He spoke as follows:

'A long time ago I went out with some Swahili friends into the forest to tap the wild rubber tree. It was in the Witu District on the mainland and not too far from Lamu. A Mboni man (a type of bushman) accompanied me. We were at a short distance apart busy at work when the Mboni caught sight of a Ngoloko stalking us from behind. He let drive with his bow and arrow and hit the creature who immediately ran off. We followed and found the Ngoloko about five hundred yards from the place where he had been hit. When I came up he was lying outstretched on the ground and still breathing. It was a male, about eight feet in height and in breadth just about the same as two ordinary men standing together. He was covered in a great mass of long, thick grey hair. It was especially long over the head and upper portions of the body — a single hair being quite a yard in length. He was built like a man but was no child of Adam. He had but one finger and one thumb on his hand, the former terminating in a single hooked claw, two and a half to three inches long. The foot possessed a very large prehensile thumb and three toes. The face was hairless, displaying a dark skin. Nose very prominent with two nostrils. The mouth was small but larger than a man's, and the teeth were big. His ears resembled those of an elephant and each were the size of my two hands fully extended when holding the wrists together. The cheek bones were prominent. Forehead low and retreating like a leopard's. Chin likewise. I did not notice the colour of his eyes which were big. The eyelashes joined on to the hair round about the face. I did not look at them particularly. The smell was awful and about ten times as strong as a he-goat.'

The foregoing statements, together with the evidence afforded by the examination of the spoor, lead to the conclusion that there exists in the district referred to a remarkable and monstrous creature hitherto unknown. The species to which it belongs, its habits and general appearance, can only be conjectured for the difficulty of obtaining reliable evidence from those who have seen this terrifying beast is much increased by the atmosphere of the supernatural surrounding it, and the more we investigate the more difficult does it become to distinguish between fact and fiction.

The statement of the man, Heri wa Mabruko, is more reliable than those of the others. Who indeed would not be able to give a more accurate and detailed account of a dead than a live Ngoloko? We may then, attach fairly considerable weight to his observations. He mentions the Ngoloko as being eight feet in height. This is corroborated by two other observers on two distinct occasions, while a third observed on another occasion that the Ngoroko he saw was 'very tall'. We may therefore be fairly confident that the height of the animal is much as stated. I ought, however, to remark, that in certain instances, proximity reduced its apparent stature — a fact which may perhaps have been due to the animal having adopted a crouching attitude when approaching its prey. Its breadth is not authenticated with such certainty. That its weight is considerable we know from the tracks.

Heri wa Mabruko mentioned the presence on the hand of a single claw and of a thumb, both of which particulars are referred to by other observers. He also mentions the presence of a very large thumb on the foot; the accuracy of his observations is confirmed by the spoor. His statement as to the ears being like those of an elephant is confirmed by Hamis wa Ishmael. His observations regarding the mass of hair about the head and upper part of the body is only indirectly confirmed. Ali Bin Nasur speaks of loose, dark clothes and conceivably he might at night have taken the mass of hair for such. Achmed bin Abubaker mentions a wild tangle of hair falling back as far as the waist. Yet another observer talks of a shuka, or scarf, an optical illusion possibly due to the excitement of the moment. Its colour is generally described as grey but the skin itself is dark.

We may conclude then, that the Ngoloko or Milhoi, is probably a variety of gorilla or chimpanzee, but more of a pure biped then either. That it is about eight foot in height and has a mass of grey hair which is especially long about the head and upper body, elephantine ears, a retreating forehead and chin, large eyes, a single claw two to three inches long on hands and feet as well as a prehensile thumb also on both hands and feet — and of a remarkable size and strength. Such is the Ngoloko or Milhoi as we can fairly reasonably picture him. A carnivorous denizen of the forest and mangrove swamps. A big and hideous brute, which one would, if alone and unarmed, have no particular ambition to meet.' End of story.

Well! Well! In my summing-up of this quite amusing imaginative story, I am taking into account that it took place about 1917. What we do know is that no variety of gorilla or chimpanzee has ever existed in Kenya and neither species is to be found here to this day. It is not a question that they may have been poached out. Kenya is not, and never has been, their habitat. It is not my wish to be unkind in my criticism of the story nor unduly harsh on the teller, but it is a pity that we do not know in what capacity he made his safari. That he was no hunter we do know or he would have followed up the spoor to the end for a sighting of the 'animal' itself. Was he an administrative officer? If so he must have been a very naive and inexperienced one to have been taken in by such lying stories (amusing nevertheless). I am inclined to think that he was not employed in any Government Department but decided on a personal safari, probably paying his 'Forty Thieves' exorbitant sums of money daily who would themselves wish to protract the safari as long as possible to this gullible *mzungu* whom providence dropped in their laps. Perhaps the kindest thing one may say that his sundowners lasted well into the night and that his retainers were floating on clouds of bhangi, or chewing miraa or possibly both, which has been the custom here since time immemorial. Both drugs, as we know, heighten the imagination and cause hallucinations and if taken in any quantity·over the years may cause brain damage.

The story of course bears some resemblance to that of the Nandi Bear in the Highlands of Kenya. Another myth for this most fearsome creature was probably mistaken for an extra large spotted hyena or possibly a man-killing leopard at night, hidden in his favourite tree and overlooking a track which people would frequent, to then drop on them with teeth and claws.

The old European settler made capital of this, for the Nandi Bears Rugby Club was started by Ray Mayers and Jimmy Bird at Nandi on Lord Kitchener's farm there (he was brother to Lord Kitchener of Khartoum and inherited the title when he was drowned at sea during the 1914-18 war). The Nandi Bears also had a cricket club in the old days and many is the game I played at Londiani followed by monumental parties! I have observed the odd leopard there and many a hyena, but the Nandi Bear I never saw!

I digress. Coming back to the Ngoloko or Milhoi, all spoor is identifiable to the trained eye of the experienced hunter or tracker. That so painstakingly and accurately described, plus the other particulars given: the pad, the claws, the weight, the height, the measurement of stride when walking and running and the booming, grunting call (so similar to that of a lion) they heard the previous night, was not the big, carnivorous, hideous brute he believed.

Had he had the determination and stamina to have followed it up and to obtain a sighting of it the poor fellow would have been most disappointed. For it could have been nothing else than an inoffensive *Struthionidae* — an ostrich!

The Old Etonian

Somewhere during my wanderings I had acquired a tatty old paperback entitled *The Perpetual Pessimist* (an everlasting calendar of gloom and woe). It was written by 'Sagittarius' and one Daniel George. It was published by Pan Books of London in 1963.

Naturally it contained relevant and expected items one would look for in a pessimist's anthology, such as:

All hope abandon, ye who enter here.   *(Dante)*
Youth is a blunder; Manhood a struggle; and
Old Age a regret.   *(Disraeli)*
In this world nothing can be said to be cer-
tain, except death and taxes.   *(Franklin)*
First murder. Cain kills Abel 3974 B.C.   *(The Book of*
Man that is born of woman hath but a short   *Common*
time to live and is full of misery.   *Prayer)*
Successful crime is given the name of virtue;
honest folk become the slaves of villains;
might is right and Fear silences the Law.   *(Senaca)*
Rain of fire and brimstone, Sodom & Gomor-
rah and so on.

Towards the end of the book and most surprisingly and unfairly I thought: Eton College: founded 1440.

I first met this particular old Etonian some thirty years ago when he was a most competent and successful cattle rancher at Nanyuki, under Mount Kenya. Before taking up ranching here he had spent an adventurous few years as a 'Jackeroo,' I believe they are called, in Australia. He was tragically killed in a car accident at Nakuru in the Great Rift Valley some years ago where he had taken a job in the commercial world.

At the time he was running his Nanyuki ranch he wanted someone to shoot off the buffalo, for they were coming out of the forest and drinking from the same troughs as his cattle, and so passing on to them every known disease they carried themselves. During the few weeks I spent with him there, under the snows of Mount Kenya, I found him to be an affable host.

He was a tall man. Well over six foot and big with it. A handsome fellow, I would say, with a craggy autocratic face. Uncertain of temper with an outspoken and devil-may-care manner. He was not one to suffer lesser mortals gladly. After some time he sold his ranch and went to live on Lamu island.

Here, though, I will let the late Ba Allen take up the story for he witnessed the incident. Ba had been many years on the island and I suppose one could describe him as the Senior Beachcomber. He was a character and for some reason was fond of Old Etonians. I seem to remember him saying that he was born near the College. He had an inane loud laugh, and when he spoke invariably ended up with the epithet of 'Old Boy'. He told me the tale.

'You will have to watch it when you come to live on the island, Old Boy, for from time to time the Police raid various houses including those occupied by the few Europeans we have here. They have nothing else to do. Haw! Haw! Haw!

'They are after smokers of bhangi and drug addicts generally, for as you have seen, most of the hippies here living in the dosshouses are usually stoned to their eyebrows. Haw! Haw! Haw! On this occasion, Old Boy, it was about midnight when they made this particular raid. First they went to the widow's house next door' (the widow being an elderly lady in her mid-sixties, I would say, and had lived most of her life in Kenya. I bought her house shortly after the incident).

'Lord, how she screeched at them for their temerity in knocking her up and looking for drugs in her house. Come to think of it, it really was a bit third eleven, Old Boy. What? What? What? Anyway, they rather ungallantly arrested her and put her in prison for a few hours to cool off. After that she couldn't leave Lamu quick enough. From the widow's house they went to his Lordship's place several yards away where they found him smoking a joint with his servant and others. Completely stoned all of them. They too were arrested. As you know, Old Boy, he is a big chap and it took three policemen to make the arrest before they finally overpowered him and chucked him in prison too.

'The following afternoon he was let out for exercise but as he was still violent they manacled his ankles together with a short chain. From that chain ran a longer one at the end of which a cannon ball was attached. Damned heavy. Y'know, Old Boy, the sort of things they used to put on runaway slaves a hundred years or so ago for we had plenty of 'em here then. Used to arrive in dhows packed like sardines. Haw! Haw! Haw!' — here old Ba guffawed again like a demented hyena.

'Well, from where we are now sitting on this roof-top verandah, I saw him exercising just outside the prison. The short chain on his ankles would only allow him to take short little steps, but you knew immediately that boy had been to Eton, for he carried that cannon ball like a King! What? What? What? Haw! Haw! Haw!'

Lamu Love Song

White and enduring the old houses stand
    On this enchanted Isle
Kiwa Ndeo, the Arab town
    Whose pulse has stopped awhile.
Ah Aziz! Let us tarry
    In this safe haven of ghosts,
See them noiselessly flutter by
    Our shrouded, mysterious hosts.
On swift galleons and dhows they came here
    Like swans upon the seas,
Persians, Arabs, Hindus,
    Steel corsletted Portuguese.
Solomon's son,
    For ivory, incense and gold,
Harun-al-Raschid
    That coloniser of old.
Beche-de-Mer and ambergris
    For Astarte, Goddess of Love;
Hearken! El Assar, the third prayer is on us
    With the Muezzin crying above.
Salaam Aleyk, Beloved
    Rest in this shade of lace
From the casuarina tree of fantasy
    To veil thy peerless face.
Here the air is soft and limpid,
    Redolent with jasmine flowers,
Gently now the Trade Winds stir
    To blow away the showers.
No longer the siwa trumpets war
    The cannons mute and silent,
Peace has come to this blessed shore,
    Ya habi Salaam Alayka!

The Hippies

I feel so sorry
    For the Hippies,
Wandering about with their beads of worry
    Like lost unwanted souls.
Searching for the Golden Fleece,
    Passing on clouds
Like a flock of geese
    Dreaming on bhangi.
Weirdly dressed they come and go
    Thinking they're doing
An epic exploration,
    You know.
Poor things, it all happened before
    For in Lamu there is nothing new
A hundred years ago they came,
    The first of the few.
We've come. We've come
    They hysterically cried
We'll call it Freeland,
    Free this. Free that.
We'll start a Colony of Love
    So long ago
And as simple as that.

Four

REFLECTIONS

Brother Mario

One day, whilst on a visit to Elephant Camp from Garissa in Kenya's Northern Province, I resolved to visit Brother Mario, renew an amusing acquaintanceship and to buy some of his renowned sweet melons. I had first met him some years previously whilst hunting in the area and had my camp at a large deshek, or water-hole, called El Lein, a favourite camping site of mine and close to the Somalia border.

Brother Mario was a character. A natural. He had started the Consolata Mission, just outside Garissa with a project he called Boys' Town. With a grant of seventy acres from Government, all desert and apparently non-productive, he had wired it in and begged, borrowed or stolen a pump to lift water from the nearby Tana River to his desolate, pathetic acres. From the United States he had obtained gifts of money and machinery so that within a couple of years it was blooming. Trees had been planted, mangoes, papaya, lemons, oranges and the like, even grapes as well as the most delicious sweet melons in the whole of Kenya.

With all his acres now irrigated, his pet project flourished due entirely to his enthusiasm, energy and vision. Permanent houses were built for himself and the other Brothers, a mess and a recreation room. All this was followed by a superb swimming pool — but above all he housed some one hundred and fifty orphans whose parents had been killed in a massive raid the shifta had made across the border a decade previously. Schoolrooms were provided for them, teachers, a football pitch and other amenities. Everything was organised on a self-help basis and he ran the whole show himself like a hard-bitten sergeant major. The other two Brothers, timid souls, were terrified of him.

In the spacious mess, deepfreezers and refrigerators hummed away happily and from the walls a few dozen or so blown-up photographs gazed down. One of Brother Mario himself showed a small man, stockily built and of southern-Italian origin, a bustle of cherubic energy, with two of the darkest, twinkling black eyes I had ever seen, like two large currants in the brown bun of his face. He affected a hennaed beard, wore a small Muslim cap and a *lungi* in the Somali fashion. Other pictures showed him with Mzee Jomo Kenyatta; with the Mayor of Chicago and with the President of the United States. Yet others with various film stars, with a family group of the Kennedys and so on. Evidently he visited the States about once every two years in order to raise funds. He had obviously been most successful.

We had arrived early in the evening from the El Lein water-hole. There were just the four of us. The client, a man whose name belied his niceness — Harold Wilson from Chicago — Buno my gunbearer, my second gunbearer, Mau, and myself. The safari lorry with old Ali in charge was already packed and on its way to Nairobi. I had also intended making Nairobi that night but Brother Mario would not hear of it. After I had introduced Harold to him and

presented him with two oryx haunches for his kitchen, for which he was thankful, he beamed at me and said how good it was meeting me again.

'You'll both sleep here in my guest house,' he said. It was an order, for in his way he was a bit of a bully, I suppose. I was happy to comply, for once in Nairobi we had a couple of days to kill before Harold's plane left, besides remembering the last time we had met I knew we would be well looked after.

'Where you say you from?' he addressed Harold. He spoke broken English with a weird Bronx-Italian accent.

'Chicago? Mama Mia! Waal. Waal. I from Chicago too — ain't dat somepin? Collins — where you say you from again? Sherwood Forest? Waal. Waal. Waddeyouknow? Robin 'Ood. Leetle John and dat dame Maid Marian. She sure was some broad. Heard of 'em all. 'Ave you seen my pool? Had a dip yet? No? First thing tomorrow then. Seen round my place yet? The schoolrooms? the shamba? The boys' 'creation room? The ball ground? The Chick Sales? Builtemallmyself. Yeah. Sure did. See my pictures on the walls?' Here he waved expansively causing one of the Brother's sitting next to him to take evasive action.

'I'm a hustler, see? Gottabe. That's 'ow I get my dollars in for Boys Town. Hey! Brother Francesco, where your manners? Vino for de guests!' Poor Brother Francesco shot up from his chair as though stung by a scorpion. He scuttled across the room to produce two enormous flasks of Chianti which Brother Mario uncorked with commendable speed and efficiency. He had obviously had years of practice. Between the three Brothers, Harold and myself, the two flasks disappeard as if by magic. At a snap of his fingers and a flash of black eyes, Brother Mario imperiously directed Brother Francesco to bring up reinforcements. The other Brother, decorously seated with a face like a harvest moon beamed his approval. Harold with a slightly dazed look on his face kept up with us. A happily-married man with children from Chicago and a great home lover — for I had stayed with them there — he had obviously not met many people like Brother Mario. I sat back happily, enjoying the company and listening to Brother Mario's gregarious chatter.

The pressure lamps were lit and then in came supper. A most delicious *Consommé a l' Italienne* sprinkled with chervil leaves. I complimented Brother Mario and out of the corner of my eye saw the fat, red-faced Brother beam and so adjudged him to be the cook. Afterwards, if I could get a word in edgeways, I made a mental note to ask him for the recipe to pass on to my safari cook, old Christopher, for future safaris. The soup was followed by a generous helping of canneleoni and then came a dozen superb sweet melons served with a little ginger. He carved us up one each, the while helping himself. The other two Brothers decorously helped themselves to smaller slices.

'Grew 'em myself,' Brother Mario boasted.

'Sure did. Got the magic seed from Israel. De best in the world.' He gobbled away happily, spitting out the pips in all directions.

'God is sure good,' he spluttered away.

'Never planted a seed before in my whole life and I ain't no chicken. I popped 'em in this desert and they just grew. A miracle. Yeah, sure was a miracle. Have some gorgonzola.' A large board with the cheese and hot rolls was placed in front of us.

'Here, have a seegar. All the way from Havana, Cuba. That sure was a miracle too.' He laughed uproariously and gave me a prodigious wink. Biting off the end of his own he spat it on the floor. The three of us puffed away contentedly whilst the other two Brothers, under the beady eye of their superior, helped the servants clear away the table. I ventured a question.

'If I may pass the remark, you are a most unusual person to be a Brother with the Consolata Mission. How did it all happen?'

'Damn right,' he replied. 'Sure is a good question. Say,' he said, addressing Harold.

'Did you ever know the so-and-so cathouse in Chicago?' Harold was quite embarrassed with little wonder and naturally denied knowing the existence of the place.

'Boy. You sure missed out there! How come you never visited the place? The best cathouse and cats in good ole Chicago. I should know. I owned it. Yeah, and a couple of Cadillacs too.'

Incredulously I asked: 'You really owned a brothel?'

'Yeah. Sure. Why not. De oldest profession in de world. We Amurrancans call 'em cathouses. Youse Limey's call 'em brothels.

So what? Waal. One night I was in bed with my favourite cat when she said "Mario, why don't you do somepin worthwhile with your life?" You know how cats are — they never stop yappin. I thought a bit. Then somepin grew in my mind, just like dose melon seeds — and I heard the word of GARD. It came to me just like dat. I suddenly got religion. I sold my Cadillacs. I sold my cathouse. I went to the local Consolata Mission boys and they accepted me. Me Mario, the cathouse owner!'

Brother Mario left his beloved Boys' Town some years ago now. More is the pity. I heard he had a disagreement with the District Commissioner, not a very pleasant character I remember. He came to collect a large supply of melons and would not pay for them. Evidently Brother Mario gave him short shrift. All credit to him for not being bullied by a Government servant who misused his authority in such a flagrant manner.

The place is still going but without his enthusiasm, energy and propensity for raising funds it is now run down.

Charlatan or true convert I do not know, but as to his achievements there, should you ever visit Garissa, stop the first *toto* you see on the road and ask him to direct you to Boys' Town.

He will probably look at you blankly and shake his head.

Ask him then to direct you to Brother Mario's place, his eyes will widen and his face light up with pleasure. With jutting chin he will point in the right direction.

'*Huko!,*' he will say. '*Huko! Huko!*' (over there, over there).

One Man and his Pig.

I had been but a few months as camp manager of Baomo Lodge
on the lower reaches of the Tana River in Kenya and loved it there.
My staff, mostly Riverine Pokomo were a happy, contented lot and
ex-Sergeant Kibwana Athman, retired from the Game Department
whom I had befriended at Lamu to take with me as a tracker, was
in his element back in the bush and being able to augment his small
Government pension. And yet — there was something missing I
thought, particularly when I had children in camp. I found it
took quite an effort to keep them amused and they were a constant
source of worry when they ventured too near the river, for the
crocodiles lurking in the depths were always dangerous. Possibly
because I missed my own two children in England and was constantly
thinking of them I was more aware of other folks' offspring than most.

It was because of this that I thought of starting a small animal
orphanage which I was sure would appeal to them. With this idea
in mind I paid a visit to the Game Ranger at Kitere, just upriver
from me. He in turn contacted his headquarters in Nairobi. After
a couple of weeks back came the answer. Yes, I could start up an
orphanage but it would have to be limited to no more than three
animals. Enthusiastically I bought a couple of rolls of small wire mesh
from Malindi on the coast and gave instructions to my station *fundi*,
the odd job man, to have him fashion poles which were placed in
the holes we had dug for each little compound. Water-holes were
then shaped in the sand to be lined with cement and each of the three
compounds had its own little lean-to shelter.

The whole orphanage was built around the enormous trunk of
a wild fig tree with ample shade. Moreover, it was only a few yards
from my own little house thereby enabling me to keep a watchful
eye on things. By word of mouth I then offered the local Pokomo
Riverines the sum of one hundred shillings for any small animal they

could find me, making it quite clear that I wanted orphans only, animals abandoned or lost by their parents. I would not tolerate any harassment of family groups. The results were negative. In the meantime my orphanage looked lonely, as did the three plastic feeding bottles with rubber teats attached which I had also purchased. I hate to see anything caged. My idea was to hand feed the babies and then release them in the hope that they would stay in or around camp. I knew this was all perfectly feasible, for many years ago in Somaliland I kept lesser kudu, gerenuk, dibatag, Speke's gazelle, dikdik, giraffe, a lion cub and two cheetah.

The two latter, along with my Great Dane puppy, Hamlet, would accompany me through the bush on my long patrols and treks, riding in style in their own little howdahs on camels. My two cheetah, I thought then, made the most admirable pets of all from the wild but I was to revise this opinion many years later. I therefore had visions of at least three of these animals for my new orphanage or even the possibility of a buffalo calf. I wasn't particulary interested in monkeys for I preferred to see the Sykes', vervets, red Colobus and mangabeys gambolling in the trees near camp.

With all the leopards having been poached there were plenty of baboons for they used to be the leopard's favourite meal but when the spotted predators disappeared the baboons increased dramatically Again I wasn't particularly interested for I had always found them unlovely with their protruding muzzles, long sharp canines, close-set crafty-looking eyes and unsightly, well-developed red buttocks.

Lion cubs? Remembering mine in the old days I knew they presented quite a feeding problem as they grew bigger and besides my old friend George Adamson was some 150 miles upriver from me with his own prides living in the wild. Also too dangerous for children, I thought. George had had his problems too when some years ago one had mauled the son of a visiting Park Warden. On top of that a large male had killed and eaten his cook. Not to be thought of, for I was enough of a connoisseur of food myself to appreciate the excellence of my own camp cook, whose cannelloni, casseroles and crêpes Suzette in particular were out of this world. No. They were out for I was not prepared to lose my African Escoffier to a hungry lion.

A potto? One of the lower primates. A little bear-like animal with a rounded head and short tail and known as 'half-a-tail' by the Riverines. Most amusing to watch as they climb the tree branches by means of a hand-over-hand action. Yes. A potto would be acceptable.

Or perhaps a galago — the bush baby with those large ears and appealing wide eyes...then again a mongoose would make a useful pet as a killer of snakes in and around camp. They tamed quite easily and we had no less than five varieties in the Game Reserve. The slender, the dwarf, the banded, the white-tailed, with the Egyptian being the largest of the species — about twenty-four inches long and

considered holy in ancient Egypt. And so as I dreamed I hoped, like Mr Micawber, something would turn up.

On 11 September 1978, William Tell did indeed turn up and proved to be the most amusing, endearing, bad-tempered and naughtiest pet I have ever had. On that memorable day I had a party of Swiss in camp including the Nabholtz family of father, mother and daughter, Christine. They were, strangely enough, all qualified veterinary surgeons. On one of the late afternoon game runs I was not able to accompany them as I was busy helping my boatman repair one of the outboard engines. I mentioned to this family about my orphanage, showed them my forlorn-looking wire enclosures as off they went accompanied by Sergeant Kibwana. They returned at sundown. Christine rushed up to me nursing something to her bosom which she held in her left hand. It was about five inches long. It had a flattened head with minute warts, little white whiskers, tiny tushes, piggy eyes and at the other end a tail like a bootlace. Christine was sucking the thumb on her right hand.

'It bit me,' she said. 'I have named it Wilhelm Tell after our Swiss folklore hero.' She handed it over to me. Holding it gingerly by the scruff of its neck, so that it could not bite me, I eyed the aggressive but pitiful bundle of skin and bones apprehesively.

'Good Lord,' I said. 'It's a pig. A baby warthog.'

'Yes,' said Christine breathlessly. 'It was alone in the middle of the bush, probably the runt of the litter and abandoned by its parents. It's terribly weak and needs milk immediately but even so I reckon you have only a fifty-fifty chance of pulling it through — for it's obviously still suckling. I would say it's only about a week old.'

All this while Wilhelm Tell was squeaking and grunting with rage and as I held him firmly by the scruff of his neck he wildly rolled his smoky baby-blue eyes. Four skinny legs, armed with sharp little trotters shot out like miniature pistons.

'Well,' I said dubiously. 'It's a start for the orphanage anyway.' Not wishing to appear churlish at being presented with this monster, I treated her thumb with iodine and Elastoplast, then offered her a whisky. I joined her. Another look at Wilhelm Tell, who was now deposited in his wire enclosure where he repeatedly hurled himself against the wire netting, stille grunting and squealing, I poured us another. In the meantime, the admirable Sergeant Athman, who had taken part in catching him, stood by laughing. I looked at him sourly. First things first, I thought, sipping my whisky.

I produced one of the plastic feeding bottles, handed it to the Sergeant who was still laughing and rather grumpily told him to take it to the kitchen and have the cook fill it with lukewarm milk. He was soon back. Christine had beaten a strategic retreat to her tent. So much for the famed Swiss Guards I thought. Squirting a little milk on the back of the hand, the temperature appeared to be at blood heat. Helped by the Sergeant I caught Wilhelm and thrust the teat unceremoniously into his protesting mouth. At least it stopped the squeals and grunts for a moment. Then full of spleen he bit the top off. Sterner measures were called for, for I was determined he would survive. Forcibly I trust his twitching snout into the milk I had now poured into a tin bowl. Kicking, squirming, grunting and squealing he resisted, but some of it went down the right way. Thereafter there was not the slightest doubt but that he would survive. Two weeks later he was on solids and would eat anything, but I had to cement his tin plate of food in the sand or he would spill the contents, either by placing his trotters in it or impatiently rooting it over with his snout. In build, personality and aggressive temperament, he reminded me of a Staffordshire terrier pup. As with all babies he was both stupid and greedy, eating until it was not possible to cram more into his now drum-like belly. Then the lapping and guzzling would become slower and slower and more laboured until he had to desist, his snout covered by food. Making comical gasps he would then stagger off to collapse in the shade.

I thought I knew all about warthogs from my days as a white hunter. I was wrong, for I had a lot to learn. What I did know that whilst it is possibly the ugliest animal in the bush, it is of much courage. An old boar will weigh three hundred pounds. It has an elongated body, enormous head, flattened face with expanded muzzle, warts, fearsome tushes and the whole face adorned with brushlike Victorian whiskers. The tushes are most unusual and can measure up to twelve inches, the upper ones turning outwards then upwards to curve inwards thus forming a semicircle. The lower wearing against the base of the upper rushes to form a sharp cutting weapon which he will not hesitate to use against his enemies. Mostly lion and leopard. The skin is greyish to black but often reddish because of the animal's habit of wallowing in red sandy mud. The coat is sparse but has a mane of stiff hairs on the neck and shoulders. A long, thin tail with a tuft is carried vertically in a characteristic way when the animal is running or alarmed. Their habitat is varied but they prefer the open savannah, especially when there is water available and there are water catchments to wallow in.

They are mostly encountered in sounders. The old boar, his spouse and several piglets in the litter. Old boars are often found alone. They often breed and sleep in abandoned aardvark burrows which at dusk they enter backwards, the better to defend themselves with their tushes should they be attacked by lion or leopard, both of which prey upon them. Their sight is poor, but as I was to find out with Wilhelm, their sense of smell and hearing most acute. A grazer, its main diet is short grasses, roots, tubers, bulbs and fallen fruit with the animal going down on its knees to eat.

From the beginning, I realised that as Wilhelm was so small and vulnerable he could not be left outside at night. In spite of the wire, lion, hyena, jackal or those fierce nocturnal killers, the caracal and serval would find him, dig under the wire and that would be the end of Wilhelm. I did not have enough wire to enclose the top and so another danger by day would be from the larger eagles — particular the martial. There was nothing else for it: he would have to live in the office. An old empty oil drum, rusty but still serviceable, caught my eye. A handful of dried grasses in this and he would think he was back home in an aardvark burrow, or so I misguidedly thought. Not a bit of it. From the moment I popped him in the drum came the usual squeaks of protestations.

Fishing him out the next morning, instead of his normal greyish buff colour he was red from snout to tuftless bootlace tail; I now had a rust-coloured pig on my hands. I had to laugh. This was a mistake for then his anger knew no bounds. He trotted to a corner of the office hiding behind the waste paper basket, baring his lip at me and making little heart-breaking squeals of disapproval. At length he recovered to discover some old files left in a corner which he began tearing to pieces with his incisors and then to stamp angrily. I picked him up to comfort him, tickling him behind his ears and rubbed his tummy.

It was then I made a momentous discovery. Wilhelm wasn't a Wilhelm at all. He was a She! I promptly re-christened her Wilhelmina. I just had to laugh when I thought of those three Swiss vets. Not very professional in their sexing and I wondered if they had pigs in Switzerland. In order to placate her after my second bout of mirth for some time afterwards, until she had grown much bigger, she slept on a rug near my bed. It was only then that I had the first squeaks of contentment.

We were inseparable, Wilhelmina and I, and at times it would become slightly embarrassing, for she followed me everywhere and would totally ignore the children who were in camp.

My house was quite small, consisting of the office, a bedroom and a shower. The door leading from the bedroom to the shower was often open but if I went for a shower and closed the door, Wilhelmina would show her disapproval by biting away at the woodwork as she grunted away in anger. Perforce she had to come in the shower with me and she enjoyed that immensely. After she grew much bigger, I placed her in the compound, comforting her by spending more time than I possibly should with her. I fed her on titbits from the kitchen as well as mangoes from a nearby tree. She really had it good.

Came the great day when I finally decided that she was sufficiently tame to be released. I was apprehensive, but she followed me close at heel like a well-trained gun dog. Well, almost. Such was her enthusiasm at being let loose that she kicked up her trotters to dash madly around in circles but if ever she lost sight or scent of me she would come rushing back for reassurance. At meal times it was inevitable that she followed me into the dining room. So as not to annoy the guests I had to chastise her occasionally with a hard slap on her bottom. After that she would lie under my table. Never would she be enticed to take food from a stranger.

At this time of the year the river was at its lowest so that a hard-packed sand beach sloped gently down to the receding water. I would jog up and down for a distance for exercise. Wilhelmina of course accompanied me, but if I put on a sudden spurt and lengthened my stride and she could not keep up then she would again squeal with rage as she pounded after me. Her little trotters working overtime.

Wilhelmina was indeed MY pig.

It has been said that beauty is in the eye of the beholder and with these sentiments I concur. Wilhelmina, to most, would appear to be a very plain Jane — but to me she had an inward beauty, possessed a courageous, independent character and, in spite of her temper and tantrums, was loyal, affectionate and faithful.

What more can one demand from any female?

The Ostrich Chicks

The ostrich chicks arrived in camp about a week after Wilhelmina. Two askaris of Kenya's National Youth Service, stationed at Bura north of the lodge, had found them in the bush apparently abandoned. They delivered them to me on foot carrying the chicks in an empty Tusker beer crate. About a week old, I judged, and they looked none the worse for their ride in their rather undignified carriage. As they craned their long necks over the edge of the box to peep at me shyly with large, enquiring eyes, I saw appealing balls of fluffy, quill-like black and grey feathers. Picking them up to pet they appeared to be completely vulnerable and helpless. A quick safari to Malindi and I ascertained that in captivity their favourite diet was chopped egg and cabbage. So it proved for this was their supper that first night with not a morsel left. As a tonic I then opened their beaks to administer multi-vitamin drops.

Having fed them I had to think of priorities and the first was for their safety by day and night. Along with the four-legged predators, there was a real danger from those massive eagles — the martial, the Verreaux's and the crowned hawk. Any one of these telescopic-eyed birds of prey could suddenly swoop down to carry them off with ease. So until they grew bigger, resignedly once again, I decided to keep them at night in the office. On a fresh bed of dried leaves and grasses and still in their original crate, they would settle down quite happily with neck and head resting on each other's back. By day they would make confidingly soft, incessant churring sounds and when drinking from their water-hole, they would do so with a curious dipping motion, so much more elegant than a domestic fowl drinking.

As with Wilhelmina, when I decided it was safe to release them, they never strayed far from camp and it was most amusing to watch their antics at being set free. They would pirouette, turning and twirling around, Charybdis-like, inadequate little wings flapping away, until quite dizzy from their dance, they would fall over blinking happily at each other as if proud of their impromptu performance. Quite charming to watch and somewhat in the nature of a fledgling ring-a-ring of roses. They were always the favourites of any visiting children. Wilhelmina would join in and play with them also but if I was walking around the camp she would always leave them to follow me.

As is generally known, the ostrich is the largest living bird, though flightless. It has only two toes on each foot. Other characteristics about the bird may not be so well known. When mature it is eight-foot in height. The adult male has a striking black and white plumage whilst the female looks dowdier, dressed in her feathers of greyish-brown. By no means is the ostrich the idiot bird it is thought to be, burying its head in the sand. Knowing that its long neck will catch the eye it lays it flat on the ground when danger threatens the nest or brood, concealment being better than flight. During the mating season, when they are anchored to one spot hatching the eggs, turn and turn about, it would appear that either the cock bird or the hen would be an easy victim for lion or hyena who prey upon them, since the same background cannot possibly suit the colours of both of them. Not a bit of it. The grey hen sits by day and the black cock at night!

They have exceptionally keen eyesight and prefer to frequent the plains, thorn-bush country and semi-desert. By choosing this open habitat they are able to see great distances and to spot their main enemy, the lion, before he can get sufficiently close to make his kill on a much-favoured ostrich supper. On the subject of gastronomical delights one ostrich egg will make a rich omelette for twelve persons.

Their nests are merely shallow depressions in the sand and contain up to twenty eggs. If disturbed near them, or when accompanied by chicks, the parents will go through all the normal bird-like motions of pretending to be hurt, by trailing a wing and so on, so hoping to lead away any would-be marauder.

In East Africa, the southern or Masai race have pink-coloured necks and thighs whilst their cousins to the north of the Tana River are coloured blue. When striding or running to expose to advantage their shapely, well-built thighs, they always remind me of ballet dancers. Except when young they are normally silent but in the breeding season the cock makes a deep booming call which many a hunter has mistaken for the grunt of a lion.

For some weeks now in camp the dark, ominous clouds had been building up over the Aberdares and Mount Kenya, the source of the river. Two days later the heavens opened, the river rose alarmingly and we were then completely cut off from the outside world. The river angrily burst its banks and the track out of camp to the main Garsen-Hola road turned into a torrent of raging red-brown water.

With all my experience of the bush I had quite forgotten one of the deadliest enemies of all who become active with the onset of the rains. The much feared *siafu*, or driver ants. They march in countless thousands to demolish all insect and animal life in their path. They march as an army, viciously voracious, with the soldier ants out scouting on the flanks.

That night was something of a nightmare. I was awakened early in the morning by hysterical angry squeals coming from Wilhelmina's little compound. The rain poured down, lightning flashed and thunder rolled as, clad in my kikoi and armed with a torch, I went to investigate. Wilhelmina was hurling herself against the wire mesh in a frenzied effort to escape. But from what? I shone the beam of the powerful torch in all directions but could see nothing of danger. At last I saw them as they attacked me, biting viciously at my feet and up my legs. I ran back to the office to beat the alarm gong. Stripping off my kikoi and sandals I pulled the vicious ants off various parts of my anatomy. The rain still poured down and underfoot was a sea of mud. Led by Sergeant Athman the staff assembled and, under his instructions, shovelfuls of hot ashes were collected from underneath the boilers supplying hot water to the tents. These were then spread over the marching ants to divert them elsewhere. We then piled more ashes around the orphanage which gave it some measure of protection. Other members of the staff had made improvised blazing torches out of old newspapers to shrivel up the strag glers. In the meantime I armed myself with a couple of pressurised cans of bug spray with which I literally doused Wilhelmina. She nuzzled me gratefully. The ostrich chicks were in a worse state, covered with dozens of bites which were bleeding profusely. I tended to them. I had arrived just in time; any further delay would have resulted in them being eaten alive.

Kabompo

An RAF sergeant helped me to clamber aboard an old Dakota. Its engines, with some help from Allah, roared into life as it staggered down and off the Alula runway like an overfed marabou stork. I looked back. Instead of the Union Jack fluttering from the flagpole on top of my crenellated white stone house, a fast disappearing flag of white, green and red mocked me. My morale was understandably low, I think, for I had previously handed over El Carre in the Ogaden to the Ethiopians. In turn their red, yellow and green flag had been run up in place of my own. These unhappy, traumatic experiences were all too much I thought, nursing my hangover. I closed my eyes. The old plane banked steeply, shuddered and headed over the Indian Ocean towards Aden.

'It's no good looking back,' I thought miserably. The last, almost ten, years of my life were finished. Over and done with. But the memories stayed with me. They always would. Ten years is quite a slice out of one's life and leaving the Somalilands was the most traumatic experience I had ever had. I had known and loved this harsh desert country, its tough inhabitants; adapting to their way of life under thorn trees is not easily forgotten.

Suddenly I remembered the letter. FM was my last Senior Civil Affairs Officer in the Mijertein Province. On secondment from Northern Rhodesia (now Zambia) to Somalia during the war, he had already returned there as Chief Secretary. He had been good enough to offer me a job as District Officer there, for I had already decided that the army in peacetime was not my glass of wompo. I took his letter out of my pocket to read it again.

'Compared to Somalia this place is civilised,' he had written in his precise, well-remembered handwriting.

'We want none of your Ogaden weaver-bird parties here.' (He referred to a wild party I had once thrown on the roof-top of the

Gendarmerie Officers' Mess. We called it The Gloom Box. This particular party had got rather out of hand with two uninvited guests being chucked off the roof-top together with an unpopular senior officer who had conveniently got in the way).

He continued. 'Your armoury. You will not be allowed to bring it in here but you may keep your shotgun. We have no shifta. Our Africans are peaceful and the country soundly administered. So get rid of your weapons. Throw them in the sea. I am not quite sure yet where you will be posted but it might well be a place called Kabompo which is close to the border of Portuguese Angola. Anyway let me know when you arrive in Lusaka, the capital, where you will report to me and I will then confirm your posting.' He signed himself 'Yours sincerely, FM.'

With the grappa I had consumed last night at Alula, waves of vertigo now hit me. Little dikdik with toylike but sharp horns seemed to be charging each other in my head.

Kabompo. Of all the places I would be posted to it would have to be called Kabompo. What a perfectly bloody name I thought. Kabompo. I pictured myself as another Sanders of the River, a film I had seen as a boy, with pith helmet resting on my ears, being paddled upriver by two dozen sweating, glistening black bodies with Paul Robeson among them in the large dug-out singing the Kabompo boating song.

Kabompo. I visualized witch doctors. Cooking pots and missionaries. Boilers and fryers. I thought it would be quite different from Somalia. Future events proved me right.

Inside the plane all was bare austerity — no seats as such and a gaping oblong opening where I assumed the door should have been. The Chief Pilot and his First Officer were up front in the cabin probably nursing their hangovers too, I thought uncharitably. With me in the flying coffin was an RAF sergeant and a couple of corporals. Cockneys by the sound of them, idly listening to their inane chatter. Unbuckling the clasp of my web belt, I took it off my waist to remove the 9 mm. Beretta automtic pistol from its leather holster. At close quarters over the years it had proved to be a snub-nosed deadly little toy. The sergeant and the two corporals looked at me with some concern. Cockneys are bright. They never miss a trick. They all knew I had been too long in the bush. Leaning over I threw the belt, holster and pistol through the opening to watch them go spinning over and over until they made three splashes in the glassy, blue-green sea of the Gulf of Aden, some two thousand feet below and behind us.

On top of my gear and just behind me were my other three weapons. Like the pistol all unofficial. A Beretta sub-machine gun I had taken off a dead shifta, my shotgun and my especial favourite — a beautiful .256 Mannlicher-Schoenauer rifle. Through the hatch went the sub-machine gun. The Cockney sergeant spoke.

'Cor blimey,' he said. 'The Major really is round the bleeding bend. He's caught that French fing. No. Not that, you clots,' he said to the corporals as they began to grin.

'Cafard' it's called. C-a-f-a-r-d. Didn't you tits ever go to school? That's why I'm a Sergeant and you two are still Corporals see? And don't either of you ever forget or I'll have your guts for garters. Ever 'ear of the Foreign Legion? Didn't you ever see Victor McLaglan in Beau Geste? The Frogs get it in them forts in the Sahara. Not from crumpet. Being too long wivout crumpet. They go mad. See. And if I don't get away from you two soon and back to my old trouble and strife on some passionate leave, I'm likely to get it too! Here, Major,' he said sympathetically. Fumbling in his pocket he produced a packet of Players and offered me one. I took it and thanked him, then remembering that I didn't smoke, flicked that through the hatch too. The sergeant's eyes widened.

'Watch 'im, Corporal,' he said to one of them as he scuttled forward to the cockpit. Lovingly I fondled the rifle. We had seen a lot together. Tribal fights or the rush of the Habash shifta on our sleeping encampment protected by the thorn zariba. The coughing war-cries of the enemy and the taunting shouts of my own men... the full-blooded charge and leap of the lion over the zariba to kill one of our baggage camels on my first safari. The shooting of plains game to augment our rations and to provide a change from camel's milk and goat meat ... the shooting of my first elephant at El Wak (the Wells of God), to keep it from fouling our one remaining water-hole of life. I was tough and hardened in those days but even so,

256

elephant droppings and urine in one's tea is not to be recommended.

'Are you all right, old boy?' I started back to reality. The Squadron Leader twitched his impressive moustache. He, too, looked concerned for my welfare.

'It was a wizard party you threw last night. Your grappa was really bang on but don't do anything drastic like jumping out of the old kite and swimming back to Alula. Far be it from me to teach you how to suck eggs but you'd never make it. You must know that the Gulf of Aden is full of sharks and it's quite a way back now.'

He looked at his watch. 'We should be in Aden in less than half an hour and then straight to our mess for a few cold beers. Take it easy and why did you throw your weapons in the drink? Are you feeling fit?' He patted me on the shoulder.

'Orders,' I said morosely.

'Not allowed to take them to Kabompo,' whereupon I threw my beautiful rifle through the hatch and lapsed into moody silence. He then asked a question. He was obviously curious.

'How long have you been at Alula?'

'Not long this time,' I replied. 'I was just ordered here to hand over to the Italians but years ago I was stationed here a long time. I love this part of the world.' Now the bitterness bubbled out.

'And then those damned United Nitwits in their wisdom decided that Somalia should go back to the Italians. The Somalis do not want it but then it is only their country and that's the way it has to be.'

'And the Military Authorities in Mogadishu decided to send you back here again to finalise the handover?' he queried. I nodded.

'Tough,' he said. He looked significantly at the sergeant, giving a slight nod of his head to that worthy as, following his unspoken instructions, he moved between me and the hatch. Fifteen minutes later we touched down at Aden. True to his word the Squadron Leader took me into their mess and plied me with ice-cold beer served in a frosted pewter tankard. It was nectar. He said that he had been detailed to keep an eye on me for a few days until I could get myself on a plane or a boat on the way to Northern Rhodesia. He mentioned that there might be a plane in a couple of days.

That night after drinks and dinner my host suggested that we go to the flicks in the Officers' Mess. This idea appealed as I had not seen a film for something like six years. It was an unfortunate choice. Olivia de Havilland starred in *The Snake Pit* and the story, in so far as memory serves, was about a woman going mad. We saw about fifteen minutes of it and then by mutual consent we returned thankfully to the bar where we did much better.

The following day I flew to Lusaka. Here, FM took me under his wing and confirmed that I had indeed been posted to Kabompo.

'Get the sand and the Somalis out of your hair and you will like it,' he said.

'You are only thirtyish and there is no reason why you should not do as well here as you did in Somalia. It's up to you. By the way, your District Commissioner is a man named Cunningham. He's a bit younger than you but you will get on all right. Both he and his wife are highly strung. Intellectuals and all that sort of thing. But that won't worry you, will it? You are the opposite. People like the Cunninghams, admirable as they may be, take things in life too much to heart and when alone in the bush this can have dire consequences. Well. They had a tiff over his wife's cooking and she went and hanged herself in the kitchen! Took it very badly poor fellow, which of course is understandable, but I'm told he's recovered now These chaps get married far too young in the Colonial Service nowadays and when they find themselves out in the blue they just go to pieces.' He poured me a gin.

'Cheers,' he said.

'Cheers,' I replied absent-mindedly. I began to feel sorry for Cunningham.

'Do you mean to say, FM?' I queried in some astonishment, 'that my District Commissioner's wife committed suicide some little time ago at Kabompo and he is still there?' FM had the grace to look a little uncomfortable.

'Er, yes. I'm afraid so. We gave him a month's leave of course, but he insisted on going back for he is a good type. Dedicated. Probably against my better judgement I allowed him to do so but as I say he is his old self again and, in any event, Kabompo is not a popular station and suitable replacements in these more remote sta-

258

tions are hard to come by. That is why you have a job.'

'Thank you very much,' I replied as I held out my glass for another gin. I hoped I didn't sound too sarcastic. Here I was, after all those years in Somalia, being posted to the most isolated station in that country, now finding myself on the wing to an equally isolated post called Kabompo. *Che sera sera.*

The safari by Land Rover from Lusaka to Kabompo took two long days and two longer nights. I motored mostly through thick bush, dreary grey stuff with the country flat and uninteresting although I had been told that the Luangwa Valley teemed with game. I saw nothing on that particular safari except on the second day at sundown, when a solitary hyena stood in the middle of the murram road and laughed at me. I chucked a handy spanner at it and laughed back. The two nights I stayed at small Government rest houses *en route*. These were small, circular whitewashed rondavals with neatly-thatched roofs. A tin of tomato soup when it was heated over a smoky fire tasted rather like a goulash gone bad by the time the sausage flies, mosquitoes and flying ants had hurtled to their doom in it. At night the tribal drums reverbrated from each cluster of nearby huts, a monotonous, meaningful pounding in the still African night. I finished my last bottle of whisky.

Cunningham, tall, dark and gaunt with deeply-sunk eyes was at Kabompo to greet me. He looked ill, harassed and unhappy, all of which I understood. He said he was glad to see me and that I would be staying with him in his bungalow pending the arrival of my gear.

At sundowner time he was pathetically eager to talk as most lonely people are. Until my arrival he was the only European at Kabompo. Under the circumstances, and after the grief-laden, harrowing time he had experienced, he had all my sympathy. He enthused over Kabompo, its problems and the plans he had for the future. I learnt that the *boma* had been built on the site of a massive graveyard where two warring tribes had done their best to massacre each other in the dim past. I could well believe it, for there was something evil about the whole place.

Like many idealists, Cunningham wanted to run before he could walk for his plans included the eradication of witchcraft and drunkenness which so many of his predecessors had failed to accomplish.

As for witchcraft, it was only after independence came many years later, when that quite remarkable woman, Alice Lenshina, achieved this. Quite uneducated, just an ordinary villager from the bush, she had a vision and ascended to heaven from whence she returned to start her Lumpa Church Movement. In the space of a few years she achieved more than the Colonial Administration had done in decades. She refused to join the ruling political party of Kenneth Kaunda, with the result that she was imprisoned and her followers killed and their churches burnt to the ground.

A long time later, when I was on leave in England, I saw Kenneth Kaunda, the first President of the new Zambia on television. He was obviously an emotional character for he said that if his people did not stop their heavy drinking then he would resign. He then burst into tears, which he should have shed for his brutality in imprisoning Alice Lenshina and killing her followers.

Cunningham chattered on.

'You can take over most of the safari work and I would like you to stay in the bush three weeks out of every month. You will get the feel of the country that way and to know the people. I have a road gang at work some twenty miles away and you can spend some time supervising them for a start. You can also investigate a case of witchcraft at one of the villages you will be passing through. Also collect tax, and that sort of thing. My tax clerk will be going with you.'

The shadows outside his house lengthened as the sun set. The Kabompo river flowed sullenly by. The drums started up. I wanted a drink.

'I'm sorry, but I forgot my usual hospitality. You will have a Cunningham Special with me before dinner?' At this I brightened up a little. He went over to a rickety drinks cabinet and after a futile effort to brush off a couple of cockroaches, mixed the drinks. Idly turning my head to watch him I shuddered. On the cabinet were two bottles and a flask of water. One of the bottles was labelled Orange Juice and the other Lemon Squash. He handed me my glass

260

which I accepted with some trepidation. 'A Cunningham Special,' he announced proudly. 'Half orange, half lemon, topped up with cool water from the Kabompo river. Cheers.'

'Cheers,' I replied miserably, fishing out with curved forefinger a half-drowned mosquito. I now felt sorry for both of us, and thought with longing of the whisky I had so wantonly consumed on the road up. Waves of nostalgia hit me and I longed for the desert country and the nomadic way of life I now so missed. The final crunch came at supper. The table was set for three I noticed. My nerves tingled at this macabre situation and I would not have been at all surprised had the late Edgar Allen Poe occupied the third chair. Cunningham's servant entered the room with a solitary candle, precariously stuck in a saucer to give just sufficient light to throw his shadow on the lime-washed wall opposite me. He silently served the soup. Away in the bush a hyena called mournfully into the night, followed by a mad cacophony of laughter and forlorn howls. The drums still beat.

'This was my wife's favourite soup,' Cunningham spoke quite naturally but in a tense, low voice. His eyes belied his forced attempts to appear normal, for they were filled with both pain and despair. Frantically I thought of something to say. A word of comfort, but the Cunningham Special had not helped me and I had nothing to give. I just could not cope with his loneliness and hopelessness. Perhaps for the best; had I spoken words of commiseration I think he might have broken down. He was obviously near breaking point and the stupidity of being left on his own in such tragic circumstances defied description. Just another little tragedy. All part of the White Man's burden that happened so long ago in a forgotten outpost of our now forgotten Empire. Silently I cursed the whole callous administration for allowing him to be left, like this. Had we been in Somalia I could have coped, but here in Kabompo I was like a lost camel. Back in the Greater Shag, in the Mijertein, I would have lectured him on the dangers of drinking Cunningham Specials, force-fed him on Cioffi's gin at five shillings a bottle, sat a nubile crumpet on his lap and told him to bash on whilst the sun shone.

For a couple of days I worked with him in the office. He was as tense as ever but I found myself completely disinterested in all he was saying, no matter how much I tried to concentrate for his sake. I now realised that I had made a terrible mistake in ever accepting the job. After the volatile, handsome, intelligent Somalis, and in spite of their deceit and lies, I found the Africans here (possibly unjustifiably so), completely negative, their country dull and uninteresting and I longed again for the open desert.

A few days later a Land Rover arrived from Provincial Headquarters far to the south. There was a message for Cunningham. Someone had woken up at last. He was to be transferred leaving me in temporary control. The Land Rover also carried the whisky I had ordered when in Lusaka. Sincerely I shook Cunningham's hand and congratulated him on his new posting for I was glad for him. He too appeared to be relieved.

'Well,' he said, 'I had better prepare some handing over notes for you. In the meantime you had better get off on safari — cut it short, say a week and by the time you get back my successor should have arrived.'

I was intrigued at the method of proceeding on safari. Apart from the Land Rover which Cunningham would obviously need himself to get back to Lusaka, there was no other transport on the station. There were no ponies and no camels. The ever-present tsetse fly saw to that.

'I suppose I walk?' I queried. Cunningham was quite put out.

'Most certainly not,' he said. He spoke a few words of the local dialect and his Orderly, like a shiny black genie, wheeled into the office a bicycle.

'The Station Bicycle,' he said proudly.

'I shall leave it in your care.' He rang the bell. It worked. That seemed to make him happy.

'Make sure the Orderly cleans the hubs every evening and gives her a little oil, particularly on the chain. Remember to stop pedalling when you change the three-speed.' I felt as though I had been presented with a battleship.

'I will lay on your safari for tomorrow morning,' he continued. 'Twenty bearers. Each man carries fifty pounds on his head. You will have a messenger-cum-tax-collector with you who knows all the camp sites *en route*. The bearers will carry your tent, poles, chairs, table, rations, lamps, eating utensils and THE FLAG. But then I am sure you know all about this drill.'

'What is the order of march, er, cycling?' I queried. 'Point sections, sentries at camp and so on.' For the first time he smiled and like FM reminded me that I was no longer in the Ogaden of Somalia.

'We have no shifta here,' he said. 'Just ne'er-do-wells, drunks and witch doctors. You cycle ahead with your messenger who is also mechanised.' Here I permitted myself a smile.

'He will show you the way, but you must keep up with him for your bearers run non-stop from village to village.'

We set off the next morning in good heart. Cunningham with a flourish attached a miniature Union Jack to the handlebars of my cycle. I thought this a dashing touch and approved. At a given word of command the twenty bearers picked up their loads, balanced them on their heads and headed by the messenger we were off. I must admit that they had commendable stamina. To the first campsite, some eight miles away, we averaged some five miles an hour, their cracked, calloused feet raising little puffs of dust, I noticed, as I adventurously looked back. They stopped for nothing. I also skidded and came off, trying to avoid a squawking fowl as we passed a village, but when I looked back the wretched bird had either escaped or was in the cooking pot one of the bearers carried. I concentrated on my pedalling for I had no wish to be tossed into a pot with a fowl and a few hot chillies which I noticed growing in the shambas as we passed. On reaching the first campsite my tent was pitched. The portable flag-pole was erected and THE FLAG hoisted. It flew lazily in the late afternoon breeze and when the messenger lowered it again at sunset I missed my Somali bugler.

That first day's safari was to set a pattern as I coped with the usual boring routine work of supervising the tax collecting, settling drunken brawls, including holding court when two drunken whores were brought up in front of me. I've always had a soft spot for whores and so I bound them over to keep the peace.

On my return to Kabompo a week later a signal was received that no less a person than the Governor (then the late Sir Gilbert Rennis) was to visit the station with Cunningham's successor. Somehow I didn't think we would hit it off. I had heard of him from District Commissioners on secondment from Kenya to Somalia when Sir Gilbert had been Chief Secretary there. They had called him Old Cookers, on account of the cheap cooking sherry he produced at his infrequent parties. Philosophically I thought that if he did offer me a drink it couldn't possibly be any worse than a Cunningham Special. As the Great Day approached I splashed gallons of whitewash around the boma, working on the old army maxim that if you see anything standing still you paint it. Anything moving you shoot it.

My meeting with the Governor could hardly be described as a success. Normally I am very fond of Scots and admire them but I found Sir Gilbert fussy in the extreme. As we were inspecting the various buildings that Cunningham had supervised in erecting, plus those in course of construction, he suddenly whipped out a penknife from his pocket and started to scratch away at the mortar between the bricks. I thought Kabompo had even sent the Governor mad until he suddenly barked at me: 'What proportion of cement to sand, Mr Collins?'

I had not the faintest idea and his question put me up the Kabompo river without a paddle as I replied without thinking, 'Twenty-two of cement to one of sand, Sir Gilbert.' I must have been thinking of the length of a cricket wicket and those entertaining games with my Somalis at Alula. He looked at me as though I were a dung beetle, gave me a sour look, and mumbled about one in three.

'Far too much cement. Far too much cement. Can't afford it. Can't afford it. The man's an idiot.'

Well, I hadn't impressed the Governor (but I could hardly blame him for that), but what was more important the Governor hadn't impressed me, I hadn't liked the country and so, with apologies to FM I resigned. I flew back north where I soon found myself in the desert counry again but this time in the Northern Frontier District of Kenya.

Old-Timers, Friends and Characters

Bunduki Gunn

Leslie Gunn, nicknamed Bunduki, was born in Brighton, Sussex, during the early part of this century. It was his proud boast that he was a direct descendant of the famous Martha Gunn, the Queen of the Brighton Fishwives in the Regency period in Brighton.

He came to Sotik in Kenya in the early twenties as a pupil farmer to a Colonel Templar and it was during this time that he became a life-long friend of 'Squash' Lemon, ex-British South African Police, who was also a pupil farmer in the same area. Adventurers both, their prosaic existence did not suit either of them and having heard that land could easily be obtained in the Toro District of Uganda they decided to go there. They gave notice to their displeased mentors and left for the Elysian life the new land promised. Their mode of travel was somewhat unusual for they rode in Bunduki's old chain--and-cog-driven Trojan with just a couple of bedrolls and half a dozen cooking pots. Squash also carried his most treasured possession, a heavy double-barrelled rifle.

After a long adventurous safari, fraught with some danger and great hardship they arrived in Fort Portal, the capital of the Kingdom of Toro, ruled by HH George Rukifi, the Omukama. The two young men then obtained land and proceeded to open it up for coffee. Their capital was minute so they supplemented it by shooting elephant, the tusks of which they sold for fifteen to twenty shillings a pound; the meat traded for food for their labour force. They also hunted buffalo for the same purpose; the meat being disposed of while fresh, dried for *biltong,* or smoked. This was bartered for grain and vegetables which they sold for cash. In addition they wandered through Toro and Ankole districts prospecting for tin and gold.

Came 1939, and Bunduki being on the Reserve, was called to the colours and joined the 4th King's African Rifles, but to Squash's disappointment, he was found unfit and rejected.

Bunduki in later years had many amusing stories and anecdotes to relate regarding the Somali and Ethiopian campaigns and the frustrating actions against the shifta and Banda irregulars. Subsequently he was found unfit to proceed to Burma and was most upset when his company and the battalion left. He had no wish to serve in East Africa or with a Holding Battalion, so when the opportunity arose he took up an appointment in the Uganda Game Department which was looking for staff.

He performed sterling work in Acholi, where he demarcated the Game Reserves physically with old *karais*. It was during this time that he earned a reputation for being a brilliant shot. He served in Acholi, West Nile and Bunyoro and he presented a magnificent pair of matched elephant tusks to the lodge in the Queen Elizabeth Park. A showpiece, chained to the archway entering the dining room and, it seems unbelievable, but those tusks are still in the lodge, not having been stolen throughout the disturbed and turbulent period during Amin's regime.

In the late forties, he retired from the Game Department as Honorary Ranger and returned to what was then his tea estate. He was active in local politics, the tea industry and was often a thorn in the side of the Protectorate and local administration. A second Colonel Grogan one might say!

He had been visiting the Kenya coast, and Lamu in particular, during his holidays for many years and in the early fifties he had the opportunity of buying Naazi Moja (one coconut), a delightful holding about a mile north of Lamu township. He bought this from 'Farmer' Owles the owner, who wished to return to his native New Zealand before he died. Bunduki used this retreat as a holiday home from Uganda and he did much to improve it; installing pumped water, electricity, extending and improving the Kenya settler-type of house, planting a garden and lawn and building a picturesque little baraza on the small sand dune adjacent to the main house. This

266

had a fine view overlooking Manda Island opposite.

He soon became a well-known character on the island, entertaining many friends there, especially from the hunting fraternity. When he was in residence the lights from the house and the baraza could be seen late into the night when he and his pards were worshipping at the Shrine of Bacchus, arguing, relating tall stories of hunting, prospecting and ribald adventures. He purchased one of the first deep-sea fishing boats from the estate of Colonel Pink. Due to declining health Bunduki then left Toro and settled at Naazi Moja. However, the quiet life there rankled him, his restless spirit craved the bush and travel. He delighted in receiving visitors who found his eccentricities, tales, recollections and reminiscences of the past so interesting. His sonorous voice with intermittent coughing and grunts, gestures and flamboyant dress made him an excellent foil for garrulous and rough Percy Petley and the dapper, suave Colonel Pink, mine hosts at the famous Petley's Inn.

Came 1972 when the tyrant Idi Amin sequestered all businesses and property in Uganda belonging to Europeans and Indians. Bunduki was among those who lost all with no compensation. His manager and other close friends then decided to emigrate to New South Wales, Australia, with their families of mixed origin. Surprisingly enough they were accepted by the Australian Government, possibly because Bunduki had been interested in that country for many years through the Fairbridge Scheme of which he was a sponsor. He could not accompany them immediately on account of his failing health and so he was left in Lamu, unhappy, restless and emotional. At his age he actually undertook cookery lessons, thinking it would be of use to him when he finally left for their little settlement.

Eventually he left Lamu by sea towards the end of 1974 for Australia, but admitted in his letters that he was unhappy there. He wrote to an old friend that he hoped to return to Africa, the land he loved, and to stay at Lamu. Unfortunately before he could return he developed pneumonia and died.

Coconut Charlie

Charles Edward Whitton was born in 1875 and arrived in Lamu from Mombasa in 1911. Soon after his arrival he left for a short visit to England to then return to the island which he never left, either for voyages or upcountry safaris until his death many years later. It may be assumed that he was in his seventies when he died and to stay on the island for some forty years without an outside break was a feat of considerable fortitude; but then he loved the place, probably more so than any other expatriate. In turn he was loved by the El-Amu who always showed him the greatest respect. Not only for himself but for his knowledge of the town, its history, culture and customs. He was an institution here, a Justice of the Peace and was awarded the Jubilee and Coronation medals. He was affectionately known as The Lord Mayor or Coconut Charlie.

He evinced great interest in the growing of coconuts, mangoes, cashew nuts and general farming and acquired thirteen shambas, or farms, on Lamu island and Witu. He also opened up a copra drying factory near Shela which commenced operations in 1912. At that time he lived in a house outside town and the other side of Hedabu Hill on which the present District Commissioner's house was built. His businesses prospered and during the First World War he was also engaged in Government activities.

Eventually, the years passed, he found all this too much and gradually relinquished interests in his shambas and his copra drying factory was closed. He then moved to a spacious flat in town in one of the old houses which had been built by Indian merchants. This was on the main street and not too far from the present Star Restaurant. Of this building he occupied the two upper floors, the front yard faced the promenade. Here he remained until he fell sick and was compelled to go to Mombasa hospital where he died.

He was a man of just over medium height; heavily built, grey hair cut short, luxuriant in growth and parted in the middle. He was always immaculately dressed in a white long-sleeved open-neck collared shirt with white or cream trousers. He had a short well-trimmed moustache stained by tobacco, for he was an inveterate pipe smoker.

In his latter years he was content with seven pipes daily of his own mixture. His seven large pipes were part of the morning ceremony. All were cleaned with a scraper and suitable feathers. The pipes, having been cleaned and charged were laid out on the table by the side of his favourite chair next to a large window which opened on to a wooden verandah which overlooked the yard and harbour. He was a most methodical man and his servants and acquaintances said you knew the time by certain of his habits. Never a gin before noon and never a whisky before sundown. To those whom he knew, and they were few, he was a most generous host. He was a fervent listener to the BBC and his massive radio was operated by 12-volt batteries which were kept in immaculate condition. The times and hours of use were carefully noted down in a special notebook kept for this purpose.

A most erudite man of Catholic tastes in literature and very well read. He had many fixed habits such as recording harbour tides and the like. He was fond of both chess and whist. He was not a recluse but he chose whom he wished to see from all races. If he did not wish to see you then his servant merely told you that he was not available. Towards the end he tired easily and hardly left his house except on Friday when he took a stroll in the street to distribute alms to the needy. He had a magnificent collection of Lamu and archipelago furniture: beds, chairs, tables, chests and everything which had been associated with the great houses of the past. This fine collection of coastal art was donated to the museum in Fort Jesus, Mombasa, as there was no museum at Lamu at that time. He also donated a large sum to the Arab and Swahili boys and girls of Lamu town for educational purposes. This was left in trust. He was very keen that the advantages of thrift should be taught to the children for this virtue they sadly lacked. Some people said that he had been married but the few who could recollect him in the early days could not remember any wife coming to Lamu and those who knew him well said that they never once saw a woman in his flat.

It seems extrordinary that in the early part of the century, such a cultured man should come to an outpost like Lamu but, with his numerous coconut shambas and other holdings, well did he deserve the title of Coconut Charlie.

Long will he be rememberd for his charitable gifts, his work in developing agriculture in Lamu and Witu and the respect given him by all the El-Amu people.

Ba Allen

The late Ba Allen was a colourful character who lived on the island for many years. Of Romany origin, he was born near Windsor a few years before the First World War. According to Ba it was his nanny who gave him his nickname. Evidently at the age of two years his parents were beginning to despair that he would ever begin to speak, but one afternoon, whilst he was being pushed along in his perambulator in Windsor Park, he saw and heard his first flock of sheep to then utter the words 'Ba-Ba'. It has stuck ever since.

An ex-Police Officer (he was the Kenya Police boxing champion), ex-Army Officer attached to the Ethiopian Army during the last war and ex-Locust Control Officer on Kenya's Northern Frontier, when he was speared in the arm by a Somali ('who knew nothing about Queensberry Rules, Old Boy — Haw! Haw! Haw!'), he was still tough and fit up to the time of his death, although his mind was beginning to wander a little. He had a shock of wiry grey hair, a largish flattened nose on a wrinkled, battered walnut of a face, deeply tanned like the rest of him, vague blue eyes with his body knotted and gnarled like an old tree. He was affable, witty and intensely pro-British, he dressed in gypsy-like fashion, yet neatly so with his Muslim hat, blue denim shorts, open-necked shirt and coloured bandanna around his neck. Somali sandals completed his attire. He used to laugh a lot and so was called *Kicheko* (the one who laughs). He adored women of whatever age ('but better when young Old Boy, Haw! Haw! Haw!'), colour or nationality and his fading blue eyes would light up with intense pleasure when in their company. He was reputed to have innumerable offspring dotted around the archipelago and to this day I am visited occasionally from one of them from Faza Island who introduces himself as *Toto ya Kicheko* (Child of Kicheko). His elder brother, Bunny, who must now be pushing ninety, has survived him. Taller than Ba, handsome, ex-white hunter and also renowned as an amateur boxer in his younger days, he lives with his wife Jeri in a delightful home on the beach near Shela called Smugglers. He, too, adores the opposite sex but these days finds trouble in catching them as he ruefully confided to me recently. The third brother Denis, older yet again, much liked and respected, died some years ago and is survived by his wife Paddy who lives on Manda Island opposite.

'Anannashee', the house in which Ba used to live adjoins my own. It was here that Mwana Kupona wrote her famous *Utende*, a long and most beautiful poem for her daughter in 1850. There is a plaque on the wall to this effect. It is a rambling, coral-built, traditional-styled house of the 17th century. Weathered and attractive it contains many pieces of old carvings and the front door is much admired. Tubs growing jasmine and bougainvillaea stand on the verandah.

Lord Nelson, resplendent in his admiral's uniform, used to hang in the sitting room. Queen Victoria on his left and the present Queen on his right, both pictures suitably adorned with tattered, miniature Union Jacks. Hung on other walls, higgledy-piggledy, were an incredible number of faded, battered pictures of rowing, boxing and soccer teams. Taking pride of place on a shelf in the dining room were a couple of dozen or so silver cups, evidence of Ba's prowess as a boxer in days gone by. Also hanging on rusty nails to fill up any odd space on the walls were several strange paintings by Ba's European son, Jesse, now a famous surrealist artist living in San Francisco.

In Jesse Allen's world nature is cast in a new order. The lush terrain is compellingly fascinating to the romantic spirit. Under red, green or yellow skies and by the light of many suns, exotic plants contend for glory with variegated fauna. Every creature is invested with grace and sensitivity as it lives out its peculiar role in this complicated ecology. It is no Utopia, this fantacism. There is both good and evil depicted in Jesse's world as our own. There is life and death. Killing and coupling, but it all seems to merge in an overall natural scheme.

Against the advice of his brother, as well as that of his friends, Ba suddenly decided he had had enough of Lamu. In his own words he would go home to England where he would be able to see the lambs frolicking about in the spring and to watch the daffodils and crocuses grow. This yearning for England became an obsession with him besides, as he confided to me, he was very friendly with a widow on the Welsh borders who had a farm. They might marry but he was against any more children. He must have been about 75 years old then. How old the widow was I do not know. He made it safely back to England, lived with his widow for a few weeks when he trotted down the path alongside the road from her farmhouse to the Post Office. A car with a caravan in tow came down the hill, lost control, hit Ba and took him through a stone wall.

Well, he had lived out his three-score-years-and-ten and a few more for good measure. When he left Lamu he was a little unbalanced so that it may be said that the timing of his death was appropriate though not the manner of his going. He was cremated and his son, Jesse, flew over from America. Together with a handful of friends they made their way to Old Windsor for, as Jesse explained, it had fond memories for his father. It was one of those miserably dark and grey mornings in October. The little party, plus a bugler loaned from the Army, set off into the woods. Still misty, still grey with more people walking about than might have been expected, for perhaps it was early closing day in Windsor. Finally they came across a glade, dominated by a large oak tree in the centre. Here they halted. Had this glade played a role in Ba's early life? Maybe Jesse remembered. He now spoke. He would scatter the ashes in this glade and then pluck a few twigs from the oak. These would be placed on a silver salver which he had taken out of an incredibly old-looking khaki haversack Ba had had from his early army days. As he lit the twigs on the salver he said that the rising smoke would symbolise Ba's final voyage. He would like us to remember our own favourite moments with his father as we watched the smoke rise.

The smoke died away and the bugler, in full regimentals, was given the signal to play the Last Post. That was all. A simple ceremony for a simple, kindly man.

Peter Hankin — Gentleman

The days, the weeks, the months passed. Guests came and guests went. Some you remembered and some you didn't for you did not particularly want to. I think it would be true to say that during my one year at Elephant Camp half the guests I entertained were personal friends of mine, either coming up in family groups or small professional parties escorted by their tour leaders whom I also knew. Such a one was Peter Hankin.

He was the antithesis of the usual white hunter for he was unassuming and sensitive and spent none of his time seeking repute or craving admiration. I seem to remember him telling me that he had been born in India and came to Africa as a boy. He was obviously an old African hand for he had spent most of his sixty-odd years further south, mostly in the Luangwa Valley of Zambia. Here, I gathered, he had a difference of opinion with his hunting partner in the safari business they ran. There was nothing uncommon about that in the hunting fraternity for they were like a lot of prima donnas.

So he came to try his luck in the hunting world of Kenya with a good clean record behind him. He was acceptable to his new colleagues but just could not get his assistant's permit to conduct hunting safaris here. Probably for a variety of reasons, he was not a Kenyan citizen and with the country being saturated by hunters and a scarcity of game due to the poaching, he hadn't much of a chance. Moreover he was not the type to obtain this necessary bit of paper by bribing or underhand methods.

He was a smallish man — but wiry and tough. Blond greying hair, clean-shaven except for a grizzled toothbrush moustache, vivid blue eyes and the usual tanned, weather-beaten face which is the hallmark of the outdoorsman. He spoke quietly with an educated accent. Invariably smiling, pleasant and cheerful in spite of his recent ups and downs. Intelligent with a nice sense of humour and charming manners. It was always a pleasure coming across him in the bush or the odd weekend in Nairobi or elsewhere.

After a frustrating few months in town he managed to get himself a job of running a tented camp on the Tana River some fifteen miles north of Garissa and about thirty miles upstream from Elephant Camp. He ran it well, was obviously popular with the guests and enjoyed himself in a country which was much different to the fauna and terrain he had known for so many years further south. And then, for no apparent reason at all, the camp folded up. He went back to Nairobi again for a longer stay with nothing to do which must have made inroads into his dwindling bank balance. His friends then found him another job north of Nanyuki. Here he would take out on safari any available, fit, enthusiastic guests on what he called his Wilderness Trails. These were all done on foot. Through the Loldaiga Hills which led to wild, rugged game country. No shooting. Just trekking, game viewing, photography and absorbing the wild beauty of the scenery hereabouts.

When we met up again he told me of a telegram from his former partner in Zambia. He had more clients than he could handle. Couldn't they settle their differences and would Peter take up with him again the old, familiar friendly partnership? Peter could and did, much to the regret of the many friends he had made in Kenya in such a short time. After tying up the few ends he was left with he flew back to his old stamping grounds where his hunting clients were already awaiting him.

Like many old timers, that first night, Peter slept with his tent awning open. Lying in bed that way it was always good to see the friendly stars and to listen to the African night sounds.

Late that night, probably emboldened by the pitch blackness of the night, for heavy cloud hid the stars and moon, a man-eating lion dragged him out of his tent and into the bush.

By the time pressure lamps, torches and the like had been organised it had killed and partially eaten him.

When I was a boy my father gave me a book to read entitled *John Halifax, Gentleman*. I cannot recall the name of the author, but

I do the title, which so reminded me of Peter and I shall let that be his epitaph. It is a fit one. Peter Hankin, Gentleman.

Sergeant Kibwana Athman

One day I was walking past one of Lamu's twenty odd mosques along a back street which was about three yards wide. It goes without saying that there are no cars on the island. The time was about ten o'clock in the morning. Petley's bar was not yet open and my own refrigerator had gone on the blink and so there was no cold pink gin available that morning. I virtuously thought that coffee might be a change and good for my soul and so I called in at one of the little makuti-roofed coffee houses. The place was quite full. El-Amu beach boys with the European girls they had in tow, Government servants and inevitably several hippies.

I sat at a fly-specked table occupied by a local; a man of about my age I would imagine, in his late sixties. He wore the usual white Muslim cap, frayed but clean. Closely-cropped grey hair, a roundish wrinkled face with faded yet humorous eyes. Big-eared, thickset, he was wearing the usual kikoi and a much-faded green safari jacket with cartridge pouches stitched under the left breast pocket. A pair of workmanlike safari sandals completed his attire.

'Jambo,' I said.

'Jambo Bwana,' he replied. I invited him to join me in a cup of buni, the local bitter coffee, which he accepted with a word of thanks and a smile. I liked the look of him but just couldn't place him nor where I had seen him before. Looking again at his old safari jacket I asked him if he were an ex-bearer to which he replied with a laugh that his name was Kibwana Athman, that he was a retired ex-Sergeant of the Game Department in which he had served for twenty-five years. I was to learn that he had a few unproductive acres on Manda Island opposite and was in receipt of a paltry pension of two hundred shillings a month on which he had to educate, feed and clothe his family of a wife and four children. He admitted cheer-

277

fully that this was quite a struggle, which I could well believe. He spoke little English and we carried on our conversation in Swahili. He also told me that he had shot, some twenty years ago, the last three lions on the island but not before they had killed and eaten 17 donkeys.

'And you?' he queried. 'What sort of work do you do?' It amused him when I told him that I had been on the other side of the fence, working as a white hunter for the last twenty-odd years, that I had two children in England and was also hard up. He looked me over and smiled. He looked at my well-cut safari suit and said, 'You are a European — how can you possibly be hard-up?' This was always the standard attitude of an African towards the European for no European could possibly be poor. All he had to do was to go to the bank and draw more money. It was of no consequence whatsoever trying

to explain that if you had nothing in your account the bank manager would view you with little favour. To save any further explanation — and I had to hunch up a little to translate it into Swahili, I replied:

'Well if you were in the Game Department as you say, you must have met many white hunters and to have seen the way they lived generally. In short, all my money went on fast women, slow horses, cigarettes and whisky.' He had a sense of humour, that old retired sergeant, and this he could understand for he laughed his head off. However, he still wasn't quite sure of me for he looked at me for a while with a speculative look, for remember, whether retired or not, a Game Ranger is rather like a policeman!

'Do you know Bwana Ya Simba and his camp at Koru in the NFD?' I admitted to knowing that much-loved figure, also retired from the Game Department, and that I had stayed with him in his camp for long periods. This really impressed him but he continued his interrogation which amused me.

'Did you know Captain Archie Ritchie?' I also admitted knowing the late, much-admired Captain whom I had first met when I arrived in the country in 1941. He was probably the most outstanding Chief Game Warden Kenya ever had. A colourful, tall, handsome man with a mane of white hair, military moustache and who sported a monocle. An outstanding soldier of fortune, for apart from his service in the Guards, he had spent some time in the French Foreign Legion. At the age of about seventy he had retired in Malindi and when a little Indian girl had got into difficulties when swimming in the Indian Ocean he had dived in to drag her ashore. This last effort had proved too much for he died shortly afterwards.

'Do you know Colonel Roger Hurt?' Another personal friend and outstanding Game Warden. Roger had won a good DSO whilst serving with the King's African Rifles in the Ethiopian campaign.

'Do you know Colonel Ian Grimwood?' Yet another much-liked Game Warden whom I knew well. 'Did you know Bwana Hunter?' I again admitted to knowing old 'JA' quite well for I was his sometime protégé.

'Do you know Bwana Ken Smith?' Another well-known Game Warden. Ken used to be the Game Warden in charge of the Coast

Province and now lived in an attractive little house in between Lamu and Shela. I thought it might be a good idea to walk over to his place as I had recently been offered a job on the lower reaches of the Tana River at a place called Baomo. Ken knew this area intimately whilst I knew just as well the higher reaches of the river. He could give me some information about the place and I also could have a word with him about the old Sergeant questioning me.

'Yes, by God, I do know Bwana Smith.' I looked at my watch. 'And in half an hour I'm going to drink his gin.' The sergeant laughed.

It was now my turn to look at him speculatively. He too had served for many years on this coastal strip and his knowledge of the lower Tana would be invaluable to me. On his modest pension and with a family to support, he was obviously hard up. He still looked fit and would be up to the job. I put the question to him as to whether he would like a job with me at Baomo. He stood up and saluted — causing the hippies to look at us both with some astonishment. A smile of happiness cracked his leathery face as he grasped my hand in both of his.

'Ahsante, Bwana,' he said. 'Ahsante! Ahsante! Ahsante!'

From the nearest mosque, the Muezzin called the faithful to prayer for the second of the day. The sergeant stood up again. Once more shook hands and hurried off to the mosque for he was a devout Muslim. No doubt as he prostrated himself he would thank Allah for His merciful bounty in finding him this entirely unexpected job in the bush which obviously he missed as much as I.

For a year we worked together at Baomo and became fast friends. When the lodge closed down after a year we reluctantly returned to Lamu and every so often we would meet for our morning coffee and talk of the old days as old-timers will.

A few weeks went by and he didn't show up. The following day I was in the same little coffee shop when a funeral cortege went past with the coffin carried shoulder high by chanting mourners. Hundreds of them followed.

Later in the day, I heard that after his customary prayers

Sergeant Kibwana Athman had had a heart attack to die on the steps leading out of the mosque.

Ali Samosa

Shortly after the death of Sergeant Athman, I found another friend as young as the sergeant was old. Life is like that and one has to have the resilience to accept the inevitable and the hope to look forward to the unanticipated.

I was walking past the Market Square under the walls of the fort frowning down on me and skipping out of the way, as far as my old bones allowed me to do, of hand-pushed *garis* (carts) and laden donkeys and warned of their approach by the raucous cries from their owners of *'Gari, Gari,'* or *'Punda,'* as the case may be. When turning left or right they would scream out 'corner, corner', which I always found amusing as the donkeys or carts were laboriously manoeuvred around these hazards.

It was quite early and I decided to look around and do my shopping in order to replenish my sad-looking larder. A cursory glance at the rickety stalls as I passed did nothing to make me enthuse about buying anything. All I could see were the usual piles of mouldy potatoes, tired-looking cabbages, squashed-in tomatoes, dried-out-looking limes, overripe mangoes past their best and caved-in papayas. Sometimes, if lucky, one is able to purchase grapefruit, carrot and suchlike. Most of this produce comes down from Nairobi on the Lunatic Express thence on the Disco Dancer bus.

But today there was no joy. Neither did I see any animation on the faces of the stall-holders who looked both bored and apathetic. Indeed, one had given up the struggle to even try to sell anything for he was lying down fast asleep on top of his produce. On the stall next to him three cats snuggled in between piles of tomatoes. Resignedly, I decided to try my luck at Shela, just up the coast.

I had first noticed him before on my daily walks there and back which I did for exercise and a swim. We had passed several times, the boy carrying a small *kikapu,* or native woven bag. He was always on his own. Like me, another loner, I thought, for never once did I see him playing with other boys or even in their company at either Shela or Lamu. For this reason he intrigued me. He obviously came from a poor family for he was undernourished. His shirt and trousers were patched time and again, but neatly so. He went barefoot. Of a copper colour with crinkly black hair and a charming, though shy, smile. He would be about the same age as my son in England at school in Sussex. About fourteen I judged. As I trudged on I saw him resting on the harbour wall about halfway between Lamu and Shela. I stopped by.

'*Salaam Aleikum*' (peace be with thee), I greeted him. He smiled. His eyes widened.

'*Aleikum es Salaam*', he responded delightedly. We chatted in Swahili but then he switched to English, obviously proud of his ability to speak the language he had been taught in Shela school. He told me his name was Ali Mohamed Abdulla Fadil and that he was of the Bajun tribe.

He lived at Shela with his mother, two sisters and a younger brother. His father was dead. He also had an uncle who sold vegetables from a stall in Mombasa market. At Shela, in between attending classes, he was the sole supporter of the family. His mother, when they could afford to buy the meat, made samosas which he sold to Peponi Hotel and to the tourists. They had a tiny garden at Shela and from what I could gather it measured about ten square yards. On it they had a solitary lime tree from which he sold the limes; also a few mealies from a few dozen stalks of maize. I asked him what he had in his kikapu. He opened it to show me five potatoes, three bananas and a piece of cassava root. He told me that this would be the family's evening meal. He also told me, and this with some pride, that he called the faithful to prayer at six every evening at Shela mosque.

On impulse I invited him to have tea with me the following day and to bring him a dozen samosas and a few limes which I would buy. I described the position of my house, telling him it was the one where Mwana Kapona wrote her *Utende* and that there was a plaque to this effect on the wall. Near the prison I said, which seemed to amuse him. I told him to come at 4 p.m. Army time, not Lamu time which could mean any time. Again he was amused. We shook hands, said our goodbyes and I watched him trudge his lonely way homewards carrying his meagre supper for the family, obtained by selling a few limes.

The following day at precisely 4 p.m. and just as the Muezzin was calling the third prayer of the day, the El Assir, from the near-by mosque, came a hesitant knock on the door. It was my young friend. We went upstairs and Mohamed my servant produced toast, butter and a jar of the local plum jam. He admitted that he had neither tasted butter nor jam before and it was good to covertly watch him enjoy himself. Thereafter he would come for tea once a week and on one occasion I baked a rich sultana cake of which he ate two large slices with an ecstatic look on his face. I enjoyed our teatime sessions immensely for I missed sorely my own boy in England. Ali's philosophical, childish way of life was so typical of the Mohammedan faith. One day I ran out of butter and so I gave him tea and a plate of tinned mulberries and custard. His table manners were always impeccable and as he cleaned up the plate, he said:

'You know my friend, when I grow up I'd like to be a schoolmaster, but if I don't grow up and die I not mind so much for I shall then go to Paradise and eat like this every day.' It was touching.

'And what do you do,' I queried, 'when you come to Lamu and you cannot sell your samosas and limes?' He replied quite simply.

'If not sell — we not eat.' Thereafter, of course, any samosas or limes he couldn't sell in town I would buy.

It has been said that poverty and suffering do not improve the character. That they make people narrow and querulous and depress the vitality, but this was not so with Ali. Except when he suffered a periodic bout of malaria, as we all do, he was always lively, cheerful and optimistic.

He told me that in Shela there were three schools. Two Arabic — one for girls and one for boys — and the Government school.

He attended the Government school daily from 7 a.m. to 10 a.m. During the weekends and when the Government school closed for the long holidays he would then attend the Arabic school but sometimes he couldn't attend, for the sale of samosas and limes had to come first.

I found him charming, ingenuous and naive and wondered how long he would remain so.

The Holy Man

John Ethelstan Cheese was known as the holiest of men throughout the Middle East, Aden, the Somalilands and Lamu Island. In 1925 he was in Palestine, a country then growing increasingly prosperous and civilised and so felt the time had come to move on to the remoter parts of the Muslim world. From that year, almost to his death, thirty years later, his work was centred in Aden, the Somalilands and Lamu and it was whilst at Lamu that he was accepted by, and lived with, one of the old El-Amu families.

Lamu then was one of his bases to which he could return from his wandering ministry to the Northern Frontier Province and beyond and throughout these wild, remote, God-forsaken parts he was simply known as Padre Cheese and he was a legend.

He came from a wealthy family but the money he inherited when he came to Africa he gave away to the needy for he did not think it fitting that a Man of God should possess anything.

In Aden for a time he ran the Danish Mission, taking charge of two schools and conducting the Arabic services. From Aden he travelled across to Africa. His normal method was to travel by dhow. Once, however, he travelled in a more up-to-date ship and asked the shipping company if they would allow him, for economy's sake, to travel in the hold registered as a piece of baggage. It was when voyaging by dhow that he lived naturally among the crew. He had his few possessions in an old tin trunk together with a sack of food, a bucket, his Bible and a Dietz lamp. Whenever the Muslim crew said their devotions he knelt down too and continued in prayer upon the deck. A contemporary tells of a safari back to the Persian Gulf at the end of the south-west monsoon. He endured for six weeks the fierce heat, the storms and becalmings of this cockleshell dhow. After the voyage most Europeans would have heeded a rest. No so the

Padre. On arrival at Muscat he found a mission in straits. One man had gone to India on sick leave, the other was ill and needed to follow him. Serenely the Padre took over the Mission and ran it single-handed for the worst months of the summer.

It was in Aden that he befriended a person who turned out to be a Somali, a race he had not encountered before, and so made contact with the Swedish Mission in Jubaland. From here after a while he set out for Ethiopia. For almost two years he got no further than the capital, Addis Ababa, for he discovered that the city was without a British chaplain. He did not allow himself to become accustomed to the greater comfort of city life but continued to sleep on a mat upon the floor. Twice he went on chaplaincy duties to what was then British Somaliland, then he was eventually free to return to Jubaland and the Swedish mission at Kismayu. This was the beginning of a mission to the Somalis which was to last for almost a quarter of a century. It was from that time too that most of the stories about him still circulate. He is still revered in memory amongst the Somali and the people of the Lamu archipelago. He also spent half his lifetime in translating the Bible into the Somali language, also part of Bunyan's *Pilgrim's Progress*. And for what would a man labour so pointlessly, you might well ask. For Padre Cheese, of course, it was not pointless for he really believed his translation would be needed one day.

He respected the Muslim religion but his own belief so filled him that he could not help feeling that one day some Somalis would at least seek what he had found in the Man who was not merely a Prophet but the Son of God. He was well aware that the Muslims considered this concept to be at complete variance with monotheism. But he lived by faith, not logic, and he never attempted to proselytize nor foister his religious beliefs on the Somalis, for perhaps in his heart of hearts he knew that these desert people could not possibly find a religion that would suit them better than the one they already had. They called him *wadaad* — a man of religion — and regarded him as a Holy Man. Whenever he was exhausted after his long waterless trekking and stopped at their encampments they fed him willingly and sustained him. He never had a car. He walked everywhere and the British in all the outstations worried about him, thinking he would be found speared by hostile tribesmen, killed by lion or hyena, which in those parts were much more aggressive than down-country. Or that he would die of thirst or sunstroke. But he never was, for those of lesser faith had not his trust in his divine bounty.

A member of the British Administration writing of the Padre's devotion to the Somalis said: 'He helped greatly and devoutly any number of Somalis so that when we asked the Somali Chiefs and Sheikhs if they knew him, they replied: "Of course He is a Christian. We don't believe what he believes. He is wrong and we are right. But he is without doubt the holiest man in the whole of Somaliland!"'

It was Jack Clive, the District Commissioner of Lamu in the thirties who gave him the affectionate nickname of St Ivel, using the brand name of a well-known processed English cheese. It was just before I met him that he was on trek in the *Jilal*, the hot season

over the vast, waterless sands of the Northern Frontier. This must have been in 1940 during the campaign against the Italians when, among others, the South Africans had a Division there. A patrol spotted his bowed and bearded figure, wearing disastrous shoes, bearing a stave and carrying a water-bottle and his customary Gladstone bag. They arrested him as a suspected spy and took him to their headquarters for questioning. Upon learning his true identity they were most apologetic over their mistake and took him on as an additional Chaplain. Until he felt the urge to move on again the Padre agreed to this. He then rested for a couple of months during which time had the odd glass of sherry in the Divisional Mess. Then came the Call of the Desert and his wandering mission once more. He decided to move on and was presented with his mess bill. An embarrassment for he had no money. A Staff Captain quickly paid him his Army pay for the time he had spent with them. He paid for his sherry and now with the little money that was left over off he trudged again.

For a short while he was once attached to the King's African Rifles as a Chaplain. His Brigadier, driving back to the Frontier from a conference in Nairobi came across him shuffling along the road some fifty miles from the nearest water.

'Padre,' said the Brigadier after picking up his Chaplain. 'I will not have my officers wandering about on their own in the bush without transport. Surely you have the sense to see that had I not chanced to come along there would have been no other transport on this road. Surely you must realize that you would be in danger, then of dying of thirst?'

The Padre was duly grateful for indeed his water-bottle was almost empty. He was also suitably humble but he assured the Brigadier that he was in no danger of dying of thirst.

'You see,' he explained, pointing to a grazing herd of camels, 'whenever I am thirsty the Somalis bring me a bowl of milk and so I have no difficulty in quenching my thirst.'

It was whilst he was in the Mijertein — that particularly arid part of what was Italian Somaliland — he suddenly decided that his wanderings should take him over the border into British Somaliland. He was only some 200 miles or so from the capital, Hargeisa, and he thought it would be good to hold a service there for the small British community. Off he trudged and this safari, if only he averaged about twenty miles a day, would have taken him ten days but without mishap he arrived to duly hold his service. The following day he was invited to stay and dine at Government House; the Governor and he had been at Rugby School together.

Like other never-to-be-forgotten characters, I first met him at Afgoi in the Uebe Scebelli (Leopard River) in 1941. I met him many years later wandering about near Wajir in Kenya's Northern Province, but that is yet another story.

He had walked in as usual carrying his usual impedimenta but this time his Gladstone bag contained his regalia: a cassock and surplice, a silver cup, a little wine and unleavened bread and a squashed sponge cake which he gave me with his blessing. I was touched. There were only two of us for Holy Communion — Ray Mayers (the Civil Affairs Officer) and myself. He must have been about forty years old then, I would imagine, but looked much older for he was as frail as thistledown, slight and fleshless. But his eyes arrested one immediately. Intensely blue and so alive.

Back to Lamu again for my last story of him for there are still many there who recall with pride the days when he lived among them. Not that many of his friends were, or became, Christians and even those who were did not receive any preferential treatment from him. On one occasion when five communicants arrived for Holy Communion in the small island church somewhat the worse for drink, he lined them up and told them that they had broken one of the Commandments so that they would not be able to receive Holy Communion at his hands. They should come sober the following Sunday.

After that he moved on as he was never one to drop anchor overlong in one place. In 1958 he gave away the six books which formed his library and shortly afterwards left Africa via the Somalilands and Aden just as quietly and unobstrusively as he had arrived. It was whilst at Aden, and unbeknown to him, that a recording was made of a short sermon he gave.

In this sermon, which was full of joy and thanksgiving he remarked: 'Take cheer! The struggle for the honour of Christ is not only from what you have seen, but from the spiritual power of the African Christians.'

The pilgrim's questing spirit then moved to him to visit other places in the Middle East where he had worked a generation before. In Beirut he became so ill that the British Consul put him on a boat bound for England. Not far from Cyprus, John Ethelstan Cheese died and was buried at sea. His itinerant mission was over and he left nothing behind save what he carried in his hand. In many ways he would seem to have achieved nothing more than leaving the legacy of a deep impression upon those he had met in his wandering life. There are still a few alive who met him, and those who had that good fortune treasure their memories and without exception feel that they had the privilege of knowing a saint. They certainly would affirm that his life was wonderfully spent and in no way wasted.

Naughty Francis

It has been said that the late Francis Bedford-Pim was the son of a bishop. I cannot vouch for the verisimilitude of this statement but I can well believe it. He ws a successful planter in the Cherangani Hills, near Kitale in Kenya, for many years and often visited Lamu, where I lived for a time, from Mombasa where he had a second home. Indeed, in the early days of the last war he was seconded to the Lamu Irregulars although what this extraordinary force did I just cannot imagine. Like so many of those legendary, colourful old-timers the country is poorer for their passing. He was known to all his friends as Naughty Francis. A kind, generous person, he never married but lived in style, and contentedly so, with a succession of handsome African mistresses, before, during and after the war.

I first met him at Afgoi in 1941. Afgoi is a small Riverine village, populated mainly by the Gheledi and Uaden tribes, straddlng both banks of the Uebe Scebelli river, the Leopard River, in what is now the Somali Republic. The township is about 26 kilometres from the capital, Mogadishu, and once crossing the crocodile-infested river, the road leads to the Ogaden and further north to the Horn of Africa, the legendary Land of Punt.

He would then be in his late thirties, I would judge. A short, broad-built man, quite bald except for a tonsure of hair of indedeterminate colour around the upper part of his neck and above his ears. He affected an immaculate moustache and wore a monocle. He had the usual Kenya planter's sunburnt, ruddy face. A merry mischievous face, for he laughed a lot but his eyes were the most arresting feature, being of a vivid twinkling blue. Wicked, naughty eyes one might so describe them. Take away his monocle, dress him in a brown cowl and robe and you would have a rotund, happy monk who obviously ate well and drank even better. As I was to find out that very day and night and in later years, Naughty Francis did all these things and more for there was nothing of the celibate about him.

At the time of our meeting I was twenty-one years old. An impressionable subaltern and quite new to the country. Indeed, Afgoi was my first posting in Somalia. He was a Major, his somewhat tubby build clad in well-cut, starched khaki drill, polished badges of rank and stitched on his shoulders blue flashes with the lettering 'Ethiopian Irregulars'. An added touch of colour were the blue flashes tucked in the top of his fawn Fox's puttees.

It was a weekend I remember well. Evidently he was at Afgoi for the one night on his way further north to rejoin his unit in Ethiopia. Could I put him up for the night as his old friend, Ray Mayers, the Civil Affairs Officer, and my superior in charge of the District, had a houseful of guests from Mogadishu and hadn't a single bed to spare? As I was to find out later, Ray Mayers, when he was not on safari, with his usual open-handed hospitality did a lot of entertaining of officers from Mogadishu from the Brigadier downwards. They would tear up the road in their staff cars to escape the rigours of the capital, for life in those days was tough in Mogadishu. Do I hear the sound of laughter from all those ghosts of the past?

I was a little flustered as he was my first guest. Nevertheless, I escorted him into my little bougainvillaea-covered cottage I had been allocated overlooking the river. The time was well after tea with the flaming sun low in the sky, yet assessing the needs of my guest correctly I produced my last bottle of whisky and, with the sun now losing itself behind the palm fronds, the whisky too rapidly disappeared. Whilst killing the bottle I told my servant, Yusuf to prepare for the Major my spare army camp bed in the guest room. We then had supper. Corn on the cob. Roast goat to be followed by the usual caramel cream, the only pudding Yusuf seemed capable of making. This was washed down by a flagon of Chianti Classico. My guest complimented me on the drinks and meal and I then fretted as to how I was going to entertain him for it was still only about 9 p.m.

I need not have worried for he suddenly roared: 'Abdalla!' As if by magic Abdalla appeared like a black genie from the darkness outside. He could have been any tribe, I thought, looking at him owlishly. Somali, Ethiopian, or possibly Eritrean.

'Splendid,' said Naughty Francis. 'Splendid.' He inserted his monocle, blue eyes wickedly atwinkle. He stood up.

'I'll just wander around the village. Abdalla here is a first rate chap and knows the type I like. Care to join me?' I demurred and aroused myself to stagger off to my bedroom, wondering what on earth this eccentric Major meant. As I have already remarked, I was very young and naive in those days.

Coping with a hangover, I was rather late for breakfast the next morning and groaned when I remembered I had to take my platoon on bayonet practice later.

Propped up by my coffee cup was a folded chit. A most courteous thank you chit from Naughty Francis who had, apparently, left for further adventures in Ethiopia. After breakfast I wandered idly into his room to notice ruefully that my army camp-bed looked rather bent. Two of the folding legs had buckled and part of the canvas sagged to the floor. An army camp-bed, I thought, was obviously a one-man show.

A few nights later, Ray Mayers, now denuded of guests, asked me round for a sundowner. I related to him my amusing evening with Naughty Francis and his little foibles. He chuckled reminiscently for he, too, farmed in Kenya and knew Naughty Francis quite well. He then told me a story about him during the campaigning in Ethiopia some months previously.

Somehow, somewhere, Naughty Francis had found himself a voluptuous Ethiopian girl who accompanied him everywhere. She carried spare water-bottles, a captured Italian Beretta sub-machine gun, extra ammunition and the like. I suppose one could call her a female batman-cum-bodyguard. It was inevitable, of course, that this phenomenon should be discussed and talked about and in due course Naughty Francis was wheeled in front of the General Officer Commanding. I have quite forgotten now whether it was General Cunningham or General Platt. No matter. He was told in no uncertain terms that the year was 1941 and that they were not fighting in the Peninsular war in Spain centuries before (shades of the gallant Sir Harry Smith and his Spanish bride!). He would, therefore, get rid of his camp follower forthwith.

When next in some skirmish or other, with the now fast-retreating Italians, it was noticed that Naughty Francis had by his side a most shapely soldier in British khaki with the stripes of a full Corporal...

After the war I met him occasionally in between hunting safaris. At one time I took up a job as hunter with Uganda Wildlife based in Karamoja. I had just married in London and my wife was with me. We stayed there a year but then decided to return to Kenya where the hunting was conducted at a more leisurely pace with fewer animals shot. Motoring south over the border we pulled up outside the Kitale Club for lunch. The first person we ran into was Naughty Francis, whom my wife had not yet met, but had heard all about him from the stories I had told her. He was at his most charming as he invited us for lunch. Off came his double-terai hat with a flourish. He bowed low over her hand which he caressed as he lingeringly kissed it.

'What a charming gel,' he congratulated her, 'and what a lucky dog you are, Collins, for I had no idea you were so discerning.' After lunch we said our goodbyes and motored on to Nairobi.

Ailsa was silent for some time and then she said, 'after meeting such a charming old world gentleman (which indeed he was), how could you have told me all those unsavoury tales about him? I shall never believe anything now you say.' Ah well. I smiled but said nothing. Some you win and some you lose.

I think the last time I met him was at Muthaiga Club a year or so before he died. As I strode in, there sat Naughty Francis with his present light of love. A handsome Nandi woman named Esther. At this time there were no African members and how he got her in I'm damned if I know. But then he was a law unto himself. He was much older of course, but still debonair with his little moustache now quite grey and grizzled. He was as charming as ever as he in-

295

troduced me to Esther.

'My dear boy,' he said rising to his feet. 'Well met, and where is that charming gel of yours? Alone! A pity but you shall have lunch with us. You may buy the wine.' Once at table it took the two of them some time to choose from the Club's excellent menu. Esther, apparently, could not make up her mind whether to have lobster thermidor or steak and kidney pudding as the second course. In the meantime I had called over the wine steward to order one carafe of white wine and one of red, thinking that one or the other would complement Esther's order when she had finally made up her mind. Not a bit of it.

'Good God!' said Naughty Francis, popping in his monocle to gaze at the excellent table wine in astonishment and indignation.

'Neither Esther nor I drink this *taka taka* (rubbish). Steward! Take it away and bring us a couple of bottles of Dom Perignon!' Naughty Francis always did things in style.

Wilfred Thesiger

One day, striding into Elephant Camp came a person with his retinue of Samburu. I thought I vaguely recognised him and yet I was not sure. He was well over six feet, spare of frame with a gaunt, hungry-looking face and a great beak of a nose. I thought he looked rather like a ravaged eagle. In his mid-sixties, I would judge, with faded blue eyes, yet still looking as though exploring the possibilities of alternative desert spaces in which to wander. He introduced himself as that most famous voyager of them all. Wilfred Thesiger.

Of course I had read his beautifully-written books and naturally was quite intrigued and fascinated to meet him as we shook hands. I gave him an orange squash which he sipped sparingly and appreciatively. Evidently he seldom drank anything stronger. He declined my offer of a tent as accommodation saying that he would prefer to sleep on an adjacent campsite on the sandy ground to which he was accustomed. In spite of his age he was obviously still tough and in good condition and intended to stay that way. I was impressed. Later that night on the bank of the Tana River we chattered away and then for long periods lapsed into silence. They were satisfying silences these, for both of us were content with the desert and bush life we had chosen. At such times, lack of speech in no way detracted from one's peace of mind.

So we sat long into the night and meditated. Simon Sykes, my friend the monkey, who did not want to be left out of things, occasionally broke the silence with a stutter of a sentence.

At length I asked him what he was doing in Kenya, which to him, at this present day and age, must be almost civilised and dull compared with the vast wilderness I imagined the Arabian desert to be. His reply was an infinitely sad one. He morosely said that the Arab desert held too many Cadillacs and transistor radios for his liking these days. We relapsed once more into a companionable silence for once again we were in sympathy with each other.

He had a dry, rather shy sense of humour for he told me a most amusing story of how he had resigned from the Royal Geographical Society many years earlier when they first proposed putting up a woman member. A stoic, yet he spluttered with indignation in the telling of it.

'A woman,' he said. As if they didn't exist and still could not believe what had happened.

'Naturally I voted against her admission but was overruled. I resigned on the spot!' At the memory of such an enormity he gazed angrily at the river but then, under its soothing influence he quickly relaxed.

Some months later Elephant Camp was closed down, for the pitiless poachers had decimated the herds; as for other game there remained lion, gerenuk, giraffe and a few other species but all wild and almost impossible to observe and photograph. I then found myself back at Lamu beachcombing and lotus-eating. Six months of this and I was soon bored and once more longed for the magic of the bush. The call came again. Would I accept the job of manager at Maralal Safari Lodge? I would and did. A short boat trip to the island of Manda opposite. Thence to Makowe where I caught the bus (the Disco Dancer) until the water-hole of Mombasa Club was reached after several tortuous hours driving. Slaking my thirst here for a couple of nights I then boarded the Lunatic Express for Nairobi. I spent a couple of nights at Muthaiga Club and then drove up to Maralal.

Mystical Maralal. Nestling on the edge of the cedar forests of the Karisia Hills, sentinel of the Great Rift Valley and Lake Rudolf — the Jade Sea, now called Lake Turkana. Crossroads of wilderness and culture and home of the nomadic Samburu, cousins of the Masai. There is but little difference in the language and customs. Being pastoralists, they own vast herds of goats and are called the 'Butterfly People', or *Loiborr Kineji* — those of the white goats.

I knew this area well from my old hunting days and so soon settled in, taking my guests to see and photograph the three resident leopard on Normotio Hill, frowning down on the lodge, half a mile away. Of the leopard one was a melanistic black, of which the area is justly proud, for they are indeed a rarity.

Stock raiding between the northern tribes, warlike and aggressive, had not been eradicated with the Turkana and Boran traditional enemies of the Samburu and the Rendille.

Once a month I normally motored down south to Nakuru to do my main shopping but occasionally I would wander in the Maralal market place to pick up a few vegetables and so on. It was there that I met Wilfred Thesiger again. He had settled at Maralal and was living in somewhat primitive fashion a few miles out of town with a Samburu family. A few years older, of course, and with the same gaunt, hungry-looking face I remembered.

He had heard of my arrival and was coming up to see me at the Lodge but, in the meantime, whilst quite content with his Samburu friends he did at times get tired of his diet of milk, posho and goat meat and could I recommend anything he could buy in the market here. He also remarked that he did miss a good hot bath for there were no facilities for one at his manyatta. I told him to buy an oxtail from the so-called butcher, a few carrots and onions and other bits and pieces also available and make himself a casserole.

'And a bath?' he said looking at me hopefully. He probably thought I was running a sort of Salvation Army hostel for famous explorers — or was this all part of the famous Arab hospitality he had been used to in the Arabian desert? I shrugged. Money meant little to me; I used to be reasonably wealthy but it all disappeared on fast women, slow horses, whisky and cigarettes. I am sure with a flat in London, a certain amount of family money and the royalties from his well-read books the famous Wilfred Thesiger could buy me out, sell me and not worry about the change. Resignedly I told him to come up to the Lodge as the sun went down every Friday and I would arm him with a cake of soap, a towel and a good hot bath. I would also give him dinner gratis. And so I did. Every Friday for exactly one year. When I left I heard that my successor had not been as altruistic. Incidentally, never once did he offer to buy me a drink. *Che sera sera.*

Years later still I heard further news of him from a mutual friend of ours. He would now be over eighty years old I thought and was still at Maralal. I smiled when my friend said he'd given him dinner at the Lodge. He also gave me all the news about him.

Evidently he was travelling from manyatta to manyatta performing the ceremonial rites on the Samburu youth in circumcising them. In spite of his age he must still have a good co-ordination between hand and eye, I thought, otherwise with this somewhat delicate operation he might take a little too much off. There might be something in drinking orange squash after all. I'll give it some thought though not, I assure you, to emulate the *tour de force* Wilfred was executing. With foresight that would not be my line of country at all.

Percival Alan Petley

I have put off writing of the last of my old-timers until the end for, surprisingly, I could not seem to find all the information such a famous character would obviously merit. I could not draw on personal recollections for he was before my time at Lamu and so I never met him. Happily I met an old character nicknamed 'Keke', a Persian-Indian who was born here, used to tipple brandy with Petley and knew him well. As a result of some of the monumental parties they used to have Keke now suffers badly from gout which, as we know, is a damned painful affliction. However, he does not blame Petley for this for when he spoke of him it was with affection and his eyes would light up with pleasure at his memories. He stressed that when I wrote of Petley I would do so as an Englishman, and he was quite emphatic about this. An Englishman — not Scots, Welsh or Irish but as English. And so I will.

He was born in Sussex in 1881 and must have come to Africa as a young man. Far from wealthy, he had tried his hand at many jobs. Hunting, though not with clients and we first hear of him in Nyasaland, now Malawi, where he was mauled and badly scarred on the forehead by a leopard which he was reputed to have strangled with his hands. Keke thought that this was the reason he mostly wore a black patch over his left eye. We next hear of him at Witu in about 1910 when he took over the management of the Witu Rubber Estate, which soon folded up as the market for rubber collapsed. Nothing daunted he then tried to grow coconuts but the soil was unsuitable. He tried his hand at saw-milling but lost money on that, too. Finally he opened up a duka, or shop, on the Tana River somewhere, from which he sold matches, cigarettes, posho, sugar, tea, beans, paraffin and the like. It was here that he was almost killed by an elephant. You should know that at that time the Tana area had the highest concentration of elephants possibly in the whole of East Africa (before the poachers came on the scene some six decades later with their automatic rifles and were allowed a free hand with their bloody work of extermination). But then in the dry season several thousand elephant would move on to the river from their normal habitat in the far bush, the now waterless scrub desert. The biggest ivory also came from the Tana and it was one of these giant-spoored pachyderms Petley had been following with his servant, and his gunbearer named Baharo. Alas! when they finally came up to the monster it turned out to be a tuskless rogue. It then came for the little party, silently and intent on killing. Petley's servant panicked and fled, dropping a large kikapu of rations as he did so. Backing away from the elephant, Petley fell over the kikapu and the elephant was upon him. He suffered broken ribs and contusions all over his body but, before the elephant could kill him, Baharo the gunbearer, picked up the double-barrelled rifle and killed it. Petley spent the next few months slowly recovering in Mombasa hospital.

After being mauled by a leopard and smashed by an elephant he probably thought that something less dangerous was called for and so came to Lamu. Here he bought, opened and ran Petley's Inn. Possibly the worst inn in the world with Petley undoubtedly the world's worst innkeeper. But now comes the most astonishing part of the legend of the man, for this ill-kept, ill-run, filthy hostelry was, and still is, as famous as, say, the Norfolk in Nairobi. Hemingway, Ruark and Perelman have all mentioned it in their books with the latter making it his headquarters whilst he searched in vain for a brothel called Eskimo Nell's, having heard of the place from some adventurer with a turn of wit in the Explorer's Club, New York. I am sure he would have been egged on by the irrepressible Petley, who for once had a regular customer.

This customer and other unfortunate victims would have their shower from two rusty buckets of water, pulled up over their heads by a rope and simple block and tackle pulley by a one-eyed El-Amu servant. They would then sluice the water over themselves by the simple expedient of tipping the filled bucket with the forefingers of an upraised hand. For supper they could expect fish or a stew (unless the rats had eaten it), with Petley as mine host at the head of the table. Here he would slice a loaf of bread by clutching it to his grubby vest as he grandly threw a piece each to his bemused guests.

He liked his beer, but brandy was his favourite drink and after half a bottle of this his great love was to make pancakes which he would toss from an old iron frying pan. Should the odd one fall on the floor, then to him this was the biggest joke of all as he would retrieve it to begin the tossing drill again.

As for sleeping quarters, each bedroom was partitioned by a piece of coconut matting hung as a crude curtain and so I should imagine privacy was at a premium.

As a sideline Petley would employ half a dozen totos, small children in a sort of Dicken's Fagin's Den — not as potential thieves but for making bracelets, ear-bobs, necklaces and suchlike out of old wire, shells, beads and shark teeth which he would bury in the sand for a few months to be then retrieved and sold as antiques to gullible tourists.

Perhaps I might mention here that this infamous inn over the years has been greatly improved; it now boasts a swimming pool on the first floor and a restaurant garden outside serving luxuries like crab, lobster, chicken, skish-kebabs, pizzas and delicious curries.

Late at night, it is said that when the town is quiet, one can sometimes hear from the old kitchen an iron frying pan being placed on a charcoal *jiko,* followed by oaths and spluttering ghostly laughter as the long-departed Percy Petley tosses his pancakes.

His greatest friend was the Sultan of Witu, but friends were not one commodity he lacked, for when he died at the age of 76 at Lamu, his coffin, suitably draped with a Union Jack was followed by a cortege, so Keke assured me, of 'thousands of people', men, women and children. One might say a second Abou Veb Adam indeed.

Bedmate

It all happened many years ago now, a few years before the Kenya Government stopped all professional hunting in the country, so give a year, take a year and 1972 would be about the time the incident happened.

Having reached my three-score-years-and-ten plus a few more, and the Grim Reaper has not yet caught up with me yet using his scythe with inevitable determination, I can claim without boasting that I have known as many as most men, because my profession often takes me to the haunts where they are to be found.

I do not love them or even like them. To be perfectly honest — for I am an honest sort of fellow — I will go even further and say that I hate them with a bitter loathing which almost borders on the verge of madness; such is my pathological fear of them. This hate was not due to any cruelty I suffered or any unhappiness I experienced during my formative years. On the contrary, for when a child in England and together with my brother and two sisters I had much loving care bestowed by parents, relatives and friends. No. I think it was in later that years bitter experience taught me they just cannot be trusted. Particularly in bed where they are all voluptuous, sensuously clinging, pliant and soft as silk. When they make a movement they become deadly. One never knows when returning their caresses whether they will kiss you and allow you to make a kind of repellent love to them, or whether they will spit in your eye or even bite you. Having been badly bitten in the past I know for this particular affair had proved a most painful and unhappy one for me; as he saying goes 'once bitten, twice shy'. Inevitably, I am now very wary, ever watchful, and avoid them where possible. One feels the urge of course, but I'd rather not if you know what I mean and so I will leave it to others to be seduced by their undoubted beauty and undulating bodies.

Now do not for a moment think I am queer. I'm not. In fact I can safely say that when our small profession was in being — and it must have been one of the smallest in the world — not more than a hundred I would estimate in Kenya, Tanzania, Botswana, Uganda, Ethiopia and Somalia, there was not a pansy among us. Ours was a tough profession and I reckon I was as tough a hunter as the next man. Anyway I survived for twenty-five years. By that I mean I survived the teeth and claws of the lion and leopard, the tusks and giant feet of the elephant, the horn of the rhinoceros and the sharp tips and wicked boss of the courageous and vindictive buffalo. I have to admit, though, that years ago I was gored by the latter.

I've never been in prison, have never been accused of anything beyond the pale and I doubt very much whether the Police will catch up with me now after all these years. Admittedly no one witnessed my shooting her, but rather stupidly I told my American clients who have obviously kept quiet over the years. Old and valued clients these, who had been out with me on safari for many years. Liking me as they did and knowing my weaknesses, I think they understood and condoned my atrocity on that fatal day after we had spoored up, from six in the morning until two in the afternoon, a large bull elephant which in the end had eluded us. We returned to camp; hot tired and a little dispirited. After a couple of gins followed by lunch we then indulged in a little Egyptian Physical Training (horizontal on the bed), in the hot afternoon. The clients to their tent and me to mine where I quickly stripped off, put on my kikoi — a sarong-like garment — to gratefully flop on my bed.

My crime? Oh, I shot her in my bed. Blew her head off as a matter of fact. Very messy with blood all over the place, ruining a couple of sheets and an expensive Witney blanket as well as blowing a hole in the tent. If ever I have occasion to kill again I shall go about things a little more carefully. She was quite beautiful but she had to die for I did not invite her to share my bed. In fact I did not even know her which just goes to show how brazen some of them can be. Of course, I'd known her and her type after a fashion but we had never been formally introduced. As I say, she invited herself and so the blame for the tragedy must be hers. Not mine for I wanted no part of her. Yes, I'll admit I panicked as I usually do with them, but feeling her body, quite naked and touching mine in several different places at once as I lay half asleep, I must admit the old thrill of desire almost overpowered me. Yet I resisted her wiles and refused to return her caresses which by this time were getting more and more demanding. An experienced female this one, I thought contemptuously. She had probably read Sir Richard Burton's translation from the Arabic of *The Perfumed Garden*.

When no longer I could stand her quiet but insistent demands I opened my eyes and looked straight into hers. They were of a golden amber colour and I read in them all her loathing and contempt for me and the unholy joy as she sensed my helplessness. Lazily she ran her tongue lightly over her lips so that her mouth trembled with a murderous passion. She did not speak. She did not have to for she could see the look of fear and horror in my eyes as she moved slowly in for that last deadly embrace.

Although almost paralysed by fear, my right arm was hanging over the camp bed. Slowly my fingers touched the loaded shotgun old Buno, my gumbearer, had placed in its usual position. By now she was lying on my left side, half in and half out of my kikoi. Slowly my right hand closed over the small of the butt, felt its reassuring familiar touch as I eased it slowly over my body. Using it as a pistol so that the twin barrels locked in between those dreadful eyes. She was obviously over-confident and possibly drugged with the power she knew she held over me for she took no quick action to save herself. Gently I eased forward the safety catch to then squeeze the rear trigger and those evil, coldly calculating eyes disappeared in a bloody mess. Her beautiful body writhed even in death. I found myself covered in blood and perspiration for the dreadful fear of her was still with me. How to dispose of her body?

My own tent and camp was pitched under huge, shady acacia trees near a large outcrop of lava rock. Nearby I knew there was a deep crevice in the rock formation. Carefully I picked her up, her body was still beautiful in death as I dropped it down the crevice where it disappeared from sight.

Yes, I suppose you could call it murder and you may think I'm just a cold-blooded killer when I say that if another of her kind crawls into my bed, I shall kill again. For with them it is kill or be killed. Judge for yourselves, but what would you have done if a large female cobra crawled uninvited into your bed? A banded cobra, one of the deadliest of the species.

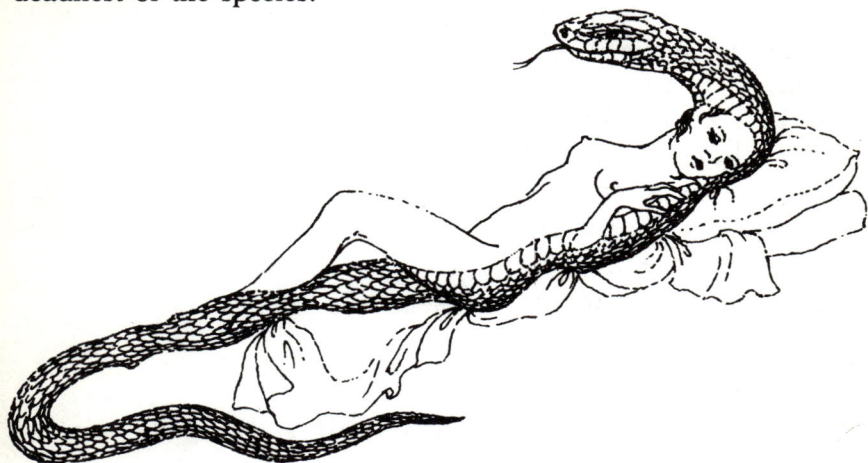

The Request
(From a dying friend)

Find me a place
    Where the sand is soft as velvet,
And where the waves make
    Foam puddles for my feet.
Find me a sea-shell
    In the shape
Of my lover's face.
    Driftwood splinters
From a home I remember.
    Find me a bird
Hiding from the world
    Of future hurts.
Find me all these things
    And that is where
You will find me.

The reply

I've found your place
    With sand both soft and velvet
Untroubled waves gently breaking
    To welcome your feet,
For they would remember.
    Driftwood too passes by
Mayhap from homes
    Now lost but once loved
And well remembered
    By you and I.
Yee! You could hide here
    Like your broken bird
To find a love
    Beyond tears and pain
As you kiss your lover's face
    On a shell of fantasy.

GLOSSARY

Non-English words which occur frequently are shown in italics - *zariba, deshek, tebed,* etc - the first time they are used. Thereafter they appear as normal. The words are Kiswahili unless shown otherwise eg Som for Somali.

askari	soldier, policeman
baraza	meeting
balwo (Som)	love poem
boma	camp, outstation
chang'aa or *changaa*	illicitly distilled liquor
dawa	medicine
deshek (Som)	water-hole
dia (Som)	blood money
dibat (Som)	dowry, given by bride's family
fundi	artisan
gabdo (Som)	unmarried girl
habari	news, information
Illalo (Som)	tribal policeman
karai	metal bowl
khanga	printed sarong-type garment, worn by women
kherif	strong seasonal wind
lender (Som)	camelman
maro addi (Som)	coloured dress, draped over one shoulder
nakhoda (Som)	dhow captain
lungi, kikoi	sarong, worn by men
panga	machete
rondavel	round hut (derived from Afrikaans)
shifta	bandits
tamaam	evening parade, as flag is lowered
tebed (Som)	dish of camel's milk
tobes (Som)	white overgarment
yero (Som)	small child
zariba (Som)	thorn fence